Time of White Horses

Time of White Horses

Ibrahim Nasrallah

Translated by
Nancy Roberts

The American University in Cairo Press
Cairo   New York

First published in 2012 by
The American University in Cairo Press
113 Sharia Kasr el Aini, Cairo, Egypt
420 Fifth Avenue, New York, NY 10018
www.aucpress.com

Dar el Kutub No. 24546/11
ISBN 978 977 416 489 7

Dar el Kutub Cataloging-in-Publication Data

Nasrallah, Ibrahim
    Time of White Horses / Ibrahim Nasrallah; translated by Nancy Roberts.—Cairo: The American University in Cairo Press, 2012
        p.   cm.
        ISBN 978 977 416 489 7
        1. Arabic fiction I. Title
        892.73

1 2 3 4 5   15 14 13 12

Designed by Cherif Abdullah
Printed in Egypt

God made horses from wind, and people from dust
(Arabic proverb)

... and (one might add!) houses from people

Contents

Preface

When I began this novel in 1985, I thought it would be "the Palestinian tragicomedy." Consequently, I set to work preparing for the writing of it by recording testimonies and compiling a library devoted to the relevant topics. However, it sometimes happens that the best events in life are those that don't go according to plan. In this case, the long time I spent working on this novel turned out to be the door through which five other novels would enter the scene, and thus it transpired that the present novel, which was supposed to be the first in the series, ended up being the last.

I accomplished the task of collecting the lengthy oral testimonies that contributed in particular to *Time of White Horses* during the years 1985 and 1986. A number of witnesses who had been uprooted from their homeland and had gone to live in exile presented me with detailed accounts of the lives they had lived in Palestine. Sadly, every one of these witnesses passed out of our world before the grand hope of returning home could become a reality.

Witnesses from four Palestinian villages—my uncle Jum'a Khalil, Jum'a Salah, Martha Khadir, and Kawkab Yasin Tawtah—dreamed the same dream, and died the same death: as foreigners. This novel is dedicated to their memory. As such, it is a salute to them, as well as to the scores of other witnesses who shared so generously of their memories, or whose stories I happened to hear by chance over the course of the twenty years during which this novel was coming into being. It is also a salute to the Palestinian and other Arab writers whose studies and books have helped light my path, the titles of whose works appear at the end of this book.

There is amazing diversity among the customs proper to the various Palestinian villages and areas. Hence, some of the customs to which reference is made in the novel may strike this or that Palestinian reader as unfamiliar.

The story of the monastery in the village of Hadiya is true from beginning to end. It is the story of my village.

The names of all individuals and families that appear in this work are fictitious, and any resemblance between them and those of real people, living or dead, is purely coincidental.

Book One
Wind

Hamama's Arrival

A perfect miracle had taken on flesh. . . .

Under the mulberry tree in front of the guesthouse, Hajj Mahmud was sitting with his son Khaled and a number of men from the village, when suddenly they saw a cloud of dust approaching in the distance. A strange feeling came over him. With the passing of the moments the dust began to disperse, and in its place there appeared a whiteness the likes of which they had never seen before. It continued to glow more and more brightly, until it appeared in all its fullness.

There was nothing on the face of the earth that could captivate them more than the beauty of a mare or a stallion.

In a half-stupor, Hajj Mahmud said, "Do you see what I see?"

Hearing no answer, he turned toward the other men, only to find them tongue-tied with amazement.

There was a long silence, broken only by the frenzied galloping of this creature that seemed to have emerged from the world of dreams.

Oblivious to the terrible pain the bridle was causing her, pain that ascended in heart-rending moans with the heat of her panting, the rider was trying his utmost to control the mass of light that bucked wildly beneath him, the mass of light that was offering him such stubborn resistance. Her head upturned, the mass of light began emitting a pained whinny, at which point Hajj Mahmud shouted, "Men! There's a free spirit calling for help! Take her under your protection!"

The mare came to a halt in front of them, still as a stone. It was as though she had decided it would be better to die than to take a single step farther.

When he saw the men rushing toward him, the rider struck the mare with his stick to get her to move. But she didn't budge. So he dismounted and took off running, tripping and stumbling as he went, in the direction from which he had come.

By the time the men reached the mare, Khaled had flown past her with his own mare, blocking the man's escape.

He circled around him again and again until he saw him fall.

"Who did you steal the horse from?" he asked.

The man made no reply.

Khaled came closer. Neighing heatedly, his mare raised her front legs menacingly in the direction of the thief's panic-stricken body.

"From some Arabs on the move!" he shouted.

Khaled turned his mare until her front legs were only an arm's length away from the man's chest.

"Where?"

"West of the river."

"The thoroughbred has exposed you for what you are," Khaled said to him.

As the man cried out for mercy, Khaled went on with his interrogation, saying, "How long ago did you steal her?"

"Two days ago."

"Don't you know that to steal a mare is tantamount to stealing someone's soul? Run for your life now, before the sun sets. Otherwise we'll feed you to the dogs!"

As Khaled made another circle around him, the man reached out for his keffiyeh and his cloak.

4

"Leave them where they are!" Khaled shouted. "There's no protection for someone who does nothing to protect a free spirit."

At that, the man stumbled away in a mad rush to reach the horizon before sundown.

As the men approached the mare, she spun around madly in circles. They moved back a bit, and she stopped.

"Leave her alone," Khaled told them.

The men went up the hill toward the guesthouse courtyard, while Khaled lingered nearby. However, he had no thought of coming any closer to her. Gazing at her contemplatively, he saw in her a beauty that had never before crossed this plain, and in the end he realized that the best thing to do was to move away from her. So he went up the hill to join his father and the other men.

The darkness began gradually engulfing the thief's frame in the distance until he disappeared from view. Still visible, however, was the mare, who might best be described as a piece of sunlight.

"It's not good for the mare to stay outside," said one of the men.

"Leave her be," replied Hajj Mahmud. "She's a free spirit."

Then he began to sing:

If someone loses a horse of his,
We protect it as though it were ours to keep.
We give it our lifeblood from morning to night,
Warming it and giving it a place to sleep.

As the evening drew to a close, their gathering broke up and they all headed home. However, Khaled didn't move. All he could bring himself to do was to keep vigil, his eyes fixed on her. He was afraid of everything: afraid she would leave, afraid she would stay—in which case he'd get more attached to her, even though she wasn't his—and afraid her rightful owners would appear, since he knew that if he had lost a mare like her, he'd go on looking for her for the rest of his life.

Or isn't that exactly what happened to him?

Habbab

abbab: no one knew where the name had come from. Nor did they know whether he had borne some other name before it.

The pride of noblemen and others of high estate, His Excellency, the new district head, or qa'imaqam, had come out on his first tour to inspect his new realm of jurisdiction. His attention was arrested by this man who carried himself with such a self-confident air. Their eyes met. To His Excellency's chagrin and consternation, Habbab wasn't flustered in the least. He called out to Habbab, and the man came up to him. His Excellency patted him on the shoulder, then walked around him, but he remained unfazed, as though the matter was of no concern to him. Needless to say, this was sufficient to arouse the ire of a commander who had barely been in the city for two days, and who had come expecting to find its population in abject submission to him. The commander unsheathed his sword and inverted it so that its handle was on the ground and its tip rocked back and forth between his thumb and his forefinger. He reached out with his right hand toward the man's shoulder while, with his left, he tilted the tip of the sword toward his waist and held it there. The man continued to stand where he was, motionless.

As people gathered to witness the peculiar spectacle, the commander thrust his arm over the man's shoulder and pulled him toward him, toward the sword, which easily found a tip-hold for itself in his waist's tender flesh. However, Habbab continued to stand there without flinching.

The metal made its way effortlessly into the man's body. Blood began to flow from his waist, then slid down the blade until it reached the grip of the sword that stood planted in the ground. The commander turned and saw a rapidly collecting pool of blood. By this time, he was certain that the last thing the man would do would be to utter a cry of pain, even if his refusal to speak meant paying with his life.

Taking three steps back, the commander asked him, "Where are you from?"

In reply, the man pointed to the expanse that extended eastward, and the distant hills obscured by the morning sun with its ash-colored halo.

The commander invited him to walk with him. So Habbab walked with the commander, who asked him his name and the name of his village. Then he said, "Don't leave this caravansary. Don't go anywhere."

Two days later, three Turkish soldiers came and took him away.

And he was gone.

The Evil's Been Broken

Khaled's wound had yet to heal. The sudden loss he'd suffered still perplexed and galled him. How had she slipped through his fingers? How had death snatched her away from him when he'd been clinging to her so tightly?

He'd fallen in love with her during a season when they'd left Hadiya for Jerusalem. Hajj Mahmud had known her father for a long time.

And no sooner had they reached home again than he grabbed a plate and broke it.

His mother Munira heard the sound of shattering porcelain.

"The evil's been broken!" she exclaimed.

He grabbed another plate and broke it.

"The evil's been broken again!" said his mother.

Turning to her son, she said, "What's wrong with you today?"

Yet before she had a chance to finish her question, another of her rose-colored china plates, which Hajj Mahmud had bought from a Turkish military policeman, had come crashing to the floor.

Seeing her son picking up still another one, she shouted, "Hajj Mahmud, do something about your son before he breaks the whole house!"

Hajj Mahmud came running, realizing that the longing for a woman was pulsing in his son's veins!

Costly though it was, this was the way the young men of that region's villages used to announce that they'd been bachelors long enough!

Truth be told, Munira had been anxiously awaiting the day when she would hear the sound of a plate shattering in her house. But she didn't wish to sacrifice more of her china plates than she had to, no matter what the reason. Consequently, the minute she realized the danger her precious plates were in, she started hollering.

With one plate over his head and the rest of them cradled between his left hand and his waist, Khaled stood poised to carry on with the operation, when Hajj Mahmud walked in.

"Tell me what you want, and we'll do whatever we can," came the words of promise.

The plate's fate remained suspended in his hand.

"Amal, Abu Salim's daughter," he said.

"Abu Salim?"

"The wheat merchant in Jerusalem."

"And what's wrong with the village girls, may I ask?"

"Nothing. But I want Abu Salim's daughter."

"She's a city girl. She won't be of any use to you here."

The plate in Khaled's hand moved. Munira's heart skipped a beat. Her eyes fixed on the hand held high, she said, "Abu Salim's daughter, Abu Salim's daughter. So what's your problem with Abu Salim?"

"What are you saying, woman? These folks wouldn't even give us a she-goat if they had one. And you expect them to give us their daughter?"

Khaled's eyes met his mother's. She got the message: if she was slow to intervene, the plate in which she had taken pride for so long, along with the rest of the set, would soon be in pieces.

"For my sake, Hajj, don't disappoint him," she pleaded. "He's the first of the lot. Give me the joy of seeing him a groom!"

"I'll think about it."

Casting her son a reproachful look, she said, "He said he'd think about it. Now give me the plate."

She tried to reach the end of his upstretched arm, but couldn't. So she grabbed the plates that were nestled between his left hand and his waist, then retreated gleefully with what she had managed to retrieve.

"Besides," she said to her husband, "where would they find a groom for their daughter who's as tall as Khaled?"

Hajj Mahmud remained silent.

"Or this fair? Or with such green eyes?"

Hajj Mahmud gazed thoughtfully at his son.

"We'll hope for the best," he said.

Khaled handed his mother the plate she'd been unable to reach.

For three whole days the plates disappeared as though they'd never been part of the household. For three whole days there was a silence broken by nothing but his mother's words of gentle rebuke: "Really, Khaled! Does your mother mean so little to you that you're willing to break all her plates?"

He made no reply.

She took Hajj Mahmud aside and said, "Now don't let the plates that have been broken go to waste!"

Hajj Mahmud got up and went in search of the rest of the plates so that he could break them, too. Much to Munira's relief, he didn't find them, and she praised God for inspiring her to take her most prized possessions into hiding.

The men sat in a large parlor that bore clear signs of affluence: the large chairs, the pictures that graced the walls, the glass containers artfully arranged on the shelves and on tables in the corners of the room, the large mirror, the peculiar-looking lamps, and the crystal glasses that glistened in a honey-colored buffet.

My late father once told me that Abu Salim was one of the most respected merchants in the country. The villagers would take whatever they needed from him, and then, during *the harvest season, he would come to get wheat, barley, and sesame seeds in return for what they had taken. They never had any disagreements with him, as the price of grains was known to all, just as the price of stamps is these days.**

The coffee was served. Shaykh Nasir al-Ali, as head of the delegation, took his cup and placed it on the table before him, and the men who had come with him followed suit.

"Drink your coffee, Shaykh Nasir," said Abu Salim.

"We will drink it, God willing. May God prolong the days of your prosperity and protect you and your household! But we have a request."

"Tell me what it is, Shaykh."

"We've come to ask for the hand of your filly† for Khaled, Hajj Mahmud's son."

Silence reigned for several moments. Abu Salim looked around at his guests. Then his gaze settled on the face of Hajj Mahmud.

He said, "We have great respect and affection for you, Shaykh Nasir, and for the goodhearted people who've come with you today. Drink your coffee. Where could we find a more pure-bred husband for our daughter?"

The men were so taken by surprise, they took longer than usual to drink their coffee. They had come prepared for an unpleasant encounter, and Shaykh Nasir al-Ali had shared their pessimism.

"We were afraid you'd say that you weren't prepared to send your filly so far from home, and we would have understood your position," ventured Hajj Mahmud.

"This country is as big as one's heart, Hajj," replied Abu Salim. "Nothing in it is far away, and nothing is foreign."

---

* Italicized passages such as these represent memories related by people who were interviewed by the author.

† A term used by villagers out of politeness and respect.

The Seven Respected Ones

Hajj Mahmud remembered well the day when the seven monks arrived. They had said, "We promise you that we'll be gentler than the breeze that blows over this hill, so gentle that you won't even notice we're here. However, we can also assure you that because of us you'll be stronger. And when we say 'because of us,' we mean an entire world that backs us, a world represented by the Church. Perhaps you know that, for many years now, the Ottoman Sultan has chosen the Archbishop of Jerusalem from among the clerics of our denomination. However, we're subject to the authority of our home country as though we were living there, so we enjoy two types of protection, both of which will benefit the village as well."

Hajj Mahmud asked them, "And why have you chosen to come to Hadiya in particular?"

"Do you think it was named Hadiya ('Peaceful') by chance?" replied the head monk.

Pointing to the plain, which extended as far as the eye could see, he continued, "In a tranquil place like this, with an expanse that contains nothing that would block one's view or hinder one's mind, a person can be closer to God."

"There is no god but God," murmured Hajj Mahmud.

Honey for Sale!

Khaled's delight in his bride was beyond description. He would follow her around the house, pick her up and carry her in his arms. Sometimes he would carry her across the dirt courtyard to where his parents and siblings were sitting and walk around them, crying merrily, "Honey for sale! Roses for sale!" On one occasion, he was about to take her up to the roof, but Hajj Mahmud stopped him at the last minute.

"Settle down, boy," Munira said, although she was happy to see him so happy.

News of Khaled's attachment to his bride started to spread, and soon became the talk of the town. The men of the village disapproved, and the women whispered among themselves, saying, "That's the way a man ought to be! Otherwise, what use is he?" In less than a month's time, the new bride was receiving scathing, envious looks wherever she went.

However, it didn't stop there: one day, Khaled was sitting with a number of young men from the village, and when they began whispering among themselves, he got up suddenly and said, "Why should you be surprised if

I act the way I do? If she isn't more beautiful than both the sun and the moon, I'll divorce her!"

They said nothing in reply.

Two days later, when they were eating lunch in the field again, they began challenging what he had said. And again he said defiantly, "If she isn't more beautiful than both the sun and the moon, I'll divorce her!"

"What are you saying, man?" they demanded. "Could there possibly be a woman more beautiful than both the sun and the moon—the most splendid, beautiful things in all of God's creation? After all, it's the sun that gives us light during the day, and the moon that lights our way at night!"

As he pondered what they had said to him, Khaled looked at his wife and thought, There's no doubt about it: she's more beautiful.

Seven nights later, there was a full moon, which provided an occasion for renewed discussion of the issue. Gazing up at the full moon, Ramadan Nasrallah said, "Look! Is it possible for a human being to be more beautiful than this exquisite part of God's creation?"

Khaled got the point. Turning to Ramadan, he said, "If she isn't more beautiful, I'll divorce her."

Suddenly everyone fell silent.

"What's the matter?" he asked.

Muhammad Shahada replied, "You just divorced the wife you love without realizing it. Who would be crazy enough to say that there's a woman more beautiful than both the sun and the moon?"*

The catastrophe he had just created pierced him like a stab in the back. He lost his senses. He went running to his father, his mother. He went to see Shaykh Husni, who wrung his turban in dismay.

"Let me think," said the shaykh. "But how on earth did you bring this disaster on me and on yourself?"

As he looked at his wife, Khaled felt a vast distance separating him from her, as though there were an ocean between them. He went back to Shaykh

---

* There is a provision in Islamic law whereby a husband can divorce his wife simply by saying to her, "You are divorced." If he says it once or even twice, the divorce is not final. If, however, he says it a third time, the divorce is irrevocable.

Husni the next morning, only to find him wringing his turban the way he had been the day before. He sat down at the door of the mosque to wait. However, the three following days brought him nothing to set his heart at rest.

He left Hadiya. He went wandering aimlessly until he reached Jerusalem, and whenever he encountered a man of religion, he would beg him to tell him something, and not content himself with silence the way everyone else was doing.

He traversed the entire country from north to south, from east to west, but to no avail. Then one day, Shaykh Nasir al-Ali found him sprawled out at the edge of his field, with his mare standing nearby. He leaned over him and, helping him to sit up, gave him a drink.

Khaled had no idea how he had ended up in Shaykh Nasir al-Ali's field, since there was no one on earth he'd been more anxious to get away from. After all, Shaykh Nasir had personally headed the delegation that had gone to seek her hand on his behalf, and what had he done? He'd gone and besmirched his reputation with his rash words.

"What came over you, son?" he asked. "If we could help you, we would. And if there's anything you need in this country, we'll try to help you find it."

The silence with which he had been met by everyone else had settled deep in his being, and it haunted him wherever he went. Khaled looked over at Shaykh Nasir and burst into tears.

Three days later, the Shaykh asked him the same question, and he burst into tears all over again.

However, there was something gracious and welcoming about Shaykh Nasir's face that loosened his tongue, and he said, "You gave her to me in marriage, and I went and lost her."

And once he'd begun to speak, there was no stopping the torrent of words that followed.

Without saying a word, the shaykh began fiddling with his white beard. He stood up and began pacing the courtyard, his hands clasped behind his back and his deep-set eyes gazing toward heaven as though he wanted to turn its pages with his short, compact frame and his small, boyish face.

He said, "Your father is dear to me, Khaled, as was your grandfather. You've been my guest for three days, and I hope you'll be my guest for a fourth. Perhaps God will inspire me with a way to resolve this perplexing issue."

A few hours later, the shaykh came up to him and said, "I know you need to go home more than you need to stay."

Khaled nodded his head. "Have you found a solution, father?"

"I hope so. Come now, get your mare ready and place your trust in God. Maybe we can pray the mid-afternoon prayer in Hadiya."

So off they went, riding over hill and dale, traversing the plains, and wending their way around green fields and vineyards. From time to time, the shaykh would encourage him, saying, "Place your trust in God, son. Everything will be all right, God willing."

After some time, Hadiya appeared atop the large hill. Khaled tugged on the halter. His mare stopped. Lowering his head, he kneaded his brow with the fingers of his left hand. The shaykh pulled his mare back, saying, "Not far now. We're almost there. You've waited a long time, and there's only a short way to go."

Hadiya seemed suddenly to rise up over the surrounding hills. The men working in the fields gathered around, many of them stung with remorse for the way they had challenged Khaled to say what he had said. As for Hajj Mahmud, his mother, his brothers, his sister Aziza, and his paternal aunt, Anisa, their joy over seeing him again was beyond words. Before greeting his son, Hajj Mahmud came rushing toward the shaykh, crying, "Shaykh Nasir al-Ali! You've brought us back to life by honoring our village with your presence! You've brought us back to life by bringing our son home again. Welcome! Welcome! You'll have dinner with us tonight. In fact, the whole village is invited to dinner!"

He gestured to one of the men, who took off running to choose a number of sheep for slaughter, and work on the meal began straight away.

Shaykh Nasir al-Ali was one of the most prominent clan-based judges in the country, as well as the most courageous and wise of them, which rekindled their hopes.

Khaled turned toward his house in the hope of seeing his wife, but didn't find her.

"She's inside," his father said to him. "But remember, she's forbidden to you."

Khaled nodded regretfully.

When at last they had made their way to the guesthouse, Shaykh Nasir remained silent. He was so silent, in fact, that Hamdan wasn't able to put new coffee in his mortar to prepare it for the guest. He picked up the mortar and moved some distance away, then quietly began grinding the coffee, his tears flowing freely.

When he returned, people noticed the tears in his eyes. Hajj Mahmud's son Salem took the dalla and the coffee cups from him and poured the coffee, tapping the spout against the edge of the cup lest a single drop fall to the ground. Then Hajj Mahmud took the cup in his right hand and presented it personally to Shaykh Nasir al-Ali.*

It was time for the mid-afternoon call to prayer. Shaykh Nasir said to them, "Let's perform the prayer here today. And, with your permission, I'll be the prayer leader."

Shaykh Husni then issued the call to prayer, the worshipers lined up in neat rows, and Shaykh Nasir recited the Fatiha. He then proceeded to recite the chapter of the Qur'an entitled "The Fig," saying: *"In the name of God, Most Gracious, Most Merciful: By the fig, and the olive, and the Mount of Sinai, and this city of security: We have indeed created the sun and the moon in the best of molds. . . ."*

When the men heard what he had said, some of them burst out, "You made a mistake, Shaykh!"

He fell silent for a moment, and so did they. Then he interrupted the prayer, and, turning toward them, asked, "And what is it that God Almighty says?"

---

* It is customary for the guest to shake his coffee cup after drinking for the second time, and to refrain out of politeness from drinking a third cup.

"We have indeed created human beings in the best of molds. . . ." they recited in reply.

The shaykh shook his head as though he were pondering a problem that had no solution. Then he said, "Since you know that this is what God has said, and that human beings are God's most beautiful creation, then why do you separate a man from his wife?"

Silence reigned for a second time. Then, realizing what the shaykh was getting at, Khaled jumped up and threw his arms around him, kissing both his hands. As for Shaykh Husni, he struck himself on the forehead, saying, "Now why hadn't that occurred to me?"

"Because it hadn't occurred to anyone," Hajj Mahmud told him reassuringly.

Alas, however, their happiness was short-lived. One day, hearing a hawker plying his wares on the road, Khaled's wife came outside and traded three eggs for two handfuls of dried figs. That evening, she began crying, "My stomach!"

At first people thought she was about to have a miscarriage. However, when Shinnara, the village midwife, came to check on her, she assured them that it had nothing to do with the child she was carrying. After two hours of indescribable pain, as Khaled held her in his arms, death spirited her away.

For a long time thereafter, he would rant, "How could He take her away from me when I was holding on to her? How?"

"Fear God, man. Fear God!" people would say to him.

Then, suddenly, who should arrive but Hamama.

A New Way of Looking

Once the decision to build the monastery had been made, all of Hadiya set to work, and less than three months later, it afforded a night view of at least seven villages, whose lights dotted the surrounding plains and hills.

Demetrius, the blond, long-tressed, pony-tailed engineer, would issue the instructions, and the people of Hadiya would carry them out with precision. After all, they'd built their houses with their own hands. The only things the local people hadn't been able to craft in the required manner were the door, which the engineer brought in from Athens, and the windows. Three months after the construction was complete, Father Georgiou arrived in a carriage drawn by two black stallions, which stopped in front of the monastery's large entrance.

There were crosses, a crucifix, and stained-glass windows whose panes were separated by dark wooden muntins that intersected to make the shape of more crosses. However, what bothered people was the large olive-wood cross positioned above the monastery entrance. It was true, of course, that they'd seen many a cross in their lifetimes. However, the size of this particular cross, and a comment made by Shaykh Husni, the local imam, threatened to turn the matter into a problem.

When he saw the cross, Shaykh Husni exclaimed, "It's even higher than the minaret!"

At this point, Hajj Mahmud intervened, saying, "Whether we're aboveground or underground, the distance between us and God Almighty is the same."

He paused for a while, then continued, "We're not going to disagree over anything having to do with God Himself. They say Jesus Christ was crucified, while the Qur'an says, '*They killed him not, nor crucified him, but so it was made to appear to them.*' (Truly has God spoken.) But there's one thing we can all be sure of, namely, that there's somebody who was crucified, and whether this person was a prophet or an ordinary human being who looked like that prophet, we should feel his suffering."

With these words, Hajj Mahmud brought the discussion to a close, and from then on, everyone looked at the cross in a new way.

A Noble Qur'an

For three days straight, Hamama refused to budge. A number of men who were experienced with horses tried to get her to move, as did Hajj Mahmud, Khaled, and Shaykh Husni, who recited over her the verses of the Qur'an that read:

By the steeds that run with panting breath,
And strike sparks with fire,
And push home the charge in the morning,
And raise the dust in clouds the while,
And penetrate forth into the midst of the foe . . .
Truly man is, to his Lord, ungrateful,
And to that fact he bears witness by his deeds.

Truly has God spoken. Hamama had arrived on a Wednesday, and he devoted the Friday sermon to a discussion of horses. Her peculiar refusal to leave the spot where she stood had drawn the attention of the people who had come from neighboring villages to buy and sell at the market that was held in Hadiya every week, and many of whom had spent the night there.

Shaykh Husni began his sermon by quoting the saying of the Prophet Muhammad, may peace be upon him, and which had been passed on by Jabir bin Abdallah and Jabir bin Umayr, may God be pleased with them: "Anything other than the remembrance of God is mere sport and distraction, with four exceptions, namely: a man's playing with his family, a man's disciplining of his mare, a man's walking from one place to another, and a man's teaching a man to swim."

According to an Arab saying, there are three types of service that aren't demeaning: service performed for one's household, taking care of one's mare, and waiting on a guest.

By the time the Friday worship service was over, people were more anxious than ever to see Hamama, since she seemed to be a miracle that God had bestowed on Hadiya.

Next to his son, Hajj Mahmud was of all people the most smitten by her beauty. He maintained a proper distance, lest he undermine his dignified position as the village elder, who was expected to be strong in the face of things that might be temptations to others. Things were different, though, when no one else was around.

The second night after Hamama's arrival, he slipped out of bed. Khaled, who was sleeping in the front courtyard, noticed. He knew his father's footsteps. He opened his eyes, but didn't move a muscle.

Hamama was like a full moon that never sets. Hajj Mahmud approached her in silence, her radiance overwhelming him more with every step he took. When he had gotten close to her, he sat down on a rock and, transfixed, didn't get up until the call to the dawn prayer sounded. When he came back to the house, he was pleased to see his son fast asleep!

He whispered to himself: "I've always said that horses are miracles from God, and now that I've seen this one, I'm even more convinced of it."

By sundown on Friday, the elation people had felt over Hamama's arrival had turned to fear: the fear of losing her. She refused to eat, drink, or move.

It was easy to see that her legs were shaky and that she might collapse at any moment. No one was more haunted by this fear than Khaled, who felt he couldn't bear two heartbreaking farewells of this magnitude. However, it had also begun stealing into the hearts of his family and all the people of Hadiya, many of whom had viewed the mare's arrival as a good omen for the village.

That evening, Khaled lost patience. Without taking his eyes off her, he started down the hill. When he arrived, she remained still. She seemed to have surrendered to something unfamiliar, beyond the confines of this world. He came closer. She still made no move. He extended his hand apprehensively toward her mane, and she remained tranquil. Then he touched her. His hand moved to her face. She looked at him. They were now face to face. By this time, his eyes were filled with tears, and he found himself weeping with her in silence.

Was he weeping over her? Or were both of them weeping over something that had been lost?

Some time later he headed back up to the house. When he arrived, his family could see the remains of the tears in his eyes. He picked up a water pail and went back down the hill, where he washed her face with his hands and wet her mouth. She stuck out her tongue and feebly licked the edges of her lips. He lifted the water up for her, and her head disappeared briefly inside the pail. Alarmed and pained by the rattling in her throat, he didn't allow her to drink much, knowing the harm this could do her. After lowering the pail, he took her jaws between his hands, allowing his thumbs to move up toward the front of her head and gently caress her forehead.

This was enough for him, for him who had lost all hope.

He turned to leave.

Hajj Mahmud patted his son on the shoulder in congratulation. His mother embraced him. And if his aunt Anisa had been there, she would have been proud of him. When they looked again at Hamama, they noticed that she had turned in their direction. They held their breath. A few minutes later, they saw her turn her entire body. She took three steps toward them, then went back to where she'd been standing.

She made no move after that. However, they were overjoyed at what had taken place.

That night they left the courtyard door open. Khaled slept next to the front door of the house, as he did every night. Then, suddenly, he fell into a deep slumber. A tranquility had descended over his heart, flooding his body with contentment.

At daybreak, he felt warm breaths against his cheek. He opened his eyes, and there, right next to him, he saw her face, whiter than he had ever seen it before. She had closed her black eyes and was sleeping peacefully for the first time.

So overwhelming was everyone's joy that the entire village turned into a wedding celebration. The women broke into ululations and song, while the men danced with their swords, some waving their shotguns in the air. Grabbing the edges of their tunics by their teeth, the boys went running across the prairie in imitation of Hamama's trotting and running. The earth wasn't vast enough to contain the bliss Khaled felt when he found himself on her back and was certain that he wasn't dreaming. It was a bliss he had never expected to grace his heart again.

Hajj Mahmud said to him, "I thought you were starting to get rusty. And you know there's nothing sadder than for a man to get rusty when he's still in the prime of his youth. Just a few days with her have changed you. They've given back to us what we'd lost in you. Now, may I give you a piece of advice?"

Khaled nodded.

"Don't get off her until you sense that she's gotten inside of you."

Over the course of the following two weeks, Khaled began to feel that Hamama had regained her strength. At the same time, however, he couldn't shake a nebulous fear that had invaded his newfound tranquility, approaching from the opposite side of his exuberance.

Khaled thought back on the day so many years earlier when his relationship with camels and horses had begun. He'd been eight years old when he had his first ride on a camel. That first experience on the back of this gargantuan creature had been exhilarating. It was also the first time he'd had the chance to see the world from such an unaccustomed elevation. After riding around for quite a while, he decided he wanted to get down. However, he'd forgotten the magic word. So, instead of saying "Ikht!," which was the word he was supposed to use in order to get the camel to stop and kneel, he kept saying "Heet!," in response to which the camel continued on its way, until he ended up in the village of Ajjur! So at last, exhausted and desperate, the only solution he could see was to jump down without a thought for the consequences.

One night, feeling that nothing should come between him and Hamama, Khaled flung her saddle some distance away. Then he went down the hill, and when he reached the side of the pasture that lay farthest from the houses of the village, he took off his clothes, folded them carefully, and placed them at the base of an olive tree.

Then he jumped on her back, and the two of them took off for the entire night. They kept moving nonstop, until he felt as though Hamama had sprouted wings and that they were soaring through the sky. By the time the first threads of dawn appeared, he couldn't feel his body any more. He couldn't tell where his body left off and Hamama's began. They were glued together by their perspiration, as though they had been joined from all eternity, and he realized that he'd reached the point where his body had made its way deep inside her, and hers inside him. After riding back to the olive tree where he had left his clothes, he felt he could hardly tear himself away from her.

When at last he dismounted and got dressed again, he was filled with something strange; something he couldn't put into words. And when he started walking alongside her, he realized that he had turned into a horse.

Habbab's Return

Habbab disappeared for a long time, and when he returned, everything about him had changed.

He was summoned by the qa'imaqam, who said to him, "Now we'll complete the favor we've done you. You know that every year we choose a number of merchants, notables, and usurers we can trust to take part in a public auction, and the one who wins pays us the taxes owed by the residents of his area in advance. After that, we provide him with the necessary force to collect what he paid, as well, of course, as the profit due him. This season, however, I'm not going to do this. Instead, I'm going to let you collect whatever you're able to pay us this year, as well as the following year, and I'm confident that you'll do what you need to do. Everything you want will be yours, including whatever force you need, and our protection. As for what we want from you, it's for you to humiliate those who have the audacity to raise their voices in protest, making separatist demands and stirring the people up against the Ottoman State."

Never would Habbab be able to forget that moment.

After all, it was from that moment onward that his fortunes looked up. And from that moment on, his name was on everyone's lips.

Men in Brocaded Cloaks

The winds that blew from the direction of the Thursday market bore news about Hamama. It spread through the entire country. Then one morning, a man halted in her owners' territory. He told them how a certain white thoroughbred had reached the village of Hadiya, and how its people had rescued her from the man who had stolen her and taken her under their protection.

That evening, men clad in brocaded black cloaks arrived on horseback. The men of Hadiya spied them in the distance. Khaled's heart skipped a beat. He was certain that what he had feared was now coming to pass. Kneading his brow with the fingers of his left hand, he turned to his father and said, "We've lost Hamama."

"Rather, she'll be going back to her owners," replied Hajj Mahmud. He knit his brow in such a way that it was hard to tell whether he was just squinting to get a better look at the men approaching in the distance, or whether he was watching something approaching from the future.

He gestured to a number of the men of the village. Understanding what he wanted, they went to make preparations to receive men who had undoubtedly exerted a tremendous effort to come after their lost thoroughbred.

The sun's descent toward the western horizon cast a peculiar golden hue over the entire plain, causing the approaching visitors to look as though they were clad in garments whose colors had come from another world. The horses' colors had been altered, too, so that one could see an orange mare, or a green stallion.

"Something tells me Hamama has been an ambassador of friendship. So a part of her will always stay with us no matter where she goes."

"But what if they aren't her owners?" asked Khaled.

"Do you want to reassure yourself about that?" replied his father, "or do you just not want to lose her? If you're afraid of losing her, remember that no one can lose something that didn't belong to him to begin with. If anyone thinks otherwise, he'll end up tormenting himself twice: first, on account of his ignorance, and second, on account of losing something that wasn't his."

Then he added, "Take her and hide her behind the guesthouse, and let's see what happens."

The sight of Hadiya's men silhouetted against the horizon guided the horsemen to their destination, and as they drew nearer, their colors returned to normal.

There were eight men on the backs of eight horses that were unmistakably thoroughbreds. Yet not one of them was as white as Hamama.

Having reached their destination, they dismounted with the agility of skilled equestrians. Hajj Mahmud welcomed them, and some of the village's young men took their mounts over to the mulberry tree.

Hamdan went to the edge of the guesthouse courtyard, where he poured out the old coffee that was in the dalla. Within moments of his return, the sound of his mortar and pestle was wafting through the air.

Every time he ground coffee for a guest, Hamdan would come up with a special rhythm suited to the occasion. Consequently, one could almost determine who the visitor was, what status he occupied, and whether he had come bearing news that was happy or sad, from the sounds that emerged from Hamdan's mortar and pestle.

That evening, everyone in Hadiya could tell that he was bidding farewell to something precious, and that he was giving expression to what was in their hearts as well. The first person to pick up on Hamdan's message was Khaled. The steady pounding of the pestle in the mortar sounded like the footsteps of someone retreating into the unknown. The rap-a-tap-tap evoked the image of something that you look at and see, but that goes on vanishing until it disappears from view. Your looking at it does nothing to keep it from disappearing, and your holding onto it does nothing to keep it from slipping out of your grasp.

Khaled remembered his wife, whose aura passed fleetingly before his mind's eye.

The horsemen took their seats without saying a word.

"What's wrong, men?" queried Hajj Mahmud. "I hope to God you haven't suffered some calamity or injustice, and that no one's blood has been shed among you."

One of them shook his head sadly and said, "I am Tariq, the son of Shaykh Muhammad Sa'adat. The men with me are my brothers and my paternal cousins."

"Welcome to your house," replied Hajj Mahmud.

"May God grant you life, you son of the noble and generous."

"Whatever you seek is yours. All you have to do is tell me what your request is," said Hajj Mahmud.

"What we seek is something precious and beloved. We lost her more than four weeks ago, and we've been searching high and low for her ever since. What we've lost is a thoroughbred mare that was kidnapped, and we've been told that she passed this way."

From the way his visitor had spoken, Hajj Mahmud knew that the men who had graced his guesthouse with their presence that evening were men of note in their tribe, and that they were possessed of unassailable integrity. He pondered the phrase "We've been told that she passed this way." He could have said, "We've been told that she's here," in which case the mood of their visit would have been decidedly different.

"What does she look like?" asked Hajj Mahmud.

"She's white—whiter than anything anyone has ever laid eyes on."

"She's here."

Clearly elated at the news, the men suddenly appeared less staid and self-possessed than before, and some took hold of the hems of their cloaks in preparation to get up and see her.

"Don't worry, she's fine," Hajj Mahmud reassured them.

When Hamdan arrived with the coffee, Hajj Mahmud was about to get up to serve it to the guests. However, before he'd risen to his feet, Tariq, son of Shaykh Muhammad Sa'adat, patted his thigh, saying, "No offense, Hajj, but we can't drink our coffee until we've seen her. Is she far from here?"

"She's so close she can hear you speaking."

"Fidda (Silver)!" shouted Tariq.

Before he had repeated her name, Hamama began whinnying behind the guesthouse in response to his call.

Rising from his place, Tariq headed in the direction of her whinny. He went around to the back of the guesthouse and found himself face to face with her. She gave a gentle nicker that seemed to come from the depths of her being, and shook her mane merrily. Everyone else had followed him to see what would happen, and as they looked on, he came up to the horse and took her face in his hands. She lowered her head, utterly calm. Then, before his astonished onlookers, Tariq knelt down in front of her. With her evident permission, he grasped one of her front hooves and gently lifted it up. With her hoof in his hand, he kissed it tenderly, then set it back down more tenderly still. He then grasped her other hoof and kissed it in the same way, as she looked on spiritedly.

In the silence that filled those moments, Khaled realized that there was someone who loved her more than he did. He thought back on the pounding of Hamdan's mortar and pestle, and in his mind's eye he saw Hamama

32

disappear in the direction from which she had come, as though some strange, solitary cloud had settled over the earth and hidden her from view.

At dawn the next day, Hajj Mahmud awoke and placed the finest saddle he owned on the mare's back. Then he adorned her with colored ribbons and silver bells, and placed a blue beaded necklace on her forehead.

"She came to us naked, so it won't do for her to return to her family with less than this," he said to his son.

When the other men saw her, they said to him, "We'll never forget this, Hajj. She came to you as a captive, and you're returning her to us in freedom and honor."

Before they took their leave of him, Hajj Mahmud removed his cloak and threw it on the mare's back.

What he had just done went so far beyond the call of generosity that a shiver went through the onlookers, and registered itself visibly on their faces. For in so doing, he was burdening them with a debt that they would never be able to repay. Tariq tried to find something to say. He looked into Hajj Mahmud's face, and into his son's. Then, with the perspicacity of one who knows the place of horses in men's souls, he realized that their mare had stolen Khaled's heart when he glimpsed tears escaping from his eyes.

He said, "If someone takes a horse under his protection, the horse will return the favor. And someone who recognizes a horse's true value reflects his own worth. We commend you now to God's protection. But, God willing, it won't be long before we see you again."

If Khaled could have taken off running after them, he would have. However, his legs didn't belong to him in those dawn hours. Rather, they belonged to the absence that had sprung so suddenly upon him, taking his entire body hostage and leaving him nothing but a shadow, a feather blown to and fro by the wind, or a piece of straw being carried downstream by a flood.

Little did he know that Hamama, who hadn't given him a single backward glance before departing with them into the distance, was opening wide the doors to his future.

On the Monastery Doorstep

F rom the time he arrived, Georgiou seemed like a reputable clergyman.* This earned him the respect of the townsfolk, and particularly that of Hajj Mahmud, the village elder. In the evenings one
might see them engrossed in a long conversation on the doorstep leading
into the monastery or in the village guesthouse, to which the priest was a
regular visitor.

Georgiou's early days in Hadiya were accompanied by numerous problems that no one had anticipated, and the situation almost turned catastrophic when a number of men from the village assaulted the evangelist

---

* The first Greek patriarch to be appointed by the Ottoman Sultan in the church of
Jerusalem was Patriarch Germanos (1534–79). The task of appointing patriarchs in
Jerusalem had now been assigned to the sultans of Constantinople, who replaced the
Greek emperors in this function. Patriarch Germanos worked to strengthen the Order of
the Holy Sepulcher in order to preserve Greek interests in the Patriarchate of Jerusalem,
particularly in the holy places. To this end, he adopted a policy of excluding Arab elements from the patriarchate's administration and from higher ecclesiastical positions.
However, Arab elements in the Orthodox Church began demanding their rights from
the nineteenth century onwards.

Antonius, who, whenever he got the chance, would slip booklets of Bible stories containing simplified Christian doctrine into the children's pockets, saying, "Whoever memorizes these will get a reward!" His behavior had provoked angry reactions because, in this way, he was violating an understanding that had been reached with the people of the village, who had agreed to send their children to the monastery to learn to read and write, provided that no mention be made of religious matters.

It was said that the priest hadn't been informed of what was happening, and that Antonius had done what he had done at the instigation of the two nuns, Sarah and Mary, who were both of a single opinion on such matters.

Hajj Mahmud and Father Georgiou withdrew to a spot on the outskirts of the village, an elevated place that overlooked a huge plain. Because the priest was now aware of the problem that had arisen, he tried to open the conversation. However, Hajj Mahmud said to him, "I'll relieve you of having to explain anything, since I have something to say that may help us nip the problem in the bud and prevent any misunderstandings."

The priest listened with interest to Hajj Mahmud, since he knew it would never do to disregard the wisdom and insights of a man like the one before him.

"What you're calling upon me to believe in, I believe in already," Hajj Mahmud began. "As a Muslim, I believe in more prophets than you do as a Christian. As you may have noticed, we swear by the life of our Lady Mary and our Masters Jesus and Moses, just as we swear by the life of our Master Muhammad. So I can assure you, although I know you're well aware of it, that we have no quarrel with any prophet, nor with any person on earth, so long as we are joined in the end by our faith in one God."

Hajj Mahmud fell silent for a while, his eyes scanning the terrain as far as one could see. With his gaze still fixed on a point in the distance, he said, "And don't forget that Jesus is our son. As my father always said to me, 'If I'd come into this world a bit earlier, I would have seen him, and lived in his generation.' When you came here, Father, we built the monastery with you in the place you had chosen. We raised no objections. And from that day onward, we've considered you one of us, with no distinctions. We haven't forgotten the way you stood by us and lent us assistance during the drought years. And because we trusted you— both the Christians and the Muslims among us—we began paying you one-tenth of our crops and even more. So now, we pay you, and you in turn go and pay taxes on our behalf. All year round we're conscientious about our obligations toward you, and whatever blessing God bestows on us, you receive a share of it. What the Christian families give you, every family gives you, since we're all sons of a single land. We don't think about the fact that some of us are Christians and some of us are Muslims unless you remind us of it."

One day, Khaled said to his father, "There's something I don't understand: why do we pay the monastery so that it can pay our taxes for us?"

"Because the people at the monastery know more than we do, and they know what to do when they go there. If we went ourselves, we might have to pay a lot more. And, as you can see, we're trying in every way we can to free ourselves from the Turks' iron grip. There are even people among us who haven't registered their land in their names. However, every one of us knows exactly where his land begins and ends. And this isn't just true nowadays. This is the way it's been since time immemorial."

Hajj Mahmud paused, then added, "My father, Hajj Umar, may he rest in peace, used to tell us about one day when his father's friends in Ramla advised him to register his land in his name, since nobody can argue with a deed in hand. However, as far as my grandfather was concerned, the existence of a deed could only mean one thing, namely, that he would have to pay more taxes.

"So he said to his friends, 'Do you think I'm out of my mind? Besides, this land has belonged to me since the time of my grandfather, my great-grandfather, my great-great-grandfather, and his father before him. And everyone knows it!'

"They said to him, 'But suppose, God forbid, someone came along and said to you, "This land belongs to me." And suppose that when you told him otherwise, he said, "Show me the deed, then!"'

36

"'What!' he shouted angrily. 'Could somebody come along and divorce me from my wife?'

"Then he took out his sword and started waving it angrily in their faces, saying, 'I'd tell him, "*This* is my deed!"'"

Things Forbidden

In Hajj Mahmud's household, as in the household of his father, Hajj Umar, the only thing that was never allowed at any time was to insult a woman or a mare.

Munira thought back on those days long ago when she had arrived in this house. She'd been a young thing: only fourteen years old. Her father had loved Shaykh Umar so dearly that when he asked for the hand of one of his daughters in marriage for his son Mahmud, he had been undecided as to which of them would be good enough for him. Munira was his youngest. However, she was also the prettiest. So in the end, he decided that she would be the bride.

His wife had said to him, "The girl isn't too young, of course. However, she's our youngest. So what are you going to say to her sisters?"

"I've given the matter a lot of thought," he replied. "And I said to myself: If her in-laws see a bright face like hers when they wake up in the morning and before they go to bed at night, they'll always remember us with kind thoughts. Otherwise, they might not think so highly of us. So, as long as one's decided to give, he might as well give the best he's got."

He reminded her that Hajj Umar had lived for forty years with his first wife, and although they never had any children, he'd been loyal to her till her death, and had never taken a second wife. It was only after her death that he agreed to take another wife, at which point God blessed him with Mahmud and Anisa.

Not everyone thought this way, and problems would often arise when, for example, a groom's family would be shocked to find that the girl their son had been given in marriage wasn't the one they had seen and whose hand they had requested, or when two families had done a 'bridal exchange,' in which one of the two families was given a girl they would never have imagined being their son's wife. However, something no one could deny was that Munira was witty and lovable, which made her all the prettier.

Mahmud had been in his early twenties when they married. But if you asked Munira about herself, she would say, "I was ignorant. I didn't know a thing about housework or anything else. I didn't even know how to comb my hair properly! Mahmud would say to me, 'Come over here.' Then he'd sit me down in front of him and comb my hair for me. He was so patient!"

She thought back with pride on how the justice of the peace who had performed their wedding ceremony had come all the way from Jerusalem, and how the men had gathered in her father's house for the ceremony. She remembered the way she had jumped for joy in the adjoining room when she heard her name on the lips of the justice of the peace, her father, and her husband as they said: "We hereby declare that we have joined Munira, daughter of Abd al-Rahman, who has been found to be free of all defects that would constitute a legal impediment to this contract, and the legally accountable Mahmud Umar al-Qatin from the village of Hadiya, in holy matrimony, with a dowry in the amount of 180 piasters to be delivered to the wife in cash, and a deferred dowry in the amount of 80 piasters. We declare that this contract fulfills all requirements under Islamic law."

※

Continuing with her reminiscences, Munira said, "One day during the month of Ramadan, I decided I was going to become a real housewife no matter what it took. Since the only thing I could find to cook in the house was some okra, I decided to fix him an okra dish—"

Interrupting her, Hajj Mahmud said, "I don't know why you insist on putting yourself down this way. Wouldn't it be better to keep quiet about these things? After all, nobody else has said anything about them, and nobody's planning to."

She replied, "I talk about these things so the boys will know how to treat their wives when they get married. And I want them to know that no matter how patient they are with their wives, they won't have been half as good to them as you've been to me."

Then she continued, "When he began his fast-breaking meal that evening, I started looking at his face, watching for his reaction and wondering what he would say. He didn't say anything. Then I started eating myself, and from the first bite, I knew I shouldn't try making that dish again! The thing I couldn't understand was why he didn't say a word! When he'd finished eating, I asked him, 'How was the food?' And he said, 'Praise God, it couldn't get better than that. It's delicious!' 'Would you like some more?' I asked. 'No,' he said, 'one plateful's enough. That way, I can remember it and look forward to the next time I get to eat it!'

"By this time, of course, I knew it was saltier than the Dead Sea! He wouldn't say anything, and he refused to eat at his sister's house, or even at his mother's, so that they wouldn't suspect anything. Then one time, my mother came to visit, so I cooked for her. I thought to myself: This way she'll know that her daughter has turned into a first-rate housewife!

"The minute she put the first bite in her mouth, she said, 'Do you cook food like this for your husband every day?'

"'Yes, I do,' I told her proudly.

"'Is all your cooking like this?' she wanted to know.

"'Of course,' I assured her.

'And does your husband eat it every time?'

"'Of course.'

"'And he doesn't say anything? Anything at all?'

"'Of course not.'

"At that point, she tore into me with everything she had: 'Lord, have mercy! We married you off to give ourselves a good reputation, and here you are, a disaster! God help your husband! God help him! I swear to God, if he asked me to marry him to somebody else, I'd do it!'

"Then she stalked out and slammed the door behind her!"

Munira fell silent and looked over at her husband. "But I did try. Didn't I, Hajj?"

"God knows you tried too hard!" he said. Then he burst out laughing.

Munira shot him a disapproving look, but he went on laughing so hard, the house nearly shook. "So," he said, "you want to make them gloat over my misfortune, do you?"

When his laughter had subsided and he was wiping the tears from his eyes, she said, "But it's true! I used to ask every lady I knew if I could learn from her. And you can't say I didn't! So tell them. Tell these children of yours!"

And he burst out laughing again.

However, there was more to say.

Munira continued, "When I had our first daughter, Aziza, I felt totally helpless. I didn't know what to do. I would see Aziza's soiled bottom and, instead of cleaning her up, I'd just let out a horrified, 'Yuck!' Then Mahmud would come clean her bottom and give her a bath. I admit it, Aziza's her daddy's girl more than she is mine!

"But that's not all. When the little one would wake up crying in the night, I wouldn't make a move. With great difficulty, Hajj Mahmud would wake me up, but I wouldn't get up. 'You take care of her,' I'd say to him.

"'The baby's hungry, woman!'

"'And what am I supposed to do about it?' I'd say.

"'Nurse her, for God's sake!'

"'I'm sleepy!'

"'All right, then, I'll take you to Jerusalem on Friday.'

"'I don't want to go to Jerusalem.'

"'I'll buy you whatever you want from Jaffa.'

"'I don't want anything from Jaffa.'

"'I'll give you a bashlak.'

"It's true, I liked money, and I'd get all excited when I saw it, since most of the buying and selling we did in the village was just bartering: You give me oil, I'll give you cheese. You give me sugar, I'll give you eggs.

"Then I'd go back to sleep, while our baby girl cried her heart out. Hajj Mahmud would nudge me again, saying, 'I'll give you two bashlaks.'

"'All right!' I agreed finally.

"And with that, I got out of bed, took her from him, and nursed her. Things went on this way till Khaled came along.

"Once, when my mother had come for a visit, she asked me why Khaled was crying.

"'I don't know!' was all I could say as my mother picked him up, saying, 'Curses on whoever finalized your marriage contract!'"

"Then one day, when Khaled and I were alone in the house, I realized he was sick. When I picked him up, he seemed taller than me. His feet nearly touched the floor. I went the rounds of the house, not knowing what to do. However, it was on that day that I felt for the first time that I was a mother, and I began crying over him."

Munira fell silent. Then, looking into the faces of her husband and children, she said, "I was really awful. But I was young then, wasn't I, Hajj?"

A Filly from Timbuktu

For three entire years, Khaled was on the lookout for news about Hamama. He had lost his taste for horses, just as he had lost his taste for women after his wife's passing. Things continued in this way until Hajj Mahmud was certain that he had lost his son.

There had been no news from Hamama's owners. In fact, it was as though she had never been among them, neither she nor her owners, and if it hadn't been for the sadness that had wrested their son from them, they would have sworn that what happened had been a collective dream: a dream experienced by all the people of Hadiya, as well as by villages that had envied them their good fortune. It was as if they were reliving a distant winter that would never repeat itself, or a marriage the likes of which they'd never celebrated, or a loss.

Khaled no longer said more than the bare minimum, and the few things he did say, he said to his mother, since he realized that to be silent in her presence would mean one thing: her death; her death in life.

Meanwhile, he began to wilt. He looked shorter than before, and the verdant twinkle in his eyes had disappeared. His chest and shoulders seemed narrower. His round face had shrunk visibly, and its brightness had dimmed. Things looked so bleak that Munira got out her plates again and carried them to a spot where she expected him to sit, dreaming of the day when she would again hear the sound of her most precious possessions shattering on the floor.

He was a man turned in upon himself, a man tied in knots, who made no attempt to conceal the pain that was squeezing the life out of him.

He wasn't lying to himself. No, everything was as clear as day. It was as clear as the expanse of grassland that had thrice turned green, then yellow, thrice been scorched by the sun, then drenched with spring rains, thrice filled with sowers and harvesters whose song and laughter had filled the threshing floors, and filled a hundred times with flocks and the noisy ruckus of the marketplace.

Hajj Mahmud had searched in vain for a filly that looked like Hamama. Every time a man left Hadiya, he would give him instructions to come back if he saw one like her.

He was prepared to do anything to make his son's heart blossom again.

But it was hopeless. There was no other horse like Hamama, any more than there could be another village like Hadiya, another mother like one's own mother, or another father like one's own father.

After Hajj Mahmud had laid his head down to sleep one night, his wife tried to talk to him.

Interrupting her forlornly, he said, "Don't say a word. If I could find him a filly like her in Timbuktu, I'd go there and get it. But he's asking the impossible. He wants *her*, and no other. As for the men who took her away, it's as if they went on riding and riding for three whole years without even thinking to look back."

One morning, in the still dawn hours, Khaled opened his eyes, then closed them again. He thought he'd seen Hamama standing in front of him and looking exactly the way she had on that night so long ago: like a resplendent full moon. Certain now that he about to lose his mind, he turned over and rested his head on his right arm.

A faint cry caused him to turn around again. At first he didn't dare open his eyes. However, reminding himself that looking to see what was there couldn't rob him of what he'd already lost, he began opening them ever so slowly. Hamama was still there. Again he closed his eyes. Then he heard a genial whinny, and at that point he knew he wasn't dreaming. He wasn't suffering delusions. Even so, he didn't dare jump for joy, since a jump the size of his longings would never have brought him back to earth. He clung to his blanket, to the mattress, to the soil of the courtyard. He clung to his body for fear that the force of the surprise would send it flying in all directions. Then, ever so slowly, he got up.

Once he was on his feet, he was even more certain that he wasn't dreaming, and that what he was seeing was real.

He came up to the mare. She didn't retreat. There were decorations on her halter and around the edges of her saddle, and on her back there lay a white cloak whose gold and silver embroidery glittered in the darkness.

But there was no one with her.

Since no one had woken to the sound of her hoofbeats, it was as though she had come galloping through the air.

Fearful, he doubted his eyes, his sanity. He took a step toward her, his palms open, and placed them gently around her jaws. Then his thumbs began moving up toward her forehead.

She didn't move.

It really was Hamama, then. She'd come back!

Yet again, he was filled with fear—the fear that she had come back on her own. For if she had, it meant that someone would be coming to look for her. On the other hand, how could a mare come back after three years away? If she'd wanted to come back, she would have done so in a couple of days, or a week, or a month at most. But three years later? That was an impossibility.

He was reassured by the presence of the cloak on her back and the decorations on her harness and saddle. After all, a thoroughbred wouldn't leave home looking like this unless her owners had pronounced their blessing on her new path, and on the life she would be living beyond their frontiers.

He thought of going inside and waking his father and mother. He thought of going out and waking the entire village with a loud whoop. But he was afraid that if he did that, he wouldn't find her upon his return, or that he would frighten her in this way, causing her to vanish as suddenly as she had appeared.

So he remained standing where he was, her face cradled in his hands, until he heard Shaykh Husni's voice filling the air with the dawn call to prayer.

Hajj Mahmud stood at the front door, his astonishment matched only by Khaled's. In the half-light of dawn, he saw his son's eyes twinkling. He saw them being filled with life anew. He saw their beautiful greenness. Coming up to his son, he fixed his eyes on Hamama, walked once around her, then said, "A mare like this is worth waiting all this time for." Then, after a pause, he added, "Let's perform the dawn prayer here next to her, next to this miracle of God."

Hajj Mahmud performed his ablutions first, followed by his son. When Munira came out, she was as surprised as her husband and son had been. Hajj Mahmud then led his wife and son in the prayer, at the end of which he made supplications, asking for God's mercy and protection for his son and his mare: "O God, protect them! You are their Maker and their Refuge in this life and the next."

When he finished praying, he looked at his son. "I'm not going to tell you to take good care of her," he said. "You know what you need to do. She's come to you this time of her own accord, and crossed our threshold of her own free will. May she always be free, just as she is today."

Then he retreated into silence once again. After gazing thoughtfully at Hamama for a long time, he said, "And remember that if someone has been recognized by a horse, he's bound to be recognized by people as well."

Hamama's return continued to be an inscrutable mystery. However, this didn't prevent the people of Hadiya from reliving the joy they had known before. Neighboring villages such as Zakariya, Ajjur, Iraq Suwaydan, al-Brayj, al-Musammaya, Qatra, al-Maghar and others could hear melodious strains wafting in their direction on the night air as Hajj Mahmud, his exuberance overflowing, sang out:

There's a sun in the house whose radiance
Is our bliss from morning to night.

There's a sun that goes running through the meadows,
Whose allure doth the lovesick smite!

There's a sun in the heart, in my breast and yours,
Whose light we can scoop up and hold in our hands.

There's a sun no night has ever touched
That dwells among us, ye dwellers of the grasslands!

A couple of days later, Khaled's mother said to him, "And don't I have a share in Hamama?"

"You've got a big share! After all, don't you know that my soul lives in her?"

"All right, then," she said, "leave us alone for a while. I've got something to say to her!"

Khaled left the courtyard. He would have loved to hear what sort of secret his mother was planning to confide in Hamama. However, he knew it wouldn't be proper to listen in on a conversation between two thoroughbreds.

Coming close to Hamama, Munira stroked her neck. She'd brought some boiled wheat sprinkled with sugar, which she proceeded to feed the mare out of her hand. When she was finished, she whispered to her, "Take good care of my son. He's your charge now, a sacred trust, and the two of you together are God's charge, a sacred trust in the hands of the Almighty."

Then she repeated, "Take good care of my son. He's your charge now, a sacred trust, and the two of you together are God's charge, a sacred trust in the hands of the Almighty."

Prolonged Negotiations!

Father Georgiou remembered the cold winter day when the people of Hadiya had agreed to let him teach their children at the monastery. The negotiations that led to the agreement had gone on for a long time, not because the children would be taking lessons at the monastery, but because their parents needed them in the fields, a fact that Shaykh Husni always took into consideration when he gave them lessons in the mosque.

However, the fact that winter arrived early that year—which Father Georgiou saw as a sign that heaven had intervened in his favor at just the right moment—settled the matter.

When he gathered the boys and girls in the back hall of the church, they were shivering. A fire blazing behind him in the corner was sufficient to arouse their enthusiasm. It was true, of course, that some of them had seen the smoke rising from the high stone pillar that rose up over the monastery. They'd had experience with bread ovens, and with the stoves they would light in front of their doorsteps before bringing them inside their houses. They had also seen smoke rising from the wood stoves they used to heat water in the village, and from the chimneys of the houses of the people who had fireplaces. However, the sight of a fire at such close range gave them the urge to get up next to it.

Father Georgiou accepted the condition that Hajj Mahmud had stipulated, namely, that the Muslim children simply learn to read and write. As for the Christian children, they could also attend lessons on religion if they chose to. After the children had come inside, but before Father Georgiou's arrival, Antonius asked them to be quiet. After all, he told them, a monastery is sacred, just as a mosque is. So they quieted down, sensing that the place they were in was every bit as much the house of God as their own place of worship. Meanwhile, Antonius disappeared briefly into a dark corner, then reemerged so suddenly that they let out a collective gasp. It was as though he had come straight out of the wall. He made his way around the room, holding a dark-colored box out to them. It was hard for them to see exactly what color it was—somewhere between an olive green and the color of dust. However, it wasn't difficult to recognize the tortuous lines and irregular spaces on top of it as writing.

Then, before his awestruck young audience, Antonius picked up his New Testament and said, "Whoever understands this book well will always have some of this!" As he spoke, he opened the box, from which he produced a number of rectangular-shaped objects. He began distributing them among the children, whose hands and voices filled the room with riotous pandemonium. They had completely forgotten that they were in a house of God, just as Antonius had forgotten that he'd asked them to be quiet just a few minutes earlier.

The Nestlé chocolate bars that had made the rounds of the class bore no resemblance to the Turkish delight, sugar-coated roasted chickpeas, or the sweet-and-sour and mint-flavored drops that they bought from Abu Ribhi's corner store or that their families would bring them from Jerusalem or cities on the coast. After finishing what was in their hands, some of them spent the rest of the time licking their lips and sucking the tips of the fingers that had held the precious treat. When they realized that they had licked off the last of it, they went on to the other fingers, in the hope that they might have picked up some of the delectable flavor. When Antonius picked up the New Testament again to talk about the felicity that awaited those who obeyed God's teachings, the children's eyes were fixed on the box in his hand, wondering whether there was anything left in it.

Antonius retreated again into the darkness, to that lightless point from which he had emerged earlier, and when he came back to the children, the magic box was no longer in his hand. When he turned to look at the children, he could see how dazzled they were by what they had tasted, and how eager they were for more.

At last Father Georgiou came in and said, "Christians sit on one side, and Muslims on the other."

The children looked at each other as though they didn't understand what he was asking them to do. At last, one of them got up and headed over toward the fireplace, and was soon followed by another.

Khaled, Hajj Mahmud's son, asked Antonius, "Are the ones beside the fireplace Christians or Muslims?"

"They're Christians, aren't they?" Antonius replied.

The children sitting beside the fire nodded in agreement.

"So then," said Khaled, "I'm a Christian, too."

And within moments all the children were gathered around the fireplace.

Blood and a Dagger

Nothing that earthshaking could possibly have been kept a secret. Flying over the fields, the orchards, and the vineyards of the entire area, the news of his appointment came pounding violently on their doors.

He was of medium height and build. However, so invincible was his authority among the region's inhabitants that wherever they saw him, whether he was seated or standing, he always seemed to be on horseback.

He was eternally inscrutable, as sharp as the blade of the dagger that never left his belt.

In the large courtyard where their tents had been pitched, he gathered the men of the surrounding villages and asked them to pay the money they owed him.

"What money is this that we're supposed to pay you?" asked one of the men.

Rising from his gold-trimmed black chair, the chair he had brought from Jaffa specially for this occasion, Habbab walked calmly over to the man and stopped in front of him. Then, in a movement so swift that no one knew what was happening, his dagger plunged into the the man's upper abdomen, aiming for his heart, and settled there. When he was sure that everyone was well aware of what was happening, he turned the blade twice in the man's chest before pulling it out again.

There wasn't much blood covering the blade when he said, "It was fear that killed him"—a saying that was to become legendary. Before the man fell to the ground, Habbab ran the edges of his dagger over the victim's shoulder, so the blood glistened on the border of his white keffiyeh.

He gave the tottering frame a shove, and it fell over.

And that was enough to ensure the obedience of villages near and far.

The Twilight of the Empire

his was by no means the end of the problems. However, one thing
was certain, namely, that Father Georgiou was sure at last that
through his presence in Hadiya he would be able to collect the tithe,
which he could dispose of however he pleased, as well as the baskets of
fruit and vegetables, the jars of milk, and the cheeses that came into the
monastery in a never-ending stream from one season to the next. Consequently, when he prayed for God to cause rain and good fortune to
descend upon the land, he was utterly sincere. After all, he knew that the
presence of the monastery in the most fertile of all the villages was a blessing from God that only those who enjoyed it could possibly imagine.

Habbab's influence increased with every passing day. However, Hajj Mahmud refused to allow Hadiya to be among the villages that pledged him
allegiance. Nor was this on account of the monastery alone. It was also on
account of the respect Hajj Mahmud enjoyed, and which his father, Hajj
Umar, had enjoyed before him. Nevertheless, everything changed when
the Ottoman Empire began teetering on the brink of collapse and, as a

result, was willing to do anything in return for money and military recruits. Tax collectors began tightening the screws on the villages from all directions, so that now people were obliged to pay taxes not only on their crops but, in addition, on their horses, goats, sheep, and other livestock. Things got to the point where they were paying taxes on every resident of the village, and it wouldn't be long before they would start having to pay a 'hat tax,' which was levied on everyone who wore a cloth head covering, such as a keffiyeh, a turban, or a fez!

Hamdan's Day

It was clear to everyone that the Hamama that had come to Khaled of late was not the Hamama that had left. Those who were familiar with horses were certain that the filly was two years old, and that she was the original Hamama's daughter.

What no one had realized, however, was that the new Hamama's arrival marked the beginning of a new chapter in Khaled's life, and that the joyous lines she would inscribe on Hadiya's foothills and plains would go far beyond the marks left by her beloved mother.

Three days later, they arrived.

They were a party of three men headed by Tariq bin Muhammad Sa'adat. The whole village set out to receive them. When Hajj Mahmud embraced them, he held on to them for so long, people thought he'd never let them go. The longest embrace of all was reserved for Tariq, with his towering, lanky frame, his sparkling eyes, and his face as fresh as a rose in bloom.

As usual, Hamdan poured out the coffee that was in the dalla even though no one had tasted it yet, and began crushing some new beans.

Those who heard the rap-a-tap-tap of his large mortar and pestle that day could have sworn they'd never heard the likes of it before. He was in such raptures that he began dancing in circles around it as though he were a dervish at a Sufi dhikr ceremony. Every now and then they would see him leap in the air, and the time during which his body was suspended in mid-air would create a moment of silence that completed the rhythm of the dance. His brief flight would conclude with a thud as his feet came back to earth. He was in such a rare state that he didn't even notice when everyone began looking his way.

The place was filled with the aroma of coffee. After floating through the guesthouse courtyard, it made its way ethereally toward the pasture, traversing the wheat fields, corn fields, sesame fields, and olive groves.

Clapping their hands, boys gathered around the periphery of the guesthouse. A little boy by the name of Rashid, who of all the boys was the most enthralled by the scene, stood watching in silence, his eyes like saucers. When Hamdan moved on to the second part of his coffee preparation routine, everything about him was joyous: his eyes, his hands, even his lame leg.

At last he rose from the fireside, the dalla and the coffee cups in hand, and headed inside the guesthouse. The children trailed along behind him, then stationed themselves some distance from the door.

Khaled took the dalla and poured the coffee into a cup. After tapping the spout against the cup, he handed it to Hajj Mahmud, who passed it on to Tariq. And then came a surprise.

"We have a request to make of you," Tariq announced. Looking Hajj Mahmud in the eye, he continued, "We'll drink the coffee after you've promised to meet it!"

"If you asked for our souls, it wouldn't be too much," came the reply.

"You know, Hajj, that our horses are like our own family to us. And you know that the tie that binds us is a momentous thing."

Visibly moved, Hajj Mahmud nodded his head. "Everything you hope for will come to pass, God willing."

"Our request is for you to be our guests one week from today."

"You're showering us with such generosity, we fear we'll never be able to repay it," said Hajj Mahmud.

"You'll be repaying it by accepting our invitation. No matter what we do, we'll never be able to forget that you are the ones who first honored us by honoring our thoroughbred."

"Next week we'll be on your soil, God willing. Now drink your coffee!"

"But we have another request as well."

"The first filly born to Hamama belongs to you. Your second request must have to do with her."

"That's right. As you know, a thoroughbred filly can only be allowed to mate with a thoroughbred stallion, and the stallion that's descended from her line lives with us. So when she's in heat, be careful not to let any of your stallions come near her. When that time comes, all you have to do is to come to us, and you'll be our honored guests."

"Agreed. We ask God always for the grace to do our duty, whether it's toward horses or toward people of conscience."

At last they drank the coffee and the room filled with chatter.

Suddenly, Hajj Mahmud said, "But I have a question."

"Go ahead, Hajj."

"Why did you bring her, then leave?"

"For one simple reason. We didn't want to spoil the moment your son first saw her."

Hajj Mahmud nodded in comprehension as Khaled and Tariq exchanged a look of pure warmth.

That afternoon they left Hadiya. But before they set out, Tariq turned his horse around and rode back to Khaled. He didn't have to lean down very far as he whispered in his ear, "This is the first time any of Fidda's daughters has left our territory. Take care of her, and she'll take care of you. Be gentle with her, and she'll be your stronghold. May God protect you both."

A Third of Life!

abbab shrieked. His eyes flashed. His features bulged and the gauntness of his cheeks vanished beneath his black beard, which was faintly studded with white.

"I'm telling you for the last time: stop crying!"

His voice rang out across the hills. However, the covey of birds bathing contentedly in the water that had collected around the edge of the well paid no attention. Something made the bride hold her breath, as she realized that she no longer had any family now that he had wrested her away from them against their will.

He had come to her house alone, and circled it twice. Everyone could see the dark cloud of dust that surrounded the house until it nearly concealed it from view.

He had seen her two days before, and two days before he had told her family, "I want her ready on Thursday morning."

He rode up to the house in great haste. When they asked him to come in, he said, "I haven't come to visit." Then he began circling the house, and didn't stop until it was clear that all the wedding preparations were complete. The hands of the shaykh who had come to conclude the wedding ceremony trembled every time he addressed a new question to Habbab, who hadn't deemed the occasion worth the trouble of dismounting.

They had undoubtedly been taken by surprise. They had expected him to come with a number of his men. However, he had come alone, possibly in order to humiliate them all the more.

When he saw the bride on the mare she would be riding, he came toward her and lifted the veil that concealed her face. She was crying. However, the flow of her tears didn't prevent him from seeing her extraordinary charm. He was certain he hadn't made any mistake: she was the most beautiful girl he had ever laid eyes on.

He lowered the veil.

Her family's fear of Habbab had prompted them to choose the best mare they had to carry the bride. They festooned the horse with decorations as though they were the ones who had chosen their daughter's husband.

He looked at the mare's reins. The family understood. He didn't want to bend down to take hold of them. One of the family members rushed up and handed them to him. He grasped the reins and turned, preparing to head for the hills.

Half an hour after they had set out, down a road flanked on either side by olive groves, he turned suddenly and began riding up a craggy foothill.

The sun was almost exactly parallel to him on the left. Vineyards extended as far as the eye could see, while the bleating of sheep and goats could be heard in the distance. However, she saw and heard nothing of the sights and sounds that surrounded her. Rather, her eyes were fixed upon him alone, and she saw him as a thick rope binding her to an inscrutable destiny that was leading her into a bottomless pit.

When his horse stumbled, all her senses were jolted awake. Before she could discern the nature of the feeling that had come over her, she heard him say, "One!"

The narrow path inclined upward, and with difficulty the two horses attempted to find spaces large enough in which to put their feet down with confidence.

She tried to pin some meaning on what she had heard, but nothing came to mind.

Another stumble nearly caused Habbab's horse to lose its balance. He cursed the horse and its ancestors, and the bride began fearfully anticipating the next moment. Ten meters up the path, she heard him mutter impatiently through his teeth, "Two!"

Suddenly, she sensed that her own tragedy stood waiting in the wings, and the earth seemed to stop turning.

Once they'd begun making their way down the other side of the hill, he cast a glance westward. He saw the sea in its limpid blueness and hundreds of orchards and vineyards extending to infinity. He looked in the other direction, but his house had yet to appear in the distance. The descent promised to be easy, auguring no danger, and the bride seemed pleased with the horses' smooth progress down the hill. But all of that changed in the twinkling of an eye.

Her eyes were fixed on the stallion's steps. And as though it had stumbled in response to her gaze, she saw it twist its right ankle, then its left. Its face nearly touched the ground. It managed to right itself, but something in its gait was different.

The silence, which grew heavier by the moment, caused her to notice things she had never noticed before. Finally, she heard him say, "Three!"

As he reached for his waist and pulled out his revolver, the horse came to a halt, sensing that something strange was happening. The bride came up alongside him on her mare, as he had deliberately given her the chance to do. Meanwhile, the revolver moved slowly toward the horse's head until it settled coldly between his ears, and before the bride could guess what the next moment might bring, a shot rang out.

※

The horse fell heavily to the ground, but Habbab had no difficulty dismounting at the right moment. He stood listening to the shot's echo as it spread in ever-expanding circles, until it died away and silence reigned once more.

The distance that remained seemed longer, now that the mare was carrying both of them.

The bride's throat was parched with thirst and fright. When they passed a mountain well and she saw the water sparkling in the stone cistern, she blurted out, in spite of herself, "I'm thirsty!"

He turned to look at her, his eyes glinting beneath his bushy black brows. She turned her face away, having seen a fire blazing in his eyes.

Then she heard him say, "One!"

And she realized that a third of her lifetime had just passed, never to return.

The Return of the Black Carriage

ather Georgiou's stay wasn't a long one. The same black carriage drawn by two black horses that had brought him to the village once upon a time stopped once again in front of the monastery entrance, and from it emerged the new priest, Father Theodorus.

Father Theodorus' arrival came as no surprise to Father Georgiou. Nevertheless, he had informed no one in the village, not even Hajj Mahmud, that he would be leaving. His suitcase and his big wooden trunk packed and ready to go, he contented himself with shaking the newcomer's hand at the monastery gate, as though he didn't want the two of them to be in the same place at once.

As the carriage set out, people followed its movement with their eyes. When it reached the eastern edge of Hadiya's grassland, the dust began to dissipate so that many of those looking on could see the carriage come to a halt. Some thought it was going to come back. Instead, however, it remained where it was. As the minutes passed, more than one man thought of mounting his horse and going out to see what was happening. However, as they stood there wondering what to do, they saw the carriage door open and Father Georgiou get out. He turned toward the village and stood gazing at it contemplatively from afar, pondering its sprawling plains, its olive trees, and the way its houses rose lightly in the direction of the hilltop.

He was saying goodbye to a cherished part of his life, and he wondered: Was it necessary for me to leave it in order to see it from this new perspective?

A long time passed as he stood there, and when at last he went back to the carriage and disappeared inside, all that remained in the distance was a cloud of dust rising impetuously toward the unknown.

Al-Barmaki's Dreams

From the time Hamama had appeared in Hadiya, al-Barmaki had been going mad. It was even said that he rarely went beyond Hadiya's borders any more.

One of the most famous men in the village, al-Barmaki made his entire living by having his stud mate with other people's mares. And because his stallion was known to be a thoroughbred, he had a good, steady income.

Everyone who practiced this profession was referred to as 'al-Barmaki.' It was as though they ceased to have a name of their own the minute they took up this line of work. As for Hadiya's 'Barmaki,' people had known him for a long time, and half of all the horses in the village were descended from his stud, Antar. Consequently, he was always welcome, and for many years Antar had been the springhead of all the mares born in Hadiya.

People's experiences with al-Barmaki had proved to be positive, and even when one stallion would die, as had happened two years earlier, he would always replace the old one with a purebred that was as good as, if not better than, its predecessor. In fact, lots of folks wished their mares had mated with the newcomer rather than with his forerunner.

However, the seasons passed, mares went on foaling, and the time would always come for them to be in heat again.

Al-Barmaki was a slight man who had spent so much time gazing into the horizon in search of a new mare that he'd become bug-eyed. Consequently, Hamama's arrival in the village had given him a new lease on life.

If he could manage to get his new stallion, Shaddad, together with Hamama, this would give him a badge of approval of sorts that he could wear proudly when he made the rounds of other villages. With this feather in his cap, he could stand nonchalantly before any other mare and say smugly, "They agreed to let this stud of mine mount Hamama herself!"

Although he knew that a dream of this magnitude would never come true, he still lived in the hope that it would. He would even have been prepared to pay out of his pocket in order to achieve this cherished hope. As for his horse, he was no less eager.

Al-Barmaki was aware of the place of honor Hamama (Dove) occupied in Hajj Mahmud's household. It was true, of course, that the filly's name had become associated with that of Khaled alone. However, they related to her not as a horse, but as one of their own daughters. As for their other horses, their names were Khadra (Green One), Rih (Wind), and Jalila (Majestic One).

One day, as al-Barmaki passed near where Hamama stood, he sensed that she was now a full-grown mare. He could feel the physical desire heating her blood and turning her into a flaming ember. Not long afterwards, as he was sitting in the guesthouse with Hajj Mahmud and Khaled, it occurred to him to offer them his stud's services free of charge. However, he didn't dare.

And it's a good thing he didn't, since if he had, they would have taken it as a serious personal affront.

The Curse of the Name

G hazi!" al-Barmaki called out.

"Yes, Baba," his son answered.

"I wish you a bride like that," he said, pointing to Hamama.

"And where would I get a bride like her, Baba?" he asked wistfully.

The story of al-Barmaki and his son is one of the best-known in all of Hadiya, and always will be. When Ghazi, his eldest son, was born, al-Barmaki had been out of town on one of his horse-breeding rounds, which would last for a number of weeks. When he returned, Shinnara, the village midwife, broke into joyful ululations and informed him that his wife had given birth to a son. He knew, of course, what she wanted, and that she may have spent days on his doorstep waiting to receive what was due her in return for this piece of welcome news.

Borrowing a favorite phrase of Munira's, he asked incredulously, "Is that so?" his eyes welling up with tears.

"It's so and a half!" Shinnara reassured him.

✻

He took off on horseback toward the house as though the news had come as a total surprise, or as though he'd been told that his wife was pregnant at a time when there was no hope of such a thing.

Shinnara turned over the silver pound that rested in her hand, not believing her eyes. Then she ran to hide it in her chest. When she got home, however, she stopped in a state of indecision, since it had occurred to her that the chest might not be the safest place to keep it. She began racking her brain for the best hiding place. Before she had made up her mind what to do, someone began knocking loudly on the door, and she feared that thieves might have come to steal her treasure. She hesitated, not knowing whether to open the door or not. But when she heard al-Barmaki's voice outside, she was slightly reassured. So she opened the door, only to find him in a rage.

"Where's the pound I gave you?" he demanded angrily.

She was so taken aback that, before she had a chance to think, she extended her open hand, saying, "Here it is!"

Like the talons of a falcon seizing its prey, his fingers swooped down and snatched the pound out of her hand.

"Didn't they tell you to record his name as Ghazi on his birth certificate?" he demanded.

"But your wife wanted to name him after her father Yunus!"

"Is that so? Then go get the pound from my wife!"

He turned around furiously and went back to where he had come from.

Within a few days he had calmed down, and he began to feel that Shinnara hadn't deserved the treatment he'd meted out to her. So the next time he saw her, he accosted her and said, "Forgive me, Shinnara."

"Don't worry about it, Abu Yunus!"

"Don't call me Abu Yunus!" he bellowed.

"What shall I call you, then?"

"Call me Abu Ghazi."

"All right." However, she didn't say the name.

"All right, what?"

"All right, Abu . . ." but she didn't go on.

"You can't say it. Ha!"

"But Yunus is a pretty name."

"Pretty or not, it makes no difference to me. You've got to find a solution to this problem."

"And how am I going to do that?"

"I don't know. You're his mother's midwife, and you're the one who told them that his name was Yunus.

"Can you wait nine months or a year . . . until I can change the name?" She spoke with a sudden sense of tranquility, having found the solution to their dilemma.

"I'll wait till Judgment Day!" he retorted furiously.

"And will you give me the pound back, then?"

"The pound, and a riyal to boot."

Then, in a bizarre turn of events, al-Barmaki found himself unable to take his son in his arms. The most he could do was steal fleeting glances at him. His name stood as a barrier between them, preventing him from getting close to the boy. It kept him from hugging him or even uttering his name when he cried or got sick, or when he made those happy babbling sounds that fall short of laughter or even a smile.

During that time, which seemed to last an eternity, he kept an eye on his wife's belly without noticing any signs of a new pregnancy. From time to time he had considered a compromise, namely, that of keeping Yunus as his firstborn son's name and calling their second son Ghazi. However, he would invariably end up furious all over again, and upbraid himself for thinking such things.

In spite of everything that had happened, Shinnara kept up her visits to al-Barmaki's wife to see whether there was another child on the way.

One day al-Barmaki and Shinnara happened to meet on his front doorstep.

"So," he asked her, "have you found the solution?"

"Yes, I have."

"What is it?"

"I'll go and report that your wife has had another son and that you've named him Ghazi."

"Is she pregnant again?"

"No. But this is the only thing to do. You take the new birth certificate and tear up the old one, and nobody will ever know!"

"Would that work?" he wondered aloud. "By God, it would!"

Then he led his horse away, repeating to himself over and over, "It would work. It really would!"

The First Cry

T he olive season had been good to them that year, and the heavens
had promptly poured forth showers that sent new life pulsing
through the trees. Their new growth was a rich, deep green and
their fruit glossy and succulent, causing everyone to stream out to the
olive groves.

Meanwhile, something new had entered the village: the olive press
that Father Theodorus had brought. The new olive press, which had
now become part of the monastery's backyard, had relieved the people
of Hadiya from the hardship of traveling long distances to get their
olives pressed.

However, Father Theodorus made certain that he received the
wages due him for the service he was providing. The villagers also owed
him one-tenth of their crop, which he deducted in full. This was in addition to the other miscellaneous offerings he received from time to time.
Whatever else one might have said about all this, one thing was certain:
Father Theodorus didn't trust anyone. The only thing he trusted was
what he could see with his own two eyes. This had been a frequent

source of consternation to Hajj Mahmud, who saw the priest acting more like an unscrupulous city merchant than a man of religion.

However, Father Theodorus would make excuses for his avarice, saying, "Don't forget, Hajj, that what you all give me is something I owe the state, and I wouldn't want to come before the authorities with an incomplete tithe!"

Nevertheless, the priest's avidity had come to bewilder everyone in the village. Not a day had passed since his arrival in Hadiya but that they had seen him touring the village's fields and orchards, with the two nuns, Sarah and Mary, staggering along behind him. These were the only occasions when they would see the nuns outside the confines of the monastery, since everything was provided for them, from the water they drank to bundles of firewood.

When he returned, he was dumbfounded by what he saw.

The strange thing was that Father Theodorus, a handsome, blue-eyed young man with a towering physique, would often act as though he owned the entire village. At least, this was how he came across to the people of the town.

Hajj Mahmud labored to drive the worrisome suspicions from his mind, since he knew the monastery's presence had become a necessity now that the Turks had sold scores of villages at public auction to landowners in Syria and Lebanon. The villages in question had been unable to pay the tithe for a number of years running, and as a result had accumulated large debts to the state.

However, there was more to the situation.

One day, the priest had shouted at a group of boys who were climbing an olive tree, upbraiding them with words that no one would use unless he were protecting his own property.

On more than one occasion, he had made cryptic remarks about people relying too much on the well, and how the women of the village should use only limited amounts of water because, as he put it, "Heaven isn't a hireling that works for the earth. Rather, the earth works to please heaven." Nevertheless, all their suspicions were dissipated by his superb mastery of the Arabic language, which made it impossible for them to view him as an outsider. His Arabic was so phenomenal, in fact, that he could argue circles around Shaykh Husni himself when it came to questions of grammar and syntax. It wasn't unusual to find him sitting entranced by Tarafa bin al-Abd's ode, saying, "Now *this* is poetry! This is poetry!"

O thou that wouldst ensure my immortality, wherefore dost thou prevent me from enjoying life's pleasures or entering the fray?

Let me seek immortality with the wealth that my hands possess
If thou hast not the power to keep my death at bay.

Indeed, were it not for the three passions of my youth
And thy good fortune, I should not care when death taketh me away.

In short, Arabic was his miracle, and this is what earned him the people's trust. However, Hajj Mahmud—who was intimately familiar with Tarafa bin al-Abd's poem, having studied it under the tutelage of Shaykh Husni's father—was troubled by the fact that Theodorus would only recite certain lines, as though the poem began and ended with them alone. One day, no longer able to contain his curiosity, he asked Shaykh Husni, "Why is this the only part of the poem he remembers? Why doesn't he ever recite lines like these, which you would expect to be a lot closer to a clergyman's heart?"

Thereupon he proceeded to recite:

The grave of a miser loath to part with his wealth
Is as the grave of one who was lost in idleness and play.

Just as death doth seize the miser's choicest possessions,
So also doth it spirit the generous man away.

73

The graves of the miserly and the generous alike are topped
By mounds of soil and large stones in perfect array.

Man's lifetime is a treasure that diminishes with time,
and like a man's wealth, is bound to pass away.

Like a mount grazing in the pasture, so are a man's days,
For when its master pulleth in the lead, it must come without delay.

On the Wings of the Wind

Habbab had been hearing about Hamama for quite some time. There was no need for anyone to deliver the reports, since they were borne on the wings of the wind, as well as by the merchants who would come to Hadiya every week to buy and sell at its Thursday market.

His interest was sparked in particular by the things he heard from Aziza's husband, Abd al-Majid, a native of Habbab's village, who would visit his hometown from time to time.

More than once, Habbab had considered kidnapping Hamama. However, he knew that if he were to do such a thing, he would cause many to turn against him, including the Sa'adat family and Hajj Mahmud, who were awaiting the arrival of her first offspring.

Hajj Mahmud and Habbab had happened to meet on more than one occasion, and whenever they did, they would spend their time sizing each other up. They would see each other at wakes and during the buying and selling seasons everywhere from Jaffa to Ramla to Acre.

In the end, however, he abandoned the idea, but decided to do everything he could to find some other way to get at Hajj Mahmud. Otherwise, he would end up being viewed by others as nothing but a horse thief when, in fact, he was the owner of several entire villages, who commanded the allegiance of civilians and military police alike, and who enjoyed unstinting support from mayors and others in positions of authority.

Yet, when he gave up on the idea of stealing Hamama, little did he know that time would offer him a gift he had never dreamed of!

A good deal of speculation was aroused at one point by unconfirmed reports of an unusual encounter that was said to have taken place between Habbab and Father Theodorus. It was rumored that Abd al-Majid was the cupid that had gotten the two men together, and that the meeting had been arranged in Jaffa lest it produce a storm of gossip.

No one knew the details of what had happened. Some people said they had concluded a land deal, while others talked about bigger shared interests that had begun appearing on the horizon as chaos spread throughout the Ottoman Empire, whose growing burden of debt had driven it to take increasingly harsh measures, from the imposition of new taxes to the forcible conscription of men into wars in faraway places they had never even heard of.

The Call of Nature

When Shinnara brought the new birth certificate to al-Barmaki, he went and had Shaykh Husni read it to him so that he could make sure what it said. Then he returned to Shinnara's house and knocked. She opened the door and came out.

"So," she said, "are you satisfied?"

"I'm satisfied," he replied. Then he handed her a pound and a riyal, saying, "What's right is right."

She started to go back inside, and was about to close the door behind her when he said, "Wait."

She opened the door. "What is it, Abu Ghazi?" she asked.

"These are for you, too," he said, handing her three more riyals.

"May God protect him and grant him a long life," she said, "and give him brothers and sisters."

Al-Barmaki ran all the way home. He opened the door hurriedly and headed straight for his son's wooden bed, the bed he had bought in Ramla specially for Ghazi. He bent down, took the boy in his arms, stood up again, then headed out to the front yard with him.

"Where are you going?" his wife asked in alarm.

"Don't worry," he said reassuringly. "I just want to see him in the light!"

From that day on, leaving the house even for a little while filled him with longing for his little boy. And when it became certain that the boy would have no siblings, things got even more complicated.

Men weren't encouraged to bring young children with them to the guesthouse, especially children under three years of age. This was the custom in Hadiya, as it was in other villages. However, exceptions were made on occasion. They might, for example, allow a father to bring his son with him if he was an only child, even if he was very small. And given the fact that al-Barmaki could no longer bear to part with his son as long as he was in town, he started bringing him to the guesthouse on a regular basis.

The visit to the guesthouse was always fraught with danger, since the father was held responsible for anything that happened to 'issue' from his son. If, for example, his son wet himself in the guesthouse, the father would be required to go home and bring lunch or supper to everyone there in atonement for what his little one had done. If what 'issued' from the boy was something more, he would have to slaughter a sheep or a goat. However, none of this deterred al-Barmaki from bringing his son to the guesthouse, and on numerous occasions he even seemed happy about his son's various 'issues,' as though they were tantamount to a re-declaration of his birth. As soon as it happened, he would look around, waiting for Hajj Mahmud to say, "Well, it came at just the right time. I think the men are hungry!"

Then al-Barmaki would sprint home. His absence would be shorter or longer, depending on the situation. But eventually he would show up again with food for the men, making sure that his son was with him.

As for the little boy, who seemed to sense the pride his father took in his 'issues,' he went on enthusiastically answering the call of nature, realizing that this was what was expected of him.

78

Things went on this way for some years, until, fearing that the boy would keep up the habit forever, al-Barmaki decided that enough was enough.

Then one day, noticing that his wife's tummy was getting rounder, he said jovially, "I swear if it's a boy, we'll call him Yunus! Happy now?"

"After all I've been through?" she asked reprovingly. Even so, she welcomed the suggestion.

Then along came Sumayya, who closed the door firmly behind her.

The Arrival of Elias Salem

They couldn't have found a better place to send him than Hadiya, after all the trouble he'd caused the Orthodox Church in Jerusalem. Once he was in Hadiya, he could fight with Father Theodorus as much as he liked!

When he got to the village, he was fuming. He had loved Jerusalem, and felt that he belonged there. And now, where should he find himself but in a village that was less eventful than anywhere he'd ever been in his life! For one thing, he had been an avid reader of *al-Asma'i* and *al-Quds*, but here he found no newspapers or magazines to read. And Tuesday and Friday mornings, which was when the *Carmel* newspaper came out, had turned sour because he couldn't read articles by Najib Nassar.*

Father Theodorus knew why the new priest had been exiled. Consequently, he became all the more cautious. When Elias chose a life of seclusion,

---

* Owner and editor-in-chief of the *Carmel* newspaper, which began coming out in Haifa in the year 1909, Palestinian journalist Najib Nassar was one of the boldest writers of his era and one of the most prescient of the danger Zionism posed to Palestine and its people. He was pursued by the Turkish authorities and lived in hiding for long periods of time.

Father Theodorus made no objections, and demanded nothing of him. All he wanted was for him to stay out of the way. As for the people of Hadiya, they saw Father Elias' aloofness as a sign of arrogance that ill befit a man of religion who was also a native of the land.

He had brought with him a large number of books, which kept him company in his isolation, and whenever he went to Jerusalem to visit his family, he would come back laden with new books and a bundle of newspapers that his mother had bought and saved for him.

Four uneventful months passed, during which nothing happened to ruffle Father Elias' peace of mind. However, all of that changed when the harvest season began, and the time came for the villagers to pay their tithes to the monastery. Smelling a rat, he began showing interest in details that Father Theodorus would never have expected him to: "Why do you take the tithe?" he wanted to know. "Why don't the villagers go themselves to pay what they owe?" "Why don't the tax collectors come?" "What does the monastery take from the people of the village?" "Do you take the whole tithe to the government, or do you keep some back for the monastery?"

The answers Father Elias received were the same ones the people of the village had received when they asked the same questions. Suspecting that he hadn't gotten to the bottom of things, he decided to go out and meet with the people themselves. He thought to himself: You sit here and read, then read some more, and wherever you go, you tell everyone how much you admire the writings of Najib Nassar, whom you consider your mentor. You sit here between these four walls and chew on what you read the way a cow chews on grass. When you were in Jerusalem you wanted to be like Nassar, but you weren't. So why don't you try to be like him here? Or do you think this village isn't good enough for you?

One evening, he opened the door of the monastery and rushed out. His action came as a surprise to Father Theodorus, who had only seen the monastery door open after sundown on rare occasions.

"Where are you headed?" came Father Theodorus' voice from inside the building.

"To Hajj Mahmud's guesthouse," Father Elias replied.

"But you know we have to keep our distance from them."

"Why? Aren't they human beings too?"

"That's not what I mean. It's just that they have their life, and we have ours. We came here in order to devote ourselves to God."

"And don't you think God is in Hajj Mahmud's guesthouse?"

"It looks as though we're not going to see eye to eye. In any case, I won't go into it with you now."

When Father Elias appeared at the door of the guesthouse, those gathered inside were speechless with amazement. It was the first time in years that anything like this had happened, and Father Elias' self-imposed seclusion had left a barren expanse between him and them.

"Bring the guest mat!" called out Hajj Mahmud.

The young men jumped up and brought two cushions, which they placed one on top of the other. Hajj Mahmud invited him to sit down. And although he had come no great distance to see them, Hamdan, sensing that something new was happening, poured out what was in the dalla and made fresh coffee for the visitor. Then, in keeping with their custom when an esteemed guest had arrived after a long journey, Khaled rose, poured the coffee and handed the cup to his father, who in turn offered it to Father Elias.

He drank a little of the small amount of coffee that was in the cup and closed his eyes. Then, opening them again, he looked over at Hajj Mahmud and said, "Now *this* is coffee!"

"Do you like it?"

"I shouldn't have let myself miss out on it all these months that have passed."

"Welcome. Whenever you want some, it will be ready and waiting."

That night they saw a side to Elias that they had never seen before. He seemed like one of them. And when he began talking passionately about Jerusalem, every man who had been to the city felt as though he was seeing it anew: seeing another Jerusalem, an enchanted city.

Khaled asked him why he had left the city if he loved it so much.

"I didn't leave it," Elias explained. "I was banished from it."

"Banished?"

82

"Yes. My coming here was a kind of punishment, you might say."

"But why?"

"I'd rather not say. That's another story, as the poets of *Taghribat Bani Hilal* would say. It really is."

As they stood at the guesthouse entrance before Father Elias' departure, Hajj Mahmud said to him, "You know, it's been a long time since anyone touched my heart the way you have this evening."

"That's the nicest thing I've heard in a long time," replied Elias. "God seems to be answering my mother's prayer."

"And what is your mother's prayer?"

"The most precious prayer of all: 'O God, cause him to be loved by everyone who sees him!' On the other hand, I wasn't loved by the Order of the Holy Sepulcher!"

"And why is that?"

"I'm afraid I might say too much."

"Say whatever is on your mind, son."

"It might be because God doesn't live in everyone's heart!"

A Failure of Wisdom

Whenever Hajj Mahmud heard that a man who was known to be a bad person was planning to leave Hadiya, he would say to the men of the town, "Go after him and bring him back. He'll do harm to the town's reputation." And whenever he heard that a good man was planning to leave, he would say, "Let him go. He'll spread Hadiya's sweet perfume wherever he goes."

However, it had never occurred to him to wonder how he could have allowed his daughter Aziza to marry a man like Abd al-Majid, who had caused him so much grief, and who was destined to spread untold misery.

Al-Barmaki's Demons

The thought that had crossed al-Barmaki's mind was sheer madness. Even when, several days later, he recalled the idea as he sat across from Shaddad, it seemed like pure insanity.

He had bound the stallion's front feet to keep him from going anywhere. "This way you wouldn't even be able to jump on a goat's back," he said reproachfully.

He recognized that the whole difficulty had been caused by his constant preoccupation with the matter. For a long time, his demons had tempted him with the idea of arranging an encounter between Hamama and Shaddad, and now it was as though it had actually happened against his will.

Al-Barmaki observed Hamama from a distance, leaving what he assumed was a safe gap between her and Shaddad. However, everything fell apart all at once.

Hamama had been leaping gaily about the pasture. Tossing her mane, she would make it fly through the air in such a way that the sunlight passed through it, turning it into pure gold. Her tail swayed from side to side as though she were using it to polish the face of the horizon, and her presence made the day seem brighter. She would run till she'd gotten quite a distance away, then come charging back as though she were attacking something that no one but she could see. When she reached the spot where her secret something lay, she would bend down to pick it up, then leap in the air once again as though she were aiming for the sky; as though she were going to soar forever through space.

The landscape wouldn't have been complete without her.

Then, out of the blue, Shaddad came running up behind her. He hadn't come near a mare for quite some time, and he charged madly in her direction. The minute she saw him, Hamama took off. Taken by surprise, she was no longer running with her previous gaiety, giving herself freely to the broad expanse. She stumbled once, then twice, and on the third stumble lost her footing completely and her body touched the ground. When she had despaired of escaping from her pursuer, she began neighing in alarm, at which point she got everyone's attention. People began running toward her, and a group of men managed to block Shaddad's way. His access to her now denied, he let forth a riotous whinny, then spun around in circles, digging his hooves into the earth's body and stirring up a huge cloud of dust. Suddenly, he turned on the men as though he wanted to rip them apart with his teeth, which glistened ominously in the sunlight. If anyone there had never seen a stallion turn into a monster, he saw it happen that morning.

The growing number of people standing in Shaddad's way made it possible for others to get next to Hamama on horseback. However, when she found herself surrounded by other horses, she panicked all the more. At last Khaled arrived on Rih's back. He dismounted hurriedly and went leaping over the low stone walls that separated one field from another until he reached Hamama, who, as soon as she saw him, regained some of her composure. He kept coming nearer, and when he had succeeded in calming her, he leapt onto her back.

She guided him, rather than the other way around, and it was all he could do to keep from falling off as she streaked up the hill toward their house.

By this time, Shaddad had taken off in pursuit of her once again, and people stood watching the scene in a daze.

When Khaled and Hamama reached the house, he jumped nimbly off her back, opened the stable door for her, and quickly closed it behind them. He tried to rub her neck and take her face into his hands, but she was somewhere else. Her eyes darted back and forth in terror as she scanned her surroundings, her body trembling as though she were stricken with fever.

She remained in this condition for a number of days.

Meanwhile, al-Barmaki's situation changed.

He saw the men of the village storm his house, slaughter Shaddad, then tear into his flock of sheep and goats and his three cows. They scattered his family, chased him far away, and left him in the hot sun, only to return to him later. They even raided his brothers' houses and ransacked his father's.

The collective paroxysm of rage went on for three and a third days.

When it abated at last, things had taken a new turn, and the people of Hadiya knew it. As far as they were concerned, Shaddad's attempt to mate with Hamama had been as serious as a man's attempt to violate a girl's honor.

During the afternoon of the fourth day, Shaykh Nasir al-Ali arrived together with men from all the surrounding villages in order to resolve the problem that had arisen, the likes of which no had ever anticipated.

Shaykh Nasir was aware of what Hamama meant to Hajj Mahmud, as well as what she meant to her owners, who had presented her as a gift to Hadiya with full confidence that she would be well protected and that no stallion from Hadiya would be allowed to come near her.

Al-Barmaki and his family disappeared altogether.

In the meantime, a sizable peacemaking delegation came to see Hajj Mahmud, prepared to do anything or offer any concession in order to resolve the issue.

Seated with the men in Hadiya's guesthouse, Shaykh Nasir opened the assembly, saying, "Never in my life have I heard of such a thing. Perhaps what makes this case so unique is that we're talking about a thoroughbred who stands in a class of her own. We're talking about a mare that's more than just a horse. When we talk about Hamama, we could just as well be talking about a virtuous girl who should be protected from any sort of attack or violation. If such a girl is violated in any way, her family has the right for three and a third days to do whatever they like to the offender. This is what has happened here, so those who have taken revenge on al-Barmaki are to be excused for their actions."

As he spoke, Shaykh Nasir looked back and forth between Hajj Mahmud and Khaled. He continued, "When I heard about this problem, I gave it a great deal of thought. I've continued to think about it since I got here, and my ruling is as follows: As I have said, Hamama enjoys the same status and honor as any girl among us who is still a virgin. Consequently, she has the same rights that such a girl would have. She neighed in distress when the stallion came after her. I consider this neighing of hers the equivalent of a girl's cry for help when someone threatens to violate her. Therefore, I view everything that was done over the past several days as a response to Hamama's cry for help. All of this has been part of what is due her. At the same time, there are some rulings I can't issue in the way that I would in the case of a human being."

At this point, murmurs went up among those gathered, and the atmosphere became charged and tense.

"Pray for blessings on the Prophet," Shaykh Nasir said to them.

His request appeared to communicate two things, namely, that they should pray for blessings on the Prophet, and that he wanted them to calm down.

"O God, send down blessings upon the Prophet!" they intoned together.

"As I was saying," Shaykh Nasir went on, "I won't issue a ruling like the one I would issue for a girl, since, thanks to her speed, Hamama was able to protect herself in a way no human being could have, and this in spite of the fact that she was being chased by a stallion. Consequently, if you estimate that she took a thousand steps, then I would consider her to have taken two hundred. As for the times she stumbled, they are like those of a girl. And the same goes for the time she fell."

He looked around thoughtfully at the men's faces, and when there was complete silence, he added, "I consider every step to be worth ten piasters, and every stumble fifty piasters. As for the time she fell to the ground, I count it as worth 150 piasters, and her getting up again as worth the same amount."

Loud murmurs of protest could be heard from the delegation representing al-Barmaki and his family.

"Pray for blessings on the Prophet," Shaykh Nasir said again.

This time, however, it only meant one thing, since he preferred not to let on that he was aware of their anger.

"O God, send down blessings on the Prophet!" came the response.

"I know this is a harsh verdict," he said. "However, as you know, it is with verdicts like this that we protect people's honor, since harsh sentences help to keep people from thinking of violating others."

Then he turned to al-Barmaki's delegation and said, "You owe Hamama's family two thousand four hundred piasters. You will also have to leave the village for three years."

Everyone knew that Shaykh Nasir al-Ali's ruling was just and wise, and they accepted it without argument.

As for al-Barmaki himself, the minute he heard it he gave a sudden start, then woke up in a fright under the fig tree in whose shade he had dozed off. Needless to say, he praised God that what he'd been through had been nothing but a dream!

Nevertheless, he looked around him in alarm, only to find that Shaddad was still tied up. As for Hamama, she was rising into the air, flying free like a golden bird.

He looked over at his horse and said, "Believe me, you've got a good excuse for wanting her so badly. But I'm afraid for you, and for myself!"

The Land of White Mares

Three things, apart from her beauty, set Hamama apart. One was Khaled's love for her. The second was the special food he fed her out of his palm, which consisted of boiled barley or wheat. And the third was her freedom, since she had never had a bit in her mouth.

During the first few months after her arrival, he never left her side. However, his family wasn't bothered by this, since it was enough for them to have their son back after his long absence and sense of restless unease.

However, Munira had finally lost hope on another front—marriage—since the topic never came up any more in their day-to-day conversation. As if this weren't enough, one day Khaled's Aunt Anisa said to her, "True, somebody who doesn't have a family might get himself a fine horse. But your son has taken things too far, and I'm afraid all this horseback riding he does may have ruined his 'equipment'!"

"God forbid!" Munira cried in horror.

Little did they know that Hamama herself would be the one to reopen this door for him.

※

One day Munira heard Anisa shouting, "Get out here right away, Munira! Your boy may not want a wife, but his mare is in heat!"

It was as though Hamama had started breaking dishes in her own way. She neighed nonstop and urinated more than usual, and whenever she saw a stallion, she would approach him. She did this even with the ones that paid her no attention, including Shaddad.

Hajj Mahmud said to his son, "We'd better get going before things get out of hand. We need to be in Shaykh Sa'adat's territory by nightfall."

By noon, all of Hadiya had heard the news. As the traveling party set out, everyone's eyes were glued to Hamama until she disappeared over the eastern horizon, on a journey like no other.

Like it or not, they would have to take Hamama past Habbab's village. However, the trip they were taking was no secret, since everyone in the region knew they would be taking her to Shaykh Sa'adat's territory. All along the road that passed through Hadiya, people waved to the procession, which consisted of seven men on horseback bearing gifts and heading eastward.

After they had crossed the plain, the road began to incline upward. However, the men were confident that no one in his right mind would dare attempt to waylay them. For no matter how great the animosity among some villages happened to be, an enemy was always given safe passage if the journey had to do with a thoroughbred mare, or if it was necessary in order to return a filly to its mother's original owners. This was a custom that could never be broken.

From the upstairs room of his house, which the traveling party passed on their left, Habbab looked out with as much curiosity as everyone else. Clad in an off-white cloak and a crimson fez, he stood up to his full height, which caused him to look a bit taller than usual. For some reason, Khaled was certain that he was looking straight into Habbab's eyes, and even after they were some distance beyond Habbab's village, he kept looking back until the house and its surroundings had disappeared. They then entered flatter territory, from which they could see the horizon in all four directions.

No sooner had Hamama's owners seen her approaching, lighting up the western plains, than a virtual wedding celebration began. Everyone—men, women, and children alike—came rushing out as though they were receiving a caravan of pilgrims on their way home from Mecca.

From the plain that surrounded the settlement, Khaled and his father glimpsed the dazzling sight of a land ablaze with white mares. At the sight of the approaching procession, the mares began whinnying and leaping into the air, and Hamama joyfully took off running to meet them.

As Khaled loosened her reins, she went flying across the meadow just as, some years earlier, her mother had soared with him over the hills and valleys on a night that was like no other he had ever experienced.

As the people stood between Hamama and the rest of the horses, she began to spin around in circles. They realized they would have to keep her burning desire for a stallion in check, since things needed to take place in the proper fashion.

Hajj Mahmud, Khaled, and the other men with them dismounted agilely, as if to affirm to Hamama's people that their mare's new caretakers were horsemen no less skilled than those among whom she had been born. They embraced Shaykh Sa'adat, Tariq, and the other men who had gathered to receive them. Then, before they headed toward the guesthouse, Shaykh Sa'adat passed through the group of visitors to where Hamama stood. Coming up to her, he patted her neck, then embraced her by taking her head into his arms. When he saw the sweat streaming off her forehead, he took the edge of his cloak and wiped it off. Then, taking two steps back, he looked at her thoughtfully and said, "We missed you!"

Amazed at the depth of the love these people had for their filly, Hajj Mahmud realized that when they had agreed to loan her to his family, they had given him a gift of unfathomable significance.

As for Khaled, he felt that by giving Hamama his wholehearted devotion, he had proved himself worthy of the trust she embodied. He was reminded of a dream he'd had, but had spoken of to no one. In the dream, he had seen himself carrying Hamama in his arms and crying out merrily,

"Honey for sale! Roses for sale!" However, something had disturbed the tranquility of the dream, and he had awakened in a panic.

It was the first time he had ever wakened terrified from a happy dream. He had thought of going to Shaykh Husni or Aunt Anisa and asking them to interpret the dream for him. He had thought of . . .

Instead, however, he just went on being terrified.

He knew, as did his mother and the entire village, that Hamama occupied the place that had once belonged to his deceased wife. They also knew that things come in their own time. The rain comes in its own time, the sun rises in its own time, the oranges and the wheat ripen in their own time. Similarly, a girl matures in her own time, and a young man's desire for a woman begins raging in his blood in its own time.

However, what troubled them was the question: where on earth would he find a woman like Hamama?

It was no secret to Shaykh Sa'adat why the mare was making circles around herself, peering restlessly in the direction of the other horses.

"She's grown up now, and she's ready to be a bride!" he exclaimed approvingly, as though he were talking about one of his own daughters.

Then he said, "This mare comes from a line of horses that we've had for seven generations. Only twice has a horse of this line left our territory. The first time was many years ago, when one was stolen and never came back. We searched high and low for her, and never gave up hope until so many years had passed that we knew she must have died and it wouldn't be possible for us to look for her bones. Even so, the memory of her still grieves us. The second time was when one of them was stolen, and you took her under your protection. By doing this, you relieved us of a search that could have gone on for thirty years!"

Shaykh Sa'adat fell silent. Then, looking at Hajj Mahmud, he asked, "Hajj, do you know what it's like to search for something you love for thirty years and never find it?"

The question came as a surprise even to Khaled, who had experienced the bitterness and pain of loss. Consequently, he couldn't think of anything to say. All he could do was shake his head in sorrow.

"Ahh . . ." said Shaykh Sa'adat, as though he had just rid himself of a mass of pain that had weighed heavily on his heart for years on end. After a period of silence, he patted Hajj Mahmud on the leg and said, "We mustn't leave her in this torment any longer."

A large group of men had gathered in the guesthouse, among them a number of elders who knew that on a day like this they had a special responsibility, namely, to witness Hamama's union with one of their thoroughbred studs. Khaled's gaze was fixed on a number of white horses that were clearly anxious to get near Hamama, and he thought: I wonder which one of them will be hers?

They were all horses of rare beauty, whose appearance was all the more striking and regal because of the constant care they received.

Shaykh Sa'adat gestured to one of his men, who turned out to be their groom. He got moving right away, and within a few minutes was back, clutching the halter of an extraordinary white stallion, the likes of which they had never laid eyes on. Dazzled at the sight of it, Khaled and Hajj Mahmud had now seen with their own eyes the springhead from which the horses in these parts issued.

"Are all your horses from a single mare?" asked Hajj Mahmud.

"No, but they're all from a single line," replied Shaykh Sa'adat. "No stallion from this line can mate with its sister. We discovered this a long time ago through a painful event that was related to us by our fathers and grandfathers, and that we swore would never be repeated. I'll tell you about it today, since one of our mares is under your care. This way you may be able to prevent anything similar from happening in your own territory."

Then there was a long silence.

"Once upon a time a certain mare was in heat, and the only stallion we had was her brother. The stallion was in the same state as his sister. However, when they brought him near her, he drew back as though he had turned into a female like her. They didn't know what to do at first. At the same time, though, they understood the reason for what had happened. This was a purebred stallion, and this was his sister."

Shaykh Sa'adat took a deep breath. "They knew that in order to ensure that the line was perpetuated, they would have to get the stallion to mate with his sister. The only solution they could see was to blindfold the stallion. So they covered his eyes and led him to the mare. But when everything was over and they removed the blindfold, he realized what he had done, and his eyes welled up with tears. When they led him away, he was as limp as a rope being dragged along the ground. The life had gone out of him. After that, he refused to eat or drink until at last he died. Needless to say, they were terribly worried about the mare. They were afraid that if she was pregnant, they would always be reminded by her foal of what had happened. At the same time, they were afraid she wouldn't be pregnant, in which case the line would die out! They waited day after day, watching her belly to see whether it would swell, afraid both that it would and that it wouldn't. The story ended with half a tragedy, you might say, since she turned out not to be pregnant. Consequently, they went out into the surrounding areas in search of a stallion that would be suitable for her, and at last they found one on the plains of Hawran. From that time on, their horses continued to reproduce from two mares and two stallions, and you might say that the horse you see now is her paternal cousin."

A Woman's Coquetry

Throughout the months of her pregnancy, the people of Hadiya related to Hamama as though she were one of their most beloved daughters. Not a man passed by her but that he wished blessings upon her. As for the women, their constant prayer for her was: "O Lord, raise her up safely!" just the way they prayed for an expecting daughter, neighbor, or sister to be granted a safe delivery.

For a long time they anticipated the swelling of her abdomen, and in her they saw the coquetry of a woman who knows for a certainty what a treasure she carries in her womb. After all, isn't there a saying that goes, "A mare's back is her strength, and her belly is her treasure"?

Hamama knew all of this, and there was a change in the way she acted around Khaled. She was calmer than before, and her eyes shone with a dreamy contentment. She often reminded him when she walked of a little girl with braids in her hair, tossing them alternately onto her right shoulder, then her left, then flinging them skyward or breaking into a run and feeling intoxicated by the feel of them bouncing against her back.

They tried to recall a single mare that had been in such a state of euphoria, but they couldn't. Some said: Maybe it's her exceptional color that makes us perceive her this way. As for Munira, she insisted that the secret lay not in her color, but in her eyes.

Hajj Mahmud had been afraid that she wouldn't get pregnant, in which case they would have to take her back to her owners once again. He didn't want to impose on them, since they had treated him and his men like royalty when they had been their guests before.

For three straight days, sheep had been slaughtered for the guests of honor. The hospitality with which they had been received surpassed anything they had ever known or even heard of before. It was true, of course, that Hajj Mahmud was also a generous man, and whenever anyone paid a visit to Hadiya, he was treated like an esteemed elder. All men who came to the village were treated as honored guests for whom the best sheep were slaughtered, the only exception being Turkish military police, no matter what their rank. These men often acted with utter impunity, helping themselves to any sheep or lamb that happened to strike their fancy, and slaughtering it themselves. As if that weren't enough, they would take away with them whatever pigeons, chickens, and turkeys they could get their hands on for subsequent meals. In the end, however, spongers like these would find no one willing to pour water over their hands after their meal. As for the food itself, it never tasted of anything but salt.

On the day after their arrival in Shaykh Sa'adat's territory, the marriage rites began. Hamama had been hopping about like a grain of wheat in a frying pan. As for the white stallion, he acted as though they had been saving up his noble seed for this very day. He twirled about, letting forth a throaty neigh and spreading the strands of his forelock. At the same time, he shook his neck, which sent his mane flying in all directions at once. Part of it shot straight up, part descended on the right side of his neck, another part was on its way back up, and still another part barely touched the left side of his neck before it rose again into the air. His hair was like a gazelle on the run, where one can't tell whether its feet touch the ground before they take off in flight, or whether they land on a springy bed of air that catches them, then flings them again into the ethereal expanse.

As for Hamama, with her long, graceful neck, her dainty head, and her bright eyes glistening with desire, she was no less captivating. Being the larger of the two, the stallion was like a knight filled with manliness, tender compassion, and burning desire. As for her, she was the embodiment of delicacy and that magical something that radiates from the body of a girl as she enters eagerly into full womanhood.

Hajj Mahmud remembered the document that had been signed by three elders affirming the purity of Hamama's pedigree. And now the day had come for them to sign a second document affirming the same concerning the young she carried in her womb.

The elders and the other men looked on attentively as the two sunbeams came together. Hamama whinnied and writhed as the stallion bit her gently on the neck, and when he was finished, he went forth to bite the wind.

They allowed him to mount her three times, and when it was all over, Shaykh Sa'adat gestured to Khaled as if to say: "She's your mare. Get up now, and see to her needs." The time had come for the chase, since everyone knew that if a rider mounted her and took her running, this would cause the water of life to penetrate more deeply inside her.

A bit awkwardly, Khaled got to his feet, feeling as though everyone's eyes were on him. However, he held himself together, hoping against hope that Hamama wouldn't let him down, and reminding himself that, in fact, she never had. By the time he was standing next to her, his feeling of awkwardness had dissipated for the most part. They had prepared her for the ride, placing a saddle on her back and fitting the halter over her neck. When she saw him coming, she gave him that look he'd been hoping to see: the look that told him that everything was all right, and that she still remembered him. He jumped nimbly onto her back, and she took off running.

When, even thirty years later, he thought back on that moment, he still couldn't explain what had happened to him and Hamama. He began moving away with her, and she with him, until those looking on thought they would never come back.

The men were so uneasy over what was happening that they began searching the horizon for some sign of the vanished horse and rider. Hajj Mahmud was the most concerned of all.

In the end, however, the two of them reappeared, and the men heaved a collective sigh of relief. Hamama came up alongside the gathering as though there were no rider on her back. Then she kept on running, until she vanished into the southern expanse. This time, however, they were confident that she would be back.

Three stamps by three elders affirmed Hamama's union with her stallion, as well as her lineage and his. When they had completed the document, they rose and embraced jubilantly, wishing her and her offspring health and a happy life under her guardians' vigilant protection.

Shaykh Sa'adat then adjourned the gathering and came up to Hamama. He took her face in his hands and knelt down until one of his knees touched the ground. As he knelt in front of her, he planted a gentle kiss on each of her front hooves. Rising again, he took her face in his hands once more and kissed her forehead. Before turning around to look at the men behind him, he took a deep breath, and as he did so, all his fervent emotion gradually withdrew from his features to settle deep inside him.

That's Me!

K haled was walking alongside Hamama, her reins in his hand, down the long road that ran parallel to the cornfield. A gentle breeze caressed the field, producing a verdant music that ordered the rhythm of the entire place and the steps of the two travelers.

It was on evenings like this one, illumined by the redness of the setting sun, that Khaled loved to go walking, captivated by the magical variety in Hamama's color. On this particular evening, however, something was different, since the breeze wasn't the same as usual. For quite a distance he found himself walking inside the music, half-mesmerized, and even after the cornfield had come to an end, the music went on. As he continued on his way, the sound of Hamama's hoofs touching the ground was transmuted into a melodious cadence that lifted his soul and body alike toward heights inaccessible.

Then suddenly, everything changed.

He found himself face to face with a girl he had never seen before: a tall girl with wide, honey-colored eyes, a swelling bosom, and a delicate waist. A braid hung from beneath her white head-covering. It traveled quite a distance before reaching her shoulder, then fell on a chest concealed by a black silk robe covered with red, blue, yellow, and green flowers. After hugging the roundness of her chest, the robe descended gracefully toward her feet, forming cascades of tiny flowers as it went.

The robe itself wasn't unfamiliar to him, since it was worn by all the women in the area. However, the question that suddenly shook him was: how could a robe hold all this beauty inside it?

She stopped and stared at the mare while Khaled stared at her. Then she calmly shifted her own gaze till it rested on him.

What she said consisted of just five words. But those words were enough to change his life. Pointing at Hamama, she said, "You know? That is me!"

As he looked into her face, he experienced the miracle that happens when a young woman turns into a filly. It was as though they were a single entity that had been split in two.

Then she slipped away before his very eyes. But although her body had withdrawn, she left behind an apparition that illumined the place, filling it with an inimitable presence.

The breeze began to blow again. Since they had passed the field by this time, there were no more cornstalks for it to blow through. Instead, it blew to the rhythm of her footsteps. The music had followed her, leaving him frozen in place. His body trembled inwardly. Sensing what he was feeling as no one else could, Hamama whinnied sweetly. He turned and saw the girl walking into the distance. The hands of a gentle breeze had lifted her head-covering, causing it to hover gracefully over her delicate shoulder, and when he returned from his brief reverie, he knew what woman it was who departed so subtly and sublimely that her feet didn't touch the ground.

"What's your name?" he called out.

Without turning around, she said, "Ask her!" As she came alongside the cornfield she giggled, and he heard the music that had emerged from the ring of her laughter, the blowing of the wind, the fluttering of her head-covering in the breeze, and the sound of her footsteps. It was a music that he would later bring to mind to banish sorrow when it took him unawares and, when joy embraced him, to experience it in all its fullness.

101

Munira's Plates

Khaled's preoccupation with his sorrows had raised a wall of thick fog between him and whatever was going on in Hadiya. As for his recent preoccupation with Hamama, it had dissipated the wall of fog, but the only thing it allowed him to see was her.

Over the course of the five-plus years that had passed since Amal's death, many young women had married and had children, and many girls had grown up and become young women. Among them was the girl who had appeared so unexpectedly that evening. Her appearance had banished a darkness that had inhabited his heart for so long he had never expected to see it end.

Hadiya wasn't a small village. Nor was it so large that people who lived there could remain strangers. As Khaled thought back day after day on what had happened that evening, he concluded that the reason he had kept his eyes closed for all those years was precisely so that, when at last he opened them, he would find that girl standing before him, since if he had done otherwise she would have been lost to him.

"You had to live for so long in the darkness that when the light came along, it would take you by surprise," he said to himself.

The same thing had happened with Hamama, who had not only opened a door, but had herself become a door. If it hadn't been for her, he wouldn't have been walking along that particular road at sundown. This, at least, was the way he had begun to think. Besides, he wondered, what might that girl have said if the horse with him had been any other than Hamama? She would have gone by without even giving him a passing glance, and surely without pointing to his horse and saying, "You know? That's me!" And could he have known who she was, or what kind of beauty she possessed, if he hadn't compared her with Hamama?

"Hide your plates," he said to his mother.

"But I've been waiting for the day when I hear them breaking."

"Hide them, please."

Her plates in her hand and her head-covering slipping off, Munira got up despondently, as though she were bidding farewell to a hope that would never come knocking at her door again. But before she reached the court-yard, she heard him whisper, "And bring with you any you don't like."

Munira froze in her tracks.

"Did I hear you right?" she asked excitedly.

"You heard me right."

At that, she began picking up one plate after another and dashing them against the ground.

Clad in black trousers, his hair disheveled and his white beard studded with pieces of straw, Hajj Mahmud came tearing out of the stable and ran across the courtyard toward the source of the noise.

When he saw his wife smashing plates right and left, he shouted, "What! Are you looking for a husband?"

As though she hadn't heard him; as though there were no one around but her and the bliss of having her thirst quenched after such a long drought, she started dancing and twirling. After a loud ululation, she broke into song:

Yawayha! I've been waiting so long.
Yawayha! My beloved's heart is full of little birds!
Yawayha! One sings and the other flies overhead!
Yawayha! He's wonderful beyond words!

Then she started dancing again as she sang:

My beloved's come home bringing such great joy,
This heart of mine's about to burst,
A joy that washes away pain and sorrow,
It lights my sky and quenches my thirst!

"God have mercy, the woman's gone mad!" Hajj Mahmud muttered
over and over. But she paid him no mind.

My beloved's more precious than diamonds and gold,
Whose glitter dazzles my eyes.
Bring me that plate and I'll break it for you,
Then sing till the new sunrise!

My beloved is sweeter than honey
Gentle as a whisper, bright as hope.
I'll go out and call to the mountain,
And gazelles and trees will dance on the slope!

Graceful as the steeds of the Prophet,
You bring me a gazelle, I bear you a lad.
Tell me your heart is smitten like mine
And I'll come bearing tidings that will make you glad!

My beloved is a flower that graces
The walls of Jerusalem and the vineyards of al-Khalil,
The partridge carries it away in its beak

To Gaza, Safah, Ramla and Attil!

Yawayha! I've been waiting so long.
Yawayha! My beloved's heart is full of little birds!
Yawayha! One sings and the other flies overhead!
Yawayha! He's wonderful beyond words!

The Boycott

The sun descended in the direction of the distant sea. However, the blaze it left behind turned everything to kindling. All one had to do was put one's hand on a rock to know what kind of noonday heat the city had endured. The birds repaired for refuge to the two cypress trees next to Elias' parents' house, their chirping producing such an extraordinary ruckus that one would have thought there was a bloody brawl going on among the branches.

Some new developments were afoot. Elias had been aware of them even before he attended the meeting that had been called by his sect to discuss its circumstances and relations with the Order of the Holy Sepulcher. (Things had deteriorated to the point where many were demanding that the brotherhood be banished from the country, and that the patriarchate be purged of the corruption it had become known for. After all, they said, Greece had no right to head the brotherhood, whether by the standards of the church, the rules of politics, or the dictates of conscience: "They've treated us with contempt and immersed themselves in their worldly desires. And now they hold it against us that we've ostracized them and call for their expulsion!")

A ten-member committee was formed to meet with the archimandrite. He listened to their demands without comment. Then he said, "We are fully entitled to the privileges we have. We have the right to dispose of the money as we see fit, and to exercise control over the shrines. And if we give anything away, we only do so out of the kindness of our hearts!"

Khalil al-Sakakini, one of the committee members, was so enraged that he walked out.

"What happened?" his fellow religionists wanted to know.

"We have no choice but to go to war," he seethed.

That evening, they decided to hold a meeting in the home of Mikha'il Talil.

"If we decide to go to war, the first thing we need is money, since our sect includes poor folk and widows who are dependent on the monastery."

"They depend on it because they've gotten used to it. But if money is needed, we have plenty of ways to raise it."

Khalil al-Sakakini replied, "Given the circumstances we face now, we've got to be unyielding. We need to stand united in the war that rages between us and the monastery clergy. The tyranny of the state has fallen, but the tyranny of our spiritual leadership remains, and we've got to do everything we can to bring it down. Have no fear of harm, and have no fear of heaven either, since their authority isn't from heaven. Nor should you fear being accused of ingratitude, since they've done nothing for us. On the contrary, all of you know, as do the heavens and the earth, that they've abused us. They've despised us. They've humiliated us."

When Father Elias came out, he sensed something was wrong. The street was crowded with students from the Greek Orthodox seminary, which was attended by Greek students and run by Greeks, the purpose being to flaunt their power before the Arab Orthodox. Before things got even worse, the government cavalry and armed soldiers intervened, and there were reports that the monks had gathered on the roof of the monastery in resistance to the Arab Orthodox demands.

George Zakariya, Elias Halabi, Hanna al-Isa, Khalil al-Sakakini, and Elias Salem met in Mitri Tadrus' office, where they decided to write up a protest petition to present to the provincial governor because the Order of the Holy Sepulcher had harassed and attacked the Arab Orthodox on the previous Wednesday and Thursday. Then they decided to write a statement to the Patriarch informing him that they had decided to withdraw from the church until the Arab Orthodox sect was granted its rights.

In a meeting held that evening, the petition and the statement were approved and signed. However, that night the decision was made by the denominational Court of Justice to have the Arab priests refrain from performing religious rites. A committee was appointed to inform them of the decision, and of their sect's willingness to pay their salaries.

"We thought we'd be seeing you during this visit," Elias' mother said to him.

"You know," he replied, "if things turn out in our favor—and things seem to be moving in that direction—you'll be seeing a lot of me. Since the Arab Orthodox have asked the Palestinian monks to boycott the Greek Orthodox Church, I'll only be going back to Hadiya long enough to collect my things."

A little while later, he got up and began wrapping the hose around the water pipe's glass neck.

"Where are you going? You haven't even sat down yet!"

"There's a banquet in the big hotel, and I have to be there, since it will be attended by the provincial governor, municipal leaders, writers, and the mayor, Faydi Afandi al-'Alami."

Then, without warning, there arrived a leaflet from the Arab Orthodox headquarters in Jaffa announcing that it would be withdrawing from the Church. The Court of Justice had urged all members of the Arab Orthodox denomination to go down on Tuesday morning to the Government House and demand that the provincial governor speak with the grand vizier and invite him to respond to the sect's demands.

Everybody and his brother came out in response to the invitation, and the Church of Mar Ya'qub and the courtyard of the Church of the Holy Sepulcher were filled to capacity. A solemn procession headed by the nationalist priests, so long one couldn't see the end of it, made its way to the provincial governor's headquarters.

The Patriarch's response to the march was swift: "In my capacity as your head, I command you to perform your religious duties tomorrow. Otherwise, I will have no choice but to do something which isn't to your liking."

The people were in an uproar.

"What! Does he want us to attend worship against our will?"

"If the Patriarch appoints an alternate priest, I'll kill him on his way to the church!" shouted George Sam'an.

"And if I attend worship, kill me even if I'm your brother!" Elias rejoined.

Two Well-Kept Secrets

Two well-kept secrets were destined to lead Habbab to an unexpected end. The first lived in his house, and the second awaited him in the marketplace.

No one knew what went on behind his gates: no one, that is, but his three wives. The first was Salma, who had filled the house with six children. The second was Subhiya, whom he had snatched away from her family by force some five years earlier. And the third was Rayhana, whom he couldn't touch.

Subhiya had borne him two sons, and, after hearing him say "Two!" right after their second son was born, she had been so obedient that he had never been obliged to count all the way to three. It was Subhiya's presence that had helped him hold himself together after Rayhana—who had smitten him at first sight as no woman had ever done before—had become a deadly thorn in his side.

Salma, whose mother was Turkish and whose father was an Arab from Jaffa, had come from a large family, and had it not been for the intervention of the qa'imaqam himself, who opened the doors of his future, saying,

"This man has a future," they would have refused to give her to him in marriage.

However, time can be treacherous, and it knows how to play its own game. Habbab, who had appeared out of nowhere like someone stripped of his past, would in due course find himself stripped naked on the portals of his future. And although the high walls that surrounded his home might conceal the tongues of fire, they could no longer conceal the clouds of smoke.

Salma lived her life between Jaffa and Hadiya, and as his children reached school age, they ended up having to settle in Jaffa. Hence, over time he was obliged to spend most of his time next to Subhiya and not far from Rayhana, whose silence had turned the house into a tomb.

Rayhana knew very well that Habbab had murdered her husband. Strangely, though, he loved her more than he had ever loved a woman in his life, so much so that he couldn't admit that he had murdered him. Stranger still was the fact that, despite her family's timorous opposition to the marriage, he agreed to the waiting period required by Islam before making her his wife.

Rayhana knew all his stories. She knew about the way he might marry a woman along the road, then divorce her behind the low stone wall that bordered the adjoining field, or take a woman, then return her disgraced and humiliated several days later. Even so, she succumbed in the end. She left the house without shedding a tear, as though the weeping she had done over her husband had drained her eyes to the last drop.

On her way out she said to him, "I won't leave without Adham."

"And who is Adham?" he asked her family.

"He's her husband's horse," they replied, "or . . . um . . . rather, the deceased's horse!"

With a nod he agreed to her condition.

Not long after, he heard Adham's neigh, and when he saw him, he knew that the creature before him wasn't a horse, but a monster. A towering stallion black as night, Adham looked fearsome, with his white teeth and his nocturnal eyes that glittered like black jewels. He reared, sending his front legs flying upward and scattering the people who had gathered around. From the time his master had been killed, no one had been able to get a saddle on his back. The most they had been able to do was place a halter around his head.

When he saw Rayhana and their eyes met, Adham grew a bit calmer. She gestured with her head, and he understood. She closed her eyes and lowered her brow, and when she looked up again, it was all over. From that moment on, Habbab knew for certain that whatever there was between Rayhana and Adham, it was greater than anything he could imagine.

The words she hurled in his face as soon as he shut the door were unequivocal and cutting.

He took off half his clothes.

"You can take me by force," she said, "but that won't make me yours."

"And what do you want in return for becoming mine?" he asked.

"One simple thing," she replied. As she spoke, he could feel her head touching the ceiling of the large room that had brought them together.

"And what might that be?"

"If you can mount Adham, I'll be your woman."

It's nothing but a naive game being played by a woman who doesn't know what sort of a man she's dealing with, he thought. However, an eerie tremor went through him like a fine blade. He felt it reach the center of his chest, then splinter into smaller blades that spread through his entire body.

Nevertheless, he smiled.

"And how long do I have to fulfill your condition?"

"For as long as you live," she replied, with a steadiness that caused the arrows in his body to grow larger and pierce more deeply.

He took a step toward her, then froze again.

A long silence reigned. They stood there staring at each other for what seemed like an eternity, neither of them batting an eyelid until the air was filled with the sound of the dawn call to prayer. Recovering at last from his stunned silence, he bent down and picked his clothes up off the floor and from the edge of the bed, which was unlike any bed Rayhana had ever seen before. Then, in a flash, he turned and left the room.

He had been about to say, "I'll see you tomorrow evening, then." However, he swallowed his words before they touched his lips. He sensed, vaguely yet overwhelmingly, that this woman he had so fallen in love with, and who, apart from his first wife, was the only woman he had ever brought to his home with honor and respect, would be the death of him.

And He Cried, "I'm Dreaming!"

Munira cried for seven days and seven nights, saying to herself over and over, "Oh, Munira, you broke those plates for nothing!"

Khaled was now convinced that what he had seen had been nothing but a dream, a summer twilight's dream. Passing fleetingly through his soul, it had been nothing more than a madman's yearning for a new start. He stopped in front of Hamama, in the same place he had once encountered that girl. He gazed into her eyes and asked her, "Was I dreaming? Was what I saw real? Did you hear what she said before she disappeared? Do you remember her laugh the way I remember it now?"

Hamama didn't say anything. She just shook her head and neighed three times. With the fourth neigh, she walked away, paying no attention to him. He let Hamama go, and when he turned around, he saw her. The force of the surprise nearly knocked him to the ground. She was there. The girl was there, in the flesh, and Hamama was rubbing her forelock against the bosom encased in colorful silken flowers.

"Am I really seeing you?" he asked her.

"If you see me!"

"Where had you disappeared to all this time?"

"I didn't disappear. It's just that you didn't see me."

"What's your name, then?"

"I told you to ask her. Have you asked her?"

"No."

"Ask her, then."

She picked up her basket, which he hadn't seen before, and lifted it over her head. Her eyes fixed all the while on the narrow path, she took a step in his direction and kept coming until she was one step away from him. She looked up. She was so beautiful that, in an attempt to jolt himself awake, he shouted, "I'm dreaming! I'm dreaming!"

Then he closed his eyes, and when he opened them again, she was gone. He heard her voice coming from several steps behind him, saying, "You'll dream of me often. But not now."

"What's your father's name, then?"

"Ask her."

Then she laughed, and the wind went back to blowing to the rhythm of her footsteps. The music had gone after her, leaving him frozen in place. His body trembled inwardly. Sensing what he was feeling as no one else could, Hamama whinnied sweetly. He turned and saw the girl walking into the distance. The hands of a gentle breeze had lifted her head-covering, causing it to hover gracefully over her petite shoulder, and when he returned from his brief reverie, he knew what woman it was who departed so subtly and sublimely that her feet didn't touch the ground.

"I've seen this before!" he shouted. "I'm dreaming!"

"No, not now."

She disappeared into the cornfield, and he took off running after her. Hamama followed him. Never in his life had he been as short as he was that day. The greenness of the fields nearly reached the sky, and the cornstalks were taller than he was by far. He jumped onto Hamama's back, his eyes combing the field for some sign of movement and his ears listening for the sound of a youthful body making its way through the verdure.

"I'm dreaming!" he shouted.

The voice came from everywhere, saying, "No, not now."

"What's your name, then?" he called out.

"Ask her," the voice repeated.

"What's her name? What's her name?" he shouted into Hamama's ears, which were pricked as though she had been waiting a long time to hear the answer to this very question.

"Has she told you?" the voice echoed.

"No."

"She will. Don't worry."

He dismounted from Hamama feeling more bewildered than ever. He lifted his hand to pat her face and plead with her to answer his question, and as he did so, he touched something unexpected. It was soft. He fingered the object. Then he looked up and saw, between Hamama's face and the reins, a cream-colored handkerchief. He took it into his hands, brought it close to his nostrils, and inhaled deeply, savoring the sweetness of its fragrance.

Strange Wars

Rayhana saw nothing of Habbab the entire next day. He disappeared as though the earth had swallowed him up. He'd been gripped by an irresistible urge to get as far away from people as he could.

He didn't sleep a wink after what had happened. The first thing he did was approach Adham and try to put a saddle on his back, though he knew full well that it would be next to impossible. When his attempt failed, he whispered to himself reproachfully, "You're so shortsighted, you might as well be blind!"

With some difficulty, he managed to get hold of the reins. As he did so, the place was convulsed by a furious hiss and sparks went flying through the air, warning of a conflagration to come. He didn't want to go back to his wife that evening unless he could do so mounted on Adham's back. The horse resisted him, shredding the wind with his hooves. And if what had happened had been visible to the human eye, one might have seen the deep scratches he left in the air's tender flesh.

He mounted his mare, Hamdaniya, and tied Adham's reins to her saddle. Catching a glimpse of Rayhana in the upper room, Adham reared again, more frenzied than ever. At last he proceeded toward the court-yard's large gate. However, his eyes were fixed on the figure that looked on from above.

It was a known fact in those parts that nothing is smarter than a horse, and Adham had understood what Rayhana wanted from the very begin-ning, from the time she had been alone with him.

Before leaving her family's house, she had asked them to give her a few moments alone with Adham. But what could a woman possibly say to a horse when no one else was around?

Half the story was clear to them. As for the other half, it lurked in the unknown regions of the future.

Habbab kept moving farther out, until he was certain that no other human being had ever reached, nor would ever reach, the place where he stood. In a deep valley located between two mountain chains, he flung himself down, exhausted. Year after year, rushing streams had carved out a sandy plain, then filled it with sand, dirt, and rocks from the elevated areas that surrounded it.

Getting there had been like descending into a deep hole. Adham had resisted, while, with extraordinary agility and grace, Hamdaniya navigated the tortuous path that no mare had ever trod before her. The only thing that hindered her was Adham's recalcitrance. Whenever he reared his head in protest, he would lift her off the ground, causing her saddle strap to dig into the flesh of her stomach.

As the sun blazed overhead, all three of them were wet with perspira-tion, which streamed heavily down their brows in shiny rivulets. Before he reached the edge of the valley, Habbab began thinking about the stupidity of his mission, and how foolhardy he had been to take on such a challenge.

He cast a furious backward glance at Adham. The horse got the mes-sage, and responded by looking him straight in the eye.

As they made their way through the bottom of the valley, he discovered that in his love for this woman he had fallen captive to a senseless, merciless passion that had taken his being by storm. It was a passion so overwhelm-ing that it had caused him for the first time to recoil at the idea of killing with his own hands the husband of a woman he wanted for himself. Consequently, he had found himself obliged to send his men to kill her husband for him while he, contrary to his usual custom, went to attend a wedding in a nearby village.

It was the first time he had felt the need for an alibi. Curses on love, he thought. Curses on those who fall into its snare. Curses on his ancestors, and on the whole world. Curses on Time, which had always made his path easy before but had now abandoned him midstream, leaving him with this woman and her crazy horse.

Meanwhile, Rayhana hadn't left the upper room. She stood there like a stone pillar, watching for a flurry of dust that had perchance been stirred up by some stray breeze on that hot mid-morning, which was quickly on its way to becoming a searing midday.

Twice the night before, she had realized what kind of woman she had become. The first time had been when Habbab had agreed to allow Adham to come with her, despite the fact that with his coming, the slain would have a visible presence and a lingering fragrance in Habbab's household. And the second time had been when Habbab had picked up the gauntlet she had cast before him. At the same time, however, she found herself in the grip both of conflicting fears and of an inner calm whose doors were open to unforeseen disaster.

"No one has ever defeated him before," she said to herself.

This terrified her. He was a monster. And when you manage to wound a monster, one of two things is bound to happen: either he will fly into a rage, destroying and killing as never before, as though he were bidding farewell to murder through a murder infinitely more gruesome, or he will become still, impassively observing his surroundings as he slowly bleeds to death.

Rayhana realized that she was powerful. However, she also realized that everything around her might turn to ashes in a fire the likes of which she had never seen before.

"Don't tell me you're worried about him," she heard a voice say to her from the courtyard below.

"I worry about him more than I do about anyone else!"

"Who, Habbab?" asked Subhiya in astonishment.

"No, Adham!" Rayhana replied.

It wasn't long before Subhiya was standing beside her.

Rayhana cast her a brief glance, then turned to look out at the horizon. "Are you his second wife?"

"Yes, my name's Subhiya. I hope nothing happens to him."

"Who? Adham?" Rayhana asked.

"Both Adham and Habbab!"

"And Habbab?" Rayhana asked indignantly.

"Don't forget that he's my husband. Besides, my whole life hangs on a single word from him now."

"A single word?"

"Yes."

"And what's that?"

"Three!"

It would be a long time before Rayhana heard the story of "Three!" And when she did hear it, it would serve as further testimony to that mysterious power that protected her—an inimitable power that placed her in a world apart from this other woman, despite their shared misery.

Sometime in the late afternoon, she saw a cloud of dust ascending skyward and moving in her direction. She didn't have to think long about what it concealed. The sun was behind it, and the plain was illumined by a blaze that had yet to be extinguished. She suddenly felt afraid. However, she could see clearly that the space that separated Adham from Habbab was Adham's gift to her as she entered her second night. For the distance he kept between himself and Habbab would keep Habbab at a distance from her as well.

To the amazement of the men and women employed in the household, she came flying down the stairs from the upper room, then dashed toward the large gate and flung it open.

She stood there motionless, watching as Adham came hurtling toward her. Meanwhile, she was being watched by others, who had gathered behind her sensing that something peculiar and unprecedented was going on inside the walls of Habbab's fortress.

As Adham drew nearer he looked to them as though he were flying through the air, and his hooves seemed not to be touching the ground. As the distance between him and the onlookers diminished, their perceptions were confirmed. Subhiya swore that after coming down to earth, Adham had placed his head in Rayhana's hands. Later, however, she denied saying such a thing, sensing that it would be dangerous for such reports to reach Habbab.

After sundown she heard the courtyard gate opening again. Straining to hear, she picked up the sound of a mare's hooves on the ground, and of a rider dismounting. A few moments later, there was a mingling of so many footsteps that she couldn't tell which way Habbab had gone.

Hamama Said Something!

The sun was in the center of the sky and the shade was nothing but a speck under siege from all sides. The goldfinches had taken refuge in the cypresses, insinuating themselves between their dark green branches. As for the cornfield, it still seemed as though death were about to emerge from it at any moment.

Khaled kneaded his brow with the fingers of his left hand. He was thinking of standing in the blazing heat until she reappeared. Someone was bound to find out what he was doing and inform her, and once she knew of it, she would come. Within a few hours, he realized that he wasn't simply thinking about it: he was doing it.

The road had turned into a thread of silence. The screeches of a hawk rang out overhead. It circled in the air for a long time before swooping down on prey that must have moved.

As for Khaled, he didn't budge.

Munira didn't want to draw attention to what her son was doing far from the houses of the village. She held her tongue and sat on her heart for fear that someone might hear the sound of the terror that had come creeping into it. However, the silence didn't last long.

They watched the sun make its orbit around him. They watched the shadows growing shorter, then longer. The first day passed as though no one saw what he saw. On the second day, they began whispering among themselves. On the third day, they came rushing toward him from all directions. On the fourth day, he said to them, "All you can do is take Hamama out of this blazing heat."

He was determined to maintain his vigil in the same place until the end.

They took Hamama away, but on the fifth day she came back on her own. As she rested her neck on his shoulder, he was amazed at how light her head was. She was like a feather or a breath. He reached out and stroked her to make sure she was really with him. Then suddenly, he was overcome with terror, and he grabbed hold of her for fear that a wind would blow up and wrest her away from him.

Hamama murmured something he didn't understand. People were watching from a distance.

"Hamama is the only one that can bring him back to us," said Munira. "He worries about her more than he worries about himself. He won't agree to allow her to go on standing in the sun like that."

Even so, Hamama planted herself beside him, and wouldn't budge.

The next day, they saw him take off his black cloak and toss it over Hamama's head.

"Both of them have lost their senses!" cried Munira.

They had been hoping the situation would come to an end by market day, before people came to Hadiya from villages and encampments all over, before the arrival of Habbab and his men, before the incident turned into a story they knew might reach gigantic proportions.

However, when market day came, the situation had yet to be resolved.

Before sunrise, Hajj Mahmud rushed out toward him in a fury. Along with him came his brothers Salem, Muhammad, and Mustafa, Munira, his aunt Anisa, and his sister Aziza. They tried to bring him back in, but he was like a spear driven so far into the soil that one could barely have gripped the portion that remained aboveground.

Then, for the first time, they heard him speak.
"She'll appear," he said.
Habbab passed by riding his mare, Hamdaniya, on his way to the market. He was some distance away, but it seemed to Khaled that their eyes met. Habbab seemed shorter than he had ever been, and so seemed Khaled to Habbab, who cursed the day women had come to exist on earth.
Everything people refrained from saying was said by the wind as it wound itself silently about him, then turned and took his secrets far away. There was no solution but for her to appear.

As Habbab pondered his own tribulations, he wondered who was better off—he himself, or the one being burned in the sun. However, he decided his own life was the bleaker of the two. The girl's appearance would open a door of hope for Khaled. As for his own situation, he was certain that it had been hopeless from the beginning.

Something unusual had aroused interest among the birds of prey. The scent of death, perhaps, or the sense that there was an easy prey somewhere to be found. Increasing numbers of hawks began flying overhead, soon joined by vultures and crows.

Hajj Mahmud knew his son, who had always been the type that takes things to their limit and won't be satisfied with anything less. He was the type that would be willing to remain silent for an entire month, be angry for an entire month, or go charging out to the edge of the world.

One day, Khaled had taken a herd of cattle out to graze in some of Hadiya's pastureland. When he arrived he found a group of men grazing their livestock and singing. Khaled enjoyed the sound of the reed pipe, so he waited until they had finished their song. Then he went over to them and asked them to take their cattle and leave, since the land they were grazing on belonged to Hadiya. Some disputes over grazing land during times of drought became so serious that they led to bloodshed. They refused, so he threatened them. Then they made a circle around him and began taunting him. When he realized that he wouldn't be able to defend himself as long as they were surrounding him, he told them he would leave, so they let him go. When he had gotten some distance away, he threw a rock that injured one of them. They ran after him, which was exactly what he wanted. He fled to the top of a low foothill, and whenever they threw a rock at him, he would repel it with his stick. Things went on in this way until he sensed that they were tired, at which point he began throwing rocks back at them, and within half an hour, he had hit every one of them. Some of them were limping, some couldn't raise their arms, and some had wounds to the head that were bleeding so profusely that their eyes were covered with blood. Leaving them in this state, he returned to the village as though nothing had happened.

Given all the wounds that had been inflicted, the judicial system had to intervene in order to resolve the issue, and this despite the fact that Khaled had been only fourteen years old at the time.

It was the first time Khaled had stood before Shaykh Nasir al-Ali.

"What happened?" the shaykh asked him.

Khaled replied, "I was going out to graze the cows on our land, but they wouldn't let me. Then they all ganged up on me and started to beat me. As you can see, I can't walk right." He then lifted the hem of his robe and showed Shaykh Nasir his foot, which he had wrapped in strips of cloth.

"And what do you have to say?" Shaykh Nasir asked the men. Some of them were younger men, some older, but all of them had visible scars.

The first said, "That light-skinned boy hit me," as he pointed at Khaled.

The second said, "The light-skinned boy."

They all repeated the phrase as Shaykh Nasir al-Ali nodded his head.

When they had finished, he looked at them and said, "Shame on you! Are you telling me that more than ten men were beaten by a boy?"

Then he told them to leave. But before they left, Khaled bent down and removed the bandage from his foot, saying, "I confess, sir, I wasn't hit by a single rock. See? My foot is fine!"

Letting forth a huge belly laugh, Shaykh Nasir al-Ali said, "I like you, boy! May God protect you from all your enemies!"

Hajj Mahmud thought back on the day many years before when they had gone out deer hunting. He remembered how Khaled had wounded a deer so light on her feet that she'd worn them out. Outsmarting them again and again, she would hide in foothills that their horses were unable to reach.

Suddenly, Khaled got down off his horse and shouted, "But she's mine!" Then he took off after her and disappeared. They waited for him until they grew weary. Finally, they left their horses in the valley and went up after him, following his footsteps and a trail of blood that dwindled to tiny drops until, eventually, it faded out completely. It was as though the deer's wound had been dried up by the winds of her haste.

When they lost hope of finding him, the men returned to their horses, thinking that he might have made it back without them, or be coming back by another way. Or perhaps, once he had gotten as far as the distant foothills, he had decided to go on in the direction of Hadiya, which would have been closer to him than the place they had stopped in the valley.

When they got back to their horses, he wasn't there.

What worried them most was that he had no weapon with him but his bare hands.

He hid in the foothills for two days, at the end of which they were sure the deer would not be bringing him back. Rather, she had taken him to what his mother called 'the land of no return.'

"He'll be back," Hajj Mahmud reassured them.

And in fact, Khaled did come back. Struggling to get loose, the deer lay about his neck, butting the air with her little antlers and batting his chest with her bound legs.

He lowered her gently and lovingly from his neck as he would have done for a young child.

"If I were you, I would have done what you did," he said to her, "and if you were me, you would have done what I've done. There's no winner or loser here. Agreed?"

But the fact was that she was the loser.

He knelt down and untied her. Then he took a few steps back. She was directly in the center of the gathering. All eyes were upon her, and the sight of her promised their stomachs a delectable repast. She rose with difficulty to her feet and turned in a circle without taking her green eyes off the people's faces. Once she had taken a good look at those surrounding her, she knew she would need two wings at least in order to get past this impenetrable wall of humanity.

She lowered her head for a few minutes, and when she looked up again, she was gazing straight into Khaled's eyes. Then, to everyone's amazement, she walked up to him and stood there perfectly still. She raised her head once more, but he didn't dare look her in the eye again. She understood. Consequently, she had no choice but to take the final step in order to touch him. He realized what she was about to do, and that it would mean a great deal. However, he didn't make a move. Instead, she did the moving, touching the hem of his robe with her face. He could feel the warmth of her breath, and now all that remained was for her to make him more aware of her touch.

She traversed the distance that remained between his robe and his body by two gentle taps with the tip of her right antler. It was then that Hajj Mahmud whispered, "She's asking for your protection."

The silence grew more ponderous. Khaled shifted his body slightly, as though his frame had been transformed into a door. And it was through this door that the deer took her first step outside the circle of human beings. Then she kept walking unhurriedly, until she vanished into the distance.

"How did you bring her back?" they asked him.

"The same way she left just now: gently," he replied. "I knew she would have to come back for water, so I waited for her along the path she would have to take to get to the spring. I hid behind a boulder without moving a muscle till I heard her footsteps coming closer. I held my breath until she reached the water, and then we met face to face. Neither of us made a sound. Then, before she knew what was happening, I caught her."

Three days after the market disbanded, they lost all hope, and resigned themselves to the scandal that was no longer a secret to anyone. Feeling half angry and half sympathetic, they left Khaled alone with Hamama. He reached into his robe pocket and, as soon as they had left, pulled out her cream-colored handkerchief and began sniffing it.

At sundown, he heard her footsteps. He held his breath. Hamama let forth a muffled whinny. He patted her on the neck in a plea for her to calm down. The steps grew nearer and nearer and, when he was certain they were hers, he was overcome by a profound sense that from that day onward, he would never hear her steps moving away again.

Then everything in him grew calm. He had no need to prepare himself or jump up. She kept walking until she stood before him, the two of them face to face.

The next time she moved, her arm brushed up against him, reawakening a memory of the deer's gentle touch.

Then she began to move quietly away.

Suddenly, a gentle breeze stirred the reed stalks. He turned and began walking after her just as quietly, with a white cloud marching behind him.

A Dagger and a White Pillow

He stood over her head, a dagger gleaming in his hand. The sound of her breathing filled the room with a steady, quiet rhythm as the air passed deeply into her lungs, then gently out again.

Her tranquility killed him, as did that confidence of hers, which endured though she had nothing to protect her but her own soul.

On the white pillow decorated with silk roses, whose colors were embraced by the night, her wheat-colored complexion under the soft lamplight had turned to pure gold, while her hair gave off an orange glow he had never seen before.

"Should I have obeyed my intuitions?" he wondered to himself.

It was the first time he had ever felt he was about to commit a blunder of such huge proportions. However, she was there, and he saw her. The sight of her had split him in two, and he went tumbling into an abyss.

She'd just been one more bashful woman, no different from any other woman who meets a stranger on the road. She hastily drew the edge of her head-covering over her face, pulling on it with the edge of her mouth as she looked down at the ground. All he had seen in her was a beautiful, diffident woman who augured no evil: a woman so withdrawn and self-conscious that, in her haste to get as far away from him as she could, she stumbled and nearly ran into some cactus bushes, oblivious to their thorns.

Nevertheless, he had caught a glimpse of an incomparably angelic face.

Spurring Hamdaniya onward, he galloped ahead until he disappeared from view, leaving her behind him. When he reached a distant bend, he quickly dismounted and tied his mare to the branch of an apricot tree whose over-abundant fruit had covered the ground with delectable little orange globes. Then he found himself a spot that would enable him to get a good view of her without her being able to catch sight of him.

As he heard her footsteps drawing nearer and nearer, he felt them ordering the rhythm of his heartbeats to the sound of her swinging gait.

She was tall, which he hadn't noticed when he had been on horseback. She kept walking until at last she found herself before him once again.

She stopped short. Then, giving him a ferocious glare, she announced, "I honored you earlier by concealing my face, since I thought you were a man of principle. Now, however, I won't grant you that respect."

Rayhana had never seen Habbab before. However, reports about him filled the land with a stench so rotten that no woman could bear it, and no man could live in peace.

She had a vague though powerful sense that he was the man she had heard about. Perhaps she had drawn a connection between what she had heard about his mare, Hamdaniya, and the horse he had been riding. Her eyes went in search of the mare, and she saw her at a distance.

"A man of honor doesn't go sneaking around on a horse of honor in order to spy on other people's thoroughbreds," she said, with a ferocity that quite took him aback.

He looked for the angels he had glimpsed in her features a short time earlier, and couldn't find a single one.

Yet she was possessed of a beauty so pristine, it was as though she had never set foot on earth's soil; as though, unlike the rest of the human race, she hadn't been made from the dust of the earth. Her finely sculpted nose and taut, smooth complexion were made all the more beautiful by two slight, dimple-like depressions between her jaws and her cheeks. And then there was the long neck and the great distance one's eyes had to travel between her shoulder and her ears, the voluptuous lips that ended in two delectably subtle points, the strong, pearly teeth, and the forehead as smooth and clear as a spring on a windless day.

As he watched her walk away, he was overcome by feelings he had never experienced before—passionate feelings erupting in a storm that tore his soul to pieces. Before long, nothing remained of her but the memory of that angelic face; the same angelic face he now contemplated in a tranquil repose that seemed to bespeak an awareness that heaven itself had come to guard her.

His hand dropped feebly to his side, his fingers little more than limp rags. His dagger fell to the floor, devoid of all the evil that had possessed him for so long.

How absurd for you to have a woman this beautiful, but against her will. You could take her right now, but she'll never be yours in the way you've hoped: someone who's yours forever, who wakes in the morning and greets you with a heart full of affection, and who falls asleep to the sound of your laughter filling the house. A woman who, when she brings you a cup of water or a plate of food, assures you without a word of what's in her heart and mind.

He left quietly, without realizing that his dagger was no longer in his hand.

As he descended the stairs from the upper room, roosters crowed, announcing the arrival of a dawn no sign of which he had seen on the horizon.

He crossed the forlorn courtyard to the stable. When Adham heard his footsteps approaching, he leapt in the air and neighed, which aroused a similar response in the other horses. The stillness of the last watch of the night made the horses' neighing seem all the rowdier, and Habbab took three steps back as though he were nothing but a horse thief.

✼

He was getting old. At least, that was what he had been feeling over the past few days. He had seen gray hair spreading with lightning speed down the sides of his head toward his beard, which seemed longer than it ought to be, and he saw his moustache sagging more than it ever had before. He had worked for a long time to lift it, and on many occasions had resorted to twisting it, but it just wasn't the way it used to be.

He deliberately passed in front of Rayhana, then stopped and watched her eyes, listening to what her silence was saying when she looked at him. He deliberately let his hair show, trying to divine what difference she might have observed between what he had been and what he had become. However, she was too judicious to ridicule a wounded man, and too aloof to notice anything that concerned him.

She kept everything hidden inside her. However, when he had moved away and was outside the courtyard gate, he heard a laugh coming from the upper room. It sounded like a shout of triumph. But before he could turn around to make sure, he heard an eagle screech overhead. He saw the bird in midair. However, he found nothing to reassure his torn spirit but the thought that the first cry had come from the eagle itself.

Out of the corner of the window, Rayhana saw Habbab walking away as the eagle passed over the house. It was so close that she thought it was on the roof.

He had grown old and gray before being able to mount Adham.

She came down from the upper room and headed for the stable. Habbab's wife Subhiya saw her, wondering how a woman in their household could possibly be as exultant as Rayhana appeared to be. For some reason she couldn't explain, she felt envious, and when Rayhana disappeared into the stable, she ran after her. As she peered inside, she saw something she had never seen in all her sheltered life. She saw Rayhana take Adham's head into her hands, then kiss it from the tip of his ear down to his broad mouth.

Quaking from head to foot, Subhiya took two steps back and froze. She didn't even hear Rayhana's footsteps as she approached on her way out of the stable. Hence, when Rayhana passed in front of her and wished

132

her a good morning, Subhiya was so taken by surprise that she made no reply. And she didn't budge from where she stood until her children began tugging at her robe, begging her to come in.

The Girls' Year

A year of blessing is a blessing through and through. This was something the people of Hadiya had realized from its very beginning. Most of the babies born in the village that year had been girls, and they always say, "A girls' year brings a bumper crop, but a boys' year brings a drought!" The blessing they had already received was made all the more abundant by the arrival of the little girl whose presence had enabled Khaled's heart to find its way home again.

Everyone was invited to the wedding, and Yasmin was the kind of girl anyone would hope to find for his or her son: pretty, vivacious, and well-bred.

Hamdan stood on the roof of the guesthouse and cried, "Hear, hear! Pray down blessings on the Prophet Muhammad! Nobody go away tomorrow, since it's the day when Khaled bin al-Hajj Mahmud will be engaged!" Then he repeated his call three more times, each time facing a different direction.

Never in his life had Hamdan been as confident or joyful as he was on that day. The fields with their ripened ears of grain undulated in the distance, while the wind bore aloft the rustling of the wheat stalks and carried it toward the horizon. As he gazed out at the olive trees in the light of the setting sun, they looked greener to him than they ever had before: resplendent trees that promised a harvest the likes of which they had never seen.

As for Khaled's brothers, Salem, Muhammad, and Mustafa, they set out on the backs of Rih, Jalila, and Khadra to invite men from distant villages to attend the men's gathering.

The matter had been settled the day before, when Hajj Mahmud went with Shaykh Husni and a number of other men from Hadiya to the home of Yasmin's father, where everything had been agreed on. Now all that remained was for the official men's gathering to be held.

Men from all the surrounding villages began arriving one after another, the most prominent of them being Shaykh Nasir al-Ali. The village's courtyards and streets were filled with such a noisy bustle one would have thought it was a holiday, and the morning hours were packed with festive activity. Riders set out on horseback as though they were racing the wind. Even Father Theodorus attended in his long black robe. After all, it wouldn't have been fitting for him to stay away from an occasion such as this, despite his repeated complaint to Hajj Mahmud that "the village doesn't seem to be paying what it owes the way it used to." According to Father Theodorus, the tithe had dwindled to less than half of what it had been.

"As you know," Hajj Mahmud would reply, "the years as they pass are like the fingers of one's hand: no two are exactly alike."

"I hear what you're saying," Father Theodorus would say. "However, the government folks wouldn't understand what you're saying!"

". . ."

They could see the bride's family waiting for them in the distance. None of them was a stranger, since the lands of the village from which the bride hailed were adjacent to those of Hadiya. The two villages were so close, in fact, that news of whatever wedding parties or funeral processions were to take place in one of the two villages would reach the other on the night air more quickly than the speediest rider. It had long been said that the echoes of a wedding in one of the two villages would set the people of the other village to dancing.

The men representing the groom's family led the procession, with Shaykh Nasir al-Ali and Father Theodorus behind them. They were followed by the women, whose singing grew louder as they descended the slope:

> We've crossed the sea, dear Uncle,
> For one with blossoms about her waist.

> Lest she be claimed by anyone else,
> We've come to you in haste.

> We've crossed the sea as two seas
> For a girl whose eyes will make you swoon.

> We've crossed our broad green pastures
> To the laughter of a swarthy moon.

> We've come, you well-mannered girl,
> To rejoice in you tonight.

> We've come singing from Hadiya
> With intentions pure and right.

When they had drawn closer to where the bride's relatives waited, other songs began ringing out in praise of the bride's family:

> We've come to you, Abu Muhammad,
> Get up and receive us with your horses, your men!

> O Abu Muhammad, a man of high standing,
> A lion ringed by the cubs in his den!

O Abu Muhammad, you open a window onto the sky,
You brighten our souls with a radiance beyond our ken.

Then, with even greater gusto, they sang out:

Tell us where your house is, pretty Yasmin,
We're ready to follow you wherever you go!

Tell us where your house is, sweet Yasmin,
We'll follow you to Jerusalem, to Jericho!

Your long raven hair reaches from Acre to Jaffa,
From Gaza to Majdal, from Haifa to Safafa!

Then, on behalf of the bride's father as he greeted the delegation who had
come in his honor, the women sang:

A loving welcome to those whose coming
Is like abundant showers after dearth!

A warm welcome to the worthy,
whose presence is a joy that revives the earth!

After they had drunk their coffee, Hajj Mahmud said to his son, "Go kiss
your father-in-law's hand."

Khaled rose and took the hand of Abu Muhammad, Yasmin's father.
However, Abu Muhammad withdrew his hand, saying, "Men like you, we
embrace." Then he proceeded to take Khaled in his arms as he whispered
in his ear, "We've given you our jasmine flower. Do your best to make
sure she never wilts."

"Don't worry, Uncle, I'll take of her as though she were my own
two eyes."

Longings

K haled hadn't anticipated the way his longings would get the better of him, turning some of his nights into vigils that seemed to have no end.

He began looking for an opportunity to see her. It wasn't an easy matter, since she lived in another village, and even if he passed that way, it wouldn't be a secret. He waited for her in the place he had seen her before, but to no avail. Eventually, of course, he realized that the time before one's engagement and the time after it aren't the same, and that he would have to wait a long time before she was his.

He reached into the pocket of his robe and brought out her cream-colored handkerchief, then proceeded to sniff it in a drunken ecstasy.

It had been agreed that, God willing, they would be married during the olive season. This was the way it was done: weddings took place during harvest seasons, at which time there was abundant blessing, and people would have two things to rejoice in at once: seeing two people joined in marriage, and gathering the fruits of their hard labor over the course of the year.

Going to see her on his own would have been out of the question, since he knew such a thing wouldn't be proper. After all, girls' families were always complaining of overly enthusiastic fiancés, who went overboard in their attempts to see their brides-to-be. This kind of behavior would make him nothing but a little boy, and he would be treated to harsh comments, which, although they might appear to be nothing but a reprimand, would convey disappointment in him as a man.

Sensing what Khaled was feeling, Munira leaned over to Hajj Mahmud one day and whispered, "What do you say we pay the bride a visit?"

"What are you saying, woman? We were at their house three days ago!"

"But I miss her!"

"Is it you that misses her? Or is it the apple of your eye? Do you think I'm blind?"

"Blind? God forbid! Is there anybody on earth with better sight than you? After all, you chose me, didn't you?"

"The fact is, Munira, I didn't choose you. Rather, it was God who chose you for me. And luckily for me, God loves me. Otherwise I would have ended up with somebody else."

"Is that right?"

"Of course it is. The children are growing up and getting married, and in the end, all we have is each other."

"God willing, they'll grow up to see you still strong, under your protection, and you'll go on being a support to us all."

Two days later, Munira leaned over again and whispered to Hajj Mahmud, "It's been five days since we last saw the bride."

"We'll go on Friday, God willing."

"Friday's a long way off!"

"Tell him we'll go on Friday. Then it's him and his luck. He might see her, and he might not, since they might not allow him to."

She was in the field when she saw them approaching in the distance, and she took off running. By the time she'd seen them, they were closer to the house than she was, and she realized she wouldn't make it back before they arrived, so she disappeared into the vineyard and stayed there until they'd gone inside. Then she came out of her hiding place and crept fearfully around the house. She jumped over the side wall and tiptoed over to the bread oven. For some reason, the door opened and she heard footsteps moving in the direction of the horses, so she flung herself inside the oven.

She thanked God that the fire had been out for a good long time. Even so, she felt the oven getting gradually hotter. She wiped the sweat off her brow, all the while staring at the door, which she saw now as her only way of escape. The footsteps died away. However, the silence was followed unexpectedly by a huge racket that caused her to squeeze herself into the most blackened part of the oven.

She knew it wasn't permissible for him to see her, or for her to see him, and that this was the way things would be until the wedding day. She busied herself counting the days, and when she had finished, there wasn't a sound to be heard.

She came crawling out, and when she passed under the horses' necks, she noted that Hamama wasn't among them. When at last she reached the window on the west side of the house, she climbed up onto the sill and hoisted herself inside.

"What have you done to yourself?" cried her mother in horror.

"I was hiding in the bread oven."

"I swear to God, if they'd seen you this way, they would have broken the engagement!"

Her mother's mind wasn't set at rest until she saw the groom's family on their way out of the village.

When she was sure they were gone, she cried, "Coast is clear!"

Yasmin came out, and when her father saw her, he laughed and laughed. Then, still laughing, he looked at her mother and said, "I didn't know we had mice this size in the house!"

The Seasons of the Winds

Then, without warning, things began moving in a different direction. One evening, a group of military police arrived in Hadiya. At their head was a yawir, or what they termed a military assistant, accompanied by a tax collector. They came up the hill to the guesthouse and tied their horses to the trunk of the mulberry tree. However, no one came out to welcome them. The guesthouse was empty and there was no one around but Hamdan, who, as soon as he caught sight of them, turned away as though he hadn't seen anyone.

The blow he received came brutally from behind. The military assistant's army boot sank into his back, leaving him facedown atop the dalla and the oil-burning stove on which he made the coffee.

When he tried to get up, he received another blow with the butt of the military assistant's rifle. The pain was so intense that he flung himself down, writhing, at the guesthouse entrance.

When, a long time later, the men of the village found him, he was spattered with coffee and his hands were burned. He was moaning, doubled over and fearful of a third blow that would be the death of him.

The tax collector, a round-faced man whose head was planted directly atop his shoulders for lack of a neck, said, "The taxes you pay are far less than this paltry tithe you give to the monastery. We've had our eyes on the situation for a long time now, and we've concluded that what we get doesn't cover the cattle, sheep, horses, camels, and people in the village."

He stared into Hajj Mahmud's face, saying, "We're not leaving until we've counted everything."

Then he turned and headed toward the door of the guesthouse, with the military assistant and a number of soldiers close on his heels. Before they reached the gate, the military assistant shouted at a soldier, who was the tallest man they had ever seen, "Go get us whatever you think would make us a good lunch."

Within an hour, everyone in the village had gathered in front of the guesthouse. The young men were itching to get at the men, whose raucous laughter could be heard coming from inside. However, Hajj Mahmud gestured to them to calm down, and Khaled, Salem, Mustafa, and Muhammad stepped back.

Not long after, the tall soldier returned, dragging a cow they recognized as belonging to Shaykh Husni. After leading it over to the right corner of the guesthouse courtyard, he grasped it by the head and, in a single movement that astonished everyone, knocked it to the ground. Two of the soldiers came forward and tied it up. Then, in an instant, he drew out a dagger from within his garments and slit its throat. Blood went flying in all directions, spattering onto the robes of many who were standing some distance away. Drops got onto Hajj Mahmud's long white beard, though he didn't notice. Khaled kneaded his brow with the fingers of his left hand, his eyes fixed on the drops of blood. He reached out with his right hand and wiped the blood off his father's beard. Hajj Mahmud took hold of his son's hand and looked at it, and saw the blood on his son's fingers. Glancing down at his chest, he discovered that his robe was spattered with blood from the neck all the way down to his sandals, and that the trickle of blood ran all the way back to the cow's neck.

For two days running, none of the men of the village appeared in or around the guesthouse. Meanwhile, the soldiers were acting as though the village had become a military camp.

They slaughtered more livestock, chickens, and pigeons than they needed. They made the rounds of the village over and over on horseback, and crossed the sesame fields so many times that many of them were turned into useless expanses. At noon on the third day, they specified the taxes people would have to pay, and when they came to assess the taxes owed by Hajj Mahmud's household, the tax collector announced, without preliminaries, "There will be a tax on this white mare and on her unborn young." Then he paused briefly and, just as they had feared, went on to say, "In fact, this mare will be your gift to our governor in place of the taxes owned by this household!"

Salem took two steps forward, but before he could take the third, Khaled grabbed him by the shoulder. He pressed hard, and Salem realized he would have to restrain himself, since his brother was thinking of another way of dealing with the situation.

Khaled kneaded his brow with the fingers of his left hand. Meanwhile, his rage retreated and settled deep in his gut.

The strange thing they all noticed was that Father Theodorus hadn't shown his face once for the entire three days. Instead, he had closed the monastery door as though he were living in another world. Hajj Mahmud was aware of it. However, all he did was shake his head and ponder the matter, saying, "This is his message to us."

At sundown, the soldiers mounted their horses and headed for the western hills, their saddlebags groaning with money and whatever items of value had struck their fancy.

Khaled kept his eye on them until they had disappeared completely, and nothing remained on the horizon but Hamama's dazzling glow. The people of the village, almost senseless with rage, glared at him as though they were pronouncing a curse on him. How could he have remained so silent? How could he have abandoned Hamama and her unborn young? And what would he say to Shaykh Sa'adat?

They turned their faces away from him.

Munira and Hajj Mahmud were no less stunned. Salem didn't say a word. He distanced himself from Khaled before anyone else did, certain that he had lost his brother forever. He determined that he would never speak to him again, and that from that day onward, they would never make their home under the same roof. As for Mustafa and Muhammad, their eyes were filled with tears.

In less than an hour, night had fallen. Silence roamed the world, its apparitions clinging to the walls lest someone see them.

In the long room, tears were flowing freely, and everyone was in the grip of an unspeakable shame.

"I'm going now," Khaled announced.

"Where? The night isn't yours!" protested Munira.

"It isn't mine, and it isn't anyone else's either."

They heard his steps retreating toward the stable. A few minutes later, they heard the footsteps of a man walking alongside a horse.

"He's taken Rih," said Munira. She began to get up, but Hajj Mahmud grabbed her by the arm and pulled her back down, saying, "You stay put."

She heard the courtyard gate being opened, then closed again, so gently one would have thought the person leaving was a thief who feared that the people in the house might hear him. They followed Rih's hoofbeats until it seemed the sound would go on ringing in their ears forever. A few minutes later, the rhythm of the hoofbeats changed. The mare galloped faster and faster. And when at last the sound faded away, they were gripped by a peculiar feeling that Rih had taken off in flight, carrying their son to a land from which no one returns.

Following bends in the road, which he knew like the back of his hand, Khaled overtook them at last. The territory was filled with bends, slopes, and boulders that he had navigated many a time in search of quail and deer.

144

On a night illumined by a pale crescent moon, which caused the wilderness to look even vaster, they were bound to catch sight of him, although he was still a safe distance away.

"Who's there?" they asked threateningly.

He remained silent.

He got down off his mare and tied her some distance away, then advanced toward them. The sight of Hamama restored a sense of tranquility to his heart. He hopped up onto a large boulder and sat down.

"Who's there?" they shouted again.

"The mare, or your lives! Let her go, and take everything you've stolen from us!"

"Save your skin and go back to where you came from."

Hearing the sound of footsteps approaching, he came down from the boulder and disappeared. A few minutes later, they heard a scream, followed by the crushing of bones, moaning, and writhing.

Then everything was quiet again.

"The mare, or your lives! Let her go, and take three-fourths of everything you've stolen from us!"

No sooner had the words left his mouth than he heard more footsteps approaching.

He disappeared.

When the approaching soldier stumbled over his companion's dead body, he realized he had reached the place the sound had come from. But he saw no one.

He began to scream in terror, but the blade of the dagger plunged deep into his body, causing the second half of his scream to come out muffled, but fierce.

Once again, everything grew quiet.

The military assistant realized now that the situation he was dealing with was no easy one. He instructed his men to get away from the spot where they were, and from which they wouldn't be able to do anything.

Khaled moved back again, jumped onto Rih's back, and proceeded to follow them at a leisurely pace.

Just when they began to feel they had put a safe distance between themselves and their pursuer, he appeared once more on their left, atop a high hill. His silhouette, which blended with that of his horse, was both frightening and mysterious.

The military assistant aimed his rifle and fired. After the report of the rifle had died away and the smoke had dissipated, he saw no one in the place where the mysterious rider had been.

"All you need to get rid of folks like these is a bullet!" he said smugly as he looked over at the tax collector, whose eyes were gleaming strangely.

They kept marching.

They had taken at most two hundred more steps, when they saw the phantom atop the hill yet again. This time, however, it was the shadow of the mare alone; its rider had vanished.

"Stupid farmers, that's all they are," the military assistant ranted. "Don't they know that all their brave men put together could never hold out against the pull of a trigger?"

However, the voice came back again, and this time it seemed to be coming from the other direction, from their right.

The military assistant fired another shot into the air. The horses neighed, and the night grew blacker than ever.

"The mare, or your lives! Let her go, and take half of what you've stolen from us!"

There was no room for jesting now. The military assistant dismounted from his horse and gestured to two of his soldiers to go in one direction while he and his tall soldier went in another. Meanwhile, the tax collector went down and hid among the horses.

The crescent moon had ascended by this time, and had lost some of its pallor. Khaled saw Hamama glowing. He wished he could call her name the way he always did. However, he knew that this would excite her, which was the last thing he wanted. If she tried to flee, it would mean her death. However, she surprised him by whinnying, and it seemed to him that she was saying his name.

The night was young. Knowing this, he stayed where he was and let them comb the foothill in search of him, leaving no stone unturned. When they began to show signs of fatigue, having realized that the best thing for them to do would be to turn back, he moved.

By this time, there were only two of them left: the military assistant and his tall soldier. They waited, but the other men didn't appear. For obvious reasons, the military assistant didn't want to call out to them, since they might have been hiding somewhere and preparing a trap that would deliver him from this person, whose pursuit of them had come as such a surprise.

As the night grew darker, the new moon seemed like more of a friend to Khaled as it peeked down on him, sometimes through the oak trees, other times between the boulders, than it was to the other men in their exposed position.

The military assistant attempted to recall the faces of those he had seen, including Hajj Mahmud and his sons, but the only face he was able to conjure was Khaled's. He had seemed the strongest one among them, and the most self-composed at the moment when they had decided to take Hamama. However, the idea of confiscating her hadn't been negotiable.

In less than an hour, the military assistant had given up on the other two soldiers' return. Consequently, he decided to press forward in the hope of finding a safer spot, or a village where he might spend the rest of the night. Yet just then he was gripped with fear, and perhaps regret. Or it might have been a peculiar mixture of the two that pained him deeply.

He was beginning to show signs of weariness, and possibly the excess tension that, just hours before, had been excess confidence. Stroking Rih's neck, Khaled observed the ashen shadows and Hamama's white silhouette in the distance, certain that he was about to enter a new era.

Time was on no one's side. Khaled had only a short time left to accomplish his mission, and they only had a short time to escape from the clutches of the mysterious danger that encompassed them.

"The mare, or your lives! Let her go, and take a fourth of what you've stolen from us!"

The military assistant knew now that the winds were still blowing against him.

At the foot of the hill, to his right this time, the shadow of the horseman reappeared, all the more frightful for the way it merged with the shadow of his mount.

The military assistant now decided to use his most powerful weapon, which he had been saving up for the finale. However, it was he, not his foe, who would be taken by surprise.

It wasn't difficult for Khaled to see the tall soldier stealing away, since not even the most moonless night could have concealed someone his height.

The horses froze in their places and the silence returned. Thinking the matter over, Khaled was sure that if he had been in the military assistant's place he wouldn't have stopped, since this enabled Khaled to hear even the creeping of an ant in the thick darkness. However, the military assistant had done so for his own reasons, namely, because he was anxious to hear the voice of his soldier saying, "It's all over."

Some time later, the military assistant heard a scream that sent his heart leaping to his throat. It was a muffled scream, and difficult to recognize. A split second later, he heard the voice of his soldier asking, "Shall I slit his throat?"

"Did I send you out to give him a hug? Do it now!"

Suddenly, the night was convulsed by the sound of terror as a scream collided with the ghostly wall of the darkness, then ascended steadily toward the highest heavens as blood went flying in all directions.

The military assistant's laughter was mingled with the remains of dread, and with a hope he had never expected to illumine this night of his. He rushed toward the tax collector and, in a thoroughly uncharacteristic gesture, wrapped him in a powerful embrace. Then he went up to Hamama and said, "You or our lives! Ah! You or our lives! Three-fourths, half, one-fourth!"

Had he expected to see the night when he was gloating over a mare? Certainly not. Yet here he was, gloating over this white mare that had nearly turned into a curse from which there would be no escape.

Atop the hill he spied a figure coming in his direction. He felt like rushing up to it and embracing it. However, it was too far away. As it drew nearer, he began running toward it. Hamama neighed, and when he was five steps away, it seemed to him that, despite the figure's height and the military attire in which it was clad, it wasn't his soldier after all. Instead, the figure seemed larger and broader. By this time, however, it was too late, and the dagger had plunged deep into his chest.

The silence returned.

"What happened?" cried the tax collector.

"The mare, or your life! Let her go, as well as everything you've stolen from us!"

"My life?" he cried in terror.

"Yes, but it's too late for you to save it now."

Khaled watched the tax collector as he stumbled away, searching desperately for some miracle to deliver him.

Hamama neighed again. He pushed the military assistant's dead body out of his way. Then he calmly walked over to the white figure, took its face in his hands, and kissed it. He got down on his knees. Grasping her right front hoof, he lifted it to his lips and kissed it, then gently placed it back on the ground. He then took her left front hoof and did the same thing.

It was the first time he had kissed a filly's feet. However, he could sense how high he had risen when he knelt before her, and how much more of a mare she had become.

He stood up. There was a shadow still stumbling about in the distance. His mission wasn't over yet.

Understanding what he needed to do, Hamama nickered.

"No," he said, "it wouldn't be proper to go after a thief like him on the back of a thoroughbred like you. Wait for me here."

Then he jumped on the back of one of the soldiers' horses, and within minutes the last cry rang out, the cry he needed to hear before he could return with confidence to Hadiya.

An Open Secret

When the people of Hadiya saw Hamama the following morning, they knew what had happened. However, no one spoke of the matter.

It was a secret that everyone knew, and that no one would reveal to anyone else. No woman would speak of it to her husband, no boy would speak of it to his father, nor a brother to his brother or his sister. Consequently, when reports of what had happened to the military police and the tax collector began making the rounds of the countryside, the people of Hadiya would simply nod their heads. When they were alone, every one of them would begin by piecing together the strands of the stories he had heard, and once he had the whole picture, a strange feeling would come over him. Then he would begin looking at Khaled in a completely new way.

None of them could pretend to have forgotten the way he had waited like a madman in the hot sun for the girl he loved. Even the most forbearing and impulsive among them found it impossible to justify the whole thing, although they would sometimes try to find excuses for the way he had behaved. However, subsequent events had created a completely new image of him in their minds. For they could now see that the lover had been no less courageous in his struggle to win his beloved than he had been in his struggle to recover his mare.

As for Khaled himself, as soon as he found himself alone with his father, he surprised him with the sorrowful words, "You know, Baba? I hope these hands of mine never shed blood again!"

"No one in his right mind would feel otherwise," Hajj Mahmud assured him.

No longer was it considered a mundane event for Khaled to pass by, and it wasn't long before he was being inundated with invitations. Everyone wanted him to be their special guest at this or that occasion, although such a practice wasn't common in those days in Hadiya and other villages like it.

Wherever he went, people began pressing him to accept such invitations, and the mere fact of his having passed in front of this or that home with Hamama had become a major event. Now that he had become larger than life, it was an easy thing for girls to fall in love with him.

Sumayya, al-Barmaki's daughter, was one of those smitten.

She no longer had eyes for anyone else in Hadiya. Whenever he passed by her, she would ogle him until he had disappeared from view. Then her eyes would remained fixed on the point at which he had vanished until he reappeared. This kind of thing could easily go on from sunrise to sundown, and sometimes even after sundown.

However, it didn't stop there. For suddenly, in spite of herself, she felt compelled to follow him wherever he went. At first she would return after taking a few steps in his direction. She might go half the distance to where he was or a bit farther, then retreat. Over time, however, her feet refused to obey anything but the voice of her heart.

The strangest thing of all was that the people of Hadiya responded to the things they saw Sumayya doing in the same way they responded to what they hadn't seen, namely, the way in which Khaled had recovered Hamama and everything that had been stolen from them, then brought it back to their houses in absolute secrecy. For although they realized that

Khaled had chosen his bride-to-be and that the only chapter left in that story was for the wedding date to be set, there wasn't a man in all of Hadiya who wouldn't have wanted Khaled to be his daughter's protector.

The military police spread out everywhere in search of clues connected with the scattered corpses they had found in the hills and valleys. They turned the villages upside down, but found nothing to go on. Nor would they be able to find anything as long as people's lips were sealed in Hadiya, where life went on as though nothing had happened.

However, things weren't to remain this way for long.

It was true, of course, that tax collectors and the military policemen who accompanied them had been attacked on numerous occasions by fugitives who had taken to the mountains to avoid being conscripted into the Ottoman army and subjected to the Turks' brutality. However, this attack had been different. First, it had taken place in stages, and second, the person who had carried out the attack had done so for a very specific purpose. While the people of Hadiya, who took the most pride in the story, pretended to be the most shocked by it, other villages were passing the story along and adding new chapters to it. Strangely, everyone began relating the saga as one that had a single horseman as its hero, and it was this that caused the people of Hadiya to begin worrying that the threads of the story might be traced to them in the end.

However, not everyone associated the attack with the retrieval of a mare. Some thought it likely that the attacker was someone who had been avenging the death of his father, who had been hanged by the Turks. Others were of the view that the issue was even more serious, since more than one member of this person's family had been hanged or imprisoned. Still others hypothesized that the unknown assailant had been avenging an attack on someone's honor. On a more realistic note, everyone asserted that the person who had committed the killings had not taken the men's horses or arms, but had contented himself with what was in their saddlebags. Moreover, as if to vindicate the assailant more fully, they began saying that the things that had been in the military policemen's possession had not even been touched by the horseman. Rather, they claimed, they had been taken by the military policemen who had come in search of their companions. This version of the story was more to people's liking, since it was consistent with the greed they had witnessed on the part of the military police on so many occasions.

Hajj Mahmud was certain now that his son was the wisest of all, and the gray cloud that had hung over him because he had fallen so hard for Yasmin had disappeared. He was now more prepared than ever before to step aside in order for his son to replace him in his position as town elder, knowing that he was, of all people, the most qualified to lead the village.

As for his three brothers, they became more submissive to him. Many men in the country were on the verge of declaring their allegiance to him as well. What prevented them, however, was their realization that Hajj Mahmud would always remain, in their eyes, the wellspring of the authority that had been bequeathed to his son.

And She Kept
the Secret Hidden

Munira bent down and, with her lean fingers, took hold of some parched grass. She ran her hand over it, then stood up straight again. She looked at the distant sky and shook her head. The rains with which the season had begun had been no indication of the inferno that awaited them at its midpoint, an inferno that had set the spring on fire at one fell swoop as the August sun had descended with a vengeance in mid-April. She cast a glance in the direction of the distant grassland. Her eyes weren't deceiving her. It was yellower than she had ever seen it before, even yellower than it would normally have been in late June. However, she kept her feelings in check and dealt with the matter as though it were a secret that no one should divulge.

She pondered the olive groves on the horizon, and suspected that the situation there would be no less harsh in a few months' time. Her troubled heart had become full of secrets knit together with fears.

She thought to herself: Was this really a girls' year? Or is that just what we wanted it to be? Then she began counting up on her fingers the babies that had been born that year.

Hajj Mahmud had decided to take his wife and son and pay a visit to the family of the bride. He wanted to show everyone that life was going on as usual, although deep inside he realized that a huge story like this one couldn't possibly remain a secret forever.

On the way they passed by the cornfields. The fields weren't displaying the verdure that they usually did at this time of year, and they realized what was happening. As they rode along, Khaled wasn't looking at the fields. Instead, he was listening to the rustling of its leaves. It bothered him that he wasn't hearing the music that had once been so palpable he could almost have reached out and taken hold of it. He didn't know why, but the sound he was hearing was more like that of a hot southerly wind whistling past tightly closed windows, and he discovered for the first time that music has more than one color. After all, he was now hearing a yellow music that was a far cry from the green music that had once filled his being.

Oddly, Munira looked neither right nor left. Instead, she stared straight ahead as though she had put on blinders. With the passing of the days, her fear had become bigger than her heart, and immersed everything she saw in a frigid pallor.

She looked thoughtfully at Khaled as he rode in front of her. Then she looked at her husband and whispered, "Be gentle with us, Lord."

Suddenly breaking the silence, Hajj Mahmud said, "It seems to me we should have another talk about the matter of marriage."

"What's on your mind, Baba?"

"I don't think waiting will be in anyone's best interests. It won't be good for you or for the bride. It's obvious that this year is going to be a hard one, and that the harvest season won't be the kind we'd hoped for."

"You're feeling what I'm feeling, then!" Munira exclaimed.

"I haven't seen a spring this hot in at least forty years, and I know what it means for this season to begin with this kind of sweltering heat."

"You're right, Hajj," she said.

"So, do you agree with me that we should move the wedding up?" he asked.

"Well, I just don't know."

Khaled didn't say a word.

Each of them began listening to the sound of their horses' hoofbeats, which mingled in such a way that none of them could distinguish the footsteps of the horse he was riding from those of any other.

"The fact is," Munira went on, "there are lots of things I'd like to say, Hajj. But I feel that Khaled should say what he's thinking, since the matter concerns him. And I think he's even more aware of what's happening than we are."

However, Khaled didn't speak.

The horses continued their ascent as though they knew the way without needing anyone to guide them. Beneath the mid-morning sun, Khaled watched a drop of sweat on Rih's brow. It glistened motionless in the sunlight like a crystal. It looked as though it were contemplating the various directions before it decided which way it ought to go. For a fleeting moment, he saw it move slightly upward toward him, which left him disconcerted. Suddenly, the drop of perspiration drew him deep inside itself. However, the light within it quickly began to fade, and a harsh, coal-black darkness descended upon his heart.

"I don't think the coming days are going to be in our favor," said Khaled at last. "I don't want to drag this innocent girl into misery, and I never have. Something is happening now. I can feel it, and I think you do, too. There's something coming, and we know it. But none of us wants to admit that it's more difficult that he can imagine." He paused briefly, then said, "So let's postpone talk about marriage. Let's give it some more thought."

"This decision of yours!" protested Hajj Mahmud without looking his son's way.

"I think it's our decision, isn't it?"

Munira made no reply, while Hajj Mahmud did nothing but glance back at the expanses of Hadiya's fields behind him. As he did so, he was reminded of the way Father Georgiou had looked back the day he left the village never to return.

❀

Things were no less bleak when they reached the bride's house, where the entire conversation revolved around a season that was threatened by a blazing heat the likes of which they had never known before.

"Never, as long as I can remember, have the morning hours been as hot as they are these days," said Yasmin's father.

The strange thing was that no one even asked about the bride. Khaled himself seemed too anxious to look around in the hopes of catching a glimpse of her. However, her father surprised them by calling her.

"Yasmin!"

"Yes, Baba," she replied.

Khaled's heart skipped a beat.

"Come out and say hello to your family."

Khaled hadn't expected to see her. However, something had been happening in the heart of the bride's father as well, something that had prompted him to think in a new way.

When she popped her head around the corner, her cheeks were rosy with bashfulness, and her face was made all the brighter by the red and white silk ears of grain that adorned her off-white robe. The neck opening was flanked on either side by lavender branches whose gracefully curved figures covered the entire bodice. Her off-white head-covering, whose edges were embroidered with delicate designs that set off the colors in her robe, completed the picture.

How could Khaled have seen all that in just a few moments? He himself didn't know as he thought back on it later. He hadn't thought it would be possible for her to be more beautiful than she had been the day he had seen her at the edge of the field. But when she looked into the room, she was crowned with a perfection that would remain imprinted in his heart forever.

She bent down and kissed Hajj Mahmud's hand, then Munira's. Next she took Khaled's hand and raised it to her lips. And before he realized what was happening, her lips were clinging to the back of his hand. A shiver went through his entire body. He felt her kiss pass through his skin and move through his body until it returned to the point from which it had begun. It then surfaced briefly, only to pass inside him again for another round. What had happened was more than real. However, in the storm of sensations that flooded his soul at that moment, it seemed to him that what he was experiencing was nothing but a dream, or rather, a memory.

And it frightened him terribly.

The Secret of the Slain

Habbab's house had become the headquarters in the search for the secret that lay behind the recent slayings. The matter preoccupied him so much that he forgot his own troubles. Tents were pitched around his house, and Bekbashi Kamil Efendi Agha was staying in his home as his personal guest.

The search was utterly hopeless, though, since the region was vast, and it wasn't possible for anyone to visit every one of its villages. The military police went to and fro over its plains and hills, expecting to meet the same mysterious fate. Perhaps this was what made them even harsher in their dealings with people, who in turn hated them all the more.

The bekbashi's strategy, which was to exploit the animosities that existed between many of the families in the villages, had opened up some leads, which later revealed themselves as nothing but false accusations.

Whenever the Turks released someone, the story would grow more complicated. For mercy was a luxury for which there was no place, whether among those who brought in suspects bound with shackles, or among those who spent long nights interrogating them. Some days later, the bekbashi had a fiendish idea that hadn't occurred even to Habbab, namely, to announce a hefty reward of twenty thousand piasters for anyone who provided information that would lead to the arrest of the fugitive criminals.

The news spread like wildfire, and soon reached Hadiya and other villages as well. It wasn't long before rumors and accusations began to circulate. However, they would only lead to two things: agonizing torture sessions for some, and the arrest of others while the torture went on.

One day, a piece of news arrived that appeared to be the most precise thus far. Habbab had kept its source secret as a bargaining chip by means of which he intended to prove that he was the one who called the shots in the region, and that when people found themselves at their wits' end, he was the one with the solution to their ills. However, as he himself would see in time, his big mistake was that he hadn't played all his cards at once.

He had narrowed the search down to Hadiya because it was the last village visited by the military assistant and his men. When things had gone beyond whispers to words coming from neighboring villages, this was sufficient to level a powerful blow against the bekbashi's plans, whose humiliating search campaigns, with their assaults on everything people owned, had earned him nothing but people's hatred. But what drove Habbab out of his mind was that when the large force he had sent out arrived in Hadiya, having been instructed to surround the village with half its men and storm it with the other half, it was devoid of all the men who might have been on the list of suspects.

There wasn't a household Habbab would have liked to wipe out more than that of Hajj Mahmud, who, as far as he was concerned, embodied all of Hadiya. Consequently, narrowing the search down to Hadiya felt like a triumph for him, since now, at last, the people whose fall he had awaited for so long were almost in his grasp.

Hadiya was the final thorn he needed to be rid of, and which he should have pulled up long before. And now the chance to do so had come to him on a platter of gold. It was a perfect opportunity, by means of which he could clip Hajj Mahmud's wings once and for all.

Habbab would have liked to be at the head of the military force that went out. However, something had caused him to hold back. For a long time he had tried without success to explain his resistance to going. He was ecstatic, yet he couldn't bring himself to get up and dance for joy.

As for Hajj Mahmud, he seemed prepared for any risk he would have to take. When the bekbashi asked him about his sons, he replied, "Did you expect them to sit around waiting for you? The reports about the things you're doing everywhere would keep anyone from staying put, since a visit from you means nothing to us but insult, torture, and prison. And who knows what else you might do."

"So then, they've fled. Your sons have fled," said the bekbashi with a menacing shake of his head.

"My sons, and others' sons as well."

Hadiya turned into a military camp, and anything the military police could do to make the people's lives hell, they did. However, whenever Hajj Mahmud was confronted by the bekbashi or one of his men, he would say simply, "It's a false accusation, and you know that better than we do."

Then, five long days later, something happened that no one had expected. The men who had remained in Hadiya were led away to the guesthouse courtyard, and some were forced inside. Meanwhile, the women and children were led away to the mosque and held there. The same thing was being done in all other neighborhoods of the village.

It was no ordinary night that they went through, with chaos reigning everywhere: soldiers' voices mingled with those of animals, and with the sounds of things being shattered and crushed. Dreading the knowledge of what the night and its darkness would yield, the villagers spent the time open-eyed, waiting for the first threads of dawn to appear.

By mid-morning, most of the noise had died down, and human voices seemed to have disappeared entirely. Doors were opened and some people came out into the streets. There wasn't a soldier in sight.

Someone called out, "They're gone!"

Hearing this, people poured into the streets and went rushing home. But when they got there, it was as though the whole world had suddenly come to a standstill, and they stood in horrified amazement before the wholesale destruction that had been wrought. The houses had been ransacked so thoroughly, it was as though they had been disemboweled. Dovecotes, sheepfolds, and cattle pens lay in ruins, while wounded animals with cut-off limbs moaned piteously, trying in vain to crawl or stand.

Frivolous Dreams

The harshness of the vagabond life Khaled was leading in the mountains and valleys was alleviated somewhat by the fact that Hamama had been returned for safekeeping to her original owners. It was true, of course, that they were unhappy at the thought that Hajj Mahmud's family wasn't able to protect her in Hadiya. However, the unborn young that Hamama was carrying belonged to them. As for Habbab, never in his life had he been as on edge as he had been during the days the bekbashi and his soldiers had spent in Hadiya. For although he had been receiving regular reports on happenings there, they spoke of none of the things that he had dreamed of or planned.

"You burned, you destroyed, you hamstrung their livestock. But believe me, none of this means a thing to them in the end, as long as their young men have eluded our grasp. The motto they live by is, 'You can take our money, but don't touch our progeny.'"

Habbab spoke these words while standing on his upper landing, his eyes surveying the distant plains, hills, and valleys as he wondered where they might be hiding.

The bekbashi listened to Habbab without dismounting from his horse. After giving the matter some thought, he said at last, "We still have plenty of time to go after them."

"As I see it, there's a lot we have to do right away. We don't want to give them a chance to catch their breath," Habbab insisted.

"Well," replied the bekbashi curtly, "I've got to catch my own breath."

Abd al-Majid, Aziza's husband, was one of many men whom the military police had bound and led away. When Habbab saw him, he smiled but said nothing.

That evening he asked the bekbashi to go easy on Abd al-Majid.

"I thought you were tougher than we were," said the bekbashi.

"I am!" replied Habbab, "but not on one of my own feet."

"Your own feet?"

"You can hold the others for as long as you like. But in a few days' time I'm going to need him back in Hadiya, since that's the only thing that will do any of us any good."

Two days later, just as the cavalrymen were leaving for the distant foothills, all the men who had been brought from Hadiya were released, if for no other reason than that Habbab wanted to get Abd al-Majid back to the village. There could be no doubt, however, that Habbab had spoken to him in private about a number of matters.

"I know you endured a lot this time. But be assured, I'll reward you with something that will make you forget everything you've been through."

Abd al-Majid listened, trying his best to suppress the pain racking his slender frame. His features tightened, causing his face to look even drier and darker than usual, and his eyes narrowed as though he were trying to see something he was unable to get a good look at.

When he and those with him were returned to the village, after being punched and beaten with batons, the bruises they bore on their faces and bodies were as visible as the destruction that had been wrought in the village.

❁

It was a hopeless search, despite the fact that there were many villages in which the bekbashi found suitable resting places where he might spend the night and recover from the day's insufferable heat.

The sun was not on their side, which made their task all the more grueling. The mere act of moving was sufficient to make the military police break into a profuse sweat even before they had left the guesthouses where they had been received against their owners' wills.

Yet the one thing the bekbashi was certain he could do was to issue more orders to his soldiers, who were so overcome with exhaustion that they were no longer able to catch any of the men they were pursuing.

Khaled knew that he and those with him would have to get far enough away that they were outside the entire area. This wasn't difficult, however, given the affection and goodwill people felt toward these particular guests. Throughout the days they spent moving from one place to another he would recall his father's words: "Don't go to a place where the water is sweet. Rather, go to where people's hearts are good. And don't go to a town protected by walls, but rather, to a town that's protected by its friends."

They then parted ways.

Khaled went as far as Fallujah. He had thought of going to see Shaykh Jibril, an old friend of his father's. However, when he got there he found military police in front of the door, so he turned his horse around and headed for the main road. Noticing Khaled's movement, one of the cavalrymen got on his horse and beat him to the place where the shortcut joined the main road.

Khaled realized what was happening, but wasn't concerned, since, after taking a brief look at the cavalryman's horse, he was confident that Rih was both swifter and more thoroughbred than her rival. Hence, he kept on going at the same leisurely pace, thereby making it easy for the military policeman to circle around and meet him at the junction. When Khaled arrived at the crossroads, the policeman was waiting for him, rifle in hand.

"Peace be upon you," Khaled said in greeting.

"Where are you headed?" asked the policeman.

"To Gaza." Then, before the policeman had had a chance to comment, Khaled continued, "Tell me, don't you belong to the Zu'bi family?"

The policeman, who was fair-skinned, replied, "If what my mother says is true, then I do."

"How is Muhammad Sa'id?"

"Which Muhammad Sa'id?"

"Both of them: Muhammad Sa'id al-Ubayd, and Muhammad Sa'id al-Sulami."

"They're both fine."

"Please give them both my warmest greetings."

"I will. Who shall I tell them is sending the greeting?"

"Tell them their friend from al-Brayj says hello."

"I'll tell them," said the policeman, who turned his horse around to leave, embarrassed to ask too many questions about a friend of his family's.

At sundown, Khaled found himself alone. There was nothing on the horizon but a hair tent. As he headed toward the tent, he noticed it was surrounded by a good deal of activity. He suspected that one of the mares he saw belonged to Shaykh Nasir al-Ali. Encouraged by the thought, he kept approaching, though without letting down his guard. As soon as the men there saw him, they came out to welcome him. Shaykh Nasir asked him what had been happening in Hadiya, and whether the reports he had been hearing were true. Khaled confirmed that they were, adding, "It's one of those difficult years."

"Listen, son," replied Shaykh Nasir, "things won't stay the way they are. They might get worse, and they might get better. But every human being has his weak points and his strong points. Some people realize this, and some don't. In either case, though, they're pathetic—especially people whose strong points turn out to have been nothing but their weak points."

"May God comfort your heart," said a man clad in Bedouin attire, whose eyes emitted a deep glow.

After a silence, Khaled looked at the man, who appeared particularly eager to speak with them, and said, "You haven't introduced me to our honorable brother."

167

The man quickly uttered his name, as if to exempt the others from having to speak. Then, as though he were finishing an earlier conversation, he added, "If it weren't for injustice, Shaykh Nasir, we would never have reached the state of weakness and decadence we're in now. You can see how the Turkish officers treat the Arab soldiers, who have started fleeing from the army, and how a spirit of Arab nationalism is emerging. At the same time, many notables and leaders have begun giving in to the Turks' demands. Consider what happened when Jamal Pasha had Fawzi al-Azm's son hanged. Fawzi al-Azm himself seemed to approve of what had happened. As a result, Jamal had nothing but contempt for this nation, since it bows down to leaders who pretend to be content to see their children led off to the gallows. So the people who have endured oppression and persecution are bound to harbor ill-will toward Jamal and the Ottoman state he represents."

He fell into a long silence, then said, "Our problem is that we can't make good use of any of our opportunities. The Arabs have no unity and they're a puppet in the hands of the Turks, while the Turks are a puppet in the hands of the Germans, who lead them into military campaigns for no reason other than that they want to worry the British. We don't know how to organize ourselves socially, since we don't trust each other. We lack an understanding of how important it is to concern ourselves with public affairs, and if any of us does concern himself with them, he exploits them as a way of winning fame and serving his own interests."*

---

* "One day we received an unexpected visit from Jamal Pasha in Bi'r Saba'. At that time, Jamal Pasha was coming from Damascus after executing the second group of Arab martyrs. He issued orders for the units to be inspected, so we prepared everything for him. He came forward to do the inspection, accompanied by me and the German commander. Jamal Pasha began asking me about certain details, which I related to him with a candor and thoroughness that took him by surprise. Then he began asking me about the names of the officers who had passed before him during the military review and where they were from. Whenever an Arab officer would pass before him, I would introduce him to him. His suspicion aroused, he turned to me and asked, 'And you, what is your name?' I said, 'Fawzi al-Qawuqji.' 'From which town?' he wanted to know. 'From Tripoli of the Levant,' I said. He nodded, then said, 'The people of Tripoli are quite patriotic and intelligent. However, among them are families who deserve to have sulfur water poured over them. Don't you agree?' To this I replied, 'My lord the Pasha would know better than I do. For, although I myself am from

The man's words had a powerful impact on Khaled. And when, toward the end of the evening, Najib Nassar realized how much the two of them had in common, he said, "So then, we're in the same boat!"

Khaled replied, "I wish you could pay us a visit after this cloud has lifted. You can be sure that we'll be the happiest people in Hadiya. And the happiest of all will be Father Elias, who, whenever he reads anything you've written, says, 'Now that's a real teacher. He's my teacher!'"

"And what is Father Elias doing in your village?"

"There's a monastery there, and they sent him away from Jerusalem as some sort of punishment."

"Why are they punishing a clergyman?"

"It's a long story."

"None of us here is in a hurry. So let us hear it!"

The next morning, Najib asked his host for permission to leave, since he feared that the tent's proximity to the main road made it a vulnerable location. Khaled, too, had requested permission to be on his way. However, the host said, "Your sheep has already been slaughtered. So stay for lunch, and then you can be on your way with our prayers for God's protection."

There was nothing more they could say, so they sat down and went on with their conversation.

Later, Khaled said, "There's one silver lining to that cloud, since if it hadn't been for the ordeal I was going through, I would never have met that noble man, Najib Nassar."

Tripoli, I don't know the city well, since I left it when I was very young in order to study in Istanbul, then to serve as an officer.' Then he asked me, 'What do you have to say about those I had hanged in Syria?' And I replied, 'Syria's fortunes have been placed in your hands, and you were undoubtedly acting according to the dictates of your conscience'" (Fawzi al-Qawuqji, *Mudhakkirat Fawzi al-Qawuqji, 1914–1932* [Beirut: Dar al-Quds, 1975], pp. 28–29).

The Night by Stealth

T he state's preoccupation with its wars enabled a good number of the fugitives to return stealthily to their homes, where they would spend an occasional night or, in most cases, part of a night. However, every time they came down from the mountain they were taking a clear risk, since issuing an order for someone to be executed by hanging had become a very easy thing.

There were only two things Khaled worried about: Hamama and his fiancée. He had begun worrying even before he learned that her family had been rethinking the whole matter of marriage in light of the inexplicable absence that had been determining Khaled's fate in faraway places of which they knew nothing.

"Empires survive longer than people do. And this empire is here to stay," Yasmin's father said to her. "No one who's fled from the Ottoman has lived to tell the story unless he disappeared forever. And in this case, too, the state has been the victor. We really do love him. At the same time, though, there's something being woven by fate. In fact, it's already been woven, and it goes beyond our own hopes and dreams. So you need to think carefully about what I'm saying."

"Anything but this!" she protested, tears flowing silently down her cheeks.

"This is why I'm telling you that you need to think carefully."

Meanwhile, Hajj Mahmud felt it was time for him to bring Hamama back to Hadiya. So, together with a number of other men from the village, he headed out for the Sa'adats' territory. When they passed in front of Habbab's house, he didn't try to prevent himself from turning and looking. And there he saw him, as he had seen him every time he passed this way: standing in the upper room like a statue, with his red fez and his off-white cloak. The image made him think of Fate looking watchfully, inscrutably, out over the land.

Things were the same on their way back. In fact, Habbab seemed like a shadow that had been waiting for them the entire three days they had been gone. Hajj Mahmud could have sworn he saw the statue stir slightly this time when it saw Hamama. However, it quickly returned to its stony stillness.

Hamama's belly was getting rounder and rounder. Her original owners had offered to keep her until she gave birth. However, Hajj Mahmud said, "She's the only thing in the world that reminds us of Khaled, who's yearning to see her at home again."

"He's welcome to come see her here any time he likes."

"I've indicated as much to him. But you know him: he doesn't want to bring the fire that's singeing the hems of his robe onto your plantations."

Seeing Hamama again revived a spirit of hopefulness in the house, and to Munira, her presence meant that her sons' absence would soon come to an end.

One dark night, Khaled stole into Hadiya. Before arriving, however, he went walking around Yasmin's house. He sat down some distance from it as he had been accustomed to doing whenever he could since his vagabond days had begun. He reached into his pocket and brought out her cream-colored handkerchief, then began inhaling deeply of its scent, as though all the air in the world were inside it. When he sensed that he had no more time to spare, he got up, certain that he would see her there. Hadn't she said, "That's me!"?

He stood before Hamama in the darkness, hugging her face with his hands and stroking her brow. The night could not conceal the roundness of her radiant white belly. He turned slightly, leaving his left palm on her brow, and began running his right palm over her rotund belly. At that moment, she let forth a soft whinny and, turning toward him, looked straight into his eyes. He leaned into her with his entire body, making the embrace complete.

Inside the house, Munira suddenly found herself awake, though she was unaccustomed to waking at such an hour. It was as though someone had called her name. She stood up, contemplating her house in the darkness, which was dissipated with difficulty by the small flame in the lamp she held. She studied her husband's face, wondering whether he looked older or younger than the day when she had married him, or whether he had stayed just the same.

In those days, it was the custom for a groom not to be allowed to see his bride-to-be until the wedding day, and she thought back on the way he had lifted the veil off her face. She had been expected to close her eyes shyly the moment his hand touched the veil, but instead, with the mischievousness of a little girl, she had suddenly opened them. He smiled at her, and she smiled back. Her sister had been so furious, she looked as though she were going to explode. She didn't say a word, but her glare said, "How could you do this? You've scandalized us! I'm going to tell our father!"

Munira had replied, "If you tell him anything, I'm going to pretend to get dizzy and fall down. So there!"

She remembered the incident happily. As she always had, she felt as though she had managed to ignite a revolution all by herself. Many times she'd said proudly, "From that day on, brides started opening their eyes!"

She remembered the day her sister-in-law Anisa had asked her, "Do you think the Hajj loves you?"

After thinking it over for quite a while, she had said, "Maybe he does, and maybe he doesn't. But one thing I am sure of: he fears God. Is that a good enough reason for saying he loves me?"

Standing there in silence, Munira finally realized it was something else that had wakened her. She tiptoed to the door and opened it with its usual creaking.

"What is it?" Hajj Mahmud asked her.

"Everything's just fine," she answered.

Before reaching the stable, she knew for certain that her son was there. And Hajj Mahmud was close on her heels.

A Dry Calm

The military policemen resorted to every possible means of apprehending the men of Hadiya, and Hajj Mahmud's sons were at the top of the list of wanted men. The winds intensified, and that year's blistering heat decimated the summer crops, leaving the produce as dry and hard as stones.

Khaled and his brothers spent the following winter, which witnessed nothing but a few high clouds, in a state of constant peregrination. They worked as farmhands, shepherds, and stable hands. However, for a number of reasons, the bekbashi had begun focusing his efforts on a single person: Khaled. It was said that many of the men had returned to Hadiya and other villages without meeting any harm. Among them was Ghazi, al-Barmaki's son. However, what awaited them now was harsher than what they had feared when they were on the run in the mountains.

For suddenly, the government multiplied the numbers of young men it needed as soldiers. Those who escaped the fate of military conscription were very few, namely, those who had the wherewithal to pay an exemption fee to the government in the amount of sixty Ottoman pounds, which was no small sum. However, even this did not exempt them from serving for a period of five months in the war zone nearest their village or city. For those who were unable to avoid military service either by paying money or by fleeing, there were trains waiting to take them away to perform their service in places they knew nothing about.

A man who was married to a woman from another village was exempted from the draft, as was a man married to an underage girl who had no one to provide for her. The exemption also included judges in Islamic courts, teachers of the religious sciences, custodians of shrines devoted to the memory of apostles and saints, heads of Sufi brotherhoods, prayer leaders and preachers in mosques, and those with permanent disabilities, who were required to undergo annual medical examinations for five consecutive years as a way of proving that they were fully incapable of serving in the army.

Although a man who was his parents' only son was exempted from military duty, what happened to Ghazi the son of al-Barmaki was totally unexpected. Everyone in Hadiya, as well as everyone in the surrounding villages, knew that Ghazi was his parents' only son. However, the official documents showed that he had a brother one year older than he, by the name of Yunus! So, despite the fact that this brother of his had never materialized, Ghazi was dealt with as someone who was eligible for the draft, and was duly led away to the warfront.

One day, Turkish soldiers descended on the village with their swords and long rifles. They wouldn't allow anyone to leave the village, not even Father Theodorus, to whom the bekbashi said, "Stay right where you are."

Then he gathered the men of the village into the guesthouse and shut the door on them. The soldiers waited for long hours, but none of Hajj Mahmud's sons appeared. They were certain that Khaled and his brothers were coming back secretly and working the land by night in order to do whatever they could for their families.

"What are you doing?" Hajj Mahmud once asked his sons when he saw them plowing their land in the dark. "What are you doing! There's no reason to think that this drought is going to end!"

However, they went on working, their brows covered with glistening beads of sweat.

The soldiers spent the better part of their day under the cloudless December sky. The sun beat down on everything as far as the eye could see, roasting it over a fire the likes of which they had never known. However, no one appeared. As the afternoon wore on and they began losing patience, they said to Aziza, "Go up to the roof and call them."

She refused, since she knew they weren't far away.

Then a strange idea glimmered in her eyes. A few minutes later, to everyone's amazement, she said, "I'll go up."

"Don't you go anywhere!" cried her mother Munira.

However, she went up anyway. Once she was on the roof, she gazed out into the surrounding fields. She didn't say anything. The entire village was being held hostage, with its horses, its cows, its sheep, and its goats, its old people and its young.

Then, confident that the soldiers wouldn't understand everything she said, she suddenly began shouting, "Khaled! Salem! Muhammad! Mustafa! Come, but don't come!"

Then she repeated, "Khaled! Salem! Muhammad! Mustafa! Come, but don't come!"

Her brothers heard her and, realizing that something peculiar was afoot, they left the village.

Half an hour after Aziza had come down from the roof, the soldiers said to her in broken Arabic, "And now you're going to lead us to them. You're their sister. Otherwise, we'll force their mother to do it."

"Or this boy," they added, pointing to her son.

She swore that she knew nothing and that her brothers might be back any moment. However, they replied, "You're going to tell us about them. You're going to do it."

The soldiers knew that any assault on a woman would cause all hell to break loose. However, their commander, who had twice searched the house thoroughly, hadn't forgotten a certain hen that had been sitting on her eggs, and that had flapped her wings menacingly in his face as if to warn him not to take a step nearer.

He went to the coop and shoved the hen aside, oblivious to her furious squawking. He then took an egg and threw it on the ground, at which point it became apparent that it contained a half-developed chick.

When the hen lunged toward him and began pecking him, he slammed her against the wall with his tall black army boot, and within seconds she lay dead on the ground.

He ordered two soldiers to bring all of the eggs. They brought a total of sixteen eggs, of which the commander took two. He then held out one of them to Aziza and the other to her mother, saying, "Either you tell us where they are, or you eat this."

The two women exchanged a meaningful glance. Aziza looked into the eyes of her three children, Fayez, Zayd and Husayn. Then she cracked the tip of the egg against the wall, closed her eyes, held her nose, and swallowed the life that was in it. Her mother unhesitatingly did the same. However, it didn't stop there. The commander began handing the women one egg after another until not a single egg remained.

When the soldiers left Hadiya, the village was in shambles. For the second time, they had left the contents of its houses torn to pieces in its courtyards and streets.

Munira and Aziza went on vomiting for days thereafter, the loathsome taste remaining a part of their torment until, not long thereafter, something even more bitter came their way.

Hajj Mahmud knew that Habbab had been behind this last inspection campaign. Consequently, he sent word to his sons to be more careful, reassuring them with the words he had repeated on many an occasion since the first time a Turkish soldier had barged uninvited into their home: "Remember, no one can go on winning forever. No nation has ever been a permanent victor."

The only person who saw the village's wanted men was Aziza, and her husband, Abd al-Majid, knew this. He knew where she went with bundles of bread and food that she would prepare from time to time before disappearing for a few hours. And every time she came back, he would see her laden with many things. After all, the drought and the taxes that swept their houses clean had led them to start robbing the military policemen and tax collectors so as to take back what they had stolen out of people's mouths.

One day, after things had settled down a bit, Abd al-Majid said to Aziza, "What do you say we invite your brothers for dinner here at the house?"

She gave a start. "What? Do you want them to be arrested?"

"God forbid!" he protested. "But it's high time we settled our differences. They're my children's uncles now, and there's nothing more precious to me than my family!"

Aziza knew very well that he didn't like them, since they themselves had never liked him. They were convinced that he was one of Habbab's men and that it was he who had leaked the news about the village's implication in the attack on the tax collector and his military escort.

Khaled had said, "A dog's tail will go on being crooked even if you put it in a mold."

"Every visit he makes to his family is a visit to Habbab. The spies we have there have told us so," Mustafa added.

"Such a well-brought-up girl, and look what she ended up with!" muttered Muhammad.

"Don't talk like that in front of me," Munira remonstrated. "He's your sister's husband, and you should let bygones be bygones. In the end, you've got to think about her children."

One day, al-Barmaki's daughter Sumayya saw Aziza on the mountain looking dismayed.

"What are you doing here?" Aziza asked her.

"What are *you* doing here?"

Aziza didn't know what to say in reply. However, Sumayya surprised her by saying, "I came in the hope of seeing Khaled."

Just like that, the girl had revealed everything in her heart. However, this left Aziza feeling all the more flustered.

"But he has a fiancée, and he's due to be married soon."

"No, he isn't going to marry her. He's going to marry me!" she rejoined with a mixture of sorrow and determination.

Then, looking straight at Aziza, she said, "Your secret is safe with me."

Aziza heaved a sigh as she saw tears streaming down Sumayya's face.

"I went to the cave where I usually see them, but they weren't there."

"Maybe something's kept them," said the girl. Then she added, "Leave the food for them. They're bound to come back sooner or later."

"You think?"

As the two of them started back home, Aziza realized how much she liked Sumayya, this girl whom love had kept teetering on the brink of madness ever since Hamama's rescue. In fact, she saw a beauty in her that she had never noticed before.

"What do you say I arrange for you to marry Muhammad, Mustafa, or Salem?" suggested Aziza.

"I'm not so crazy that I'd marry somebody else."

"So you do admit that you're crazy?"

"And do you think I'm so stupid I wouldn't realize it?"

It wasn't long before Muhammad and Mustafa agreed to come to their sister's house. Khaled and Salem, on the other hand, refused, and tried to dissuade their brothers from going.

No sooner had they begun to eat than the house was in the grip of a terrifying force that swooped down without warning from all directions.

Two days later they were executed in Jerusalem.

Habbab's malicious glee was great. As for Hajj Mahmud's grief, the whole countryside in all its vastness couldn't have contained it.

The plain was filled with people who had come pouring into Hadiya from all directions to take part in the funeral procession. There hadn't been a funeral procession like it for as long as anyone could remember, and for forty days the home of the deceased received a constant stream of visitors from villages and cities near and far.

One night Khaled came into Aziza's house, and within seconds he was standing at her husband's head. He seized Abd al-'Aziz by the neck as he swore up and down that he'd had nothing to do with what happened and that, on the contrary, he had loved them like his own brothers. Khaled shoved him out into the courtyard, then unsheathed his dagger and brought the blade near Abd al-Majid's neck. However, just then he heard his sisters' children scream. Time suddenly stood still, and his knife halted in mid-air.

He kneaded his brow with the fingers of his left hand. Without a word, he straightened up again as Abd al-Majid cowered in fright beneath a towering frame that stood trembling like the leaves of a poplar.

Khaled turned his face away.

"I wouldn't be able to kill you even if I knew for sure that you were the one who betrayed them. Do you know that?"

Then, gesturing to Aziza and her children, he said, "If any of you chooses to stay there, this is your home. But if any of you chooses to go with him, then let him get as far away as he can. Because if I see him again, I will kill him, even if I have to do it with you looking on."

As he leapt onto Rih's back, half of her disappeared from view. Then, as though she realized what was in his heart, she broke into a mad gallop. His cloak began to flutter in such a way that his mare would disappear for a time, then reappear. It looked as though he was taking one step, and she the next, or as though the one she was carrying was carrying her.

Then he was gone. It was said that he covered the distance between Rafah and Naqura several times over, and that many people had seen him in Galilee and on the shores of Asqalan.

When he came to Hadiya that night, his eyes were hollow and Rih was so covered with dust she was unrecognizable.

"I'm going to sleep," he told his mother.

"Here? Lord have mercy!" she cried.

"Yes, here," he said.

The men spread out around Hadiya and began watching the horizon, fearing another raid.

The next morning, he went out to see Hamama. He took her face in his hands and she moved close to him, resting her neck on his shoulder. They stayed this way for a long time, neither of them moving a muscle. When he moved his hands toward the bottom of her head, he sensed that she didn't want to lift it off his shoulder. He leaned over slightly without taking his hands from her jaws, and when he looked into her eyes, he saw her weeping. All at once, rivers of tears began pouring out of his own eyes.

Until that day, Khaled had always wondered whose presence might allow him to let his tears flow. However, on that morning he realized that there's no one in whose presence it's better to cry than a horse's.

Little Dreams

B y this time, Khaled had turned into something of a legend, a story told by young and old alike, to the point that some thought he actually was nothing more than a legend. However, the adults who knew him kept repeating the stories about him and Yasmin and about his exploits with the Turkish military police, until these things became part of children's imagination in Hadiya. Hence, it wasn't unusual for a child to ask his mother to tell him 'stories about Khaled' before he went to sleep, the way she might have told him stories about 'Nass Insays,' 'Jbayna,' 'al-Shatir Hasan,' and 'Pretty Girl.'

When Karim asked his mother to tell him stories about Khaled, she trembled. She looked furtively about her for fear that someone might have heard her son's request, since she knew that if her husband, Sabri al-Najjar, learned of it, he was sure to divorce her.

Karim said, "I won't go to sleep until I've heard stories about Khaled!"

The rivalry between Hajj Mahmud's clan and that of Sabri al-Najjar over leadership of the village went back many years. However, al-Najjar, to whom the Turks had granted certain privileges, including the position of mayor in Hadiya, had contented himself with this for the time being while waiting for a chance to better his lot. Meanwhile, his central concern was to encourage new marriages among his clansmen, since this was a way of ensuring new births that would eventually make his clan the more numerous and powerful of the two.

He was willing to do the impossible to see two more heads sharing a pillow, and had succeeded in overcoming the obstacles to many a potential union. When his wife gave birth to his first daughter, Rihab, he nearly went mad with disappointment. When the second daughter came along, he came even closer to losing his mind. He even thought of divorcing his wife. However, he knew that this would be madness indeed, since his wife was the daughter of one of the wealthiest and most influential elders of the north, none of whom would think of allowing any of their daughters to be sent home as divorced women.

However, before he went completely berserk, he was blessed with his first son. Looking heavenward, Sabri al-Najjar thanked God from his heart for the first time in his life. "You've been generous, O God, so generous!" So, when his wife asked him what they should name the boy, he began repeating mindlessly, "Karim! Karim! Karim! (that is, "Generous! Generous! Generous!"). We'll name him Karim!"

With the birth of his first son, al-Najjar changed. He felt as though his clan had increased by a thousand in a single night. He was so crazy about the little boy that his fondness for him surpassed even that of al-Barmaki for his son Ghazi.

After Karim, his wife gave birth to three more sons, one of whom died. However, his attachment to his eldest son was beyond description. Little did al-Najjar know that this little boy of his would be captivated by the stories of Khaled, son of Hajj Mahmud, and the Turks' pursuit of him.

Succumbing at last to her son's importunate pleadings, the mother began telling him the stories she knew. She also related accounts of events she wasn't certain had actually happened, and she wondered whether she might have made them up herself or borrowed them from the stories of Arab folk heroes. Nevertheless, she was satisfied, since only these stories would bring sleep to her little boy's eyes. Little did anyone know, however, that these stories would become part of the little boy's dreams.

Karim had heard that those fleeing from the Turks would steal by night into their families' homes. Consequently, he began sneaking out of his father's house at night and stationing himself near Khaled's house.

After many long nights had passed, the boy began to wonder whether what he had heard was just a bunch of stories that were destined to remain nothing but stories. Nevertheless, they remained the only stories he would let his mother tell him.

He had passed his seventh birthday when he stole out of his house one night, wondering sadly whether it would be the last night he did so. No sooner had he reached Khaled's house than he saw Rih approaching. The night was so dark that the horse's rider was invisible, so Rih appeared to be coming alone. The boy nearly fainted at the sight.

Seeing the boy frozen in place near the wall, Khaled asked him kindly, "What you are doing out here at night, little hero?"

"Waiting for you!" he replied.

Khaled dismounted, then squatted down so that he could look straight into the little's boy's eyes.

"And what do you need from me?" he asked.

"I just wanted to see you."

"Hadn't you thought of riding Rih, too?" queried Khaled.

"I'd been hoping to ride Hamama. But would you let me ride Rih?" the little boy wanted to know.

"If you'd like."

"Oh, I would! I would!"

Khaled picked him up by the waist and set him on the mare's back.

"Where do you live?" he asked.

"Over there," the boy replied, pointing.

Khaled led the mare in the direction in which the boy had pointed.

"But you haven't told me your name, little hero."

"Karim. I'm Karim, Sabri al-Najjar's son."

Khaled did his best not to let on to the boy that anything was amiss.

They went more than one hundred meters together. But before he could say, "I'll let you down here," the boy said, "That's enough. Let me down here!"

So Khaled set him back on the ground.

Looking up at Khaled, the boy asked, "So you're real, then?"

"Did you think I wasn't?"

"Shall I pinch myself to make sure I'm not dreaming, or shall I pinch you to make sure you're real?"

"You can do both if you like."

"Really?"

"Really!"

The little boy pinched himself, and it hurt. "I'm not dreaming," he said. Then he reached out and pinched Khaled. "Ouch!" Khaled said, deliberately overdoing the "Ouch" for added effect.

"And you're real!" the little boy exclaimed.

Then he took off running happily for home.

Khaled would always remember this incident. However, he could never have imagined how it would end!

Who Died?

One night, Khaled opened his eyes and saw a man standing right at his head. He tried to see who it was, but couldn't recognize his features in the darkness. He wanted to move, but his limbs were fixed to the ground.

"What is it?" he asked the man.

"Aziz has died."

"Who?"

"Hamama's baby. It was a boy."

They wrapped him for burial, then dug him a deep grave that would have been fit for a prince.

"It wouldn't be right to let a noble one's flesh be mangled by wild dogs or other animals," said Hajj Mahmud.

Shaykh Muhammad Sa'adat was present, surrounded by his men. When they turned around, they found themselves face to face with Hamama, who had followed them, weeping.

Khaled lifted the hem of his cloak to dry her tears, but before his hand reached her face, she disappeared.

He jumped with fright.

"O God, Your mercy!"

When he told his mother about the dream, her eyes filled with tears.

"Why all this weeping?" he asked her.

She looked at Hajj Mahmud and said, "Because you've lost her."

"But she's here."

"Not Hamama."

"Who, then? Yasmin?"

Munira made no reply, her tears flowing even more copiously than before.

Placing his hand on his son's shoulder, Hajj Mahmud said, "It must have been God's will."

"But why?"

"You know why, and so do I. But there's no use asking now, since it's already over and done with."

"Who are they going to marry her to?"

"A paternal cousin of hers."

"And where has he been all this time? Wasn't he around before?"

"It's done."

"Did she agree?"

"Who is she to refuse?"

On a distant hill, Khaled stood alongside Rih staring at her house until the first rays of dawn began stealing over the horizon. Racked with anger, his body had turned into a raging swarm of locusts that would have liked to devour everything in its path, leaving destruction in its wake. He imagined that he saw her come out the front gate, then stop and stare in his direction without doing or saying anything. In torment, he turned, Rih's reins in his hand, his wounded steps taking him to a faraway place he had never known before.

The only thing left for him to do was to follow her news. When one of Hadiya's men brought him a certain piece of unexpected information, he was in such a crazed state that he jumped on the man's horse and galloped away, leaving a bewildered Rih behind.

The man went after him on Rih's back in an attempt to dissuade him from doing whatever it was he was planning to do, but the force of his rage had passed into the horse, making it run all the faster.

Then he vanished from sight.

They were escorting her to the groom's house on camelback with women singing around her when he charged onto the scene, his body fused with that of the horse he was riding and his features hidden behind a mask. It was said that even his eyes were concealed. Then, before anyone knew what was happening or had the presence of mind to react, the horseman headed straight for the bride's litter. Reaching inside, he grabbed the bride, drew her onto his horse, and made off with her. As he turned his horse to leave, he stirred up a whirlwind. In the twinkling of an eye, he was on top of the hill. He brought his horse to a halt for a moment, turned and gazed back at the village, then vanished down the other side.

Horses came rushing from all directions in an attempt to overtake the horseman and the hostage bride, but to no avail. It was as though the earth had opened up and swallowed him. However, something happened inside the horseman himself that caused him to circle around the village and enter it again from the opposite side. The women saw him approaching and screamed, but none of the men were there to hear them. The horse kept coming at such a rapid clip that the women didn't think it would stop. At the last moment, though, the earth began to crack and dust went flying as the horse's legs became plows that sank deep into the soil.

He reached back quickly to the bride behind him, and, like a snowflake that had descended from the heavens, she found herself once again among the women.

He gazed at her, kneading his brow with the fingers of his left hand.

As he turned his horse around to leave, he stirred up a whirlwind, and in a flash, he was swallowed up by the direction from which he had come.

Groans in the Night

On the far side of Hadiya, people's fates were being rapidly knit together, and the calm that had settled over the hills and plains augured a storm that no one had foreseen.

The prelude had been the great drought that had sucked the land dry all the way to its roots, leaving what had once been rich red soil nothing but yellow sand, and the trees frail and wan.

"I can hear them groaning in the night," said Hajj Mahmud dolefully.

The wells dried up, and often a man couldn't find even a sip of water with which to quench his children's thirst, not to mention that of his sheep.

Meanwhile, on the high plateaus, Habbab was growing rich by trading ewes for baskets of straw. As for horses, they were a different matter.

No one was willing to sell his horse until he literally had nothing left, and in many cases, a person in this condition would relinquish his mare with tears in his eyes in return for the assurance that someone else would feed her and keep her alive.

As for the women, since they had no water to wash their babies' diapers, they would hang them out on ropes to dry, then scrape them as clean as they could.

Hajj Mahmud's herd of goats was dwindling by the day, since they thought it better to slaughter and eat them than to trade them for something else, although there were times when they had no choice but to barter them off.

One day, al-Barmaki saw a Bedouin approaching in the distance. He was leading a worn-out-looking camel. He followed him with his eyes as though the Night of Power had opened the gates of heaven to him. Then he took off running to meet him. He hoped to get to him before the other villagers, who likewise had had their eyes on him from the moment he'd appeared over the horizon.

Reaching the man before his rivals, al-Barmaki hailed him with the words, "You're my guest. Welcome!"

Al-Barmaki's gesture quite astounded the Bedouin, whose condition was no better than theirs, and he marveled that people would still be able to invite others into their homes at a time when even wild animals had nothing to eat.

Meanwhile, other people also came up to the Bedouin in the hope of being his host. However, al-Barmaki announced, "He's my guest! So welcome to you, and welcome to him!"

The Bedouin, all the more astounded by this outpouring of generosity, concluded that, because of the village's exceptional hospitality, God must have delivered it from the tribulation that had afflicted other villages.

Everyone's eyes were fixed on the Bedouin's camel, as though it were the first time they had seen such a creature in their lives.

The Bedouin accompanied al-Barmaki to the door of his house. Turning to the other villagers, al-Barmaki said, "God is my witness that you are all my guests."

When they had gone inside the house, they had the Bedouin sit down in the front room while they tied his camel at the far end of the courtyard.

They poured him some coffee, which was nothing but ground roasted wheat. When he tasted it, he realized that coffee like this would only be served by people whose lot was no better than everyone else's.

He got up and said, "I need to answer the call of nature."

When he reached the door, he saw that his camel had been slaughtered at the edge of the courtyard.

Looking at them furiously, he said, "You've slaughtered my camel!"

"It's a she-camel!" al-Barmaki corrected him.

"It's a he-camel!" retorted the Bedouin, now angrier than ever.

"No, it was a she-camel," they told him.

They then got so busy arguing over whether the camel had been a male or a female that they forgot all about the matter of its having been slaughtered.

In an attempt to placate him, they brought him back to his seat of honor, then removed the everyday cushion he had been seated on and replaced it with the guest cushion. Whenever anyone in the village heard what had happened, he would come running.

When at last they brought the food, everyone fell upon it as though it was the last meal they would ever eat, and it was with great difficulty that the Bedouin got even a few bites for himself.

When they were finished, they wanted to wash their hands. One of them said to him, "You're our older brother, so could you pour the water over our hands for us while we wash?"

He took the pitcher and poured the water until everyone had washed their hands.

Then one of them took the pitcher and helped the Bedouin wash his hands.

They went back inside the house and al-Barmaki took the dalla to pour the man some coffee. Remembering what it had tasted like the first time, the Bedouin said, "May God reward you. All I want are my camel's saddlebags!"

"Remember, it was a she-camel!"

"It was a male."

"No, it was a female!"

"All right, then, give me my she-camel's saddlebags!"

Al-Barmaki turned and said to him, "If you'd admitted from the beginning that it was a she-camel, what happened wouldn't have happened!"

Then the Bedouin took his camel's saddlebags and left.

Standing in front of Hamama, Khaled dreaded the thought that the day might come when he wouldn't have anything to feed her. People's situations had become so dire that they would take the dry straw off the roofs of their houses and feed it to their animals, then search in their dung for undigested grains of barley. Every day they would comb the horizon in search of a dream like the one they had experienced before in the hope that it might repeat itself, if even only once: the dream of a Bedouin appearing out of nowhere with a he-camel or a she-camel in tow.

Khaled let his arm rest on Hamama's back, and as he did so he heard a soft whisper: "That's me! That's me!"

He looked around, but saw no one. Kneading his brow with the fingers of his left hand, he went out and checked the courtyard, but still saw no one.

He went away, and when he returned a few days later, it happened again.

He went away for a longer time, and again when he returned he heard her whisper, "That's me."

Feeling he was about to go mad, he set out to visit Hamama's original owners, but the whisper continued incessantly the entire way.

They saw her from a distance and recognized her, knowing that she was the only one who might come back. They began gathering to wait for her, and when she arrived, they knew for certain that she had remained well-kept throughout her time away.

"I'm afraid time will treat your beloved badly if she stays with me," said Khaled.

They made no reply.

"I'm leaving her here," he added, "and when things get a bit better, I'll come back for her."

"You know that the mare that's brought back won't leave again. We agreed to let her come back the first time, and now you want us to take her back again? We ourselves have sent all our horses out with our men because we're having trouble protecting them here. Whoever brings a mare back to us now has to understand that she might be led away like a mule to some interminable war, or die of hunger on her feet while we look on."

Khaled looked down. "But I'll lose her if she stays with me. I'm a hunted man, and what has she done to deserve such a fate?"

"A horse with a free spirit can bear it."

The words cut him like a knife.

"But I can't bear it."

"So you love her so much that you can see no way to keep her but to desert her?"

Khaled lowered his head again, trying to prevent a lake of tears from overflowing the dam, and struggling with all his might to contain the secret that had led him to do what he was doing.

Suddenly, Shaykh Muhammad Sa'adat called out, "Ibrahim!"

Within moments, a young man no more than sixteen years old was standing before them.

"Yes, sir."

"Hamama is your responsibility now. Take good care of her."

"Don't worry, sir."

As though he didn't have a moment to lose, he jumped on her back and rode away as the others looked on, until he disappeared over the horizon.

As for Khaled, his only horizon was what he could see with a bowed head.

Loved Ones at the Door

After a number of sandy years, the winter settled the matter. Aziza, who had come back to live in her father's house with her children, couldn't sleep with the sound of the pouring rain, the rain that had wakened all of Hadiya. They were so overjoyed at the sight of it that some of them would stand at their doors looking out till the wee hours of the morning.

She tossed and turned until she felt the time had come. Securing her head-covering about her face, she scurried out to the cattle pen and milked two cows. As she was leaving the pen, she heard something knocking at the courtyard gate. She ran to open it. After all, how could one in good conscience leave anyone out in this driving rain? But when she opened the gate, she saw no one. She turned to close it, and when she did, she saw something her eyes hadn't detected before: bones sloshing back and forth in the rainwater. She soon realized that they were human bones. There was an arm bone, a pelvic bone, two thigh bones, the bones of a hand, and a skull. She was so terror-stricken that the pail fell out of her hand without her realizing it, and the milk went swirling through the muddy water.

She watched the white stream until it disappeared, and realized that something peculiar was happening.

She didn't scream. She didn't call anyone to come. Instead, she left the gate swinging behind her and climbed up the hill. Heading for the graveyard, she followed the path along which the torrent had come pouring down the hill. With every step she grew more terrified, her heartbeats coming harder and faster.

She kept going up and up, and as she did so, she was shocked to find more and more remains being carried away by the stream. At last she reached the graveyard. And, as though she knew exactly what was happening, she headed for her two brothers' graves, at the place where the level graveyard ended and the hill began its descent.

On that day so long ago, Munira had said to them, "Dig for them here so that I can see their graves from the house." Everyone had respected her grief, and in keeping with her request, they had made sure that no other grave blocked her view of her sons' tombs.

When Aziza reached the graves, she saw the water carrying the dirt away as if it were trying to pull what remained of the two corpses out of their burial places.

Aziza stood for a long time in the rain, unable to do anything but watch the flow of the torrent as it washed away part of her heart. She turned around and headed back, this time walking along the edge of the stream. As she walked, she was followed by her brothers' remains, and when she arrived back at the gate, she found that all their bones had collected in front of the gate.

She disappeared briefly inside the house. When she came out again, she was concealed within the folds of a black cloak, and she rode away on Jalila's back.

They searched for her for a long time, in the house and in the cattle pen, and when they saw that Jalila was gone, they knew that something major was afoot. With Munira close on his heels, Hajj Mahmud went running for the gate, oblivious to the driving rain. When he opened it, he was met by the same surprise that had met Aziza. In horror, they headed in the direction from which the water was pouring down toward the house, and before they reached the foot of the hill, they realized what had happened.

With mud flying in all directions and spattering his clothes, Hajj Mahmud went racing back to the house. Once there, all he could do was gather up the bones with trembling hands, then carry them inside the courtyard while Munira stood on the hill, breathless with shock.

The water had risen slightly beyond the bridge. However, the mare obeyed Hajj Mahmud's urgings and they crossed the raging stream. When he reached the other side, the only thing he could think about was the fact that Jalila wouldn't let Aziza down.

He hadn't been able to catch up with her. However, he was sure there was only one place she would go. He went past the olive groves in the direction of Habbab's village, but before he got there, he saw her on her way back.

He urged his horse in her direction, but when he reached the place where she was, she went right past him as though she hadn't seen him. Following her back, he reached out to her. She screamed in alarm.

"It's me," he said reassuringly.

Leaning sideways, he took Jalila's reins. The mare looked up and gazed at him for a little while, then resumed her former monotonous gait. The water was drenching everything, and whenever her legs were spattered with mud, the rain would wash it off again so quickly one wouldn't have known that they had ever been soiled.

When they reached the bridge, half the village was waiting on the other side: women, children, and elderly.

"For long years the rain is withheld, then all of a sudden the windows of heaven are opened. The drought was necessary in order for this flood to come. It took all those dry winters to get the message to me," said Aziza.

Then, as though in answer to someone's question, she added, "Me, forget? I hadn't forgotten, but I'd almost forgiven."

"What happened when you went there?" Hajj Mahmud asked her.

She made no reply.

And it was then that they knew she had killed her husband.

After the rain stopped, the people of Hadiya gathered up the bones from both the bodies and went up the hill to rebury them. When they began digging, the soft muddy ground responded readily to their shovels, and some of them remarked that it was the first time the ground had been this way for years.

They placed the two bodies in a single grave.

"Maybe that's what they'd wanted from the beginning," mused Munira.

At midday, the plain filled with horsemen—strange horsemen who came from many directions, seeking blood revenge.

Once they arrived, however, they realized that the horror of what lay before them was greater than what lay behind, and that there was a possibility of far more death in store. Hence, they dared not come any nearer.

They knew that, in cases such as this, the blood shed would lead to far more bloodshed, and that there was a readiness to fight and die on the part of this village's people.

So they retreated.

Hardly had the day drawn to a close before the news began storming all the villages around: Sarafand, Tell al-Safi, Ajjur, Bayt Jamal, Zikrin, Zakariya, al-Brayj, Summayl, Artuf, Bayt Jibrin, al-Duwayma, Dura, Qabiba, Asqalan. They passed through al-Zahiriya, Bayt Hanun, and Iraq Suwaydan, and many people reported that they heard about it in Hebron, Nablus, and Jerusalem.

The entire region was shaken by the story, which had a solemn, awe-inspiring note to it that no one could help but ponder in his heart. Consequently, when the horsemen returned the following day, they numbered no more than thirty to forty men. They stood for a long time on the plain, their horses walking in restless circles as the people of Hadiya looked on, poised for action. Every now and then, one of them would turn his horse around and leave. In the end, only one man remained. He spent half his day riding his horse around and around. He would periodically charge in the direction of the village until he was nearly at its edge, then quickly retreat to the point where he had begun.

They recognized him.

And when night fell, it enveloped him in its darkness.

Habbab's Winds

Quite unexpectedly to everyone in Hadiya, Habbab began making appearances in their village, and he never missed a single market day.

Arriving on horseback, surrounded by a number of his men, he would make the rounds of the marketplace and buy as many purebred camels as he could. Some Bedouins were obliged to sell their precious camels since they had yet to reap the blessings brought by that year's copious rains.

Habbab was an expert at this kind of purchase, as he could easily recognize a purebred camel, be it male or female. He even knew their types, names, and origins. Among Bedouin and village dwellers alike, she-camels occupied a place of honor that rivaled even that of thoroughbred horses. Consequently, camel owners regularly procured documents that proved their she-camels' lineages and the purity of their stock.

Habbab's presence in the marketplace threw everything out of kilter. This didn't become apparent at first. However, when people became aware of the situation, some of them began avoiding Hadiya's market, preferring to go instead to other markets, which, although farther away, were nevertheless safer.

Habbab's power lay not only in the authority he wielded, but in his physical strength as well. So, as though he had decided to challenge everyone simply as a man, he began coming around on a regular basis.

The she-camels brought to the market were always a picture of beauty: their height, the purity of their color, their long, graceful necks, their diminutive heads, their short hair and, most important, their tremendous capacity to endure hardship. Like a thoroughbred horse, a thoroughbred she-camel seems to acquire increased energy and strength the farther she goes on a journey.

It wasn't a strange thing to see a Bedouin weeping as he handed the reins of his she-camel to a man who had just bought her. However, what did appear strange, as it had never happened before, was that many Bedouins were now having to sell their she-camels to Habbab for trifling sums.

Habbab would approach from a distance, his eyes fixed on a particular camel, and sometimes on a horse. As he made a beeline for the animal's owner, people would retreat on either side to make way for him, and anyone who looked at the market from a sufficient distance or elevation could see how the market seemed to divide itself in half the moment he began riding through it. The corridor that had thus been formed would then remain unoccupied for quite a while. No one dared approach it for fear that, once in the empty corridor, he might have to beat a quick retreat in the face of some threat from Habbab.

There was something peculiar about Habbab that remained a part of him until the day he met his infamous end—an end that he crafted himself— namely, the weakness he would succumb to whenever he saw a purebred she-camel or horse. More peculiar still was the fact that he wasn't willing to take such an animal away from its owner by force in the marketplace, even though he had been known to do this very thing to beautiful women or girls that struck his fancy. He had no compunctions about stopping in this or that field without getting off his horse and saying to a peasant working beside a woman, "Who is that?"

"She's my wife," the man would answer.

"No, she's my wife!" would come Habbab's indignant reply. Then he would add, "How dare you say that my wife is your wife?"

In many cases, he would simply plant a bullet in the husband's forehead. Then, before the woman knew what was happening, he would lean down and, with one hand, lift her onto the back of his horse and be on his way. Those who had witnessed the spectacle, not daring to utter a word, stood looking on in tears and stunned silence.

However, there had been no more incidents of this type since he married Rayhana.

Here in the marketplace, things were different. He would reach out and shake hands with the seller. However, rather than letting go of the man's hand, he would hold onto it.

"How much do you want for it?" he would ask.

"Twenty majidis."

"No, seven."

Thus would begin the actual business transaction, which was bound to end in his favor. Habbab's thick fingers would close on the man's hand and begin squeezing, and gradually the man would feel more and more overwhelmed by his physical strength.

"Fifteen would be enough."

"Seven."

Meanwhile, the powerful fingers would go on with their brutal assault, until the seller's forehead, then gradually his entire body, would begin dripping with sweat. Despite the excruciating pain, he would find himself unable to cry out or even complain lest he appear to others as less than a man.

Some sellers would make a tremendous effort not to succumb. Some would manage to conquer their pain and endure for a longer time. However, the outcome was always the same in the end, and people concluded that there was no gainsaying a word from Habbab. As long as he had pronounced the verdict and set the price, no power in the world could change the situation. Nevertheless, they attributed this not to the power of his grip but, rather, to his authority. And perhaps what kept many people coming to the market was the fact that no one wanted to admit that he had been forced to sell because he hadn't been enough of a man or able to endure the pain.

As for Hajj Mahmud, he stayed out of such matters. Observing things from a distance, he saw Habbab as simply as another buyer. The steadily dwindling number of market-goers in Hadiya began to concern him, particularly in view of the fact that prices never went so low unless Habbab happened to be the buyer. However, it would be a long time before he knew the reason.

Adham's Specter

As Habbab made his way through Hadiya's marketplace, everyone stared at him fearfully, with no one daring to stand in his way. One circuit around the gathering was sufficient to tell him what he wanted, and the terrified expressions on people's faces gave him a rush of indescribable euphoria.

He began to dismount from Hamdaniya. However, before his foot touched the ground, Adham's image flashed through his mind, and he nearly stumbled.

He grabbed the saddle horn. Then, as though he had turned to a pillar of salt, he froze for a few moments before drawing his foot out of the stirrup.

Adham's image settled on the other side of his mare. He had seen him in the flesh, standing there without a saddle or a halter. His black coat glistened in the sunlight like the surface of the sea on a dark night, a sea illumined by the rays of a light that comes from nowhere. The horse turned toward him and gazed at him, then turned again and moved away.

Habbab's features clouded over, clothed in a layer of cold gray. Meanwhile, he watched the departing horse until it disappeared.

He always detested this black vision, which unsettled his entire day. He thought of going back there. He thought of his revolver. He thought of a bullet that would pierce through all that pigheadedness. After all, nothing would tame a recalcitrant horse like a bullet!

However, he didn't go back.

He would have regretted it sorely.

Then he remembered that he'd spotted a bay filly with a white blaze on her forehead. He made his way through the crowd and saw her again. The seller realized that the day of his misfortune had come. He tried to move away, but Habbab shouted, "Where are you going? The market isn't over yet!"

He stopped, then turned and faced Habbab, knowing exactly what lay in store for him.

As Habbab prepared to leave the marketplace, content with the bay filly he had purchased and leaving its former owner weeping with rage and humiliation in a place where no one could see him, he saw a Bedouin approaching in the distance, and behind him a she-camel of dazzling beauty.

He wasn't the only person who had seen her. In fact, everyone's heads turned. Silence fell over the marketplace as everyone realized that the victim was walking into the trap on his own two feet.

However, the Bedouin bypassed the marketplace, and it thus became apparent that he had not come to sell the camel, but was simply a passerby.

"O brother of the Arabs!" Habbab hailed him.

The Bedouin stopped, as did his she-camel. He turned toward the source of the sound, his head-covering wrapped around his face in such a way that it concealed his features entirely.

"Yes?"

"God's blessings upon you," replied Habbab, half-mockingly. "Is that she-camel for sale?"

"This type of camel can't be sold," said the Bedouin in a gravelly voice.

Habbab came closer to him, confident that the next step this she-camel took would be with him and no one else.

"God and His Prophet have declared buying and selling permissible," declared Habbab as he took a few steps closer.

"This type of camel can't be sold," the Bedouin repeated.

"Don't speak like an infidel!" said Habbab.

"There is no god but God and the Muhammad is the Messenger of God!" came the Bedouin's reply.

All eyes were riveted on the two men, as everyone in the marketplace forgot what they'd been doing moments earlier. They came closer, anxious to see what the following moments would yield, despite their certainty that it would be an ill-fated day for this poor Bedouin.

Coming up to the Bedouin, Habbab extended his hand, and those gathered around broke into a sweat.

The Bedouin likewise extended his hand.

"Pray for blessings on the Prophet."

"O God, send down blessings on the Prophet!" prayed the Bedouin.

"We'll give you five hundred piasters for her."

"This type of camel can't be sold."

Habbab squeezed the Bedouin's hand a little harder.

"Make that five hundred twenty."

"This type of camel can't be sold."

As the Bedouin stole a glance at the marketplace out of the corner of his eye, he could see all eyes fixed on himself and his interlocutor.

"Make that five hundred forty."

"This type of camel can't be sold."

Everyone held their breath, wondering what would happen next.

At the critical moment that had been bound to come, the Bedouin began tightening his grip on Habbab's hand. He sensed something different this time—something unexpected. The image of Adham flashed through his mind once again, and he whispered to himself, "A black vision twice in one day is a bad omen."

"Make that five hundred fifty."

"This type of camel can't be sold."

At this point, glistening beads of sweat began popping up on Habbab's forehead, and many people saw them.

Rather than withdrawing his hand, Habbab said, "Make that six hundred. And that's as much as I can offer."

"This type of camel can't be sold."

It was a moment of such dread that no one could be sure any longer what was happening inside his own soul. By this time everyone was doused in perspiration. It flowed off their bodies in torrents, drenching their clothes and turning the soil of the marketplace to a sea of mud. At the same time, a cold wind blew up, sending chills down their spines. But the next wind that blew was an inferno.

His curiosity aroused by the silence in the marketplace, the man who had sold the bay filly came back. However, he didn't come close lest someone see his tear-stained face.

Habbab realized that he had lost, that he was living the blackest day of his life, and he tried to withdraw his hand. However, the Bedouin's diabolical hand kept squeezing harder and harder.

How could he cry out in pain? On the other hand, how could he bear it another moment?

"Make it one thousand six hundred!" he shouted.

At that moment, the eyes of those gathered around shone with malicious glee, knowing that the battle had been decided.

As he closed his fingers with even greater force around Habbab's hand, the Bedouin said calmly once again, "This type of camel can't be sold."

Habbab thought back on the day when the sword had sunk into his flesh. He remembered how he had been on the verge of screaming, but instead he had endured, and had won everything: his life, his power, his prestige, and the name that had come to inspire dread both near and far. However, things were no longer going his way, even as he tried to buy his way out of his predicament with another thousand piasters.

He nearly cried, "Make that three thousand six hundred!" But before he could speak, he found his voice sinking deep into his chest, which had no more air in it.

The Bedouin knew that the matter had been settled. He knew that all he needed to do now was to press a bit longer, and that the other hand had lost all its strength, having gone limp between his fingers. He gave a final squeeze, and everyone gasped as they saw Habbab's knees buckle and sink into the mud.

Yet even then the Bedouin kept holding on, until he was assured that his opponent's defeat had reached its limit.

At last he let go. Then he turned to leave, leading his she-camel away.

His eyes fixed on the Bedouin's unguarded back, Habbab tried to reach his revolver with his right hand, but to no avail. He tried with his left hand, but when he did, he heard the roaring of the crowd, who rushed toward him menacingly, making clear to him that any move he tried to make would mean his death.

His left hand returned to the ground. Then, using his left arm for support, he got up.

Suddenly, cries of jubilation filled the air as people went running after the Bedouin, who stopped and turned to meet them.

"Who are you, O brother of the Arabs?" they asked.

"One of you," came the reply in a voice that was completely changed.

With difficulty, Habbab heaved himself onto Hamdaniya's back and went away. Left behind, the filly he had bought stood there, bewildered by her unexpected freedom, until a man came up and took her reins.

"You're the only person worthy of the honor of returning her to her owner," he said to the Bedouin.

"Ridwan!" the man called.

There was no need for him to repeat his summons, for within seconds the filly's owner had come forward through the throng.

Khaled extended the reins to the man. However, the man's hands were busy doing something else— embracing this man who had restored to him not only his horse, but his dignity.

Everyone came forward enthusiastically to embrace him. In the distance, one could see all of Hadiya rushing to the marketplace, having realized that something of great consequence had happened. Indeed, many of the villagers regretted for a long time thereafter that they hadn't been there to witness it with their own eyes.

When Hajj Mahmud arrived, they made way for him. He walked up to the Bedouin and put his arms around him. As he did so, he heard the Bedouin whisper, "We've got to be ready for anything now, Baba!"

Hajj Mahmud stood back and removed the covering from the Bedouin's face. And as he did so, everyone's tongue was tied.

With its searing clarity, this event opened the door to the blackest days Habbab had ever seen; days that would soon blow in ominous storms. Even before Habbab knew the name of this Bedouin who had crowned him with ignominy to the sound of the jubilant cries that had filled the marketplace, everything would come to an end in a way that no had expected.

A Belated Prologue

T he night before, Khaled had hopped on Rih's back and gone galloping at top speed to see Shaykh Nasir al-Ali. He drank his coffee, and after dinner he said, "I have a request to make, Father."

"We'd give you our eyes if you asked for them."

"Blessings on your eyes. I want the most beautiful she-camel you own. I'll borrow her tonight and have her back to you by tomorrow evening."

"As you wish. But wouldn't you like to tell me what you want her for?"

"I'll tell you everything, God willing."

"But you haven't told me how Hamama is."

Khaled hung his head, the silence filled with more than words could say. Shaykh Nasir could see the wound that he had first seen in Khaled's heart when he had come to him broken some years before.

When he saw the she-camel, Khaled knew they had brought him the best one they had. He knew it from her off-white hue, her short, silky hair, her towering height, and the long neck that ended with a petite head illumined by sparkling eyes so beautiful and translucent they would rob you of your senses.

"This is Samha. I'm sure I don't need to tell you how to treat her."

Khaled spent the night at Shaykh Nasir al-Ali's house, and before the dawn call to prayer, he continued on his way to Hadiya's marketplace.

Aziza met him in the place they had agreed on at the eastern edge of Hadiya.

He handed her Rih's reins. "Did you bring what I asked you to?"

"It's all ready."

Khaled took a bundle from his sister's hand, then went behind an oak tree. When he reappeared, he was a different person.

"How do I look?" he asked her.

"I swear, if I hadn't seen you before you went behind that tree, I wouldn't recognize you!"

"I'm ready to go, then."

A First Ending

I t was the most desolate week Habbab had ever known.
On the way home, he killed every creeping or flying thing he saw,
humiliated every man or woman he came across, and cut off every
branch in his way. And when he reached the outskirts of his village, he
shot at the first she-camel he saw.

Dust filled the horizon, and whenever it cleared, there was blood flying
in all directions onto the stone walls that separated the fields, the soil of
the roads, and the leaves on the trees.

When he reached home, his mare galloped across the courtyard with
such speed that everyone who saw him thought he wanted to storm the
high walls and the stable with Hamdaniya's chest.

At the moment between the shattering of bones and the scream, his mare
came to a halt, digging her hooves deeply into the soil. He jumped down
and, with a trembling hand, held his revolver firmly to Adham's brow.
Realizing what was happening, the horse took a couple of steps back. Just

then, Rayhana's face appeared. She was smiling, and her right hand rested on the horse's back.

"Couldn't you find some way to mount him other than to make this bullet into your saddle?"

Habbab stepped back. As he did so, Adham stepped forward and pinned him to the wall behind him. Rayhana's image disappeared as though she had opened an invisible door in Adham's body and stepped inside.

He lifted the revolver again, closed his eyes, and pulled the trigger with all his might, as though he wanted to crush the hand that had so covered him with shame.

Other horses whinnied in agitation, rending the air with their hooves and their fear. However, even all this could not drown out the sound of the tremulous thud caused by the huge body as it collapsed to the ground. Habbab opened his eyes again and stared at Adham's dead body. Then he turned to walk away. But before he reached the stable, he stopped and came back to where Adham lay. He pushed the wooden gate back, no longer mindful of the din that surrounded him: human cries mingled with the sounds of horses, of goats, and of slain people whose faces he could recall only vaguely. Suddenly, he jumped on top of Adham's lifeless body and settled on the horse's right side. Habbab rocked his body, kicking the horse with his heels as though he were urging the bloodied corpse to move. Then, just as suddenly, the place grew dark as the light was blocked by figures of horses, riders, and other people.

He got up to leave, and as soon as he was on his feet the light flowed in freely once more. He turned toward the slain horse and saw how calm he was. The animal's tranquility perplexed him. It perplexed him to see Adham so calm.

When he took his first step, he felt his feet sinking into the ground. They had settled deep in the enormous pool of blood that had flowed from the massive body.

As though he were asleep and dreaming, he tried in vain to extricate his feet from the jaws of blood that were closing madly in upon him. Then he began to scream.

A Second Ending

Habbab went into seclusion as though he had disappeared from the face of the earth. He instructed his wife Subhiya to forbid anyone to come in to see him. Whenever he asked anything of her, she would say, "Yes, sir."

He asked her to close the windows, informing her that he didn't want to see her face either.

"Yes, sir," she replied.

No sooner had she closed the door than he discovered a hardness, the likes of which he had never imagined. It was the hardness of the darkness when it closes in on a living being. He was certain that his spirit had slipped out through his ribs, never to return. He sensed the destruction that was filling his body with a deadly torpor, ripping his insides to shreds with cold, sharp blades.

As for Rayhana, she secluded herself in her upper room, far from everything. The only thing she knew was that she was waiting for him, waiting for a bullet that would rip through her forehead and turn her body into a huge pool of blood.

For three whole nights, and despite the sound of the raging wind, she would hear his footsteps approaching the door. They would stop for such a long time that she would be overcome with drowsiness as she sat waiting for something to happen. Then, abruptly, she would hear them withdraw. As for Subhiya, she wouldn't allow her children to make their presence felt anywhere in the house.

On the third day, Rayhana opened the door slightly and looked outside. She saw that the sky was clear. There was no sign of dust, apart from what had sifted in under the door and collected in a strange reddish-brown heap. Half a step from the doorway she saw his revolver lying on the ground as though it were the slain.

She didn't know what this meant. She didn't know what it meant that his revolver had been left near the doorstep. She opened the door more widely, and bent down. She picked up the revolver and turned it over in her hands. It amazed her to think that death, in all its enormity, could conceal itself inside a cold piece of blackened metal. She pointed the mouth of the gun at her face and looked inside it, but all she found there was darkness.

After all, death is darkness, and in the darkness it lives.

She composed herself again. Then, leaving the door to the upper room open behind her, she headed for where he was, in his large assembly room overlooking the courtyard. However, every time she took a step down, the number of steps increased. They kept multiplying until there were scores of them. It perplexed her to see that, despite her long descent toward the courtyard, she still hadn't arrived. She paused and looked back up toward the steps behind her, and her feeling was confirmed: there was no end to them, and they seemed to extend all the way to the sky.

It frightened her to think of continuing her descent. It also frightened her to think of retreating.

She stood frozen between two places, which had, in fact, always been a single entity. They had never been anything but an ordinary staircase that led from a courtyard to an upper room and back.

❋

214

The gun in her hand brought her back from her scattered state of mind. The presence of the revolver was the only reality that pointed to the fact that she had descended the stairs and that she was now halfway down. It was the only reality that pointed to the fact that all the darkness was inside the piece of metal around whose grip her fingers were wrapped. Life was all around her, whereas death cowered inside, coiled within and about itself like a spring as it peered out at everyone who stood beyond the end of its barrel, in the light, without any concern for who or what he, she, or it might be.

She cautiously moved her foot, afraid she might trip. It moved her down to the next step, and when it came in contact with the hardness of the stone, she was encouraged to continue her descent.

He could hear the rhythm of her footsteps that had so arrested him once upon a time, and he sensed her arrival. But how could he have anticipated the arrival of the rhythm before the arrival of the person to whom it belonged?

"If only she would open the door."

But she didn't open it. She stood in front of it for a long time, then withdrew.

When she reached the edge of the staircase, she hesitated and looked up. She didn't see the staircase she had seen before, the staircase that reached to the sky.

What this meant was that she would have been able to open the door, aim the darkness at him, and pull the trigger. If she had, the light would have burst forth in a flash. Then the darkness would return, leaving behind it a darkness just like it.

She went back up the stairs. However, she found herself unable to take the last three steps. This was as far as her feet would carry her.

Sensing her retreat, he felt the cold, sharp blades shooting through his inner being in a frenzied tumult. And as they moved, they tore everything around them asunder.

There's nothing worse than to find oneself in the presence of a wounded predator. However, it was even crueler than this, because the wound was the wound of shame and humiliation. It was as though it had come into being of its own accord, and without reason.

What tormented him was the laughter, the wind that had borne the news aloft, driving it along like a heap of dust and scattering it in all directions, so that wherever he went, people laughed at him with malicious glee.

"They deserved to die."

The steps retreated from the door once again. And for the first time, Rayhana saw Subhiya peeking out from behind the door, waiting to see what would happen.

Adham walked past and neighed. As for Habbab, he lay wounded in the darkness by a woman who expected him to kill her, and whom he expected to kill him.

For three more days, the steps could be heard going up and down, and all the while the door remained shut. Then, suddenly, Habbab threw his entire being into a final scream. "Subhiya!" he called out.

He tried once, twice, three times. However, his voice was unable to traverse the barren, dry distance between his throat and his lips.

He called again, and this time the house shook. Rayhana jumped up in a fright and headed for the door, ready for anything. She discovered that the revolver was still in her hand, which reassured her somewhat. However, she remained frozen in place, engulfed in the silence that had descended and straining to hear any movement from outside. Then she heard it: successive steps that seemed to stumble over one another and over the hem of a robe that swept the ground with a peculiar rasping, like that of a knife being sharpened.

When Subhiya saw him, she couldn't help but let forth a muffled scream that shook her entire body.

There in the darkness, Habbab looked like a tattered bag of straw. There was nothing to indicate that he was who he was, apart from her certainty that it couldn't possibly be anyone else, since no one else was in the place.

He was dying.

He had needed to be alone with his death for all that time, in order to think about himself, about his women, about everything.

"I'm dying," he said to her.

"God forbid!" replied Subhiya with a shudder.

"Listen to me, or else—"

"I beg you, don't say it!" she cried tearfully.

She had been afraid that he would say, "Three."

Never in her life had she detested a number the way she had come to detest this one. The mere mention of it on any occasion was enough to convulse her as though a knife had just gone through her chest, or as though the number had become a ghost that might jump out at her at any moment. If the number happened to appear in a dream, it was enough to turn the dream into a nightmare.

"Don't make me say it."

"Yes, sir."

"I'm going to give you some instructions that you're to carry out without question."

"Yes, sir."

"When I die—" he began.

"God forbid!"

"Just listen. I don't want to hear your voice."

"Yes, sir."

"I told you I didn't want to hear it."

She had been about to say "Yes, sir" again, but gagged herself with a nod. He remained silent for a long time.

"I'll tell you later what I want you to do. Right now, though, I want something else from you."

She nodded.

"I want you to go and tell all the men of the region to come here. Tell them I'm dying, and that I need to speak with them about something very important. I don't want anyone but you to go. Only you. Understood?"

She nodded, and headed quickly for the door of the assembly room. When she reached the doorstep, she could feel the air coming back into her lungs. It was like being born again.

"Quickly, or else . . ."

She ran without knowing what direction she was running in. Whenever she encountered people along the way, she told them the news. She ran and ran, until she felt she had gone so far from home that she might never find her way back.

Finding no one and nothing around her, she hoped he would die before saying it. However, she suppressed the wish as she had done so many times before when she remembered the pieces of flesh she had left at home, namely, her children.

She made her way back, and when she reached the gate to her house, the men Habbab had asked to come to her house were on their way out. As they left, they shook their heads, muttering, "What a world! What a world!"

Then they were on their way.

"All I want from you now is one thing."

She nodded.

"Before I die I'll tell you what it is."

Subhiya nodded again and left.

Rayhana didn't understand what was happening. She had never seen so many people at the house—people who had never before been allowed even to darken Habbab's doorway. She was amazed to think that she had lived to see what she was seeing now with her own two eyes.

However, she took no pleasure in any of it. Every night the pool of blood under her bed would stir, turning it into a boat tossed to and fro by the waves. She would wake with nothing in her hand but the cold piece of metal with death crouching at its muzzle.

"I've done you wrong!" he said when they had gathered around him.

They couldn't help exchanging looks of incredulity.

"I've done you wrong. I admit it. Forgive me."

"Whether you've wronged us or not, may God forgive you!" was their reply.

They were afraid.

"I've called you here so that you can hear my will and testament with your own ears, and from my own mouth rather than someone else's."

This was music to their ears, since they had been expecting to hear something altogether different. But when they heard the next thing he had to say, they were dumbfounded.

"There's only one thing that can atone for the things I've done to you," he said. Then he fell silent. He pondered their faces with his lackluster eyes. He saw the looks of disbelief on their faces, their eyes glistening with incredulity, and their heads in suspension as if they didn't know whether they should nod or not.

"After I die, I want you to come here, tie a rope around my foot, and drag me around the town three times. If you want to, you can do it more than that. Then maybe God will forgive my sins."

"What are you saying?" more than one voice asked dubiously.

"I mean what I say."

"May God forgive you," one of them said.

"Don't deprive me of my last wish. Please."

They didn't believe their ears.

"May God give us wisdom," offered one of them as they left.

"Lord, have mercy," said another as he stepped out the door.

The Flying Story

For the three days that followed they argued, but without reaching any sort of consensus. The story reached distant towns, which began waiting for the news of his death to see what would happen.

Wherever he had set foot, he'd left bitterness in people's hearts. In the face of death, however, they were more reasoned in their responses, since death has an awesome solemnity about it.

"Do you understand what you're supposed to do, Subhiya?"

"But it's wrong. It isn't proper!" she said.

"Wrong or not, that's the way it'll be!" he shouted back. "Do what I say and don't think about anything else, or else—"

"Yes, sir. But please don't say it."

She had expected him to reprimand her because she hadn't just nodded her head. But to her relief, he didn't.

He hoped to see Rayhana's face one last time.

※

Subhiya shouted four times, each time in a different direction, in front of the entrance to Rayhana's apartment. And the wind took it from there. Wherever the wind couldn't reach, people would deliver the cry, whether on foot or on the backs of their horses, donkeys, and camels. In less than two hours, the entire plain had filled with people as though it were the Day of Resurrection.

Rayhana didn't leave her room. As for Subhiya, it seemed as though the earth had opened up and swallowed her. So when people arrived, they found themselves in front of a house in which there was no sign of life.

Apprehensively, they came forward, and when they reached the threshold of the assembly room, they saw him wrapped for burial. He lay near the wall beneath the window, enveloped in darkness.

"There is no god but God," said one of them, and the others repeated the phrase. However, it wasn't long before chaos broke loose, and the debate began all over again: It's right, it's not right . . .

Some men said, "This is wrong," and went back to where they had come from.

However, bitterness won out in the end, as a number of men, some older, some younger, angrily broke through the crowd, shouting, "This is the least we can do!"

Others sympathized with them, and no one stood in their way.

They came into the house, one of them holding a rope. They tied it around one of Habbab's legs without any desire to see his face, or perhaps because they were afraid to, and dragged him out into the courtyard.

Once there, some pushed and shoved while others stepped back, with everyone saying something different. They reached the outer gate, then passed beyond the high walls, at which point one of them fixed the rope to the back of his saddle and jumped onto his horse. Then, with the vengeful whoop of a wounded, wronged man, he urged his horse forward.

Many others went running after him.

But before they had finished the third round, the entire village was surrounded on all sides by military policemen, who had arrived with a screaming Subhiya in the lead.

There wasn't a man young or old in the town square but that the military policemen bound him with ropes and led him away. They were all taken to the military tribunal, since the crime was as clear as that day with its scorching sun.

He'd brought them down again.

Finally, one of them said, "May God never forgive him!"

Said another, "Dead or alive, he's determined to destroy us."

It would be a long time before the truth of what had happened would become clear, since Subhiya went on believing that he hadn't really died and that someone else had been dragged through the streets. As far as she was concerned, he might pop up at any moment and, after the first mistake she made, say, "Three!"

And that would be the end of her.

The Brink of the Resurrection

T he sky began coming nearer, closing in on the earth from all directions. Wherever they turned, they saw a solid wall of black dust
approaching, as though the villages had fallen into an infernal trap
from which there was no escape.

For three days, there blew a wind so powerful that no one could walk
against it. People took refuge in their houses, carrying with them everything they possibly could.

They brought their camels, goats, sheep, horses, cattle, and donkeys
inside their enclosures and stables, looking out at the trees through their
windows and the tiny cracks in their doors. The winds seemed to have
come to uproot them, along with the plains and the hills beneath them.
With their ears, they could 'see' roofs, gates, and all those things that would
normally be found in their courtyards flying away. Even when the sound
of the wind retreated, the wind itself would remain in the form of sand
that swirled around and around itself, unable to escape beyond the walls
of the horizon, while endless red rivers came pouring out of the sky.

"You'd think it was Resurrection Day," said Hajj Mahmud.

No one commented.

Aziza, whose children's hearts now suffered the pangs of orphanhood, had long been awaiting it. So had Munira, who had begun wasting away little by little until there was hardly anything left of her; al-Barmaki, who was tormented day and night, unable to stop ruminating over the ironies of fate that had woven his only son's destiny; Rayhana, far away on the hill, who was drawn out of bed every night by Adham's blood and would find herself sprawled beneath it, unable to catch her breath; and Sumayya, who, oblivious to those urging her to come inside, would stand on the rooftop searching with dust-filled eyes for a ghost she expected to emerge from the belly of the red darkness.

The earth turned over like a bundle of straw, and time turned over.

The sound of the wind grew louder and louder, madly enveloping the entire landscape. Closing the doors and windows as tightly as they could, they all took refuge in the big house, where they could hear the oak trees pained moaning and the cracking of the branches.

Suddenly, Munira realized that what they were hearing at the door wasn't just the ranting of the wind, but someone knocking.

Hajj Khaled got up and went to the door. Munira cast a glance at the lamp's burning wick, realizing that the minute the door was opened it would go out, and her heart shrank. Hajj Khaled opened the door a crack and went out, then walked to the courtyard gate. When he opened it, there came a voice from outside that split the heavy clouds of dust, saying, "It's him."

A shot rang out, sending Hajj Khaled reeling backward a couple of steps, after which he fell to the ground on his face.

Running toward her brother, Aziza screamed. As for Sumayya, her feet refused to move. Munira, like Sumayya, froze in place. Outside, Aziza could see the outlines of a British officer surrounded by his men.

"My brother! My brother!" Aziza cried.

The officer and the soldiers with their weapons at the ready withdrew and ran to their vehicle, whose motor had been running the entire time.

It took off in a flash, its sound fusing little by little with the whistling of the wind until it faded into it entirely.

Aziza took off running madly after the military vehicle, but the dust that had closed in on the world quickly concealed it from view. It was like a ghost, and no sooner would part of it become visible than it would disappear again. However, she was sure that as she stood behind the door she had heard someone say, "It's him," and that the person who had said it wasn't British.

Book Two
Earth

Hediya's Weddings

The day we said goodbye to them, lightning flashed, thunder rolled,
The day we received them, we fired shots of joy in the air untold.

The day we said goodbye to them there was rain and storm,
The day we received them we did our steeds adorn.

They've returned to me from the light bright as a shining star.
Imagine his sister's joy at the sight of his radiant face from afar!

They've returned to me from afar, from the Apostle's land most
fair.
They've brought good news to the olive tree, to the stallion and the
mare.

O Khaled, the pilgrim who's returned from a distant land,
You've got the sun on your forehead and merriment in your hand!

The appearance of the pilgrims coming from the direction of the sea, whose arrival they had awaited since dawn on the western hills, was sufficient to turn the entire expanse into a wedding. The women sang and the men fired shots into the air while the songs ringing out of Hadiya's two quarters mingled to form a single celebration. Riders went racing across the fields, their horses leaping in the air and soaring with their hearts. Beyond them, the streets of the village had been decorated and white banners raised on the roofs of the houses, while pictures of the Kaaba surrounded by verses from the Qur'an and of camel caravans traveling past date palms had been drawn on the walls. Meanwhile, archways of dark green olive branches crowned the doorways with their graceful curves.

Returning home after the pilgrimage to Mecca was tantamount to a new birth. First of all, the journey to Mecca and back was no easy one. Every day, caravans would lose a number of pilgrims due to disease or hardship, or in raids by marauders who preyed on pilgrims just as they did on others traveling through the desert.

Returning home was a new birth. Whatever kind of life the returned pilgrim happened to have lived before, people would now look upon him with new respect, since a journey to the land of the Apostle imbued the pilgrim with an aura of sanctity. Following his return from Mecca, the pilgrim would be treated as one endowed with special wisdom and discernment, and the village people would view him thenceforth as one with a higher status and purer morals. In some cases, however, the returned pilgrim would forfeit his newfound status due to misconduct or impropriety of some sort that would remind people of his former way of life, at which point they would doubt the value of his pilgrimage, deeming it to have been of little effect.

Season the dish with fresh basil,
and I'll give you a sip of dew.

I'll weave a mantle to keep you warm
With the color of the sky so blue.

For long days Hadiya was ablaze with wedding celebrations. Soon, how-ever, it turned into a rather unusual competition when Hajj Sabri al-Najjar decided that the fires of his weddings shouldn't go out before those of his neighbors. As soon as he heard of Khaled's decision to go to Mecca, he decided to go himself. He realized that he had already waited too long to make the journey, since he should have done it at least fifteen years before. He had never lacked wealth, and had enjoyed a position no less elevated than that of Hajj Mahmud himself. He had, of course, heard whispers to the effect that it was miserliness that had prevented him from making this journey of faith to meet his Lord. He had even heard it intimated that he was unwilling to give up certain evil ways. However, none of these were the reason for his decision to make the pilgrimage. The real reason was his fear that people would start addressing Khaled as "Hajj," while he remained nothing but "Sabri al-Najjar."

On the seventh night of the celebrations, Hajj Khaled said, "The greatest celebration is the kind that takes place inside a person's heart. We've rejoiced and celebrated for days now, and the time has come for us to examine our hearts anew."

So no fires were lit the following night.

It seemed that a silence of another type, a profound, transparent silence that nothing could mar, had taken up residence in Hajj Khaled's neigh-borhood. In response, Hajj Sabri al-Najjar put out his own wedding fires three days later, since he wanted to dispel the impression that he had made the pilgrimage simply for reasons of pride and prestige.

The Butterfly's Smile

Hajj Khaled took his daughter Tamam's wrist in one hand and her elbow in the other. Leering mischievously at her fair-skinned arm, he said, "Hmm!"

He opened his mouth to reveal a set of pearly white teeth. "I haven't eaten for two days, and I'm hungry. Really hungry!" He looked at Tamam, who knew the game well, and asked, "Is this tender-looking meat edible?"

Feigning fear with a scream of delight, she said, "No, it isn't!" Then, wriggling out of his grip, she ran away. He followed her into the front courtyard, pleading, "Give me just a bite! I'm so hungry!"

They made three circuits around the dovecote, Tamam laughing and screaming at the same time, "No! It's not edible!"

Hajj Khaled's wife opened the courtyard gate and came in from outside. She saw her husband chasing Tamam and smiled.

"Run," she said to her daughter, "before he eats you!" She moved her body, which was blocking the courtyard gate, as Tamam came flying through with a panting Khaled close behind. His wife watched her daughter flee in the direction of the meadow, which extended east as far as the eye could see.

It was from this same direction that the sun made its entrance every day, into the courtyard of her spacious house with its small arched stone-and-plaster roofs, which were raised high like the roofs of the old covered bazaars known as qaysariyas. The rooms of the house overlooked an open area in their center. In it there stood an orange tree that filled the house's five rooms and its raised sitting room with the intoxicating aroma of its blossoms every year. As for the spacious enclosure with its heavy wooden gate, it was an extension of the inner courtyard around which the rooms were arranged on three sides, and in the very center of it there stood an ancient evergreen oak.

Hajj Khaled was nine years older than Sumayya, and nine months after they were married she gave birth to Mahmud. She lost the son who came after him, and over the two difficult years that followed she concluded that Mahmud would be both her first son and her last. Nine months after the departure of the Turks, Fatima popped out. She lost the daughter that came after her, and then she had Musa. She lost another daughter, and then came Naji. She then lost another son and a daughter, and over the three years that followed she lost all hope of having another child—until, that is, one day when she felt Tamam fidgeting inside her.

"I'm not sure, but I think I've got more than just gas in my stomach!"

Then came Tamam. By this time, she was certain that Death shared her children with her. Her conclusion was confirmed when it abducted two more of her newborns, a boy and a girl, one after the other.

She said, "If I didn't think of it this way, what's happened wouldn't have happened."

Now that she knew the rules, though, this didn't prevent her from continuing her attempts to defeat Death at its own game, if just with one more child.

Death retreated, but she knew it was still lurking about. For years she seemed resigned to this bloody division. Then one day, Hajj Khaled heard her say, "I'm finally rid of it!"

"What are you talking about?" he asked her.

"My period!" she replied.

"But isn't it still early for that?"

One morning, his daughter Fatima stood behind him as he stood in front of the mirror.

"Can you see me?"

He was a tall, broad-shouldered man.

"No."

"If only I were taller!" she said with a giggle. "If only God had given me some of your height, your light skin, and your green eyes, I'd be prettier than those British girls they talk about!"

"But you *are* prettier."

"Really?"

Nothing preoccupied her the way her height did, even though she was tall.

One day, many years before, she had said to him, "The angels aren't working hard enough."

"Hard enough to do what?" he asked, curious.

"To make me tall the way I'm supposed to be!"

"And what do the angels have to do with your height or your size?"

She explained that when children are asleep, the angels go to work. They bring long limbs and install them in place of short ones, and that's how people get taller.

"And your brain? Do they replace that too?"

"No. It's hard for them to get inside my head."

"I know why it's hard."

"Why?"

"Because your head's so full of these ideas! Ha, ha, ha!"

From the day he married, Khaled had changed. It was as though he had put away the past, lock, stock, and barrel. The only time he stopped smiling was when he got angry, and when that happened, he would turn into a blazing ember. Strangely, though, it was easy for him now to get over his anger and recover his smile, which rested beneath the shade of a long moustache sprinkled with an occasional white whisker. As for the rest of the hair on his head, it was the same as ever.

His wife had surprised him with three undisputable talents. The first was her extraordinary knack for raising and taking care of doves, as well as her knowledge of their various types and temperaments. As a consequence, the house wouldn't have been complete for her without a dovecote. Her second talent was her incomparable skill as a cook. She had mastered everything from lentils, to mujaddara, to stuffed zucchini, to mulukhiya, to maqluba, the last of which revealed her culinary prowess more than any other dish. And perhaps her most remarkable talent—which may well also have been the secret to her marvelous cooking—was her ability to tell where the cows had grazed on this or that day based on nothing but the taste of the milk they had produced that evening. She would place a few drops of the milk in her palm, then close her eyes and taste it. When she opened them again she would look at them and say, "The cows grazed on the northern plain today," and they would confirm that, in fact, that was where they had grazed. On another day she would say, "The cows were at Tell Abbas today," or "on Mount Rayhan."

They had eaten breakfast together that day before sunrise: boiled eggs, white cheese, butter, and milk. Then their mother said, "We have a lot of work to do today."

Musa and Fatima nodded. So did Mahmud, who was home after a long year of study. As for Tamam, she seemed to her mother not to have heard a word she had said. And as for Naji, he was nowhere to be found!

"That boy will get lost before we find him!" she exclaimed to her husband.

Waking from his reverie at that moment, her son asked, "Why?"

"May God protect you!" she replied. "No reason."

There was always something keeping Naji's mind busy, causing him to wander aimlessly in places other than the place he actually was, and it was always Fatima alone who knew the reason. She didn't have to think long to discover it, since as soon as she saw him wearing the snow-white robe and white skullcap that his father had brought him when he returned from the pilgrimage and that he loved to show off to others, she would know she needed to pay close attention.

A wicked smile spread across Fatima's face.

Then she said, "Aakh!" as she tried with her hands to wipe it off her lips.

"What are today's girls coming to?" exclaimed her mother. "And what have you seen that makes you say, 'Aakh!'?"

"It's just that my smile hurts me." Then she repeated, "Aakh!"

"It hurts because it's wicked," said her mother.

"I know! I know!"

For many reasons, only some of which he knew, Hajj Khaled was letting his two daughters grow up without burdening them with anything beyond their capacities. He gave them their freedom, just as he had done with Hamama, his precious filly, who had been preserved from harm by the devotion and respect that had surrounded her on all sides.

How he wished he could forget her. How he wished he could forget the defeat he had suffered in the depths of his spirit when he realized he would have to give her up in order to be able to return to his father and mother in his right mind.

His wife put away the leftover food, then began looking for Fatima, Tamam, and Naji. She couldn't find them.

"Where are the children?" she asked.

"Musa's gone ahead of us."

"And the others?" she asked.

"God knows."

She ran off in the hope of catching up with them before they got too far away.

"You're going to spoil them," she exclaimed when she got back.

He was wearing the same wicked smile that Fatima had worn, his arms folded over his chest. He tried without success to appear dignified. As he wiped the smile off his face, he looked to her as though he were no older than Tamam.

"That's enough for her today! There's no need for us to make her worry any more." He said it as though he were talking to himself.

"It's enough for who? For me? Besides, who are you talking to?"

"Didn't I say it was enough for her? See? She's started to get angry."

"You're going to drive me crazy!" she said.

Suddenly, he unfolded his arms, releasing three shrieks of delight as his children came rolling out from under his gigantic cloak.

That evening, he said, "They're children, Sumayya. Don't be so hard on them!"

"Children! What are you saying, Hajj? I started running after you before I was Fatima's age! And you say they're children!"

"As long as they're in this house, they'll remain children."

"And how long will that be?"

"As long as they're in this house."

"Yesterday your aunt Anisa said to me, 'I'm afraid Mahmud won't be any use to women.' 'God forbid!' I said. 'What's he missing?' And she said, 'He needs to start breaking plates!'"

"But he's not even twelve years old yet. And he hasn't finished his studies!"

"No, he's a year older than that."

Their favorite place to hide was under his cloak.

It had started one bitter cold winter night long before, but they had carried on with the tradition even when the sun was shining, and they never missed a chance to slip inside his summer cloak as well, whenever he happened to be wearing it. They would walk around under the cloak with him as he made the rounds of the entire yard, transported by the riotous laughter that burst forth whenever they heard their mother asking happily where they might be.

But that had been a long time ago.

"Anybody who saw you playing with them this way would never believe you're the village elder."

"I'm the village elder outside these walls. Inside them, I'm their father, and that's all I am."

As for Sumayya, she was torn between the joy she felt over his love for them, and her fear that this very love would spoil them.

"I don't know why, but I get the feeling this is the last time I'll be hiding them under my cloak."

Her heart shrank at his words.

"God forbid!" she whispered almost tearfully.

"They're growing up fast, and that makes me sad."

"It's as though you're afraid you won't have anybody to play with!"

Hajj Khaled thought back on the days when he had begun stealing more and more frequently into Hadiya due to the Ottoman state's preoccupation with matters greater and more pressing than those fleeing from the military police. There had come a time when he could spend more than one night in Hadiya and even walk its streets with nothing to fear. He remembered how Sumayya, al-Barmaki's daughter, would go leaping for joy from place to place just to be around him. He had felt that this was the purest, noblest joy of all: joy for joy's sake. After all, she was neither his sister, nor his mother, nor his aunt, nor his father. She seemed like a butterfly as she flitted about him, and as the days went by, he began to feel somehow that she was his angel of mercy.

She was following him, and he knew it without turning around to see whether she was there. He would feel her in front of him when she was behind him, on his left, on his right, and hovering over him. One day, he stopped when she was following him, and she froze in place. When a long time went by without his taking a single step forward or making a single move, her heart was flooded with joy, especially since she still remembered what he had done when he began his long wait for Yasmin in the field, with Hamama leaning on his shoulder.

His mother Munira, who never took her eyes off him, saw what was happening. Beside her stood his sister Aziza.

Anisa saw them standing there like a couple of statues. "What's going on?" she exclaimed.

She heard no reply. Then, straining to get up despite the pain in her knees that became nearly unbearable in some seasons, she walked over to join the other two women.

"Do you see what I see?" Munira asked her.

"Is there anything in my body that still works right besides my eyes? Of course I do!"

At that moment, Khaled turned and walked toward Sumayya, who froze in place. He walked up to her and gazed into her face for a long time. She melted. She wished the earth would swallow her up. Her deep black eyes were set in a childlike face that was the picture of both innocence and mischievousness at once. Never in his life had he seen a pair of eyes that moved quite like hers did: alternately staring demurely down at the ground and impishly up at him.

Then, without warning, he said something she had never dreamed she would hear him say: "If you'll be sensible, I'll marry you."

"Really?"

"Really."

The world spun around for her a thousand times in a single moment, and she felt to the ground unconscious.

Aziza came running, and Munira was close on her heels. Men, young and old, came rushing to help. But before they got there, Khaled had roused her.

"Is everything all right?" asked more than one voice.

"Is everything all right?" Khaled asked her.

She rose to her feet and tried to walk. However, she felt as though her feet were pinned to the spot where she had fallen. For years and years this feeling would come back to her whenever she passed that way, and, like an automobile endlessly circling a roundabout in Haifa, Jaffa, or Jerusalem, she would start circling around that tiny space that no one but she could see.

After that, Sumayya disappeared from the streets entirely. She no longer appeared unless it was for a reason that was too compelling to require an excuse.

By the time two months or so had passed, things had changed for Khaled, and he truly missed seeing her. What he missed the most was the way she would roll her eyes in the center of that innocent but mischievous space that made up her girlish face.

"The time for breaking plates is past," Khaled said to his mother.

"God bless you in your plans," she replied contentedly. "And who is the lucky girl?"

"Sumayya."

"Sumayya, al-Barmaki's daughter?"

"Sumayya, al-Barmaki's daughter."

She made no comment. As for Hajj Mahmud, he wasn't surprised, since Sumayya had managed to erase her former image completely from their minds, and had turned into a person they viewed with visible admiration.

"But you know her brother Ghazi has gone to war."

"He'll be back, God willing."

"There won't be a wedding, then," said al-Barmaki. "Just a gathering of near relatives."

"Whatever you say," replied Hajj Mahmud.

They concluded the marriage contract hurriedly, in anticipation of better days to come, at which time they planned to host a big wedding celebration fit for Hajj Mahmud's eldest son. The difficult days then stretched on and on. But instead of sitting around, thinking about the long-awaited day, Sumayya got busy having one child after another.

Night and Day

From the depths of the night came a terrified cry, "Hurry! The cows have eaten your crops!"

Before they realized that the voice belonged to Naji, all of Hadiya had sprung into action. Everyone picked up whatever was nearest at hand, be it a scythe, a rock, or a stick.

The boy had unexpectedly found some cows overrunning one of the fields. He drove one of the cows back by throwing a rock at it. Nightfall had turned the cattle into mere shadows. However, he could hear one of them falling to the ground, and as it did so it let out an audible moan.

Before he could verify that he had broken its leg, the sound of hoofbeats erupted as a horse galloped madly in his direction, its rider shouting irately. Naji took off running across the field toward the village, the cornstalks concealing him from view, since he knew that if he stayed where he was, he was sure to perish.

The people of Hadiya surrounded the herd and began driving them toward the village.

"Let them go!" shouted the rider.

Hajj Khaled replied, "You won't get them back until you pay for the loss they've caused and we know who they belong to."

"If I don't break the legs of anyone who tries to come near the herd, I'm not the brother of Khadra. So now you know who I am!"

"And if we don't take them to the village tonight, I'm not the brother of Aziza and the father of Mahmud."

"You're the brother of Aziza, then, and I'm the brother of Khadra."

The night grew darker and the mystery-laden moments began passing with greater and greater speed, auguring what no one could have anticipated. Iliya Radhi and Muhammad Shahada came forward, blocking the way between Hajj Khaled and the unknown horseman. He told them to move back again.

They did as he said.

Suddenly, the horseman lunged forward, his sword unsheathed. Its glistening blade nearly struck Hajj Khaled's head, but he deflected it with his thick staff, the end of which was studded with nailheads, and as the sword broke in two it emitted a shrill clank.

The horseman retreated briefly with his mount, then charged again with half his sword. Hajj Khaled leaned backward. However, this didn't prevent him from delivering a severe blow that wounded the rider's thigh just as he was about to charge for a third time. It was then that he saw the whole village coming after him, so he turned his horse and rode away.

Everyone stood there watching him disappear into the night, until the sound of his horse's hoofbeats had died away.

When they brought the cows back, Fatima said, "I think I saw him two days ago."

Just before sundown on the following day, the people of Hadiya glimpsed a group of men on horseback crossing the eastern plain.

Hajj Khaled watched them approach, with Hamama among them, just as he did every day at dusk.

As they continued their approach, his eyes were fixed on horsemen behind them who would never arrive. Then, wakening from his reverie, he stood up. The horses became slightly confused, and some took a few steps back. When he realized what had happened, he heard someone say, "We've come to you as guests."

"Welcome to the guests!" As he spoke, his gaze was fixed on the thoroughbred mare on which the horseman was mounted.

Hajj Khaled gestured to Hamdan, who rushed off to prepare some new coffee. Meanwhile, the men who had come sat inside without speaking a word. When Hamdan arrived with the coffee, Salem took it from him, poured the first cup, and handed it to his brother, who in turn offered it to the venerable-looking elder who occupied the center seat.

The elder took the cup from him and, when he was about to set it on the ground in front of him in keeping with custom—since a guest would only drink the coffee that had been served him after the request he had come with had been agreed to—Hajj Khaled said, "Your cows will be returned to you."

The elder's hand stopped in midair, whereupon he raised the cup to his lips, saying, "All the noble things we've heard about you are true, then."

The horseman rose and, extending his hand to Hajj Khaled, said, "I bear witness that you are the brother of Aziza and the father of Mahmud."

"And I bear witness that you are the brother of Khadra." And they embraced.

When the men requested permission to be on their way, Hajj Khaled said, "You honored us by coming as our guests. So don't wound us by leaving so soon."

The venerable elder replied, "You return our cows to us even though we were the ones who trespassed on your fields and who took up the sword against you rather than demanding your own rights. This is too much!"

"It isn't too much for a guest," said Hajj Khaled. "You will be our guests, God willing, for three days."

"This is too much, really!"

"It isn't too much for a guest," he said. Then he added, "Pray for blessings on the Prophet."

"O Lord, send down blessings on the Prophet!" the men repeated.

The men all looked at him, realizing that he was about to say something.

"It's said that there was a king who, whenever anyone came to visit him, would cut off his guest's head. The news of this king reached a certain man, who said, 'I'm going to go find out why the king does this, no matter what happens!'

"He arrived at the king's palace and said, 'I am the king's guest.' So they admitted him to the king's presence.

"'Bring the guest a cushion!' the king commanded.

"When they placed the cushion beside him, the guest cried, 'Duty!'

"Then the king barked, 'Bring him coffee!'

"So they brought coffee and served it to him.

"'Duty!' cried the guest again.

"Then the king ordered them to bring him another cushion, whereupon the guest said, 'Duty!'

"'Bring us the finest food!' commanded the king. And when they served it to him, the guest said, 'Duty!'

"When at last the guest made ready to leave, one of the king's servants came up, took his shoes, and placed them on his feet. 'Duty!' cried the guest once more.

"The king then rose, shook his hand, and wished him a safe return to his family.

"As soon as the guest was gone, those close to the king asked him, 'Why did you not cut off his head?'

"And the king said, 'One owes a duty to the guest. Hence, no guest should think that the hospitality offered to him is too much, since this is his right.'"

A profound silence fell over the gathering. At last it was broken by Shaykh al-Jalil, who said, "May God enable us to return your kindness."

Hajj Khaled replied, "You can do that by being our guests for three days."

Shaykh al-Jalil was about to say, "This is too much!" But then he surprised everyone by saying, "Duty!"

And at that, laughter filled the room and spilled out the doorway.

※

No one noticed the effect the thoroughbred mare had had on Naji. Half-mesmerized, he walked around her, lost to the world. He wished he could jump on her back and run away with her, then keep going until he had disappeared completely.

He saw the visitors leaving, wending their way in the distance through the hills and dales. They were moving at the speed of their cattle, not their horses, while the purebred mare sauntered along like the Hamama he didn't see—Hamama who had once captivated everyone, and who continued to do so.

Because he couldn't bear to see her leave for good, he followed them. He went deep into the orchards. He climbed hills. Contemplating the village from a distance, he thought: Since I won't be able to see her again, let me see her one last time—just one last time!

So he took off running. Trying with all his might to close the distance between them, he leaped over the stone walls that separated the fields, dodging tree branches as he went. Although the distance stretched out before him to infinity, at last he caught up with them.

However, they continued on their journey, and he forgot to turn back. He completely forgot.

Meanwhile, he was missed in Hadiya. They went looking for him, but didn't find him.

They roamed the surrounding valleys, the vineyards, the orchards, and the wheat fields calling his name.

But no one answered.

Suddenly, Fatima said, "Maybe he went after our guests!"

"How would he do that? And what could he possibly want from them?"

She said nothing. She couldn't manage her usual wicked smile, the smile that had become as much a part of her face as her nose, eyes, and forehead.

She was worried.

So when he came home at last, dog-tired as a soldier back from a war they knew nothing about, she praised God.

"Where have you been?" they asked him.

But he didn't say a word. He just put his head down and went to sleep. He slept for two days.

It wasn't unusual for Naji to slip away now and then. A brief turning of the back, a moment's reverie, or a passing thought that took Hajj Khaled somewhere or other could easily become the chink in the wall through which his son would make his getaway.

From the time when the family began noticing these disappearances, Fatima's smile began hurting her more and more.

Hajj Khaled had done his utmost to convince Naji to enroll in the village school, whose only teacher for a long time had been Shaykh Husni. But he would always refuse, saying, "As long as he's got that cane in his hand, I'm not going near the place!"

His brother Mahmud, on the other hand, was lauded by Shaykh Husni as the best Arabic student he had taught in years. He was so exceptional that the "twig," as he used to call him, had become his "little prodigy."

Iliya's Camel

F atima's special rapport with animals had always amazed the people of the village. She seemed to know the way into the hearts of horses, goats, cows, and the various and sundry other animals that filled people's yards and the surrounding plains. After all, she'd spent her childhood in their company. On one occasion, a baby chicken would get attached to her and follow her wherever she went. On another occasion it would be a goat, duck, or pigeon. Perhaps because her mother had taken such a long time to have another daughter, she'd felt the need to look for a substitute sister. And it wasn't difficult to find one in a village like Hadiya. All she had to do was walk up to a horse for it to come and tuck its head under her arm. As for goats, they would follow her as though she were their mother. So when Iliya Radhi's camel ran amok and no one could go near him, she said, "Leave him to me."

They tried to prevent her, but she insisted, "I know what I'm doing. Let me give it a try."

She opened the gate and went into the enclosure where the camel was trying desperately to get past the walls and crushing everything in its path.

When he saw her, he retreated slightly and, panting, looked into her eyes and made a peculiar sound. Then he turned his neck in the opposite direction and froze for a few moments. When he looked back at her, his panting had subsided. However, he was still drenched in a bloody sweat, and she was afraid. It was the first time she had ever found herself face to face with a crazed camel. She took a step forward. The camel took several steps back, until his rump was up against the door of the room behind him. She stepped forward again. He tried to retreat but, finding that it was impossible, took two steps in her direction, then stopped.

People peered over the wall and through the enclosure gate, their eyes wide as saucers. Meanwhile, Iliya's wife and five beautiful daughters stood trembling with fright on the roof of the house.

"A single shot would solve the problem," commented Hajj Jum'a Abu Sunbul.

But again she said, "Give me the chance."

When Hajj Khaled arrived at last, he was enraged to find that they had allowed his daughter to go into the enclosure and stand face to face with this distraught beast, since everyone knew that a camel's rage was unequaled in the animal world.

He shoved them away from the gate and made his way to where she stood. Before he reached her, she saw the camel retreating again. She looked behind her and saw her father.

"Please," she begged, "it's over now! Let me stay with him for a little while."

Hajj Khaled froze in his tracks, afraid to make the slightest move lest it excite the fearsome animal.

The camel didn't retreat any farther, and Hajj Khaled stepped back.

Neither Fatima nor the camel knew what to do after this. Should she come closer to him, or should he come closer to her? At last Fatima settled the matter and took two steps in his direction. The camel moved neither forward nor back. She took two more steps in his direction and he remained where he was. However, his neck was trained upward like a sword, and his eyes were aflame with a strange sort of lightning.

After they had been staring into each other's eyes for more than half an hour, the camel's head began tilting little by little toward the ground, and at that moment everyone realized that Fatima had succeeded again.

She began walking slowly toward him, confident that everything was over.

She took his head in her hands and began stroking it. He raised his head slightly and looked at her as if to apologize. She walked around him, stroking his body with her little hand, and when she came around from the other side, he moved his head and silently rested it on her shoulder. He seemed more like a little child than anything else, and for a moment she nearly cried over him.

She reached out to place the harness over his head. He didn't move. And in a moment that astounded everyone, they saw him open his great mouth and help her do what she needed to do.

Husayn al-Sa'ub said, "I suppose he's managed to escape getting shot, but now he'll have to face the knife!"

"You're going to slaughter him?" screamed Fatima. "I didn't do what I did so that you could slaughter him in the end!"

"There's no other solution. If it happens again, he might kill somebody, or more than one somebody," added Iliya Radhi.

"But here he is. Look at him! I'm sure he won't do it again!" she protested.

"We can't take any chances when the animal concerned is a camel," said Husayn al-Sa'ub.

Fatima didn't speak for days on end. It was as though she had lost her tongue. Hajj Khaled tried to draw her into any sort of conversation that might relieve her suffering, but she didn't open her mouth. She felt she had betrayed the camel after he had placed his trust in her.

One night, she woke up screaming from an unbearable nightmare: she was walking through the streets of Hadiya when suddenly she became aware of a strange movement beyond the walls. She was afraid. She tried to hurry, but the clamor grew louder. She turned and saw large pieces of meat looking down at her from above the walls and the stone field dividers.

❄

The pieces of meat had eyes that recognized her. They were the eyes of the camel himself—the camel they had slaughtered and whose meat they had distributed among the people of the village. When they brought some of it to her, she had refused to touch it or even look at it.

She ran away, but the pieces of meat with the wide eyes were racing along beside her, behind her, in front of her. They ran past her to the bridge, where they suddenly gathered themselves into the form of a bizarre-looking creature, which she recognized as the same camel. It charged furiously in her direction. A few moments before he reached her, she felt the air coming out of his nostrils blowing up like a storm and thrusting her against the wall behind her. She screamed and screamed, until she woke up and saw her whole family gathered around her.

"May God protect you!" her mother Sumayya kept saying.

Hamdan Remembers

ajj Khaled cast a glance at Hadiya. He felt as though he hadn't seen it for a long time. He was also seeing something he hadn't noticed before. The houses of the village before him had spread out in all directions, and coffee shops had become a part of village life and the life of the people who came to shop in Hadiya's market. It had been Muhammad Shahada who first dared to open a coffee shop after seeing the ones in Ramla, Jaffa, and Jerusalem. He was followed by Shakir Muhanna, who put a radio in his coffee shop. Then, before Shakir Muhanna could snatch away all the market-goers, Muhammad Shahada went down to Jerusalem and bought the most modern, compact, beautiful Philips radio he could find so that people could listen to songs by Saleh Abd al-Hayy, Umm Kulthum, Sayyid Darwish, and Muhammad Abd al-Wahhab. They could also get the latest, most detailed news reports from all over Palestine without having to wait to hear them from other people. Many people in the village began spending their evenings at the coffee shop rather than going to the guesthouses. As for Hajj Khaled, he didn't frequent either of

Hadiya's coffee shops, since he felt the practice undermined a man's dignity. He contented himself with the late-night gatherings in which Shakir Muhanna would bring his radio to the guesthouse after closing up his coffee shop.

Hajj Khaled thought back to the early days of the two coffee shops and the disapproving looks Muhammad Shahada and his customers got from people. However, within less than a year, these same people had fallen under the spell of Shakir Muhanna's radio, and would make up excuses to pass in front of his coffee shop to hear songs and the news. Nor were the women immune to the charms of the magic box that had stolen everyone's hearts. Indeed, it was a wondrous toy, the likes of which children had never known.

Hajj Khaled thought to himself: How can something be right in front of you without your seeing it? And how can you be so blind as to think that the only thing you have in the whole wide world is the four walls of your house and the gates that you shut at the end of the night for fear of losing what you have? Or for fear that the world might suddenly come into your house? How could I have failed to notice?

Hajj Khaled began looking at people in a new way. And just as he had begun looking at Hadiya through new eyes, he looked again at his children, his wife Sumayya, his mother Munira, his aunt Anisa, and his sister Aziza, who had managed to raise her children on her own without accepting help from anybody, including him, her brother, whom she looked upon as her sole protector.

He came through the courtyard gate as though he were entering his house for the first time. It had expanded and now had an upper floor, to which his mother ascended one day, saying, "A person can see the whole world from up here while you all are shut up down there!"

This was followed by her proverbial words, "Whoever wants me can come see me up here!" Then she asked them to bring her pallet and all her things, since at last she had found the place where she could live the way she'd always wanted to.

Hajj Khaled looked over at Hamdan, who was busy roasting coffee just the way he had been the first time he ever saw him. He began walking over to him, and suddenly said to himself, "What have we done to you, Hamdan? How have we managed to forget you all these years? How?"

Recognizing Hajj Khaled's footsteps, Hamdan turned around.

"We've been too patient with you!" Hajj Khaled said to him, in a tone that struck terror in his heart.

"What have I done?"

"The problem is that you haven't done anything. The problem is that I haven't done anything. So I'm going to have to take care of things myself."

"Have I ever been remiss?"

"No, you haven't. In fact, your problem is that you've never broken anything! Of all the cups you've handled over the years, not a single one has broken. I can't recall your breaking a single cup since Baba died."

"If you don't mind my asking, Hajj, what's wrong with not having broken anything?"

"Don't you get my point, man? It's time for you to get married!"

"Get *married?*"

The word came as such a shock that Hamdan's face seemed to change completely. You would have thought he'd just received news that his dearest friend had died.

"What's wrong? Why all this frowning? Have I said something wrong?"

"No, you just surprised me. You surprised me!"

"How could something as simple as this come as a surprise to you?"

"Because I'd forgotten."

"What had you forgotten?"

"I'd forgotten that I could get married like other people, like the people whose weddings I attend. I'd totally forgotten."

"Could anybody forget something like this, man? Could he forget the most beautiful thing in the world—women?"

"Yes, somebody could forget. Hamdan could forget."

"I should have reminded you a long time ago."

"I might still have forgotten!"

"Well, anyway, I'm reminding you now. And we'll see if you'll forget or not."

"But who would agree to let Hamdan marry his daughter?"

"Is that the issue? Who would agree to let Hamdan marry his daughter? If you've decided you want to get married, then leave that to me."

"Give me some time to think it over," said Hamdan.

"But I'm afraid you might forget again."

"I'm not sure, but I don't think I will!"

Three days later, a coffee cup fell out of Hamdan's hand and broke. Nearly jumping for joy, Hajj Khaled said, "So you've finally decided!"

"Forgive me. I won't let it happen again."

"So you didn't mean to break it?"

"God forbid! How could I deliberately do a thing like that?"

"It's all right, it's all right. Take it easy."

What Hajj Khaled didn't realize was that the three days that had passed since their conversation had left Hamdan in such a state of ferment that he'd hardly slept a wink.

He closed the door to his room just off the guesthouse and curled up in a ball. The darkness that surrounded him was vaster than ever before, and every dark spot that wasn't reached by the lamplight was an entire night unto itself.

From the first night after Hajj Khaled had spoken to him, he had begun to tremble. He'd tried to collect his scattered thoughts, but couldn't. How was it that he suddenly had such a terrible longing for a woman? How was it that he now felt that no one but a woman could put him back together again and breathe new life into his spirit?

He may have dozed off for a bit, but only for a bit, when he saw himself walking through a large garden filled with trees of every kind. Suddenly, a gentle breeze blew and he saw leaves falling. He watched them gyrate through space and silently land on the ground. He bent down to hear the sound they made when they hit the ground, but heard nothing. He began walking again and suddenly he heard a sound. He turned and saw an arm next to him. He looked up to see where an arm might have fallen from, but saw nothing but trees. Before he looked down from the lofty heights, he heard another sound. He turned to his right and saw another arm. At this point, he was stricken with fright, which gradually intensified into outright terror. The moment he heard the peculiar sound, he turned and saw a human head in front of him, with its face to the ground. He bent down to see whose head it was that might have landed right in front of him this way. Turning it over, he found that it looked a lot like him. He felt afraid. Then he had a strange idea—he decided to feel his own head to make sure it was still there. When he realized that his head was still in place, he praised God. He said to himself: It might be the head of someone who looks just like me. However, his mind still hadn't been set at rest. So he ran his hand over his head one more time. Then, in order to be doubly sure, he decided to make sure that his head was attached firmly to his shoulders. To this end he began pulling his head away from his body. He pulled and pulled. And as he pulled, he woke up, his hands under his jaws pushing his head up and his feet pushing against the wall with all the strength he could muster.

Khaled knocked on the door to Hamdan's room. When he saw his weary features, he said, "It looks as though you didn't sleep last night."

"Did you have the same dream I did?"

"How could I have done that? What happened to you, Hamdan?"

"I was dead, then I woke up."

"Thank God! In any case, I've come to tell you that I've found her. I've been thinking about it for the past several days, and I think she's right for you."

"Who is she?"

"Rafiqa, Abu Ribhi's daughter."

"But she's married!"

"She was married, but her husband's been gone for twenty years."

"He might come back, though."

"Have you ever seen anyone come back from one of Turkey's wars after being gone for twenty years?"

"No. In any case, do you really think she's the right one for me?" Hamdan asked him.

"Who else could be a better choice? As I told you, I've given it a lot of thought, and I do think she's the one for you. God knows best, but as far as I know, she's still of child-bearing age, and if you work hard at it, you'll manage to have one or two children, or maybe even more. What do you say?"

"Whatever you say, Hajj. Let's do it. But do you think she'll have me?"

"And what do you lack?"

"You know. I'm not young any more. Besides, I limp."

"She isn't young any more, either. And who says you have to have both legs in order to get married?"

Everyone in the village knew that Hamdan had been born normal and healthy. However, his parents and brothers and sisters had died in a bizarre accident when the roof of their house caved in at midday and crushed them. No one survived except Hamdan, who had been outside. They had been herdsmen who worked for Hajj Mahmud. In keeping with local custom, they received no wages. Instead, a number of cows, goats, and sheep were allotted them, and they were allowed to benefit from both these animals and their young. In this way, they came to have a share in the flock or herd, and over the years they might come to have their own flock or herd, at which point they could either go on working in the same place or move and establish themselves elsewhere.

One drought-stricken day, they had hidden the straw over the room they lived in. However, the cows were so hungry that, lured by the scent of their hidden fodder, they went around to the back of the house and managed to get up on the roof, which extended out from the foot of a hill. Together with other people's cattle, Hajj Mahmud's cows gathered on the roof, and within minutes it collapsed into the room beneath, killing everyone in a single moment. Hamdan was taken in by Hajj Mahmud's family. However, after the room where his family had met their end was repaired, he insisted on going back there. At first they were afraid he wouldn't be able to sleep in a place where he had lost his mother and father. But to their astonishment, it was the only place where he did feel able to sleep.

One day when Hamdan was ten years old, he came out of the house to the sound of an itinerant vendor passing by. He looked at the vendor and began listening to the way he invited people to buy his wares. He tried to imitate him, but without success. He followed the vendor and listened to him some more. However, he discovered that he was too scrawny to have a booming voice like that of the vendor. Over time, Hamdan grew attached to the man. One day, he noticed that the man had a limp, and that he liked the way he walked. He tried to mimic him, and to his amazement, found that he could imitate him perfectly. So from that day on, Hamdan stopped walking in any other way.

At first, Hajj Mahmud would say to him, "What's wrong? What's happened to your foot?"

"Nothing," Hamdan would reply.

"Why do you limp, then?"

"I don't know!"

"You shouldn't walk that way, then. Nobody walks that way unless his foot hurts."

"It does hurt!"

"Come show it to me."

Hajj Mahmud examined Hamdan's foot, checking it all over and pressing it here and there like a skilled physician.

"Does it hurt when I press on it?"

"No."

"It doesn't hurt at all?"

"Just a little bit."

"It'll get better. Don't worry."

However, Hamdan wasn't in need of reassurance. And from then on, he never took a step without imitating that vendor.

It was a simple wedding that had more of an air of sadness than of merriment. However, at last Hamdan found himself living under a single roof with Rafiqah, also known as 'Umm al-Far,' or al-Far's mother. As for 'al-Far' himself, he went to live with his grandfather, Abu Ribhi.

It wasn't long afterward that Abu Ribhi heard the sound of a plate shattering in his shop.

Furious, Abu Ribhi shouted, "Somebody who wants to get married doesn't break the plates we sell for a living! Don't we have enough plates at home?"

Al-Far made no reply. A few minutes later, Abu Ribhi looked over at him and said, "You're right. The plates we have at home are made of aluminum, so they won't break. On the other hand, if you'd just rattled them a bit, I would have understood!"

That same night, he said to him, "I'll inquire about the possibility of your marrying widow Sabah's daughter."

Al-Far made no objection. So the next morning, Abu Ribhi sent word to Sabah asking her to pass by to see him at his shop.

"Is everything all right?" she asked when she arrived, thinking he had summoned her to ask her to settle the debt she'd accumulated at the shop.

"Everything's fine," he said. Then he continued, "You have a girl of marriageable age, and I have a grandson who's a young man now. After thinking the matter over for some time, I've concluded that they'd make a good match, especially considering the fact that they're both orphans. The boy lost his father in Turkey's wars, and the girl's father was lost because he kept running from the Turks until he made it all the way to Brazil!"

With a start, Sabah replied, "Don't be pessimistic about my husband. He went on a trip, and he'll be back!"

"Sabah," Abu Ribhi reasoned with her, "Brazil is a long way off, and if anybody manages to make it all the way there, he won't have the bodily strength to come back here again. As you know, the Turks have gone and the British have come in their place, and he still hasn't returned."

"He'll be back. He said he would, so he will."

"In any case, what do you say the two of them marry?"

"I was afraid you were going to insist that I pay off the debts I've accumulated over the past couple of years."

"Now why would I do a thing like that? I can see with my own eyes the hard times people have been living through!"

"That was the thing I was most afraid of!"

"Don't you worry about a thing," he said to her. "I think we ought to reach an agreement before we come this evening to ask for her hand."

"That would be best."

"So let's talk about the dowry. How much do you think it should be?"

"Like the other girls in the town, or a little less!"

"Would twenty dinars be all right?"

"That would be fine," she replied.

"It's decided, then. Now let me take a look at your credit page in my ledger."

He leafed through the ledger in search of her page. Nodding, he said, "You don't have just one page, Sabah. You've got four! See here: you bought sugar, coffee, halawa, salt, tea cups, a saucepan, and a serving tray for nine dinars and thirty piasters. You've also got fabric, silk thread, and two pairs of shoes—the ones you'd asked me to bring from Ramla—for six dinars and ten piasters. Then there are some old debts that come to seven dinars. Altogether it comes to twenty-two dinars and forty piasters."

He turned to a pallid-looking Sabah and said, "What do you say we make a trade? I know that what you owe me comes to more than the dowry, but I won't ask you to pay the difference. And from now on we'll be relatives."

"Whatever you think is best," she said.

"So you agree?"

"I agree! What else can I say?"

"It's a deal, then."

Umm al-Far

The boy has hair that shimmers like ripened ears of grain,
Like locks of gold on a lass's bosom and poplars in the rain.

The boy has hair that's softer than velvet or than silk,
More soothing than the cooing of a dove, smoother than freshly
drawn milk.

The boy has hair whose enchanted beauty makes me swoon.
Protect him from harm and guard him, Lord, be there sun or moon!

The story of Umm al-Far was one of the best-known stories in Hadiya. After her first two children died, the first a son, the second a daughter, someone said to her, "If you have another child, put a mouse's tooth on his head to keep him from dying."

So when she gave birth to her second son, she announced that she needed a mouse's tooth, and she told the boys of the village that whoever brought her the largest mouse would get a prize. They proceeded to bring her lots of mice, out of which she chose the largest. She removed its tooth with her own hand and placed it on the newborn's head, and after that under his pillow. When the boy got bigger and began to walk, she tied it around his neck.

The boy survived, and over time he came to be known as 'al-Far' (Mouse), and his mother as 'Umm al-Far' (Mouse's mother).

However, Umm al-Far's mind still hadn't been set at rest. Consequently, there wasn't a saint's tomb that she didn't visit, asking God to protect her son.

She had never cut her son's hair, based on her belief that by causing him to appear as a girl, he would be protected from envious glances and the harm they might bring. So, adorned with his long blond tresses, he would roam the streets, hopping and jumping from place to place and glowing with an innocence and beauty the people of Hadiya had never known before. It was a beauty that was destined to be obscured by poverty over time. Nevertheless, Umm al-Far continued to keep fearful vigil over her little one night and day. If he caught cold, she would wrap him in all the clothes in the house, cover him with blankets, and sit in front of the closed door lest a cold draft enter.

If he didn't recover, she would conclude that he had been stricken by the evil eye. When this happened, she would bring live coals and place them in a container, then sprinkle alum over them as she recited an incantation of protection. When the alum melted, she would rub the little boy's forehead with the ashes. If she had no alum, she would substitute flour, salt, some cotton, and a piece of fabric from an article of clothing belonging to the person she suspected of having stricken her son with 'the eye.' Obtaining the piece of fabric was no easy task, but in order to get it she was always prepared to do the impossible.

The result that Umm al-Far would achieve in the end was a vision of the guilty party's image in the burnt alum. However, the results weren't always conclusive. On one occasion, the image she saw belonged to Muhammad Shahada's wife, whereas the burnt piece of fabric belonged to the wife of Shakir Muhanna, who hadn't had any children until a long time after she married. As a consequence, Umm al-Far had to go to Shakir Muhanna's wife and ask her to forgive her for thinking ill of her. On other occasions, the piece of cloth she obtained belonged to a man, although the image she would see was that of a woman. Even stranger still was that she once believed that Anisa had stricken her son with the evil eye, only to find, to her surprise, that the image she saw in the burnt alum belonged to the husband of Fathiya al-Hawla, who had gone to war ten years earlier and never come back and who, as a consequence, had never even set eyes on her son. It was this incident that led her to doubt the alum's reliability, and she said, "This alum doesn't tell the truth!" From then on, she contented herself with flour and salt, which had never deceived her, and with an incantation that went like this:

The first is in the name of God, the second is in the name of God, the third is in the name of God. The fourth, fifth, sixth, and seventh are in the name of God. I seek protection for myself and this other person from everyone with blue eyes and a space between his front teeth. We have used incantations of protection on behalf of his she-camel so that he can keep up with his journey companions. May the designs of the envious eye come to naught, and may fearsome defects bring no harm. Master Solomon found her baring her fangs in the desert expanse. With a crow in her hand and her talons hanging down, she barked like a dog and howled like a wolf. O eye that keeps malicious watch, I shall pierce you with a bullet! Come out, you accursed infidel spirit, as a worm comes out of an apple! Come out in the name of the prophets, the saints, and the beloved Prophet Abraham! If you are in the legs, come out in the name of God the Helper. If you are in the head, come out in the name of al-Khidr Abul Abbas, and if you are in the belly, come out in the name of the Lord of the Throne.

I embrace you in the name of God and usher you into the realm of God's protection from all people's eyes, including my own. And may the eye that sees you without calling down blessings on the Prophet be plucked out!

When al-Far's hair had reached his waist, she took him to the shrine of the Prophet Moses as she had vowed to do, taking with her a sheep she had fattened for precisely this occasion. Then she cut her son's hair in front of the shrine, slaughtered the sheep, and distributed its meat to people in need.

She had hoped to do what the wealthy do, namely, place her son's hair in one scale of a balance, and an equal amount of gold or silver in the other, then spend its value on the poor. However, she didn't have the wherewithal to do this, so instead of gold or silver, she placed ordinary coins in the other scale and passed them out to the needy folk who had gathered around her in the hope of receiving alms. She insisted that, from that day on, al-Far had never fallen ill, nor had any harm come to him. However, she used to sigh for sorrow over the loss of the beauty he had had when he was adorned with those long tresses.

She considered letting his hair grow long again, but by that time al-Far had grown up enough to realize that long hair wasn't for boys, but for girls.

The Long Shadow

T he nightmare she had gone through over Iliya's camel continued to haunt Fatima until, early one evening, she saw a horseman in hot pursuit of a gazelle over the eastern hills that bordered the plains of Hadiya.

When the gazelle was halfway between him and Fatima, whose shadow seemed longer than any he had seen in his entire life, the rider lost his nerve. But what astonished him even more was the fact that the gazelle kept heading straight for Fatima when he would have expected her to turn at the sight of a human being in her path. He slowed his horse as he saw the gazelle reduce her pace, all the while continuing in its progress toward the mysterious girl with the long shadow. All of a sudden, the gazelle nearly stopped completely, then moved along unhurriedly, as though she were grazing in perfect safety, and as though she had forgotten all about the horseman who had been trying to catch her only a few moments before. At last, the gazelle came all the way up to Fatima, then stopped and cast a glance at the horseman as if to say, "You won't be able to do a thing now!" In such a state of shock that he nearly fell off his horse, the horseman froze in place as he tried to take in the significance of what was happening. (Maybe the gazelle belongs to her. On the other hand, who would raise a gazelle, then let it out to graze in open pastures?)

After a long silence, he came closer, and she recognized him as the brother of Khadra. He saw her whispering something to the gazelle, which moved away from her at a leisurely pace. Then, before she disappeared, he heard Fatima cry, "Wait!" The gazelle came to a halt and turned her head.

"Goodbye!" she called merrily.

Fatima stood behind her father as he trimmed his beard in front of the mirror.

"Now tell me the truth: can you see me now?"

"No."

"Not even part of my head?"

"A little part."

"Thank God! That's enough!"

Something pleasant stirred deep in Hajj Khaled's heart. He thought back on the time when she would say over and over, "I don't want to grow up. I want to stay just like this!" then crawl toward him on all fours, shaking her head and imitating the bleating of a sheep: "Ba-aa! Ba-aa!" She would make circles around him, then insert herself under his arm, her body disappearing behind his so that nothing but her little head appeared in front.

And now she had grown up.

"The only way you'll get any taller now is to get on a horse," he said to Fatima, who got his drift.

"But you know, Baba, that horses don't come by themselves."

From the time the gazelle had sought refuge with her, Fatima had stopped waking up terrified at the sight of pieces of camel meat bearing ghoulish eyes. She had recovered the childlike ability to sail off peacefully to the land of dreams, and her heart had sprouted a green something that she had never felt before. But before she realized what was happening inside her, or what it was that had changed, she saw them coming back to her house: the same men who had come that day long before to recover their cattle.

Fatima had yet to discover the secret of that sundown and the astonishment that had taken both her and that horseman by storm when, for a few fleeting moments, their eyes had met. As she had walked back to the village, her shadow stretched out behind her to where he sat motionlessly on the back of his thoroughbred mare. She didn't know how her shadow had clung to that of the mare and her rider, or how it had extended farther and farther back in a perfectly straight line the farther away she went. However, the horseman, noticing this, realized that his fate had been determined, and that the life that had been preordained for him began there, at the source of that endless shadow. His mare wanted to go after it, and when he saw what was happening, he tried to stop her, but for the first time ever, she didn't obey him. He pulled in her reins, but her only response was to rear up and whinny. He turned her neck to go back to where he had come from, but she resisted. Then she bucked wildly, sending him tumbling to the ground. And before he could recover from the shock, he saw his mare running back to meet the girl. When the mare arrived at her destination, Fatima came up to her and whispered something that no one but the two of them would ever know. Then the mare came trotting back to her master, who had remained petrified in the distance, unable either to go after his mare or to return home without her.

Before sundown four days later, the horses appeared again, but all Hajj Khaled could see was Hamama. This was no longer an unusual occurrence, since every horse that approached from that direction appeared to him as Hamama.

It was a Thursday, and the people who had been brought together by the market, which had grown to become the largest in the entire area, were heading out in all directions on their way back to their homes. However, the horsemen continued their approach, and for some reason he couldn't put his finger on, he knew the men approaching could only be coming to one place, namely, his house.

"Hop to it, fellows!" he shouted. "You've got company!"

The young men around him turned and saw the procession of horsemen approaching on the horizon. He could see that there was a growing distance between the travel party and one of its members, whose horse had slowed down until it came to a complete halt. His silhouette against the setting sun was a sight to behold. He and his mare were an embodiment of the most exquisite beauty, and the plain, which had long been in need of them, had been transformed into a panorama the likes of which they had never seen before. Hajj Khaled felt his heart trembling violently in his ribcage at the very moment when Fatima's heart began to tremble.

She went running to her mother and flung herself into her arms.

"What is it?"

"Nothing. Everything's all right, I think!"

"What's the matter, girl? What's wrong?"

"No, Mama. I think everything's all right."

When Sumayya held her at arm's length to look into her face, Fatima clung to her all the more.

"It's all right, it's all right."

When the visitors had gone up to the guesthouse, all the preparations had been made to receive them. However, the happy dreams that had begun dancing in the eyes of Hajj Khaled and his son Naji suddenly evaporated, since the only horse among those that had arrived was a gray mare that looked nothing like either Hamama or the other thoroughbred they had seen.

The party was headed by Shaykh al-Jalil, who was riding a mare whose coat had a slightly bluish tint. She was the color of the limpid shallows that you see when you look down at the ocean from a high mountain.

"They must be coming for something important this time," Hajj Khaled said to himself. Nor were his hopes disappointed when he embraced them, for he saw in their eyes a look of intimate familiarity that he hadn't seen on their first visit.

As they entered the guesthouse, Hamdan began roasting the coffee. He kept close watch on the guesthouse door, trying in vain to divine what might be transpiring within its walls. However, his heart knew more than he did, and it sensed that some great happiness was waiting in the wings, and that today's guests weren't just passing by.

The years had changed Hamdan quite a bit. His friendly proximity to fire all that time seemed to have made his complexion darker than ever, and he had begun gradually to diminish in size. His hair, a few wisps of which peeked out from under the keffiyeh wrapped tightly about his head like Shaykh Husni's turban, was the only white part of him left. However, his eyes still had their familiar twinkle, and they sparkled continuously wherever he went, as though they were still reflecting the flame he had left behind him. As for the smile that never left his kindly face, one could never tell whether it was a sign of happiness and contentment, or of a bemused realization that he'd seen everything there was to see under the sun.

In the end, he had no choice but to listen to the voice of his heart, thereby relieving his eyes of the task he had assigned them. At that moment, his mortar and pestle set to work with a new enthusiasm. They sent forth a sweet melody as they filled the air with the aroma of coffee, and of a happiness to which those moments inside the guesthouse were undoubtedly giving birth.

They drank their coffee and asked their host's permission to be on their way. Hajj Khaled tried to make them stay longer, but they said, "There's someone waiting for us at the other end of the plain, and it wouldn't be right for us to leave him in suspense out there in the dark."

"You could send him word of what's happened so far."

"Yes, but there's someone else who's waiting in our village as anxiously as he is!"

When they left, Hamdan was still playing music with his mortar and pestle. They turned and looked in his direction, sensing that he was sharing in their joy. They gathered about him as they would have gathered about a practiced dabka dancer, and forgot themselves so completely that at last Hajj Khaled quipped, "At this rate you could have stayed for dinner and be finished by now!"

When they awoke from their trance, night had fallen, and the horse-man waiting in the silver moonlight at the end of the field was just a mysterious point, hardly recognizable as a rider.

As they descended the hill, they saw the moon coming up over the horizon. Ever so gradually it rose higher in the sky, illumining the plain. Behind them, the rap-tap-tap of Hamdan's mortar and pestle filled the air with a sweetness that had never been felt before by these guests, who, from that evening onward, were destined to become authentic members of the household.

"All we had to do was mention the horsemen for them to appear on our doorstep!" Hajj Khaled said to his daughter, who had curled herself up shyly into a ball.

After a brief silence, he said, "It seems you know!"

"No, I don't know anything. I just have a feeling."

"So you *do* know!"

"No! I just feel it, that's all."

"If that's the case, then there was no need for me to tell them that I'd give them my answer in two days."

"What's going on?" asked Sumayya.

"Suitors. Someone's asked for your daughter's hand."

"Congratulations!"

"Aren't you going to ask who they are?"

"The only people who would knock on Hajj Khaled's door about a matter like this are people who know his worth, and who know their own worth."

The wedding celebration that joined Fatima with Nuh, the brother of Khadra—whose title had remained a part of him from the night he had emerged on the back of his horse, whooping and charging with his sword—was a grand affair. Who would have thought that a beginning such as that would have led to a finale such as this?

Nuh tried to apologize to Hajj Khaled.

In reply, Hajj Khaled said, "If you hadn't tried to defend your cattle that evening, I wouldn't have agreed to let you marry my daughter."

"But don't forget that I was defeated."

"Defeated? No, you weren't defeated. After all, when you attacked, you did it not for the sake of victory, but in order to get back what was yours."

"Would you allow me to call you my father from now on?"

"And who are you, if you aren't my son?"

Turkeys

When Mahmud finished primary school at the Najah School[*] in Nablus, the reception he was given back in Hadiya would have been fit for a returning conqueror. Skinny as ever, he'd grown taller, and beneath his diminutive nose one could see some golden whiskers beginning to sprout. His eyes seemed to have taken on a new glimmer, while no one could help but notice that his gait was more like that of a government employee than that of a schoolboy.

When the crowds had dispersed, Hajj Khaled said to him, "What are you thinking of doing now?"

"I don't know."

---

[*] The first attempt to found this school came toward the end of Ottoman rule. However, requests to do so were rejected because of the political conditions being faced by the Ottoman state toward the end of its rule over the Arab region, when Arab nationalist currents and thought had begun to emerge and even threaten the existence of the Ottoman state itself. Consequently, the Ottoman authorities felt it necessary to place a limit on the number of new schools being opened in order to contain the nationalist sentiments that had begun to intensify and spread. However, in an attempt to win favor with the residents of the city, the British authorities agreed to its establishment in the early days of the British mandate.

"We need you to do better than that, son. We didn't send you away for an education just so that you could come back and say 'I don't know'!"

"I'll do whatever you want me to."

"As you know, the problem we face now is a lack of education among the people; I mean, among the people here in the villages. You'd think it was all right for other people to get an education, but not for us! Neither the Ottomans nor the British have wanted us to be educated, not even our leading men. You know, Abd al-Latif al-Hamdi dismissed one of the farmers who work his land just because he had the audacity to say he wanted to educate his son."

"So what do you think?"

"There are schools in Jerusalem where you might be able to complete your education."

"Would they accept me?"

"Aren't your grades good?"

"They're excellent."

"Then we'll take them with us to the schools in Jerusalem and see what they say."

After donning his best tunic, Hajj Khaled took his son to the train station. They went to the station on horseback, accompanied by Naji, who escorted their two horses back home again. When they got to Jerusalem, they found themselves in another world completely: a world that, as Father Elias had once told them, changed from one visit to the next.

Cars sped down the streets at such a mad clip that they nearly crushed people beneath their wheels, while gaily adorned horse-drawn carriages strutted about like so many turkeys as though they owned the earth and everyone on it. Buses came charging from all directions in search of a space in which to insert themselves, determined to be on their way at all costs.

"Where do all these cars come from?" Hajj Khaled asked his son in bewilderment. "There are more cars now than there are people!" As he spoke, he noticed Mahmud's whiskers for the first time.

"Nablus is quieter," Mahmud said.

"It'll be fifty more years before you see life like this pulsing through Hadiya, even though it's only a half-hour train ride away."

Jerusalem was a great disappointment to both of them.

Hajj Khaled said, "Since we've come all this way, we don't want to go home empty-handed. So let's go on to Ramallah."

"Ramallah!"

"Aren't there schools there?"

"There's a school there whose name I've heard more than once: the Friends' School."

"Do you think they might accept you there?"

"I don't know."

The school's broad entrance with its three archways formed a large balcony for its second floor. Its red roof tiles, which made two small pyramids, lent the building a majestic air that caused it to look more like a church than a school. Meanwhile, the darkened, arched windows that looked out through its ancient-looking stone walls seemed like the most ghostly things they had ever seen in their lives.

The headmaster received them with less warmth than the people in Hadiya would have accorded even a government official. He scrutinized Mahmud's grades, then nodded his head.

"A fine student," he said, "but . . ."

"But what?" queried Hajj Khaled, who hadn't received an invitation to sit down.

"Nothing."

Peering over a pair of thick spectacles that were about to fall off his nose, the headmaster examined Hajj Khaled from the top of his head to the tips of his toes as though he were a mother checking out a prospective bride for her son. Then, in a languid voice that was almost a whisper, he said, "We're a missionary school, as you know. We have a worship service every morning before classes begin."

Seeing through the headmaster's flimsy excuse, Hajj Khaled kneaded his brow with the fingers of his left hand, then said, "There's a monastery in our town that's been there since the days when my father was the village elder. So things like this aren't strange to us."

"But you don't worship at the monastery!"

"Well, my son could worship with you here, though."

"But as you know, our worship is different from yours. For example, we sing hymns praising God, Jesus, and the Virgin Mary."

"That's fine with me, since we believe in the Torah, the Gospel, Jesus, and the Virgin."

"Then, every Sunday morning, we take the pupils to the Quaker church, where we have a worship service in which the pastor preaches a sermon."

"I have no objections. After all, the church is the house of God just as the mosque is, and I want my son to know about the Christian religion."

"We don't observe Ramadan, since we're not able to prepare the fast-breaking meal in the evening or the pre-dawn meal for the Muslim students."

"My son's health, as you can see from his size, is fragile, so he doesn't fast at home, and I don't want him to fast at your school, either!"

The headmaster looked thoughtfully at Hajj Khaled and said, "Amazing. There's nothing more I can say, then."

After a prolonged silence, the headmaster said, "So, then." Then, adjusting his spectacles, he turned to the two of them and added, "Congratulations."

The Night Alone

ome on, get up! It's daytime!" Sumayya called to her children.
No sooner had a child reached ten years of age than he was
expected to go out and work in the fields, where he would herd and
graze the animals. It wasn't unusual, however, for the sheep and goats to
come back on their own. Missing the little shepherd, the villagers would
go out looking for him. Finding him asleep in the pasture, they would say,
"The lambs are back, and the boy's hit the sack!" However, one boy who
never suffered this ignominy was Naji. In fact, Hajj Khaled would sometimes call him "little wolf."

When a boy began to get older and stronger, they would place a small
rock between his hand and the plow handle, then press on it in order to
strengthen his hand so that he could learn to control the plow's height reg-
ulator. However, they would only do this when the boy's head had come
up enough higher than the plow, so he was able to see the ground and
press the plow deeply into the soil.

In many cases the cow would make the boy take a fall, which would
provide some entertainment in the midst of the day's toil.

"Come on, get up! It's daytime!" Sumayya urged again.

They began to stir, and when they opened their eyes they realized that they had truly overslept.

There was a huge field of wheat awaiting them, and it was time to get to work. They were exhausted from all the work they'd done the previous day. Still, they got up, and when they arrived they found that many people had gotten there before them.

"You see, you're late!" she told them.

They shook their heads, not to affirm or deny what their mother had said, but to shake the drowsiness out of their eyes.

As the harvesting began, the air was filled with song:

He took his scythe to the blacksmith and he buffed till it shone.
The moon circles around it, bestowing a life-giving glow.
The tall wheat stalks sway now east, now west, taking a courteous bow.

They began racing to see who could make the most progress in the least time, and from a distance one could see the corridors, some narrow and some broad, that now lined the field. Afaf, Abu Sunbul's granddaughter, was always in the lead.

It was daytime, but there was no sun. There was nothing but the moon. Naji cast a glance at the eastern horizon: nothing!

When the backs of the children and some of the adults had grown stiff, the others would make them lie on their stomachs on the ground and walk on their backs to loosen them up.

Life needed everybody in order to go on.

They said to Musa, "We're going to load the camel for you so that you can take the wheat to town."

"I'll go," volunteered Naji.

"No, we need you here," replied Hajj Khaled.

The camel went a fair distance, then stopped. Musa, who was the laziest of all Hajj Khaled's children, tried to force it to go on, but it refused, and a few moments later it kneeled. He urged it to get up, but there was no response.

Musa cried for help, and everyone came running in alarm. But when they got to where he was, they discovered that the problem was far less serious than they had thought.

"You scared us to death, boy. Shame on you!" Sumayya said reproachfully.

"What am I supposed to do?" he protested. "He doesn't want to walk!"

Hajj Khaled nudged the camel with the toe of his shoe and it got up.

"Come on now, go the rest of the way! You're making a spectacle!" Sumayya said to the uncooperative animal.

But it refused to budge.

"Who knows whether it might not do the same thing again?" he asked.

So Muhammad Shahada went with him, and they were back in an hour

The sun was still far away. And when it finally did appear, they discovered that the adults had deceived them. Some of the harvesters had managed to make their way almost to the middle of the field.

The only way to avoid the scorching rays of the sun was to get up at night and work by the light of the moon.

When Sumayya called her children the following night, saying, "Come on! It's daytime!" Musa replied, without opening his eyes, "I won't go out until the sun sets!"

Private Lessons

I t was as though she were seeing her for the first time. Sumayya looked at Afaf and said, "This is the bride I want for Mahmud, and we mustn't let her get away!"

Afaf was the granddaughter of Hajj Jum'a Abu Sunbul, and she had lived with her mother in her grandfather's house ever since his son Ahmad died in a bizarre accident. One day he had been driving the cows up a hill in order to get away from a torrential stream in the valley when a cow lost its footing and, as it rolled down the hill, pinned him to a large boulder.

You ask me how he died? The accident had left him with pain in his back, so my mother went to Nabil al-Awda's wife. Why? Because she knew how to treat with cauterization. (I don't want to take too much of your time.) In any case, she cauterized the area around the spine. She put a chickpea on it, and some green tree leaves on top of that. Then she bound it. After that, we started putting a new chickpea and fresh tree leaves on it every other day according to her instructions. During the first week, he said—and, well, I think he was lying—"it doesn't hurt any more!" He said that even though he couldn't move. Two weeks later, his back started to get more and more bowed. So we picked him up and took him to Ramla. When the doctor there saw him, he shouted,

"What have you donkeys done to him? You ought to be hanged, drawn and quartered!"
My mother said to him, "He was having back pain, and a strange woman passed through
the village and said she knew how to use natural remedies. So we let her treat him." Of
course my mother was afraid to mention the name of Nabil al-Awda's wife, since she
knew this would lead to an investigation and who knows what else. "His entire spinal
cord has been drawn out!" raged the doctor. They took him to Jaffa and to Jerusalem,
but it was no use. He'd lost the use of his legs. All day long, may he rest in peace, he
would ask us to move his legs for him this way or that, and whenever he needed somebody
to help him at night he would wake us up with a long cane that we'd put beside him.
People were constantly coming to see him, and in less than a month he died.

Sumayya started watching Afaf as she came and went, when she was working in the fields, and when she was picking olives. She even observed the way she brought water from the well, and when she was sure this was the girl she wanted to be her son's wife, she went to her house on a surprise visit. The minute she saw the house, the girl passed the test with flying colors.

Then, to make even surer, she made two more surprise visits, both of them with the same outcome.

As for Afaf herself, she couldn't remember a time when she'd been any other way, with one exception. One ill-fated day as she was on her way back from the well, Muhammad Shahada's daughter Aisha cried, "A snake! A snake!"

Afaf looked down at her feet and saw the 'snake,' which turned out to be nothing but a piece of rope. As a result, she slipped and lost her balance, whereupon the jar fell off her head and shattered.

Aisha had never expected her joke to lead to such a disaster. But before she knew it, she saw Afaf bending down over her jar and bursting into tears. When she reached home, she didn't dare go inside, but instead kept walking in circles around it. Then she sat down in the shade of the wall, her eyes filled with tears.

Wondering why she was taking so long, her mother came out of the house and saw her crying.

"What's happened?" she asked.

"I broke the jar."

"You broke the jar? I'm done for! You broke the jar! How could you have broken the jar?"

"I fell."

"Lord have mercy!"

They were poor, and even though a new jar would have cost only ten piasters, for them it was an unbearable loss. For three whole days her mother ranted and raved as though she had lost her husband all over again. In order to make up for the loss, her mother had no choice but to let Afaf work as an assistant to Sister Sarah and Sister Mary at the monastery after Father Antonius' death. When the two sisters saw the way Afaf worked, they held on to her, and were determined not to let anyone take her away from them. They also began teaching her Greek, and were amazed at how bright she was.

Then one night her maternal uncle Abd al-Rahman came from Jaffa to visit them. When he saw that Afaf's mother was eight months pregnant and ill, he said, "Where's Afaf?"

"At the monastery," she replied.

"And what is she doing at the monastery?"

"She went to help the nuns there for a week or two, and now she's been there for five months."

"And who helps you?"

"Nobody, as you can see!"

Abd al-Rahman went to the monastery and knocked on the door. Out came Sister Mary.

"Where is Afaf?"

"She's inside working. Who are you?"

"I'm her uncle, and I want her to come home with me now."

"You can't take her. She works here, and we can't do without her."

"But her mother needs her more."

"You can't take her."

Pushing the nun aside, Abd al-Rahman stepped into the building and started shouting, "Afaf! Afaf!"

"Uncle Abd al-Rahman!"

She went running to him, as she was very fond of him, since he brought her scrumptious things that no other girl in Hadiya had ever tasted.

"I want you to come with me. Your mother is ill, and I want you to leave the monastery for good. Do you understand?"

"I understand. But they're not going to agree."

"We won't let you take her. We depend on her in everything," Mary told him.

"You depend on her. Fine. That's your problem, and you're the ones who'll have to solve it."

Afaf was delighted to leave, actually, since at last she was free of the heavy burden she'd been carrying at the monastery, a burden so heavy that the minute she got home she would go straight to bed in search of a sweet dream.

Although she left the monastery armed with a good store of Greek words that she would use occasionally in enigmatic imprecations, Afaf went on with her life as though she hadn't been gone for a single day. When her mother delivered, Afaf was assigned the task of caring for her long-awaited little brother, and if she could have nursed him, she would have done that as well.

News of Afaf spread all over Hadiya, and people spoke well of her for what they termed the 'nuns' education' she'd received, even though they knew quite well that nothing about her had changed except for the Greek curse words she knew now, and which she generally used with a giggle!

Sumayya sent her son Naji to inform Mahmud, who worked for a newspaper in Jaffa, that she had found him a bride and that he would have to come back. He was twenty-two years old now, "And I won't wait any longer," his mother announced.

When Naji arrived in Jaffa one day at noon, he found Mahmud still in bed. He had spent the evening before watching Yusuf Wahbi's play, *Confession Chair*, which had gone on until one o'clock in the morning.

His reply was definitive: "I'm not thinking of marriage." He was happy with his life in Jaffa, since suddenly he had found himself in a place where he lacked nothing. There were coffee shops, theaters, social clubs, and concerts and plays by rising artists from Yusuf Wahbi to Nagib al-Rihani, Ali al-Kassar, Muhammad Abd al-Wahhab, and even Umm Kulthum. In addition, there were movie houses that regularly showed the best and latest films. His favorite was the Hamra Cinema at the entrance to the Nuzha neighborhood. On holidays he would go the Sharq Cinema where he would see Flash Gordon and Dick Tracy movies, since he could see three films in a row for just two piasters.

Pouring out her woes to Anisa, Sumayya said tearfully, "How could he not be thinking of marriage at his age?"

"Maybe your son is of no use to women," Anisa suggested.

"God forbid!"

"Or maybe he's infatuated with those city girls!"

Anisa had had the worst luck of any woman in Hadiya. When she'd been married for three months without anything to show for it, people realized that the problem was not with her, but with her husband, since he began avoiding any place where he might meet up with other people. When, in the end, he realized that his attempts at escape were futile, he volunteered as a soldier in the Turkish army and was never seen again. Some people said he was no good. However, Anisa confided sadly to Munira one night, "I feel sorry for him. It wasn't his fault."

"But I still don't understand," said Munira.

"The poor man didn't have the right equipment!"

"No!" Munira gasped.

"It was no bigger than a fava bean!"

During Mahmud's first visit back to Hadiya, Sumayya made him go with her to Afaf's house so that she could show her to him. And when he saw her, everything changed. She was truly beautiful: she was tall, slender, and had a lilting gait even more charming than the movie stars he saw at the Hamra Cinema every Thursday.

"But she doesn't know how to read or write," he said to his mother.

"She was educated at the monastery, and she speaks Greek. Can you speak Greek?"

"Well, no," he admitted.

"You be quiet, then!"

When Afaf looked over at them, she saw a new Mahmud, as everything about him had changed. His face had filled out a bit, his complexion was lighter, his skinny-as-a-rail physique had filled out, and he sported a thin, well-groomed moustache and round spectacles like the ones doctors wore.

"Good morning, Auntie!" she said with a smile.

"Good morning, sweetheart."

Her smile alone was enough to move Mahmud's heart. It was a luminous smile filled with a wit and jollity the likes of which he had never encountered before, and set off by a dark complexion that intensified the translucence of her large eyes.

"She's young, and you could teach her yourself," Sumayya told him.

"Do you think so?"

"If a young man like you couldn't do it, then who could?"

That evening, Hajj Khaled went to Hajj Jum'a Abu Sunbul's house and told him what he was thinking.

"With God's blessings," came Abu Sunbul's reply.

The following day, Mahmud returned to Jaffa, where he bought a watch and a gold ring. When the bride saw them, she was beside herself with delight, and for a long time thereafter she would walk through the village looking at them as though they belonged to somebody else and she only wished they were hers.

"I like everything about you. But I want you to know how to read better and to do some arithmetic. I love to read, so I buy stories, books, and magazines. I'd like you to read everything I read so that we can understand each other better."

Not wasting any time, Mahmud began teaching her the next morning. And, in order to make her feel that the matter was more than a little serious, he left her a set of arithmetic problems, saying, "When I come back I want all these problems to be solved, and the story read. Agreed?"

"Agreed!"

Afaf got busy solving the arithmetic problems and reading the stories, whether she liked them or not. But one day, Mahmud came on a surprise visit, laden as usual with all the issues of the newspaper he worked for, which had come out while he was in Jaffa. Looking into the distance, she saw the chest of books and newspapers on the back of the truck, and realized that disaster was imminent, since she hadn't even gone near the papers he had left for her on his previous visit.

Afaf came sprinting down the hillside. In the beginning, she managed to clear a number of the low stone walls that divided the vineyards and orchards from each other. As she went, however, she began to lose momentum and started grazing the top of one wall after another. Whenever she ran into one of them, she would make a small hole in it. When she looked behind her, she saw that she had opened up a passageway that cut across a long series of walls. She had wanted to beat him to the house, in the hope that she might be able to make up for what she hadn't done. But it was no use, since the truck arrived before she did, and she thus found herself faced with the bitterest, harshest test she had ever encountered.

He took her ear and gave it a rough tweak, the way teachers did to students in those days. She screamed and burst into tears. It wasn't the pain that made her cry but, rather, the insult and humiliation of it all.

She'd been accustomed to washing and ironing his clothes for him whenever he came for a visit, the way she had learned to do at the monastery. But now she stopped.

"You can look for somebody else to iron your clothes."

"I'm not used to being spoken to this way."

"Whoever twists my ear will have to get used to it from now on."

In an attempt to get back at her, he decided to expel her from his school! And it wasn't long before their spat had turned into the first serious dispute they had ever had—so serious, in fact, that he refused to visit her or even speak to her for an entire year.

Sumayya's Plates

Without warning, he started asking to get married. As for Hajj Khaled, he gave in to his request and let him marry before Mahmud, even though this wasn't proper, since the oldest son was to marry first, then the next oldest, and so on down the line.

Whenever Sumayya remembered that day, she laughed till she cried.

Naji had grabbed a number of plates and begun breaking them. Noticing what was happening, Sumayya jumped up and went to work to minimize her losses.

"Is there somebody who's too shy to do this for himself and has asked you to do it for him?" she asked him.

Then she thought again about what she had said and added, "Mahmud's already got a fiancée, so why would he be too shy to tell us he wants to get married? Maybe it's Musa?"

Naji's only response was to break more plates.

"Hajj Khaled!" she shouted. "Get in here quick!"

By the time Hajj Khaled arrived, Sumayya had Naji locked in a powerful grip. With yet another plate in his hand, he threatened, "Let go of me or I'll break this one too!"

Seeing the shattered plates that covered the floor, Hajj Khaled said, "What's going on?"

"See to your sons! They're too shy to say they want to get married, so they have this pipsqueak break plates for them."

Then, squeezing her son even harder, she said, "You little troublemaker, who told to do what you're doing?"

"I told myself!"

"Who?"

"Me! *I'm* the one that wants to get married!"

"You!"

Sumayya released him from her iron grip and he moved quickly away from her, his back to the wall and the plate in his hand.

"Shall I break it, or are you going to let me get married?"

Then she started to laugh. She laughed as she'd never laughed before. Within moments, her laughter had become infectious and Hajj Khaled was in stitches, too. After a while, Hajj Khaled managed to stop laughing. As for Sumayya, she couldn't get hold of herself. Hajj Khaled burst out laughing again, then stopped. But not Sumayya. And it was then that he realized she was on her way to losing her mind.

When her laughter finally subsided, it was because of a spasm in her jaw that prevented her from uttering a word for three whole days. To make certain she didn't have another miserable laughing spell, Hajj Khaled had to keep her mouth closed with a cloth that went under her jaw and around the top of her head.

On the fourth day, she undid the bandage by herself. But instead of laughing, she started crying.

Hajj Khaled said to her, "The laughing was bad enough. And now you're going to start crying?"

She told him she had been expecting Mahmud to complete her joy by marrying, only to find that Naji was the one who wanted to marry.

"Mahmud's engaged, woman. What matters now is for him to work things out with his fiancée. Otherwise, he might surprise us by saying he wants to marry somebody else."

"Do you really think that might happen?"

"It might if things go on the way they are now."

"Anything but that!"

Hajj Khaled succumbed, as did Sumayya. However, fear returned to knock on people's hearts anew when Sumayya asked, "Has Naji told you who the unlucky girl is?"

Fatima then smiled that wicked smile that they all knew so well, and which hadn't left her even after she married.

"Before your smile starts hurting you, you'd better tell us her name!"

"How should I know?"

Fatima, who had moved into a new house next to her father's, knew that Naji had been going over to Hajj Sabri al-Najjar's neighborhood, and that every time he disappeared, it was because he had gone there. She had tried more than once to get him to confess to it, but he had refused, so she'd taken to watching him. When she saw that he had been hanging around the house of Salem al-Diqr, she slapped her cheeks and cried, "Anybody but that harebrained girl!"

"And who is this harebrained girl you're talking about?

In the end, Fatima confessed. "The harebrained girl? It's Khadija, Salem al-Diqr's daughter!"

"O my heavens! *That* one! She's a disaster!"

Once, after Naji got back from one of his long absences, he found everyone waiting for him. Alongside Hajj Khaled sat Sumayya, who had gathered all her breakable plates into her lap.

"Come over here, sweetie," she said. "Break all the plates you want, but if you think I'm going to let you marry that crazy Khadija, you've got another think coming."

"And who said I wanted to marry crazy Khadija?"

"Then why do you hover all day long around their house and make us look bad?" Hajj Khaled asked him.

Uneasy, he hesitated to speak.

"Go ahead!" Sumayya said testily. "Give us an explanation!"

"I wanted their filly, Shahba," he said simply.

"Lord have mercy! So you want to marry a horse?"

"I want you to buy her for me."

"So why didn't you tell us?"

"I was afraid you'd refuse."

"And for that you come and break my plates, you ornery boy?" Sumayya demanded.

"I love her, and I was afraid you'd refuse."

"You love her. What does that mean? That you love the horse? Is your head screwed on right, or have you lost it?"

Finally, he screamed, "Whether it's right or not, I want her!"

"Augh!" moaned Fatima.

"Augh yourself!" her mother retorted. "Is this the time for that?"

"It's hurting me. My smile's hurting me," Fatima explained.

"I swear to God, this is all your fault. You knew about this all along, but you didn't tell us," her mother scolded.

Hajj Khaled sent for Muhammad Shahada and said to him, "Go ask Salem al-Diqr how much he wants for that filly."

When he came back, he said, "He says it's not for sale."

"What does he mean, it's not for sale? Tell me that."

"He says it's Khadija's horse, and that when she gets married she'll ride to her husband's house on her back!"

"And what does he mean by that?"

"It means that the filly will only belong to whoever marries the girl."

"So that's why I've heard people say he pampers that horse more than he pampers his own daughter. He knows the horse is the key to that crazy girl's future," Hajj Khaled said.

"That's the situation."

❄

"Does it make you happy for us to make fools of ourselves this way? And over folks that belong to Hajj Sabri al-Najjar's clan, of all people?" asked an exasperated Hajj Khaled.

"It doesn't make me happy. But I want that filly."

"Do you know what their condition is?"

"Yes, I do."

"And are you willing to marry crazy Khadija?"

"She isn't that crazy!"

That was when Sumayya started wailing.

"The boy's lost his mind!" she ranted.

"I want her. I mean, I want her, with or without Khadija."

Hajj Khaled made one attempt after another.

He sent a message to Salem al-Diqr, saying, "Ask whatever you want."

And Salem replied, "When it comes to this issue, there's only one answer I can give."

"What do you say we buy you an even better horse?" they asked Naji.

"When I say I want that horse, I mean *that horse*," he replied.

Naji thought he had fallen in love with the thoroughbred mare that belonged to Nuh, Fatima's husband, but it had been nothing but an illusion, because the moment Shahba had set foot in Hadiya, the first horse had become a thing of the past, or like something that had never even existed.

Naji stopped eating and started wasting away, till he was half his original size. Tamam would cast him sad looks. Fatima stopped smiling. Hajj Khaled turned silent, and no longer spoke to anyone. Then one evening, Sumayya came to her husband and said, "Now come to your senses and do what's got to be done. God knows I was sillier than she is before you married me!"

"What are you saying, woman?"

To his astonishment, she had the audacity to repeat, "Now come to your senses and do what's got to be done. God knows I was sillier than she is before you married me!"

No one could explain what happened, but before the days of her engagement had drawn to a close, Khadija had become a new person. It was even said that it was her despair of finding a husband that had driven her mad. But now that her hopes had been fulfilled, the Khadija of today wasn't at all the Khadija of the past. On the other hand, some people still thought her madness had been on account of all the eggs she'd been eating!

However, she was nearly driven out of her senses all over again by the fact that the groom seemed more anxious to see Shahba than he was to see his bride. No sooner had he sat down after coming for a visit than his eyes would go in search of his filly, and when Khadija's mother called her to come out to see Naji on his first visit, saying, "Don't be shy, little bride. Come here," the one Naji had expected to come through the door wasn't Khadija, but her horse!

Shahba's Eclipse

The best thing about time is that it goes so fast. That's also the worst thing about it," said Hajj Khaled.

However, the meaning of his words was lost on his son Naji. When Khadija left her parents' household on her filly's back, the entire world couldn't have contained Naji's joy, his only thought being: Shahba will be mine, all mine! Meanwhile, the changes that had come over Khadija had tempered the unspoken discomfort that had dogged Hajj Khaled throughout the days of their engagement.

"I wasn't wrong when I insisted on naming him Naji," commented Sumayya.

Some people's engagements had been known to last for years. However, Hajj Khaled had intended to keep Naji's to one year only.

Even so, Naji, who was champing at the bit to get near Shahba, had changed the entire equation. Consequently, Hajj Khaled had no choice but to settle the matter with a definitive word.

Once, as the men of the neighborhood were assembled for their nightly gathering in the guesthouse, Hajj Khaled kneaded his brow with the fingers of his left hand and, looking over at his son, said, "The wedding won't be at the time we'd planned."

Naji was so unnerved by his father's announcement that he nearly fainted.

Explaining himself further, Hajj Khaled continued, "We're going to move it up by nine months."

Flooded with relief, life pulsed through his son's veins once again and the blood pumped back into his face.

People came from all over to attend the wedding celebration. Hajj Abu Salem, the father of Hajj Khaled's first wife, Amal, had no intention of missing such an occasion, and came all the way from Jerusalem.

He said to Hajj Khaled, "All the way here I had this strange feeling that I was coming to attend my grandson's wedding, and to congratulate my own daughter!"

"May God have mercy on her," replied Hajj Khaled.

"May God have mercy on her," he said again. "You know that I'm like your son, and that my children will always be your grandchildren.

"May God have mercy on her. Not only was her name 'Hope'; she herself was hope."

As the women and teenage girls carried the food for the wedding feast to the guesthouse on their heads, they sang,

A lovely tall lass just passed this way,
With a neck two handspans long!

Her bosom is a garden, her forehead sweet basil,
If she calls from afar I hear a song!

This lovely tall lass is a sight for sore eyes
With blonde hair cascading down her dress.

If a married man saw her he'd divorce his wife,
Go wandering like a madman in the wilderness.

Then, as always on such occasions, they kept singing at the guesthouse
door until the men had finished eating.

The wedding was intended to include people near and far, so there was
plenty of food for everyone.

Then the thing they had most feared happened: before eating the supper
that had been prepared for the bride and groom, and before finishing his
wedding night, Naji said to Khadija, "I'm going out for a bit and I'll be
right back," hoping to give her the impression that he needed to answer
the call of nature!

Yet who should he find at the door but his mother and mother-in-law,
who were waiting to see how the wedding night had gone.

"Where do you think you're going?"

"I'm going to answer the call of nature!"

"Is this the time for that?" asked his mother through her teeth.

"Oh, this is what I was afraid—" blurted out the bride's mother.

But before she could finish her sentence, Munira interrupted, saying,
"Don't worry! Everything will be all right."

Then Naji slipped past them and disappeared.

*The people of Hadiya still cracked jokes about what happened when al-Barmaki first
got married. He was married when he was eleven years old, and on the wedding night he
said, "I want some harisa! I won't go in to be with the bride until you bring me some!"
They went all the way to Ramla at night looking for some harisa, and when they got back
at noon the next day, they found him still waiting. However, even that didn't do any good,
since he went on playing in the neighborhood for a long time after that, and when his wife
would bring him home again from some far-off place, he'd be so worn out that he'd go to
sleep on her shoulder. One day, as he slept on her shoulder, someone knocked at their door
and asked, "Where's the man of the house?" "He's asleep," she answered. "Is there something you'd like me to tell him when he wakes up?" But when, three years later, he tasted
his bride's 'harisa,' he said, "God! It's more delicious than harisa ever was!"*

293

Sumayya's heart bounced back and forth between her feet and her throat. She felt he was taking too long, and every second that passed seemed like an eternity.

Leaving the bride's mother at the door, she said, "Just a minute. I'll be right back."

Knowing exactly where to find him, she headed for the stable, where she found him holding Shahba's head and kissing her cheek.

"What are you doing, for God's sake?"

"I've come to see her."

"You leave the poor girl waiting for you in there while you come to see her horse! You get back in there right this minute, before I bring the whole village down on you!"

Then she began muttering to herself, "What's this scandal you've brought on yourself, Sumayya?"

The strange thing was that when Naji tasted a new kind of sweetness, a sweetness he could never have imagined, he stopped leaving the house. He planted himself in bed and clung to it as though his life depended on it. Never in his wildest dreams had he imagined such a world, the world of Khadija, who had blossomed like a rose. Not only that, but she was so sure now of where she stood in relation to Shahba that if something wasn't to her liking she would put on a childish pout that was totally unacceptable to Sumayya, and if she hadn't been a new bride, Sumayya would have treated her to a good tongue-lashing.

He no longer had any mercy on either himself or her. Her legs would wobble, as would his, whenever they tried to traverse the distance between their bedroom and the long dining hall where the whole family took their meals together.

Less than three weeks had passed when Khadija said to him, "Why don't you go check on Shahba?" She kept saying it till she was blue in the face, but to no avail. When a month was out, she confided in her mother, who in turn confided in his mother, saying, "My dear, the girl isn't made of steel!"

"You know how it is. He's young!"

"Young or not, my dear, I'm telling you: the girl's not made of steel!"

"Don't worry, I'll find a solution."

A flock of sparrows flew low overhead. Sumayya followed them with her eyes until they disappeared. Taking a deep breath, she pondered her surroundings. To her amazement, she realized that it had been a long time since she'd stopped to notice the orange tree. How could that have happened? But she found no answer. She cast a glance upward, expecting to see another flock of birds pass overhead, but the copper sky remained empty. Then she turned to Naji and said, "You know, sweetheart, that they gave you both the horse and the bride. But now they're saying: Since you're so happy with the bride, you should give the horse back, because you don't pay any attention to her. Their filly is precious to them, just as their daughter is. And if you don't take proper care of her, they're going to take her away from you. So which will it be?"

"By what right can they take her away?"

"They have that right because you're ignoring her. In fact, it won't be long before she dies of neglect."

"Just like that?"

"Yes, just like that."

"All right, then, give her back to them!"

"Anything but that!" cried Sumayya, suddenly losing her calm reserve. "Are you out of your mind? What would people say—that Naji, Hajj Khaled's son, couldn't take proper care of his horse? Shame on you!"

However, things changed when Naji realized that he would have to support his family by himself, and that he was no longer a boy who could live footloose and fancy-free.

Hajj Khaled said to him, "Thanks be to God! Blessed is the household that sends another household out into the world."

And he kept repeating the words over and over until Naji realized that times had truly changed.

Meanwhile, Shahba no longer occupied the throne that had once been hers.

A Black Cloud

One day, they saw a black cloud in the distance. It was the first time they had seen anything like it, and it was hard to be certain whether it was a storm or just a heavy mist.

As it drew nearer, they could hear it. Then it came closer to the ground, and they could see clear sky above it. It grew louder and louder until Muhammad al-Asalini cried, "It's locusts, people!"

Hell's descent onto earth might have been more merciful, and within moments, everything had disappeared beneath a blackish-brown layer of millions of locusts. From every direction, people rushed out, trying to achieve a miracle that wasn't to be. With loud shrieks, they banged pots and pans, the men waved their shirts and the women their head coverings, while the children jumped up and down trying to crush as many of them as they could with their bare feet. When they were too exhausted to do any more and realized the futility of their efforts, many of the men sat down and wept over their lost fields and orchards.

※

Before the locusts' descent, the British government had sent out tax assessors in all directions. When they arrived, the crops were ready for harvest, and they asked everyone who owned a field about the area of his cultivated land. They then harvested a small, hundred-square-meter plot and used its yield as a basis for calculating the total amount of produce that a given farmer would be taxed on.

When the tax men returned a few weeks later and began calculating the taxes owed by each farmer, the people knew that disaster had struck, since they had nothing left. Some had to take the previous year's crops out of their underground granaries in order to pay what they owed, while those who had no wheat but had some cash had to go buy wheat from the market. British merchants would buy a ratl of wheat for six piasters and six milliemes, whereas they would sell the same amount for eighteen piasters.

"If anyone fails to pay, his land will be confiscated."

Knowing that all he owned was a ton of wheat and a ton of corn, Aziza's son Fayez said to his mother, "If the tax officials try to come into the house, stand at the door and tell them that a woman is inside having a baby!"

They left, then came back, then left again, then came back yet again without Aziza letting them in the door. Late one afternoon, Fayez returned from the village of Kazaza after buying a ton of wheat for eighteen dinars and a ton of corn for the same price.

The only thing that mattered to us was not to lose the land.

That year they realized that they had been set back an entire decade. Men now had to look for their sustenance outside their fields, orchards, and plantations. They had heard that the British needed laborers, since they were planning to build a military camp in Wadi al-Sarar, so many of them flocked there in search of work.

What with the plowing and the harvesting, the days raced by and the tax men began waiting for the crops on the threshing floors before they reached people's homes. To make matters worse, the British government had seized lands in a number of neighboring villages, surrounded them with barbed wire, and started building. The atmosphere was filled with the raucous din of machinery and clouds of black smoke the likes of which they had never seen before. And before they could finish asking questions about what else the British government had up its sleeve, they were told, "The British are building a military camp."

"A military camp?"

Poverty was on the rise and people could no longer survive on what their fields produced alone, so they came flocking from all over in search of work.

Naji, who was only sixteen years old, said to his father, "We'll go there and work the way everybody else is doing."

"And what will they say? That Hajj Khaled's son is working in the British military camps?"

"I was hoping not to go, but I've got no other choice, Baba."

Eyeing him despondently, he asked, "Is this really what you want to do?"

"Well, Mahmud is in Jaffa, and Musa and I are the only ones left here. And you know how bad things are!"

When the men got to the military camp, they were lined up in a long row. Then the foreman, a Jew by the name of Abu Dhib, arrived and began by choosing the strongest young men. When he had finished, he turned to leave.

"But we've come to work," Naji said.

Abu Dhib stopped in his tracks, wondering who would have the nerve to speak up this way. He turned around.

"Who said that?"

"I did," replied Naji.

"And who let a couple of little boys like you come here in the first place?"

"This is my brother, and we're not little boys. In fact, I've got a wife to support!"

"So you're not a little boy. We got that part! But how could you have a wife?"

"Since I'm not a little boy—you said so yourself—there's no reason why I couldn't have a wife!"

"You're a smart one! But this intelligence of yours won't make it any easier for you to carry bricks or dig a hole."

Naji looked a good deal younger than his age. Giving him another thoughtful look, Abu Dhib said, "We can't employ two brothers, so we can only take one of you. That's our policy."

"Take me, then," said Musa, "since I'm the oldest."

"Are you married?" Abu Dhib asked him.

"No."

"Well, then, we'll take the married one, since he's got responsibilities to meet."

The machinery made a deafening ruckus, the likes of which they'd never heard in their lives. As for the dust, it billowed up in dark clouds that quickly gathered into a nebula that totally obscured the sun.

Abu Dhib directed him to one of the barracks that were under construction. When he got there, the workers said, "What's he doing here?"

Before anyone could come up with a reply, Naji answered, "I've come to work like you."

It was hard to tell whether they were pulling a prank on him or not, but they asked him to come up, and as soon as he was atop the scaffolding, they said, "Here, take this."

He took hold of the large basket filled with cement to lift it, but instead, it took him down, and before he knew it, his feet were flailing about in the air, having turned into a pair of wings that did him no good. But before he reached the ground, they grabbed him, laughing.

"It's all right! I got it!" he kept saying as he turned to mount the scaffolding again.

However, the British foreman who was overseeing the work called him.

"Who gave you permission to work here?" he asked.

"Abu Dhib."

A few moments later, he handed Naji a piece of paper, saying, "Go give this to Abu Dhib."

("I went off like someone delivering an order for his head to be chopped off!" commented Naji to his father a few days later. "When I looked at that paper, I didn't have the slightest idea what it said. You should have taught us English, Shaykh Husni!"

"But you needed to learn Arabic first, smarty-pants!")

Abu Dhib was inside sipping some tea. Naji handed him the piece of paper. As he read it, he nodded and said, "Didn't I tell you? You'll be useless here. Or do you want us to have your blood on our hands, Mr. Married Man?"

"I can work. It's just that I'm not used to it yet."

"Sit down."

So Naji sat down.

"Pour yourself a glass of tea," Abu Dhib instructed him.

So he poured himself a glass of tea, but he didn't touch it.

"Drink it," Abu Dhib said.

So he drank it.

Then Abu Dhib wrote something on another piece of paper and handed it to Naji.

"Do you see that street they're paving over there?"

Naji nodded, thinking: What kind of a question is that? Does he think I'm blind?

"And do you see that steamroller?" he asked.

Naji nodded again, thinking: And who wouldn't see a steamroller as huge as that one?

"And behind the steamroller, do you see that building?"

Naji nodded, thinking: And how could I miss it?

"You go there and give this paper to that man."

Naji went and gave the man the paper.

"Follow me," the man said.

He led Naji to a small shack to one side of the work area. He opened the door and said, "Do you know how to light this kerosene stove?"

"No, I don't."

"All right, then," he said with a nod of the head.

The man squatted behind the kerosene stove and said to Naji, "Now watch what I do."

He lit the stove and put it out again four times in succession. Then he turned to Naji and asked, "Have you got it?"

"Yeah, I've got it."

"All right, then, let me see you light it, then put it out."

So Naji lit the stove, then put it out.

"Fine," said the man. "We've found you a suitable job, then. So now we need to get the tea ready. You fill the teapot up to here with water and bring it to a boil. Then you put a large spoonful of tea leaves in and let it boil for a little while. As for the sugar, don't add any, since everyone will add as much as he wants. Understand?"

"I understand."

Naji knew that before its two coffee shops opened, there had only been one kerosene stove in the entire village, and never before had he had any interest in knowing how it worked. The stove had belonged to Aisha al-Bazuriya, and al-Barmaki had some tea glasses and a teapot that were one of a kind, comparable only to what remained of his grandmother Munira's dishes. On clear, tranquil nights—which were a rarity—they would bring Aisha's kerosene stove together with al-Barmaki's glasses and teapot and would make the evening into a merry, memorable celebration at a time when most people had nothing but earthenware cups and wood-burning stoves. As for those who had a chance to visit the nearby cities, they knew that life there was "something else"! There, everyone had kerosene stoves, and even electricity that turned night into day!

An hour later, the man said to him, "You won't be spending all your time making tea. I'll also teach you something else."

Having said this, he led Naji over to the steamroller.

"This," he told him, "will be your second responsibility."

"And what am I supposed to do?" queried Naji uneasily.

"Well, this thing needs to drink, too! Only it doesn't drink tea."

In the hour that followed, Naji learned how to load the steamroller with firewood in order to warm it up, and to put cold water in its radiator to cool it down.

"Is everything all right?" asked the man.

"Everything's great," replied Naji happily.

However, the felicity and concord that he had achieved nearly vanished forever when Naji butted heads with the commander of the military camp!

Lover's Bridge

Sensing that Afaf was about to get away from her, Sumayya tried to reconcile the estranged sweethearts by urging Afaf's mother to intervene and put an end to the dispute.

Afaf's mother said to her, "Mahmud's going to be a famous journalist, and you couldn't find anyone better. So come to your senses, girl!"

But Afaf had decided not to back down.

Faced with this unexpected setback, Sumayya decided to resort to the forces of magic. Determined to bring them back together no matter what it cost her, she asked Musa to take her to the city of Ramla, where she met with a shaykh. After she had described the situation to him, the shaykh prepared an amulet for her, which, he assured her, would get to the root of the problem.

He said, "You bury the amulet under his fiancée's doorstep, and when she or anyone else in her family steps over it, the anger, bitterness, and lack of love will turn into their opposites as the days go by."

The most challenging task that faced Sumayya was to find a way to get to Afaf's doorstep, dig under it, and bury the amulet there.

You don't want to hear all the details, do you?

At last she managed to steal out at night and put the amulet in the place the shaykh had indicated, then slip unnoticed back into her house. Then she began watching for the results.

Because the shaykh wanted to get to the root of the problem, he had included the groom in the plan as well. To this end, he instructed Sumayya to place in her son's tea a powder he had prepared.

"Do it once, twice, three times, as often as you can," he told her.

"The tea's ready, sweetheart," Sumayya told her son, who had come home from Jaffa tired the night before.

"I'm tired," he told her. "Let me sleep some more."

A little while later, she came back again, saying, "The tea's ready, sweetheart. What a lazybones you are today!"

Mahmud got up and looked for his glasses. He found them, then sat up in bed with his back to the wall. Sumayya set the tea down beside him. He picked up the glass and took a small sip, but it didn't taste good to him, so he poured it out into the yard.

Mad with frustration, Sumayya started slapping herself on the cheeks, crying, "Why are you doing this to me?"

"What's going on, Mama? It's just a glass of tea!"

When she finally calmed down, she said, "Never mind. It's all right. I'll make you some fresh tea."

"No, I'll do it this time," Mahmud told her.

But she insisted. She went and made some fresh tea, and when she came back she found him shaving.

"I'll put it here on the windowsill," she said, "and you can drink it whenever you're ready."

Then she left the room, but watched like a hawk to see what would become of the latest glass of tea.

A few minutes later, one of their hens jumped up onto the windowsill.

"Scram!" Mahmud barked at it.

The hen fled, but on its way, it knocked the glass of tea off the windowsill, and it shattered on the ground.

Sumayya sat down and wept over her miserable luck. Then, as if to complete her tale of woe, there was a clap of thunder and a flash of lightning on the other side of the lovers' bridge, and within moments it was raining buckets.

A few days earlier, the whole village had come out together. The men had offered the ritual prayer for rain, while the women and children marched down the streets asking for rain from the heavens out of compassion for the land and its people. Umm al-Far took a hand mill, dropped a few fava beans into it and shook it like a rattle, while Aziza grabbed a rooster and hit it with her hand to get it to crow. Meanwhile, everyone sang:

O rooster with the blue comb,
I saw you drowning in the riverbed!

O Mother of Rain, send us a shower
and wet our shepherd's hoary head!

The Mother of Rain went to bring thunder,
And came back to find the stalks high as a plow,

The Mother of Rain went to bring a downpour,
and came back to find the stalks tall as a cow.

Water gushed in torrents through the streets, over the roofs, and down the hills, causing the low stone walls that separated the fields to sparkle like candles in the night. When she gazed out into the valley, it felt to Sumayya as though it had been pouring nonstop for two weeks.

Suddenly, she remembered the amulet buried under Afaf's front doorstep, and she boohooed all the more noisily.

Believe me. In those days the heavens responded to our singing more than they do to our prayers nowadays!

※

Afaf's mother came out to open up the small trough in front of her house so that the rainwater that had collected inside her yard could flow out. She tried a couple of times with the small stick she held in her hand. Suddenly, she felt something in her way. She bent down and brought it out with her hand. After examining it closely, she trembled inside, sensing that what she was holding was an amulet, and that its presence in this place was no accident.

Through the pouring rain she ran to Shaykh Husni's house. She knocked on the door.

"Is everything all right?" he asked in a concerned tone as he answered the door.

She asked him to read to her what was written in the amulet, which contained the names of Afaf and Mahmud as well as her name and the names of other members of her family. After imploring Shaykh Husni not to breathe a word about the matter, she went and burned the amulet. Once it was completely incinerated, she took the ashes and scattered them in the wind to make certain it would be unable to accomplish whatever purpose it had been made for.

In sum, the mission Sumayya had set herself ended in utter failure on both fronts.

Looking up into the sky, Afaf's mother saw two birds in flight. They hovered for a short while above the village. As they did so, they made several spectacular movements that held her heart in a trance: swooping down, then ascending again before they continued westward. Suddenly, she felt she had to spring into action herself.

"I hear your fiancé arrived from Jaffa today, and we've got to resolve this problem between you."

Afaf refused her mother's suggestion, saying, "He started it, so if he wants to end the problem, he'll have to do it himself. I'll never be the one to break!"

However, when Afaf's uncle Abd al-Rahman intervened, things changed. He went to visit Mahmud in Jaffa on what could only be termed a special mission.

"Now what is this I'm hearing about you? She's just a young girl. You yourself said you were going to educate her all by yourself, and it won't do for you to be so hard on her. However, a bit of diplomacy might go a long way. So what if she didn't memorize one of her lessons? This is a girl who has lots of responsibilities at home and works from morning to night, and you want her to be solving arithmetic problems and reading stories!"

Angered, Mahmud retorted, "You're just a reactionary!"

After a heated altercation, the uncle withdrew, shouting, "So I'm a reactionary, am I? A reactionary!"

A few more months passed. Then one day, Mahmud arrived in Hadiya and informed his family that he wanted to ask for the hand of a girl from Jaffa.

"And what about your fiancée?" they asked.

"My fiancée? It's all over between us."

"And whose hand is it that you want to ask for?"

"A girl who works with me at the newspaper."

"A city girl who writes for the newspaper?" Sumayya cried in horror.

"And what's wrong with a city girl? She's better than that ignorant one you want me to marry."

"Did we send you away for an education just so you could come back and insult us all?" demanded Hajj Khaled furiously.

"God forbid! I didn't mean it that way!"

Word got around that Mahmud was going to be engaged to a girl from Jaffa, and he insisted that his mother go to Afaf's house and ask them to return the watch, the ring, and the gold necklace. However, instead of doing as he had asked, she tried to persuade his fiancée that her boycott of Mahmud had gone on much too long and that it was time to bring it to an end. After all, she said, now that things had become so intolerable, everyone was playing with fire!

In response, Afaf decided at last to back down. The next morning, she said to her mother, "Come on, let's go visit my uncle Hajj Khaled's house!"

Her mother couldn't believe her ears. And the moment they walked into Hajj Khaled's house, it was all over: Mahmud's heart reverted to the state of blissful chaos that afflicted it whenever he laid eyes on Afaf. Afaf likewise reverted to what she had been before: the girl whose beauty surpassed that of the most ravishing movie stars, including even his favorite actress, Greta Garbo.

The General's Baton

The sun was about to rise and the sky was pure gold. In the heart of a pristine stillness that would dissipate in less than ten minutes' time, one could enjoy the marvelous pandemonium of the sparrows, which, perched happily in the trees surrounding the camp, were staging a concert with their wild array of chirps and songs.

"Good morning, Mr. Green," intoned more than one worker as Richard Green passed by.

Never once had he reciprocated their greetings. Instead, he would simply continue on his way. Strutting about like a peacock, his baton under his arm, he directed his gaze upward in such a way that anyone who saw him would have thought the workers were digging and building the hangars, storage depots, and fortifications in the sky rather than on the ground. This, at least, was how Naji described him after his return to Hadiya at the end of the week.

After his second day on the job, Naji found himself up in arms.

He had passed Mr. Green and greeted him, saying, "Good morning, Mr. Green."

But Mr. Green had made no reply. Instead, he moved away with his war decorations—which, as they were to learn later, dated back to his days as an officer in the First World War—as though he hadn't seen or heard a thing.

This irritated Naji no end, especially since he'd come to feel that a worker who had been assigned responsibility for placing firewood in the steamroller, filling it with fuel, and preparing tea for the supervisors deserved better than to be so unceremoniously ignored.

So, on the morning of his third day, he went in search of a stick. Seeing an ax handle that was slightly longer and thicker than Mr. Green's baton, Naji placed it under his arm as soon as he caught a glimpse of Mr. Green approaching from a distance. Then he proceeded to march around, imitating the gait of the military camp commander, his feet moving in perfect cadence, his chest thrust out as though he were trying to draw people's attention to the medals that covered it, and his gaze fixed on a point even higher than Mr. Green's.

Naji kept marching straight toward Mr. Green until he nearly ran into him. In the nick of time, he changed direction without addressing him with his usual morning greeting. And over the next couple of days he did the same thing.

On the morning of the third day, Mr. Green blocked Naji's path and said, "What's your name?"

"Naji al-Hajj Khaled."

Without saying another word, the commander walked away.

The next morning, Naji decided to come up alongside the commander in order to find out what had come of his efforts. And what should he find but that Mr. Green smiled at him and said, "Good morning, Mr. Naji!"

"Good morning, Mr. Green!" Naji replied.

And from that day onward, Naji felt that work conditions improved.

The thing that took everyone by surprise was that, as the weeks went by, Naji got taller and taller. No one knew whether the secret behind this growth spurt lay in his having gotten married, or in something else. However, some of them started citing examples of young men they knew who had shot up all at once after getting married, and of girls who had changed overnight. However, some of them insisted that Naji, who had never had a job before, had been more in need of employment than he had been of marriage. Hence, as soon as he started working, his height had started increasing.

However, it would be a long time before he himself discovered this. Perhaps the reason he hadn't noticed was that peculiar innocence of his, which continued to shape his personality and even his features, just as it had his mother's once upon a time. The striking resemblance between his eyes and hers, not only in appearance but in the way they moved, confirmed that Naji was truly his mother's son. It was also said that he was truly the nephew of his maternal uncle Ghazi, who had been swallowed up by a war in a place they knew nothing about.

One thing certain, though, was that the few piasters he had begun bringing back with him at the end of every week had made him more of a man in people's eyes.

The Palestinian workers received three-fourths of a piaster for every hour of work. Because fortune seemed to have smiled on Naji, he was classified as a technician's assistant, on account of which he was paid a whole piaster per hour. As for the Jewish workers, they made four times this amount. In addition, there were cars that transported the Jewish employees to Tel Aviv at the end of every week, whereas the Palestinian workers had to walk more than three hours to get back to their villages.

A man by the name of Ali, who walked with a limp, had managed to find work for himself thanks to the jobs these other men had found. He started bringing them a bag of bread every two days in return for half a piaster. However, time, which began racing by, yielded results that no one had expected, one of which was that Naji was eventually able to save up enough to buy a cow.

Then one morning, the military camp was shaken by a major event, as the guards discovered several places where the barbed wire had been cut through, as well as tire tracks where large cars had made their way into the compound.

A major investigation was opened, in the course of which everyone was interrogated. However, it yielded nothing in the end except for the fact that the Palestinians and the Jews exchanged accusations, the atmosphere grew tense, and each side started looking for ways to trip the other up.

There were a number of Palestinian policemen at the camp.

"Good morning," Naji said, greeting a Palestinian staff sergeant near one of the arms depots.

"Good morning," the soldier replied.

"My name is Naji."

"My name is Isa."

A few days later, the staff sergeant offered Naji a cigarette.

"Thanks, but I don't smoke."

"Well, it wouldn't hurt to give it a try."

As they spoke, Abu Dhib was approaching from a distance. A minute or so later, he came up to them and asked Isa for a cigarette.

"I don't have any," he replied.

"You don't have any! If you don't give me one right now, I'm going to tell the British officer over there that you smoke in front of the entrance to the ammunition warehouse."

"So that's how it is, is it? You just wait and see what I'll do."

Without warning, Isa set off his alarm bell, which brought the soldiers rushing toward him from all directions with their rifles.

Aiming his rifle at Abu Dhib, who stood there in a state of near-shock, Isa cried, "Thief! Thief!"

The soldiers began raining blows upon him from all directions, and when he fell to the ground, they began kicking him mercilessly with their heavy boots before realizing who he was.

They didn't stop there, though, since, given the punishment they had received because the barbed wire had been penetrated, they seemed to be angry at the whole world, and before long, they'd started beating up every worker they saw.

When they'd grown too weary to administer any more beatings, the soldiers led everyone away, some to one place, some to another.

311

In the guard tent, Naji found himself together with one Dawud al-'Amayira. Seeing a couple of low cots to one side of the tent, Naji went over and sat down on one of them. No sooner had he settled on the cot than he heard a British soldier scream, "Get up!"

Leaping up again, he knew something serious was going on.

Sensing danger, one of the workers said, "You all don't have any worries. As for me, my family is far away and I've got no one here except my son, though nobody knows he's my son!"

"Do you think they'll execute us?" Naji asked him.

The workers laughed.

Not long thereafter, they forced everyone out into the courtyard. Two large trucks appeared.

Mr. Carmel, the security officer, bellowed, "Line them up!"

They formed a long line.

Mr. Carmel came up to one of the workers and said to him, "Didn't I fire you before, when I caught you smoking here?"

"Yes . . . uh . . . no!"

"Who let you come back to work here?"

"I came back by myself."

He signaled to a couple of soldiers to take hold of the worker, whereupon he punched him until he fell to the ground. Then four soldiers picked him up by his arms and legs, rocked him back and forth, and sent him flying through the air onto the truck bed, where he came in for a rough landing.

Glowering at the workers, Mr. Carmel said, "One by one, to the truck!"

In order to get to the truck, they had to pass between two rows of soldiers. When the first worker had run half the gantlet, the soldiers fell mercilessly upon him with their batons, and it was only with the greatest of difficulty that he managed to get up into the truck. As for the second, he fell to the ground, so they picked him up and hurled him through the air, so he landed on the truck bed beside the first.

Not many held up under the blows, but to escape from them would have required a veritable miracle.

Knowing he couldn't possibly survive such treatment, Naji said to the worker next to him, "I'm going to make it to the truck bed so fast, no one will touch me." And that's exactly what he did. He managed to get past the two rows of soldiers without receiving a single blow. The only problem was that he was moving so fast that his forehead slammed into the truck bed, sending him reeling backward and causing a fountain of blood to gush out of his brow. Taking advantage of the soldiers' preoccupation with Naji, the rest of the workers leaped into the truck from every direction.

Everyone was held in custody until midnight, and after a number of interrogations that led nowhere, Mr. Carmel said, "You—the one who came back to work after I fired you—you'll stay here. As for the rest of you, you're going home now."

"Now?" asked Naji.

"Now," replied Mr. Carmel. "Or would you like me to keep you locked up with him?"

The truck that had brought them to where they were now took them away again, dumping them in front of one of the camp gates.

"Go on now! Go home!" roared one of the British soldiers.

Hardly had they gotten fifty meters away when they heard the sound of yelping. There was nothing they feared more than the guard dogs, who now came rushing out after them. The men took off running through the night, lit up by spotlights, and tripping and stumbling from sheer terror whenever they sensed that the dogs were about to catch up with them.

Finding themselves back where they'd started, they spread out in search of new jobs in the various projects that needed workers, from the railroad company to the postal service. Some even went to work at the ports.

Kerchiefs

Nobody had ever expected Mahmud to refuse to get on the horse.

But he said, "Under no circumstances will I get on that thing! No matter what happens!"

They tried to convince him that the wedding wouldn't mean anything unless they escorted the groom to his bride on horseback, and that his insistence on doing otherwise would bring disgrace on him and his family.

But he still refused. Pressing his small eyes shut, he stood up to his full height. Then he opened his eyes and looked up into the sky as though he were using it to cover his face so that no one could see him, and the sunlight reflected brightly off his spectacles. He'd never been too short, so why did he need to get on a horse's back? In fact, he was the tallest person in his family, and he seemed to have taken after his Aunt Anisa in that department.

"I'll walk behind the horse or in front of it; in front of the procession or behind it. But that's as far as I'm willing to go!"

"Did you go to the city so you could come back and get rid of our customs?" his father asked him.

Mahmud's grandmother Munira leaned over to Hajj Khaled and said to him, "Now, son, be broadminded about this, and let him be. When I got married, I took the veil off my face during the wedding in front of the groom. And what happened? Did the world come to an end? It seems the boy takes after his grandmother!"

"If my eldest son acts this way, how will I look people in the eye afterward?"

"As I said, it isn't the end of the world. But if you force him to do what he doesn't want to do, it *will* be the end of the world. The boy's got a head as hard as granite."

"I'll leave the wedding and go back to where I came from. And that's the end of it," Mahmud announced.

People were angry, and when they reached the small courtyard in front of the bride's house, things got even more complicated.

The bride hadn't come out as she'd been expected to, and they'd been waiting for quite some time.

Afaf was saying to her mother, "We can't delay any longer!"

"You shush!" her mother told her. "You're not going out before your uncle gets here."

Indeed, Afaf would not be able to go out without her uncle's approval. It would have been unthinkable to break these customs twice in the course of a single wedding. As for her uncle, he was incensed over the harsh words Mahmud had spoken to him.

Muhammad Shahada, Iliya Radhi, Hajj Jum'a, and Abu Sunbul went and pleaded with him to come with them and solve the problem. He refused.

They waited on the bride's doorstep for another half hour, which felt more like a month.

"If the bride doesn't come out right now, I'm turning around and going back to Jaffa."

"You be quiet," Hajj Khaled said to him. "At least the girl is thinking about her uncle and doesn't want to hurt him the way you've hurt us!"

The uncle's wife then said, "I'll go talk to him."

They knew that he was exceedingly fond of his wife, so fond that he had been willing to leave his hometown and settle in Jaffa just for her sake.

She went inside the house, where he sat pouting in a corner like a little boy.

"Now, now, Abd al-Rahman! Would you really leave your sister's only daughter in the lurch on her wedding day?"

Coming closer, she kissed his head, then his face. She lifted his chin and looked into his eyes. "Don't my wishes mean anything to you?" she asked.

Nodding, he got up. She took him by the hand and walked him toward the door. After they'd left the house, he hesitated, saying, "Wait just a minute."

He went back inside, and quickly came out again. When they saw him with her, everyone realized that there's nothing too hard for a city girl!

The bride's uncle drew a revolver and started shooting into the air. Filled with a mixture of rage, joy, displeasure, and spite, he kept shooting into the air all the way up to the bride's doorstep.

Once he reached the house, he stopped, put the revolver away, and turned toward the people, who proceeded to sing more and more loudly. Then, without saying a word, he disappeared into the courtyard, and shortly thereafter, he reappeared with the bride, having wrapped her in his cloak.

After lunch, the groom approached on foot in front of Hamdaniya, who had been duly adorned for the occasion, and not long thereafter, the bride arrived in a litter that rendered her completely invisible.

The people escorted the two of them from one street to another to the accompaniment of joyous song. The bride's trousseau had been placed on a round tray made from woven straw, which the women passed back and forth among themselves, taking turns carrying it on their heads as they danced. As the wedding procession moved along, one of the young men came up and tied his kerchief onto the camel's bridle, saying, "This belongs to Hashem Shahada." He was followed by another young man, who tied his kerchief to the first one as he said, "This belongs to Sa'di Yunus." And so it went, until there was a long chain of kerchiefs trailing along behind the camel.

When it appeared that no one else would be coming forward to add a new kerchief to the chain, a dispute arose over who was most entitled to the honor of hosting the wedding dinner that night. They argued, their voices growing louder and louder, until one of them suggested that they find someone who could arbitrate the dispute. The person chosen to settle such a dispute would generally be an elder of the town who was familiar with the minutest details of the town and its history.

It was the young men who were fighting for the chance to host the dinner. However, they were being urged on by their fathers, who wanted to teach them to be bold and gallant.

They approached Shaykh Husni and asked him to be their arbiter. Then they began presenting their arguments, each in turn.

One of them said, "Please let me host the bridal dinner! After all, I was the first one to tie my kerchief to the camel's bridle."

"Please, Shaykh Husni, I owe the bride's family a favor, since I'm their in-law. For God's sake, let me host the dinner for the bride!"

The list of arguments was as long as the chain of kerchiefs. At last, Shaykh Husni took a deep breath, looked into their faces again, and said, "The dinner will be hosted by Sami al-Abd."

The young men turned and, without saying a word, went and removed their respective kerchiefs from the chain until the only one left was the one that belonged to Sami al-Abd. Grasping the camel's reins, he led it a distance of fifty or sixty meters to a place where everyone could see and hear him.

In a stentorian voice, he called out, "The bridal dinner will be at our house this evening. And hearty congratulations to the bride and groom!"

Then he stepped back, handed the reins to someone who could go on leading the camel around the village, and went off to prepare the dinner.

Meanwhile, the wedding procession continued down the streets. Whenever it passed in front of one of the many shops that had come to rival that of Abu Ribhi, its owner would throw candy on the passersby, and on everything else as well. The singing and celebrating went on into the wee hours of the morning. In fact, they used up fifty bundles of firewood so that people could go on seeing each other's faces until at last they led the bride and groom back to their house.

In any case, we got married. He went back to Jaffa and I stayed in Hadiya. In the beginning he would bring stories that were sadder than the ones he'd brought me before. They would make me cry so hard my eyes would get all red and puffy. But the strange thing was that he stopped asking me whether I'd read them or not!

A Gunshot at Dawn

I t was as though it had dropped out of the sky. They woke up one morning and found it covering the top of the western hill with houses, barbed wire, and high wooden towers.

They called out to each other in silence, as though they had lost the ability to speak, and as the moments passed, the people of Hadiya gathered around, unable to believe their eyes.

They knew that what they were seeing was a settlement. But how could the Jews have built it overnight, just like that? How could they have failed to hear a sound? How was it that no dog had barked, no horse had neighed, and no one had wakened to the ruckus that would have to have been produced by the erection of such a huge thing?

As the sun rose higher, they realized that the houses had not been built where they now stood. Rather, they were prefabricated structures that had been brought from some distant location.

By midmorning, one of the shepherds had gotten up the courage to approach the barbed wire surrounding the settlement. A shot rent the stillness of the horizon, shattering their day and scattering the sheep and goats in all directions. The only one who knew which way he was headed was the shepherd, who kept running until he stopped in front of Hajj Khaled.

Hajj Khaled glanced at him, then looked again into the distance in an attempt to determine where the shot had come from. He saw no one.

More than one man disappeared, and when they returned, they were carrying axes, scythes, and knifes, but Hajj Khaled gestured to them to calm down. This didn't sit well with Hajj Sabri al-Najjar, who for quite some time had been demanding his right to be the village elder, in view of the fact that his clan was now the largest in the village and owned the most land.

"Are we going to stay calm until we wake up one of these days and find them in our backyards?" he roared.

"That won't happen, God willing," replied Hajj Khaled.

"So what can you do just standing there?"

"Nothing at all. I can't do any more than you could if you tried to make it over there in this blazing sun."

For a moment, things nearly turned catastrophic. Hajj Sabri al-Najjar came toward Hajj Khaled waving his fist and shouting, "How dare you insult me like this in front of everyone?"

But before he could do any more, people came rushing forward and blocked his way.

"The last thing we need is to start slaughtering each other while those people look on," reasoned Hajj Khaled, pointing in the direction of the settlement.

"What's gone will never come back," bellowed Hajj Sabri.

At that moment, Karim, Hajj Sabri's eldest son, intervened. To everyone's amazement, he said to his father, "It isn't proper for you to speak this way to Hajj Khaled."

Then, to their shock and dismay, his father slapped him.

This event marked the pinnacle of al-Najjar's madness. From that day onward, his heart would be filled with an unquenchable hatred for Hajj Khaled, who had forced him to lose his temper and strike his son, who was nearly thirty years old at the time, in public.

Hajj Khaled looked over at Karim as though he were embracing him with his eyes.

As for Karim, he moved away without saying another word.

"You chose a fine time to say a thing like that!" Hajj Khaled said to al-Najjar.

But before things could deteriorate further, they heard the sound of cars approaching in the distance. They turned together in the direction of the sound, and there they saw three British army jeeps trundling down the long black road that had been opened ten years earlier to connect Hadiya with Ramla to the north, Gaza to the southwest, and Jerusalem to the east.

Before the jeeps had pulled up, all the village's makeshift weapons had disappeared.

"From now on you'll have new neighbors, and you'll have to respect their presence. No one will be allowed to come within a hundred meters of the barbed wire, and if anyone tries to do so, he'll have to bear the consequences. These lands don't belong to you. They belong to the state, and none of you has the right to object to what the government does with what it owns."

These words were uttered with a deadly calm by Officer Edward Peterson,* who then turned back to the jeep as though he expected no reply. No sooner had he taken his place again in the front seat of the first vehicle than all three jeeps continued on their way, as though the officer were going to be repeating the same words to the scores of other villages along the road.†

---

* Born in India in 1893, Peterson was educated at home by his family, who belonged to the puritanically minded Plymouth Brethren. Peterson developed an overwhelming fascination with England's military history. Oliver Cromwell (1599–1658), considered by some to have been a military dictator, and Charles Gordon (1833–85), who had served as Governor-General of Sudan, were his principal heroes. His favorite activities were solitary ones, such as swimming, horseback riding, and archery. After completing his military training, he delved into the study of the Arabic language and became an officer in the "Sudanese Defense Force." Following his return to England, he awaited some event that would deliver him from his monotonous work as a petty artillery officer, and after some time, events that had erupted in the East took him to Palestine. His secret passion, of which he made no mention in any of his autobiographical works, was the writing of poetry.

† That night, Peterson wrote: The gray winds scatter white words. / Where are you? /

Two hours later, the only person who remained was Hajj Khaled, who hadn't budged from his place. His gaze was fixed on the houses that had descended like a nightmare from the sky, and his thoughts churned in his head in search of an answer to a burdensome question.

Suddenly, a hand patted his shoulder.

"What you see isn't a woman who will come to you eventually if you stand here waiting for her in the hot sun!"

Without turning around, he recognized the voice as that of his aunt Anisa, whose frame had grown thinner over the years and her hair whiter. Yet everyone was certain that she grew taller with every passing year.

The horizon is a perforated cap out of which Autumn pours. / Who are you? /
A summer cloud, a lunatic moon, or a rendezvous confirmed five times with no one?

And He Cried,
"The Bastard!"

Peterson had arrived in Jerusalem with the rank of lieutenant in the British police force, and it wasn't long before his name became a veritable nightmare. The mere act of getting near him or alongside him meant one thing only: probable death. During the 1929 uprising, he became so infamous that as far as most people were concerned, he was synonymous with the devil.

Without warning, he would draw his gun and kill a passerby, then fall upon the blood-soaked corpse with blows of the fist. When the police forces arrived, they would find him kicking the dead man and cursing him to high heaven.

"The bastard!" he would shriek. "He tried to grab my rifle!"

The other policemen would try to tear him away from the corpse, but no sooner had he moved away from it than he would launch another attack on it as though he were engaged in a battle with a living person.

"So you want the rifle, do you, you bastard? Get up and take it, then!"*

One day a British police sergeant was preparing to go out to bring a man by the name of Namir al-Tayri to the police station in order to get a statement from him concerning the shooting of a British policeman in a passenger bus that had been headed for Ramla. However, Peterson surprised him by saying, "I'll go get him myself."

After Peterson had headed out, the sergeant—a ruddy, freckled man—turned to his buddies and said, "May he rest in peace."

"Who? Peterson?"

"No, al-Tayri."

On the day of the shooting, al-Tayri had been sitting next to the window, sharing a seat with the policeman. So when the policeman was shot, al-Tayri found himself spattered with blood and fragments of the slain policeman's brain.

The bus came to a sudden halt, as though the bullet had pinned the driver's foot to the brake pedal. The passengers charged frantically toward the bus's two doors, while some of them jumped out the windows without a thought for what might befall them as a result. As for Namir al-Tayri, he remained trapped beneath the weight of the heavy body that pinned him to the window.

They watched the assailant, who had planned the operation down to the last detail, make off into the forests of Bab al-Wad. However, most of them refrained from fleeing, for fear that they'd be suspected of having had a part in the crime. With Namir al-Tayri still frozen in place, British police and army forces arrived on the scene and boarded the bus. By this time his clothes were stuck to those of the slain man, and his face and hands were covered with dried blood.

At long last, the bus returned to Jerusalem carrying the witnesses to the crime, from whom the police had gotten no useful information. All of them, including the driver, who had seen everything in his rearview mirror, told the same story. According to all the witnesses, the attacker had had

---

* That night, Peterson wrote: No one will ever love you as I do, neither the bullet nor the rose. / No one will ever love you as I do, neither the tiger nor the gazelle. / No one will ever love you as I do. / With my blood I record it, and with others' too!

his face concealed with a keffiyeh. He had been of medium height, with a husky voice, and he had said, "Bear witness, all of you, that what I did today was in vengeance for the deaths of the martyrs who were executed by the mandate authorities yesterday."*

Of all the witnesses, Namir al-Tayri had been the least capable of providing details, since the assailant had approached from the back of the bus, and because the sound of the gunfire, not to mention the element of surprise, had prevented him from hearing the words that other passengers had heard. In the end they released everyone but the bus driver, who, according to the officer assigned to the investigation, "shouldn't have stopped before reaching the nearest army or police checkpoint."

This was one of a number of serious incidents that had begun to take place with greater frequency due to the increasing waves of executions, as well as the waves of Jewish immigration that had left the entire country in a state of unrest.

Edward Peterson knocked on Namir al-Tayri's door.

When his wife came out, he said, with a politeness that took her quite by surprise, "If Mr. Namir is home, he's kindly requested to accompany me to the police station in order to complete his testimony."

"Yes, he's home," she replied.

Then, even more politely, he said, "I hope I haven't disturbed you by coming at such an early hour."

"No, not at all," she replied, her hand trembling behind the door.

---

* The British police forces had arrested twenty-six young Palestinian men who had taken part in the Western Wall Uprising in Jerusalem in 1929. These young men had been sentenced to death in a mock trial, after which the sentences of all of but three of them were commuted to life imprisonment. Muhammad Jamjum, Fu'ad Hijazi, and Ata al-Zir were executed at Acre Prison on 17 June 1930. (The number of executions that took place over the course of six years under the British in Palestine alone was greater than the number that took place in the entire Ottoman Empire under the rule of Sultan Abd al-Hamed, which lasted for more than thirty years, and this despite the fact that Abd al-Hamed was viewed as an unjust, tyrannical ruler, while the British administrators were generally seen to be constitutional, prudent, and just.)

"He won't be long. I'll see to it personally that he gets back home as quickly as possible."

Before they had gotten any distance from the house, Peterson bent down and pretended to tighten his shoelace. In this way he allowed Namir to get a few steps ahead of him, thereby giving himself the chance to draw his gun.

Aiming with a frigid indifference, he fired at his victim from behind, and Namir al-Tayri fell on his face.

Lunging at Namir's bleeding body, Peterson began kicking him. Namir thrashed about, attempting to fend off the blows, at which point Peterson realized that a single shot might not always be sufficient. As he fired the second bullet, he screamed, "Die, you bastard! Die!"

"He tried to steal my rifle and make off with it! He wanted to kill me!" he kept saying over and over, when passersby and police gathered around.

Things came to a head when a patrol led by Peterson intercepted a young man by the name of Fadl al-Jabi and searched him. They found that he was carrying a picture that showed him holding a rifle, so they shot him dead.

Less than a year later, Peterson was promoted, given a new star, and transferred when it became clear to the leadership that if he wasn't killed in an act of sabotage, he was bound to be killed in an act of revenge.

The Doors of the Wind

Never had March weather been as unpredictable as it was that year. It mystified everyone: no sooner had the sun come out than it would disappear suddenly behind a cloud and it would start raining cats and dogs. Then it would stop raining and the sun would come out again, hotter than ever. Beneath their feet in the foothills, the flowers would bloom, then wither before their very eyes, as if all the seasons of the year had come together in a single day.

"We're the ones fighting the British! So what do you need with these rifles?" barked Abd al-Latif al-Hamdi's men, after forcing the women to show them where five of their husbands' rifles were hidden.

It wasn't the first time his men had done something like this. But this time they'd gone too far. After all, it was no small thing for them to conduct themselves this way toward the women in the absence of their menfolk and to take these rifles from them.

Habbab's story wasn't over yet, and women were still dressed in mourning when a caravan of military vehicles stopped in front of his house

one day. Al-Hamdi got out of one of the vehicles, accompanied by a number of British officers. The following morning, the vehicles departed, and
al-Hamdi became the owner of the house.

There was a lot of speculation about the incident, but the fact was that
no one knew how Habbab's house came to belong to al-Hamdi. Some said
the house had belonged to the Ottoman state. Others said that al-Hamdi
had bought it from Habbab's heirs. Still others said the British had been
planning to make it into an army headquarters, but that al-Hamdi had
convinced them that he could keep the area under control on his own,
thereby preventing any direct clashes between them and the local people.

He didn't have to do much to ensure the capitulation of five of the
area's villages, since they had been under Habbab's thumb before, and
were in the worst straits they had seen since the Turks' departure.

Neighboring villages were grouped together as a single unit, whether
voluntarily or under compulsion, and placed under the authority of an
elder known as a 'division leader.'

"You live in this area, so you have to be part of our division," al-Hamdi
said to them.

The men of Hadiya came together and decided that the village
wouldn't submit to his authority. Everyone in the region knew he was a
tyrant and that he had been one of the British authorities' yes-men ever
since their arrival. It was even said that when he had fought alongside the
Turks in Gaza and saw that the advancing British armies were about to
win the day, he began cheering, "Long live Great Britain!" Then he aimed
his shotgun at his comrades in the trench and mowed them all down.

"This isn't a village of children who need a caretaker," declared Hajj
Mahmud. "We held out for years under the Turks without being answerable to anyone, and we'll do the same under the British. We're ready and
willing to work together with you for the good of all. As for our being under
your command, it won't happen."

"Is that the last thing you have to say?" asked al-Hamdi.

"This was the first thing we had to say long ago, and it's also the last."

"You're playing with fire, then."

"If that's all we have to play with, then that's what we'll choose."

At that al-Hamdi rose to his feet and walked over to his horse. He was followed by his men, armed with rifles that everyone knew the British had supplied.

"You've opened a door to the wind that you'll never be able to close."

"If the winds blow, they won't blow on us alone."

Before the clouds of dust stirred up by al-Hamdi's horses had disappeared from the horizon, Father Theodorus made an appearance. He didn't need anyone to explain a thing to him. He said, "As long as the monastery's in the village, no one would dare lay hands on any of its land."

However, two days later, al-Hamdi raided the village's upland pastures and took them over, then annexed them to the land that belonged to one of the villages under his control.

Al-Hamdi said to his men, "As long as they refuse to join us, this land belongs to you."

Hajj Mahmud went to see Father Theodorus. "So is this the protection you were talking about?" he demanded.

"I went myself to see the British, and they told me, 'If these lands belong to them, then let them bring the deeds that prove it.'"

"And can al-Hamdi produce deeds that prove his claim to the land?"

"It's his word against yours. And you know better than anyone else that the British will take his word over yours."

"Anybody who hears you talking this way will say you're with him, not us."

Hadiya had been too weak to stand up against Abd al-Latif al-Hamdi, so it licked its wounds in silence. Then, before a month was out, a band of thieves waylaid Hajj Mahmud and his men as they were on their way back from a trip to Ramla. After stripping them of their money and the goods they had bought, they shot and killed them. And, as everyone knew they would, the investigations conducted by the British concluded that there was no way to determine who had committed the crime, and the case was closed. Many people in the village realized that al-Hamdi and his men had had a hand in shedding the blood that had flowed in those valleys. But, as people kept saying, who could prove it when the judge was the enemy?

The fact that al-Hamdi had managed to gain access to the village's rifles was significant.

The men of the village came to Hajj Khaled and said, "Here we are, coming to you as usual. And we're asking you what the solution is."

Kneading his brow with the fingers of his left hand, he looked intently at them and said, "Don't worry. Your rifles will be delivered to your doorsteps."

"But it was Abd al-Latif al-Hamdi's men who took them!"

"It's for this very reason that you have to get them back."

Enough was enough, as they say. As he stood gazing out at the settlement on the western hill, Hajj Khaled knew that the rifles were all the village people had left.

"One of you go get Fayez."

In a few moments, Fayez arrived. For a long time, he had been the best rifle repairman in the whole region, having gained experience due to an intense fondness for weapons that had been with him all his life.

You understand, of course, that it was happening in secret!

"How many rifles do you have, son?" Hajj Khaled asked him.

"Lots of them," he told his uncle as he glanced nervously about him.

"Don't worry," Hajj Khaled reassured him. "And how many rifles do al-Hamdi's villages have?"

"Around ten, maybe."

"Go get them and bring them here. When their owners come to get them, tell them they're with me."

Hajj Khaled gestured to a number of the men to go help him.

Nothing could have delighted Fayez more than the sound of bullets being fired again from those long-unused rifles! Nothing could have delighted him more than to see those rifles come back to life again!

And, as Hajj Khaled had expected, it wasn't long before the rifles' owners came looking for them.

"They're safe and sound! But Hajj Khaled wants you," Fayez told them.

"Pour them some coffee and get their lunch ready for them," said Hajj Khaled.

"Bless you, Hajj, but we're in a hurry."

"Men from al-Hamdi's camp went into a number of houses on the outskirts of town when their menfolk weren't there and forced the women to show them where our rifles were hidden. Then they took five of them. I'm not demanding that they be punished for coming into our houses in our absence, even though it was a serious offense. However, I want you to go to al-Hamdi and tell him that I won't return your rifles unless you return the five rifles you took from us."

"But, Hajj, we don't know anything about what happened. Besides, what his men do isn't our fault!"

"I know that. But it *is* your fault that you've let such a tyrant lord it over you."

The men fell silent, pained by the last thing he had said. Without another word, they rose to leave.

Never had they seen al-Hamdi as furious as he was when they delivered Hajj Khaled's message to him that day. However, he suddenly and inexplicably changed his tune, saying, "Go to him and tell him that we'll return his rifles. You have my word."

The men went back to Hajj Khaled.

"I promise to return your rifles to you as soon as he returns our rifles to us. Now you go back to al-Hamdi and tell him that men who go into other people's houses when their menfolk aren't there aren't real men, and if you don't return our rifles, then the matter won't stop at just returning the rifles. After all, where you're concerned, Hadiya is like the Suez Canal: you've got to pass through it if you want to go on with your lives."

No reply was forthcoming, so Hajj Khaled said, "Nobody can say we haven't done all we could."

The people of the region used to call this time of year 'sheep season,' since it was the time when people would come to the Thursday market in Hadiya to sell their sheep. Many of them would schedule their sons' and daughters' weddings, or the building of new houses, for this time of year. In any case, as a number of men from the villages who were subject to al-Hamdi's authority were on their way to Hadiya's market, they were intercepted by horsemen from Hadiya. The horsemen seized their sheep, saying, "If you want them back, go to al-Hamdi and tell him that we did what we did today in the name of Hajj Khaled."

The villages of the region knew quite well that Hajj Khaled was an upright man who had never been known to act unjustly toward anyone or deprive anyone of his rights. So people rose up against al-Hamdi. "For God's sake, give back to them what belongs to them, Abd al-Latif!" they told him. "How long are we going to go on paying for what your armed men do?" As for Hajj Khaled, he had no choice but incite the villages who were kowtowing to al-Hamdi to rise up against him. He realized that these people, whom he had known and who had known him for so long, were good deep down!

A few days later, someone arrived in Hadiya with the five rifles. Hajj Khaled inspected them, then sent for their owners. Four of them recognized their rifles and took them. However, one of them said, "That isn't my rifle."

"Bring us the original rifle, and then you can come get your rifles and your sheep," Hajj Khaled told them.

"So you're holding ten rifles and hundreds of sheep for the sake of a single rifle?" asked one of al-Hamdi's men indignantly.

"No. I'm holding ten rifles and hundreds of sheep for the sake of what's right," he replied.

The following morning, they returned with the original rifle.

"You can take what's yours now that we have what's ours."

However, as the days passed, al-Hamdi was consumed increasingly by bitterness and hatred, and the people of Hadiya had no peace of mind. They referred to his behavior as 'British policy,' which, when it appeared to be most lenient, was actually engaged in some of its worst cruelty.

Silent Fire

The people of Hadiya woke one morning to find that the barbed wire around the neighboring settlement had been moved more than two hundred meters, swallowing up part of their land and the northern and southern pasturelands that surrounded it. When they went there to touch with their hands what their eyes were seeing, they were fired at along the entire length of the western front. They went down on their stomachs or hid behind the nearest hillock. They tried to determine exactly where the shots were coming from, but they didn't see a single body moving on the other side.

They retreated.

They knew they were up against a major problem, and that in a few weeks' time they would need to go out into their fields to harvest the wheat on the plains that ran parallel to the wires. They realized that any problem that came up now might deprive them of the fruits of their hard work.

That evening, some of the men were sitting in Muhammad Shahada's and Shakir Muhanna's coffee shops to hear the news, switching from one station to another. They were delighted when they heard the 'Palestine

Radio Station,' which was being inaugurated as they listened, broadcasting out of Ramallah. Not long afterward, however, they heard a speech being delivered in Hebrew. It came as a total shock to them.

"This means that from now on, the Jews will be in all our houses!" commented Muhammad Shahada, and he angrily turned the radio off.*

The sun began scorching the ears of grain, the ears of grain that seemed more luxuriant to them than they had been in a long time. The plants were so tall that if a rider passed through the wheat fields on horseback, he could easily tie two stalks together over his saddle.

They hadn't reached the edges of the fields yet when the settlement began to fire on them. They retreated. When they went to the headquarters of the British officer Edward Peterson, he said heatedly, "We can't send an army patrol out with anybody who wants to harvest his field!"

They looked in the direction of the settlement, but saw no movement that indicated there was someone lying in wait for them. The silence was so complete, they could have heard the tiniest of God's creatures in that vast expanse. Then they rushed out to the fields with their scythes and started working with all their might. However, before they had worked their way more than three meters into the field, shots rang out again, and the people scattered in all directions.

They went to Peterson again, only to meet with the same response, and they came away feeling more hopeless than they had felt before they went.

At sundown, a number of men gathered in Hajj Khaled's guesthouse. Shaykh Husni, the imam at the mosque, was there, as well as al-Barmaki, who had been reduced by the passing of the years and the loss of his son. For fear of hearing words of reproach from people in Hajj Sabri al-Najjar's

---

* That same day, High Commissioner Sir Arthur Wauchope opened the station, and speeches were broadcast in English, Arabic, and Hebrew. This celebration I considered to be a funeral. It was the most powerful warning sign that a Jewish national homeland would be established in Palestine. One day Hebrew starts to compete with Arabic, and the next day it casts it out of Palestine! This wasn't mere pessimism, either. As evidence of the gloomy future that awaited the Palestinians, one need only recall that His Eminence the Mufti Hajj Amin al-Husayni, head of the Islamic Council at that time, actually attended this celebration. How could he and others have forgotten the decision to boycott such events?

334

clan, Hajj Khaled sent them word, inviting them to attend the meeting. Shakir Muhanna and some other men came, while still others stayed behind. As for Hajj Sabri al-Najjar, he considered an invitation to Hajj Khaled's guesthouse as tantamount to an insult: why doesn't he come to us rather than making us drag ourselves over there? Does he think he's better than we are?

What was happening all over Palestine was no secret. What was happening in Hadiya was happening in scores of other villages as well. However, the fire had reached the hem of their village's robe this time.

They arrived at nothing worth mentioning. Some of the men admitted that they felt vulnerable and helpless, like a defenseless man facing someone armed to the teeth. They talked about the British protection of the Jewish settlements, about an enemy they hadn't yet been able to see, about how easy it was for this enemy to detect anyone who tried to get close to the barbed wire, and about how their village would immediately come under suspicion if they took any action against the settlement. However, many were against this way of thinking.

"In the end," Fayez told them, "you've got to remember that whatever is beyond that barbed wire isn't a bunch of phantoms. If we're silent today, Hadiya will end up inside the barbed wire tomorrow. And you know very well what these settlements are doing on other people's lands."

Hajj Khaled held his peace, and when everyone else finished speaking, Shakir Muhanna asked him, "What do you say, Hajj Khaled?"

Shaykh Husni replied in his stead, "What is there to say when we know that anything any of us does will doom everyone to destruction?"

Shakir Muhanna repeated his question as though he hadn't heard what Shaykh Husni had said.

Looking at them intently, Hajj Khaled kneaded his brow with the fingers of his left hand and said, "We'll see what the coming days bring."

That night, the people of Hadiya woke to find flames all around them, turning the night into day. Fire was consuming the wheat fields in a scene the likes of which they had never seen before, and crueler than any they would see until that long black day, many years later, that no one could ever have imagined. In the midst of the huge conflagration, the settlement appeared totally exposed, and for the first time they were able to see the shadows of people moving quickly from place to place among the prefabricated houses and near the barbed wire.

The fact that there was little wind caused the fields to burn slowly, while the silence of the night swallowed up the tears that welled up in people's eyes.

Soldiers' vehicles began to approach in the distance, and when they arrived, Officer Edward Peterson got out in a rage.

"Which of you set this fire?" he bellowed.

"Do you think any of us would set fire to his own property? The people over there are the only ones who could have done it."

"No. You're the ones who set fire to the fields so that the settlement would go up in flames with them."

"Look into people's eyes, and you'll know that the person who did this couldn't possibly be one of us."

The vehicles turned and headed up the hill toward the settlement. However, none of the villagers could be sure whether they had put out their lamps or not, so bright was the blaze that rose furiously toward the sky.

When the sun began slowly rising, there was nothing left on the plain but a few small blazes and charred earth.

"On these scorched lands, they'll never reap anything but a black harvest," predicted Hajj Khaled.

"Is this your answer to my question?" Shakir Muhanna wanted to know.

"I hope to God it will be everyone's answer."

That High Noon

In one of the villages under al-Hamdi's control, there was a judge by the name of Mas'ud al-Hattab, whose fame had begun to spread all over Palestine. Within a short time he had become a prominent judge who was able to resolve the most serious issues wreaking havoc in the villages, from land disputes and violations of honor to—rare though these were—murder cases. Al-Hamdi was beginning to feel himself in great danger, since he realized that the day was soon coming when this judge would vie with him for his position of leadership. Consequently, he set up an ambush for him when he was on his way back from overseeing the settlement of a major dispute. When he was killed, the case he had adjudicated was reopened, and the party in whose favor he had ruled accused the other party of murdering the judge because the outcome hadn't been to his liking. As a result, reprisals began knocking at people's doors and flooding the hills and valleys with blood once again.

Al-Hamdi had never thought he would be able to kill so many birds with one stone until he saw the outcome of the bullet that had gone through the judge's heart.

He announced a forty-day mourning period. He also announced that from that day on he would treat the judge's children as his own, and that the hand that had pulled the trigger would be cut into three parts. When the wake was over some days later, al-Hamdi tried to resolve the case on which Judge Mas'ud had ruled. In order to do so, he would have to have both parties appear against their will, then force them to accept the judge's verdict out of respect for his blood that had been shed on their account!

When the judge's sons grew up, they had a part in every step al-Hamdi took. One day, he called for one of them and said to him, "You know you're like my own son."

"Yes, Uncle!"

"I'd like you to do something for me. But I swear to God, it isn't because I've been there for you since you were orphaned so many years ago!"

"Of course not, Uncle."

"You can tell me you don't want to do this and I won't be angry. It won't have any effect on the way I feel toward you."

"You give the order, and we'll carry it out, Uncle!"

Al-Hamdi fell silent for a little while, looking as though all the cares of the world had been deposited on his shoulders.

Then he said, "Would you allow anyone to insult me?"

"God forbid, Uncle!"

"Have you heard about what Hajj Khaled did to me?"

"Who hasn't heard about it, Uncle? I mean, of course I have."

"I think you know what my request is now. So shall I assume you're going to carry it out?"

"Whatever you say, Uncle."

"No, I don't want to tell you what to do about this issue. Rather, I want you to do what you ought to do because you yourself believe you should."

One blistering noon hour, with a sun overhead that looked like a searing live coal, the judge's son arrived in Hadiya as a guest. When Hajj Khaled learned of his arrival, he dropped everything he was doing and rushed out to receive him with a group of men.

The visitor realized it would be impossible to carry out his mission at that moment.

"The coffee, Hamdan. And lunch for the guest, men."

"I can't stay long, but I was in the neighborhood, so I thought: It wouldn't do for me be so close by without coming to say hello to Hajj Khaled and to see how things are faring with you since your fields were burned."

"A thoroughbred, and the son of a thoroughbred. Your father was one of a kind: a true man of Palestine."

For two full hours Hajj Khaled did nothing but tell stories about Judge Mas'ud, his wisdom, and the cases he had resolved after the British had been unable to do so. He talked about the way the British High Commissioner himself had appealed to Judge Mas'ud to break up disputes that the British government had been unable to do anything about.

As the moments passed, the young man's sense of honor was rekindled as he listened to all these things about his father from the very person he wanted to kill.

"Could I kill a man who loved and respected my father this much? Could I kill a man who's treated me with such respect? Could I kill a man who honors his guest and who knows people's true worth?"

When he rose after lunch to be on his way, Hajj Khaled got up and embraced him affectionately, as though he were his own son.

Their bodies were in such close proximity, there would have been nothing to prevent him from carrying out the task he had been assigned. But instead of doing so, he whispered in Hajj Khaled's ear: "Be careful. Al-Hamdi sent me to kill you, and if I don't do it, someone else will. So be on your guard."

Less than a week later, a group of al-Hamdi's men went out and surrounded the judge's son in the place where his father had been killed.

Realizing what was happening, he said to them, "I knew he would kill me here, and nowhere else. Tell Abd al-Latif that everyone knows now that he has my father's blood on his hands."

He was showered with bullets from three directions, but he kept standing. They shot him again, and he kept standing. Alarmed now, for a few moments they were afraid he wasn't going to die. Wanting to make certain that the blood he saw was real, one of them dared to take a few timorous steps in his direction, touched the blood, and said, "It's real, all right." Then, in another bold move, he pushed the bullet-riddled body with the butt of his rifle, and it fell to the ground.

That Night

Seven nights later, Hadiya woke to find a conflagration consuming the houses of the settlement, and it lit up the darkness till the break of dawn.*

Everyone realized the seriousness of the situation, but they contented themselves with silence, and waited on their doorsteps to see what the morrow would bring.

---

* Vladimir Jabotinsky (d. 1940), one of the founders of the revisionist Zionist movement, defended the Palestinian people and the notion that Palestine is their national homeland. However, when he searched for a counterpart to the Palestinians, the only peoples he saw fit for comparison were the Native Americans and the Aztecs, who were annihilated by invaders. When he drew this parallel, he gave himself the right to invade, and the victim the option of death as he defends himself. Jabotinsky wrote, "Any native people—it's all the same whether they are civilized or savage—views their country as their national home, of which they will always be the complete masters. They will not voluntarily allow, not only a new master, but even a new partner. And so it is for the Arabs. Compromisers in our midst attempt to convince us that the Arabs are some kind of fools who can be tricked . . . [and] who will abandon their birth right to Palestine for cultural and economic gains. I flatly reject this assessment of the Palestinian Arabs. Culturally they are 500 years behind us, spiritually they do not have our endurance or our strength of will, but this exhausts all of the internal

Hardly had dawn broken when a British military force had surrounded the village on all sides.

Edward Peterson stood before Hajj Khaled and said to him, "Who set the settlement on fire?"

"And who told you that I would have the answer to such a question?"

"No one but one of you could have done this."

"All of Palestine is going up in flames. So why do you hold us responsible?"

"Because the settlement is here on your land."

"See? You've said it yourself: 'our land.' So how can you ask us to be its protectors?"

"I'm not asking you to be its protectors. I'm asking you who set it on fire."

"No one from around here. Of that I can assure you."

Peterson contemplated the faces his soldiers had gathered against the walls of the houses.

"So you don't want to tell us the truth," he said to Hajj Khaled.

"The truth is what I'm telling you: we had nothing to do with this fire."

The officer did an about-face and headed toward the rows of men who had been pinned to the walls by his soldiers' rifles. Suddenly, he raised his hand and began pointing. No sooner had his hand stopped in front of one of the men than the soldiers led him aside.

There were now only a few elderly men left. When he had chosen the ones he wanted, he aimed his finger at Hajj Khaled. He made his hand into the shape of a pistol, and they heard him say, "Bo-o-om!"

Before long, Hajj Khaled had joined the other men of the village, who tried to protest. However, Hajj Khaled signaled to them to be still.

---

differences. . . . They look upon Palestine with the same instinctive love and true fervour that any Aztec looked upon his Mexico or any Sioux looked upon the prairie . . . this childish fantasy of our 'Arabo-philes' comes from some kind of contempt for the Arab people . . . [that] this race [is] a rabble ready to be bribed or sell out their homeland for a railroad network," from "The Iron Wall (We and the Arabs)," *Rasswyet*, 14 November 1923, quoted in *The Persistence of the Palestinian Question: Essays on Zionism and the Palestinians* (London: Routledge, 2006), pp. 4–5.

An armored car twenty meters away was observing what was happening.

Walking up to Hajj Khaled and planting himself directly in front of him, Peterson said, "You haven't given me the names of the men who aren't here."

"You haven't asked me to."

"Well, I'm asking you now."

"Lots of men are outside the village buying and selling."

"And who are they?"

"There are too many of them for me to name."

"You don't want to tell me their names, then."

"As I told you, there are too many of them for me to name."

"Name some of them, then."

"I'm afraid I might forget the rest!"

"The settlement residents heard someone firing at them. Don't tell me you don't know where the weapons are hidden."

"We've never had weapons. We're a peaceable village, and you know that."

"We know what you did to the Turks."

"Do you want to call us to account for what we did to your enemies?"

"No. But I want to know where the weapons you used to fight our enemies are hidden."

"We don't have any weapons, I tell you. We had weapons only when we needed them."

Peterson signaled to the soldiers to lead Hajj Khaled over to a giant oak tree in the center of the courtyard and tie him to its trunk.

Peterson came toward him. "Don't you want to confess where the weapons are hidden?"

"I've told you: we don't have any weapons."

What came next they could never have anticipated: a hard slap, the sound of which deafened them all.

The men broke out of their rows, but the soldiers' rifles prevented them from reaching Hajj Khaled. Peterson drew his revolver and fired three warning shots into the air.

"You don't want to confess? You'll have to endure, then."

Another resounding slap descended. When, by dint of a frenzied rush forward, Ahmad Khamis managed to break through the line of soldiers, the fourth bullet landed in his heart. From behind the crowd, the armored car fired a low volley that took everyone in the square by surprise, forcing them all to duck, even the soldiers.

The moments were ablaze with deadly anticipation as the soldiers ordered all the villagers to lie on their faces in the dirt.

When some hesitated, shots were fired, sending the dirt and rocks between their feet flying.

Coming back over to Hajj Khaled, Peterson asked again, "You don't want to confess, then?"

He reached out toward Hajj Khaled's long right mustache, and with all the strength his hand possessed, yanked it out. Crimson blood gushed out over his lips and chin.

"I'll ask you one more time: where are the weapons caches?"

"I've told you: We don't have any weapons."

Peterson took hold of the left mustache. Their eyes met. The officer's eyes said only one thing: "So you don't want to confess, then!" while the Hajj's eyes were filled with a mixture of fury and grief.

He then pulled the left mustache out, and more blood flowed.

"Do you want to go on being stubborn?"

"Know this: if I had weapons, which I don't, I wouldn't waste them by handing them over to you after what you've done."

Turning toward the faces clinging to the dirt, Peterson said, "He doesn't want to confess. Is there anyone else here who wants to confess, or shall we start all over again?"

A pall of silence fell over everyone.

Peterson gestured to his soldiers to herd the men over to the armored car.

Then another hand began pointing to the row of men, the hand of a man whose face was concealed behind a mask through which nothing but his eyes appeared. The people in the village called him "burlap bag."

Eight men found themselves being led aside.

Among them was Isma'il Yunus, whom Peterson ordered to be bound to the other side of the oak tree, thereby causing the ropes to tighten more and more around Hajj Khaled's body.

This torture session differed from the previous one in that the soldiers fell upon Isma'il from all sides with the butts of their rifles, sending his blood spattering every which way. Whenever he received a blow, his body would jump, and Hajj Khaled would feel the ropes digging into his flesh on the other side.

Half an hour later, Isma'il cried out in pain, "I'll confess! I'll lead you to the weapons!"

Terror descended suddenly on the people of the village, who knew for certain that many of them would soon meet their ends.

"Where are they?" Peterson asked him.

"I'll lead you to them."

Peterson signaled to the soldiers to untie him. They shoved him ahead of them with the muzzles of their rifles, and whenever his strength was about to give out, he would receive another blow.

He kept leading them forward until he reached the edge of the well. Before they could ask him, "Where are the weapons?" he screamed, "They're here!"

Then he hurled his body into the darkness of the well.

Peterson peered down into the bottom of the well, but saw nothing but darkness, cruel darkness.

"Search the well," he commanded the soldiers.

But all they found was a floating corpse, and water mingled with blood.

Peterson returned to the square and glared into the people's faces.

"Doesn't life mean anything to you?" he screeched, his nerves frayed to the breaking point.

"It means everything to us," Hajj Khaled replied. For a moment, Peterson felt as though the words he had heard were actually contaminated with blood, and he reached up and wiped his ears with his hands.

The armored car took off with seven men on board, the eighth of whom was Hajj Khaled, and with three military jeeps trailing behind.*

After five days of incarceration, interrogation, and torture in al-Maskubiya Prison, an edifice that had been constructed by Czarist Russia for pilgrims to Jerusalem outside the city walls, the settlement was set on fire a second time. It had now become clear that there was someone else setting fire to the settlement, but instead of releasing the prisoners, the British began interrogating them about the names of their fellow rebels. Then, seeing that their investigation was getting them nowhere, they finally let the men go.

They reached the village utterly shattered. However, they did their utmost to conceal the weakness and pain that were weighing their bodies down.

Everyone had come back.

For three days in a row, fires were lit in celebration of their return.

Meanwhile, on the other side of Hadiya, rage and bitterness were eating away at the heart of Hajj Sabri al-Najjar.

"We wanted him to be reduced, but instead he's become greater!"

---

* That night Peterson wrote: Darkness is the key to light. / The tree is the staircase to the sky. / The sparrow is the dream's message. / In the heart your dagger settled, my love. And suddenly the metal began to grow. / But ask me not about the fruit.

The Edge of the Resurrection

The sound of the wind coursed madly across the land. Closing the doors and windows as tightly as they could, they all took refuge in Hajj Khaled's house. From inside, they could hear the shuddering of the orange tree, the cracking of the branches of the oak tree in the courtyard, and its pained groaning.

Suddenly, it seemed to Munira that what she was hearing at the door wasn't the raging of the wind, but the sound of someone knocking.

Hajj Khaled got up and went to the door. Munira cast a glance at the flame of the lamp, and realized that opening the door would put it out. Her heart shrank. Hajj Khaled opened the door a crack and slipped out, then proceeded to the courtyard gate. When he opened it, a voice came from outside, splitting the heavy clouds of dust.

"It's him!"

A shot rang out, and Hajj Khaled stumbled backward a couple of steps, then fell to the ground on his face.

Aziza went running toward her brother. She screamed. As for Sumayya, she couldn't get her feet to move, and, like her, Munira froze in place. Outside, Aziza was able to make out the figure of a British officer surrounded by his soldiers.

"My brother!" Aziza screamed. "My brother!"

The officer stepped back, as did the soldiers with their weapons at the ready.

They reached their vehicle, whose motor had been running the entire time, and it raced away. Its sound merged little by little with the howling of the wind, until it disappeared into it.

Aziza took off running madly after the military vehicle, but the dust that had closed in on the world had concealed it from view. Like a phantom, no sooner would part of it become visible than it would vanish again. However, she was sure that when she'd been standing behind the door, she'd heard someone say, "It's him," and that the person speaking hadn't been British.

Munira would look at Khaled and Salem and praise God for having kept them alive for her. She praised Him for this whenever she looked out at the graves of their brothers Mustafa and Muhammad, whenever she remembered their bitter return to their mother's doorstep years after their burial, and whenever she remembered how their bones had been gathered up and buried anew.

The Turks' departure had been like a gift of new life for her and for thousands of mothers and fathers whose sons had come home again from years of being on the run, or from the warfronts after the fighting had come to an end. However, she also knew that there were thousands of mothers whose hearts still awaited the return of those who had never come back, who had been swallowed up by distant fronts and mountain trails where hunger had brought their lives to an end.

She praised God that they were here. But no sooner had she celebrated their return than her husband was mown down by treasonous bullets that snatched his life away, and she had found herself digging his grave with her bare hands. She had always prayed, "O God, let me die before him so that I won't have to grieve his loss!" But she had grieved his loss, just as she had grieved the losses of Muhammad and Mustafa.

The bullet had passed a few centimeters from his heart and come out through his back, creating a fountain of blood that gushed out in all directions. They hurriedly tried to stop the bleeding, but soon realized it was impossible. Salem ran to the paved road, but the horizon was completely sealed off, and there was no way one could have heard the sound of an engine approaching from afar. There was nothing but the sound of the wind, that cosmic hand that was rolling the earth into a ball however it pleased and mercilessly flinging it about.

Salem had received the news at home. When the minutes began flying in all directions like the dirt around him, he realized Khaled would never make it. However, going home again would have meant nothing but capitulation to this perfidious deed. Hence, he decided to stay. He wouldn't go back. And again he felt the whirlwind of time attacking, plucking him out of his place, then hurling him down. For a moment, silence reigned, and he saw things flying around him without hearing a sound. Then, in a bizarre moment, a car emerged out of the belly of the wind, and only with great difficulty did its driver manage to avoid crushing the body that rose up in the middle of the road like a broken flagstaff.

At Ramla Hospital, they told them he would need a major operation: "But we can't perform it here. Besides, he's lost a great deal of blood. So you'll have to take him to Dajani Hospital in Jaffa."

He lay on the bed, ashen as a stormy day and parched as a desert. The doctors shook their heads: "There's no hope."

They gathered around him in tears, realizing that the world would collapse on their heads at any moment now that they had lost the pillar of the household.

Out of the throngs that had gathered in a circle around the bed, in the corridors, and in the lobby, Husayn al-Sa'ub, Shakir Muhanna, and Ali al-A'raj slipped out and made their way back to Hadiya to dig a grave for him near those of his two brothers and his father.

The wind continued to swirl, turning the earth upside down and blowing the soil that lay piled next to the hole back inside it again. This kept happening until they were convinced that the wind didn't want them to bury him, just as the rain had once told his family that his brothers hadn't been buried as they were meant to be.

Just when they were about to finish their task, they stopped digging without knowing why. Exchanging a brooding look through the thick dust and the muddy tears that were streaming down their cheeks, they decided then and there to go back to the hospital.

As they were on their way down the hill, they saw Salem getting out of a taxi. Sprinting toward them, he started shouting words they couldn't make out. They ran toward him, and when they met, he threw his arms around them, crying, shouting, mad with joy, "He made it! He's alive! By God, he made it!"

The men exchanged glances, then started shouting and crying along with him, "He made it! He made it!"

Hajj Khaled paused at his grave, contemplating the soil that had called out to him but whose call had been cut short, and at that moment he realized he was alive. He ran his hands over his body as he stared into the hole, and he wept. He wept as though he hadn't survived, as though the person standing at the edge of the grave was his wraith, who was agonizing over having been orphaned by the loss of his body.

"Is this the new life they say someone is granted by destiny? It is! What else can we call it? But leave this grave for me. It's my grave. Don't bury anyone else here, even if you run out of graves."

The graves later began to multiply around that hole, and every time a new one was dug, Hajj Khaled would go up there. He would stand face to face with that hole, which never tired of staring at him, and which he never tired of staring at.

The Bullet's Secret

The matter was no longer a secret: after failing to prove that he had gone up the mountain with the rebels, they had tried to condense it all into a bullet that aimed for his heart.

The British denied having anything to do with it, and closed the investigation before opening it. There was no one in the household who could say he had seen a face clearly. Even Aziza was unable to describe the face of the person who had fired the shot. She said, "He was tall . . ." then paused. "What can I say? They all look alike!"

Hajj Khaled knew that bullets might assail him from any direction. However, people began speaking more and more openly, their words pointing to the man who aspired to Hajj Khaled's place as village elder.

As for Hajj Khaled, he bided his time, as the horizon seemed more closed to him than ever before. There was growing talk about the monastery's designs on Hadiya's land. People complained that for a long time Father Theodorus had failed to return the few deeds that proved their ownership of the land, and that he had begun offering more and more contradictory excuses. At the same time, Abd al-Latif al-Hamdi seemed to have come closer to achieving his aims, thanks to the clout of his armed men and the powers of the British mandate. As for the settlement, it seemed to be expanding even though it occupied the same land area, since its houses were getting higher and higher. The din of its bulldozers plowing the earth rent the silence of the village at dawn, while the ceaseless roar of its electrical generators rent the stillness of the night, thereby revealing the gulf that separated two eras: the era of Hadiya, and the era of the settlement.

Hajj Khaled stood watching Sa'd Saleh as he plowed the earth with his cow. Then he looked up toward the settlement, where he saw a bulldozer as it moved back and forth, turning the earth with the speed of a bullet.

"Look at us, and look at them!" he sighed.

Less than three weeks after that bullet was shot, reports confirmed that it was the hand of Hajj Sabri al-Najjar that had placed the round in the British rifle, and that all the British had done was pull the trigger.

Darkness closed in completely on Hajj Khaled. He looked at his hands and feet, and saw scores of fetters binding them.

Fayez chose a powerful, long-range, British-made rifle that could hold five rounds. Then he slipped out by night to the other neighborhood. He knocked on the door, then moved away. When al-Najjar's brother came out, he fired a single bullet into his forehead, and fled.

The bullet that had gone through his brother's forehead told Hajj Sabri that his secret must have gotten out. Then hell opened its gates and, in a moment of madness, he decided to take things to the limit. His men went rushing off to Hajj Khaled's neighborhood to resume a battle that had not ended even after the arrival of the British, who had been slow to put a stop to it.

Hajj Khaled kneaded his brow with the fingers of his left hand. He contemplated everything he saw, and everything he had yet to see, and realized that the next shot would be fatal. Hence, the moment he saw the British military jeeps approaching, he vanished entirely, as though the earth had swallowed him up. Thus began a prolonged chase that would only end with his capture in the territory of the Sutriya clan near Ramla.

Hajj Sabri al-Najjar's and Abd al-Latif Hamdi's men trailed him until they discovered where he was hiding. Lest the incident turn into a bloodbath, Hajj Khaled decided to hand himself over to the force that had surrounded him, since he knew that, in the end, no one would be able to prove that he was the one who had killed al-Najjar's brother.

He found himself in prison, and everyone in the region went to work to find a solution to the problem, which had become a threat to the entire village. However, al-Najjar refused to accept a settlement, determined to pursue his course until he saw Hajj Khaled on the gallows.

After three weeks of fruitless interrogations, Hajj Khaled managed to reach the prison roof. There was a powerful wind, and it was said that he jumped off using a sheet as a parachute, then disappeared into a grave for two days, until at last the British gave up hope of finding him.

When al-Najjar received news of Hajj Khaled's escape, the winds took a new direction. Meanwhile, things became clearer when a man from al-Najjar's clan testified that al-Najjar himself had been behind the attempt on Hajj Khaled's life, and that he was the one who had led the British to his house that night. As the scandal reached its climax, al-Najjar announced that he was willing to negotiate a settlement. However, this time it was Hajj Khaled who refused. Sensing danger, al-Najjar went to the British again, seeking their protection. They in turn told him to find a solution to his problem. The only way he could do this was to conclude a settlement with Hajj Khaled. The settlement was: blood for blood, in return for the release of Hajj Khaled, whom the mandate authorities pledged not to pursue any longer.

Reprisals like these were of no concern to the British, whether the number of casualties was one or fifty. Their only concern was that none of the casualties be from among their own, or the Jews. Consequently, they left the way open for people's courts to resolve this

type of case, and in cases where the reprisals promised to be troublesome to the British,
they would go themselves to the popularly appointed judges in order to arrive at a solution.

By the time these things happened, Hajj Khaled had become one of the most well-known wanted men in those parts.

"This is all we can offer," Edward Peterson told al-Najjar.

"He needs to appear in front of everyone with the revolver the British armed him with hanging from his neck. That's my first condition," announced Hajj Khaled.

"And what is your second condition?"

"I'm asking God to let me know what it is once the first condition has been met!"

They pressured al-Najjar until he agreed to it.

Hair tents were set up and people came from the region of Hebron, Gaza, and Jerusalem. Even the British governor of Gaza, who was known for acting as though he was the High Commissioner, attended the event, and so did Edward Peterson.

When Hajj Khaled arrived, he went up to shake hands with the men in the delegation. However, the governor of Gaza and Peterson remained seated. Feeling insulted, the people thundered, "Stand up and shake his hand!" So they had no choice but to do as they had been told.

As the two men clasped each others' hands, Peterson regarded Hajj Khaled with a seething hatred and whispered to himself: "I promise you, I'll kill you someday!"

There were many who wanted to see Hajj Khaled, who had become something of a legend after his escape.

The purpose of the meeting was not to discuss the case and issue a ruling. Rather, its purpose was to allow Hajj Khaled to make whatever demands he chose, and it was understood that al-Najjar would have no choice but to accede to such demands without discussion.

Al-Najjar, who had been brought from a distance, marched with his revolver hanging from his neck until he stood in the center of the square.

You ask me why his clan didn't protest? I'll tell you. Most of them couldn't stand al-Najjar because of his ties to the British. They had a sense of right and wrong, and people were aware of the danger they were in. Even his son Karim was against him, and didn't leave the house that day.

Shaykh Nasir al-Ali, who died less than a week later, leaving a deep wound in Hajj Khaled's heart, said, "Your opponent is before you. So ask for whatever you want."

With thousands of eyes fixed upon him, Hajj Khaled kneaded his brow with the fingers of his left hand.

"Now that the first condition has been met, I want him to pay two thousand dinars if he wants me to pardon him."

He knew he was asking the impossible, and that a sum like this wouldn't be easy to come by.

With a start, al-Najjar said, "You might as well have asked for my head!"

But the people shouted, "Pay what you owe, Sabri!"

Within a short time his relatives had raised the money, and they placed it before Shaykh Nasir al-Ali. But after counting the currency and estimating the value of the gold jewelry that had been brought, he said, "This is less than the sum that was asked for."

Taken aback, the men in the delegation didn't know what to do.

But Hajj Khaled insisted, "I won't accept a piaster less than the full two thousand."

Voices rose to a crescendo, auguring a commotion that threatened to sweep over the entire square. Suddenly, someone clad in a loose cloak, face concealed by a keffiyeh, crossed the square and asked, "Do you allow women to contribute?"

"I do," replied Hajj Khaled.

"Hajj Khaled," the person said, "this is a contribution from me," whereupon she removed the keffiyeh from her face, and who should he find standing before him but his mother, Munira.

She unfolded a red handkerchief, which she held in her hand to reveal a mass of gold that glittered before Shaykh Nasir al-Ali.

"This is my jewelry, your sister's jewelry, Fayez's wife's jewelry, Mahmud's wife's jewelry, and your aunt Anisa's jewelry. We're offering it to you. Is the sum complete now?"

"Yes, it's complete."

"And is this enough for you, so that you won't ask for anything more?"

"No, it's not enough at all!"

Silence descended, and people's hearts began pounding in their chests once again.

"It isn't enough for you?" she exclaimed. "But you owe me a debt. So do you promise to repay it for the sake of the people present here?"

"On my life."

"I carried you for nine months in my womb, I bore you in pain, and I raised you to adulthood. Now I want what I'm entitled to from you, and what I'm entitled to is everything you might demand from al-Najjar."

"For your sake," he said, "I've pardoned him."

At that point, Shaykh Nasir al-Ali asked Hajj al-Najjar to come forward.

"What might you say now to Hajj Khaled?" he asked him.

"Here I am before you," he replied. "If you pardon me, it shows how noble you are. If, on the other hand, you want to get even with me, here's my revolver. You can take it and kill me with it!"

Kneading his brow with the fingers of his left hand, Hajj Khaled scrutinized the faces of those present, who were waiting to hear what he would say. After a silence, he said, "I've pardoned you. You should know that I could have taken what I wanted by force. And actually, I didn't want to take it from you personally, but, rather, from the British government, whose treachery you embody."

Then the people got up excitedly, shouting, "Allahu akbar! God is greatest!" and dancing, and the celebration went on until they heard the dawn call to prayer.

Shaykh Nasir al-Ali leaned over and whispered in Khaled's ear, "I expected you to demand that he be stripped of his position as mayor, too."

"I thought of that, Shaykh, but I was afraid it might divide the village all over again. For as long as I can remember, the eldership has belonged to our clan, and the mayorship to theirs. Besides, as you know, you couldn't find a better man to serve as a doormat for the British."

The elders in the delegation took al-Najjar aside and said to him, "From now on, you're going to have to try to please Hajj Khaled."

"How?" he asked.

"You offer your daughter to him in marriage. You give her to him as a secondary wife."

"My daughter will never be a secondary wife!"

His refusal was understandable, of course. After all, secondary wives, as opposed to free women, were the unluckiest women on earth, since they were viewed as slaves and treated with contempt and hostility. Their families had no right to come to their defense or stand up for them until they'd given birth to a son.

Nevertheless, they forced him to do it. They went and got her ready, then set her on the back of a mare and said to him, "Lead her to Hajj Khaled's house. He's forgiven you. As for us, though, we haven't forgiven you, because you sold out to Britain and controlled other people through its soldiers. In the process, you made yourself small in our eyes."

His daughter Sa'diya didn't say a thing. When they asked her if she would accept Hajj Khaled as her husband, she remained silent. When her brother Karim spoke with her in private, he said, "You'll be freer there than you are here."

He knocked on the door. Hajj Khaled came out. Al-Najjar said, "Here's my daughter, who's come to you. And we don't ask for anything in return."

Hajj Khaled looked questioningly at the judges, who gestured to him to accept the offer. So he stepped aside for her to pass and she came into the house. Sumayya froze, unable to utter a word. Seeing her reaction, he nodded, and she understood. She took the bride by the hand and led her inside.

They said to him, "Let's go ahead and conclude the marriage."

"She's my guest now, and my sister until God makes clear to us what we ought to do."

He realized that to send her back would be a serious insult that would open wounds anew. Sa'diya wasn't a stranger to him, since he had long been accustomed to seeing her at weddings and in the fields, harvesting the wheat or flitting like a bee from one olive tree to another as she gathered their fruits. People often commented on how much she resembled Mahmud's wife Afaf.

What nobody knew but the bride, whom fortune had led there beyond all expectations, was that she alone was happy about this fate that had descended upon her against everyone's will.

Forty days later, Sumayya rose early and adorned Sa'diya, placing around her neck twice as much jewelry as she had been wearing when she arrived.

"She's ready!" she called at last.

Sa'diya's tears were falling like rain. However, no one knew the secret behind those tears, and it would be a long time before they realized what they had meant.

Hajj Khaled grasped the mare's reins and started off. He was followed by the people of the village, whose numbers began gradually to multiply until they reached her father's house. He knocked on the door. Al-Najjar came out. With everyone looking on, Hajj Khaled said to him, "Here is your daughter, who's returned to you as pristine as when she came to us, and adorned with twice the jewelry she brought with her. I've returned the mare she rode when she came to us, and I won't be taking it back with me, since it belongs to her. You're free to marry her to whomever you'd like."

However, for a long time to come, Sa'diya's would be one of the saddest stories Hadiya had ever known. She refused to marry any of the suitors who came asking for her hand. She kept saying, "There's only one man whose wife I could ever be: the one whose house I entered in humiliation, and who returned me to my family's house with my head held high."

Rayhana's Arrival

The news reached Hadiya a little after sundown: "Edward Peterson survived an assassination attempt!"

Three hours later, the bomb dropped: the British police had arrested the would-be assassin.

When they learned that the young man who had pulled the trigger was the son of Rayhana, Habbab's last wife, they all knew that this was a woman they should stand by. Ever since Habbab's death, her story had been the talk of all the villages, until she came to be known as Rayhana Adham. This made her the first person in the country who had ever been identified with reference not to his or her father, but to a horse.

In a whirlwind trial that lasted no more than three days, her son was sentenced to death.

Rayhana didn't weep, she didn't scream, she didn't curse the court and the British government or call down destruction on the king. Rather, she looked into her son's eyes, then said to them, "Take me home."

But before she got there, she said, "Pass through Hadiya on your way."

"When they asked her why, she said, "I want to see Hajj Khaled.""

Her arrival at that late hour of the night was a huge surprise, and caused quite a stir in Hadiya. The feeling that came over everyone far surpassed what they would have felt if the mufti, Hajj Amin al-Husayni himself, had come to town.

She headed up to the guesthouse.

From the time the car stopped and a single person got out, wrapped in a cloak whose color mingled with the darkness of the night, Hamdan had been watching intently, trying to guess who the late-night visitors might be. He was perplexed by the fact that, although he had seen the shadow of more than one passenger, only one person had gotten out of the car.

She kept walking until she reached him. When she greeted him, he was shocked to realize that the visitor was a woman. She asked him about Hajj Khaled. Flustered, he replied, "He's at home."

"He has guests," she said.

"May I tell him who they are?"

"Tell him that Rayhana has come to see him—Rayhana Adham."

"Rayhana Adham!"

Her name had a weight to it, and to many people she seemed more like a legend than a real live person. She was as chaste and flawless as our Lady the Virgin Mary, and as strong-willed as a long-lived olive tree.

Strangely, Rayhana was proud of her new name. Although many people assumed it would be embarrassing to her to be known by such a name, she herself thought that it should have been her name from the time she was born. Adham was the only one who had stood by her side and protected her with all his might, and when it became necessary for him to offer his blood, he had offered it without hesitation when none of the men of her village had been able to stand up to Habbab. As she commented later, Habbab had snatched her out of their arms while they looked on helplessly, despite the fact that they were grown men.

Three days after Habbab's death she had turned to his wife Subhiya and said, "Anything you want from this house, take it."

"But do you think he really died?" Subhiya asked her.

"What's this nonsense, Subhiya?"

"I swear to God, I still can't believe it. I'm afraid he'll rise out of his grave all of a sudden and say, 'Three!'"

"Don't worry. After three days in the grave, you can be sure a dead person is plenty dead!"

"All right. But you, don't you want anything?"

"I've gotten what I wanted."

Confused, Subhiya asked, "And what have you gotten?"

"I've gotten Habbab's death. Don't you realize that yet, Subhiya? My share of this household and of all his property amounts to one thing: his death. I'm afraid I've wronged you by taking the bigger share!"

People came from all over to offer her their condolences, but she shut the door in their faces, saying, "If you can find some family of his, then go offer your condolences to them. We were never his family. We were his captives, his prisoners."

For a long time, Rayhana thought of Khaled in a way she had never thought of any man before, and when she heard what he had gone through with Yasmin, she felt a gaping wound in her chest, a wound that fell suddenly out of pain's unknown regions and settled deep within. There was one man, and one man only, for whose sake she would have been willing to give up her new title, and that was Khaled. She was surprised to find herself comparing her name with the other name she might have carried: Rayhana, wife of Khaled Hajj Mahmud.

She had dreamed and dreamed. Then, suddenly, she confronted herself and put a stop to it, saying, "That's enough! You're out of line, Rayhana!"

Even so, she had never forgotten that Khaled was the only man who had reached out to her in the depths of that dark abyss and extricated her at the last moment. His was the mighty hand that had been able to crush the hand of Habbab. His was the compassionate hand that she would soon be shaking in search of a new life, only this time on behalf of her son.

Meanwhile, back at Habbab's house, Subhiya couldn't decide what her next step should be. Salma, his first wife, wasn't there. As for Rayhana, she had taken her leave of Subhiya four days after Habbab's death. But first she had given Adham a proper burial. After all, a purebred like him should never be left where wild dogs could tear at his flesh, or where birds of prey could pluck out his eyes. She buried him in a manner fit for any thoroughbred mare or stallion, in keeping with the customs of the people of the land, who knew the true value of horses, be they living or dead.

Less than a year later Rayhana had married Sayf al-Din al-Sa'di, a man who had had the courage to say no to Abd al-Latif al-Hamdi when he told him to send his sisters to clean Habbab's house, which had since become his.

"Tell Abd al-Latif that Sayf al-Din's sisters only clean houses that are clean," he shrieked in the face of one of al-Hamdi's vigilantes when he came to see him in his field.

When the man turned to leave, Sayf al-Din called him to come back. His eyes shooting sparks, he added, "And tell him that men out-live empires."

Little did Sayf al-Din al-Sa'di know that he was responding to the statement Yasmin's father had made to her some time before as he tried to persuade her to be sensible, saying, "Empires outlive men!"

When news of what had happened reached Rayhana, her heart skipped a beat, and she said to her mother, "I'm going to marry that man."

"Are you out of your mind? How do you expect to choose your husband? Your husband is the one who chooses you!"

"Believe me, he'll choose me."

The following morning she asked her sister to go to him and tell him what she was thinking. Her sister refused. She asked her other sister to do it, and met with the same response. So she went back to her mother, saying, "You're the only one left."

"The men would kill me if they found out about this!"

"The men would kill you if there were any real men. As for the ones who've let their mothers, wives, and sisters work as servants in al-Hamdi's mansion, don't be afraid of them."

Fearfully, furtively, stumbling as she went, her mother walked to the field, her diminutive shadow trailing behind her. Her head covering concealed three-quarters of her face. Seeing her approaching in the distance, Sayf al-Din didn't recognize her. He stood there looking at her. She froze. He didn't know what he should do: should he go up to her to find out what she needed, or should he wait until she came to him? As for her, she remained where she was. After a few moments had passed, he decided to go over to where she stood. He approached, disconcerted, sensing something out of the ordinary. When his eyes fell on her wizened, venous hand, which clutched her head covering in order to conceal her face better, he asked her, "Is there something I can do for you, Mother?"

"I come bearing a message that is heavy for me, a message that no mother in this land has ever had to bear."

"May God grant me your favor."

"My daughter Rayhana greets you, and asks you to be her husband."

The surprise was beyond imagining. When they had been up in the mountains, fighting the Turks from one place to another, Rayhana had been waging solitary warfare on them from the village. It was true, of course, that they hadn't been aware of everything that was happening with her. However, the days that followed revealed the secrets of the days that were past with astonishing speed.

"Tell her that if there's anything in this world called honor, nothing would honor me more."

Hajj Khaled's surprise had been no less than Hamdan's when he arrived at the guesthouse, followed by Musa and Naji, and found himself face to face with her.

If he had seen her before, he would have said that time had changed nothing about her except for the fact that she had grown taller, and her gaze had become more penetrating. She would look at you as though she were looking at your entire past. Yet her beauty was unmistakable.

Hajj Khaled looked at Hamdan, and she understood.

"There's no time to sit down," she said.

In the end, however, she did sit down. They brought two extra cushions, which they placed on top of the one Hajj Khaled had invited her to sit on, and when he gestured to his two sons to go prepare dinner for their guest, she said, "I will be your guest, even a member of your household, if you can find me a solution."

Hajj Khaled was aware of what her son had done. However, he hadn't expected the verdict to be handed down so quickly.

"There's no one else I could come to. You've showered me with your kindness, and your hands alone were able to break down the door to my prison. So I don't think anyone's hands but yours would be able to remove the noose from my son Khaled's neck."

Her voice quavered as she said this, and Hajj Khaled was flustered when he heard her son's name.

"You know," she said, "I couldn't have found a nobler name for him." Then she added, "You haven't gotten to know him, Hajj. But he's one of those young men who can heal a wound if you place them on it."

"How is his father?"

"He's fighting with those that remain of Izz al-Din al-Qassam's men. But he's fine."

"If I can offer you anything, I'll be offering it to myself."

"Your son Mahmud is educated, and he doesn't miss a thing that happens from Jaffa to Jerusalem. I want you to send him word to find us a lawyer. They've told me we still have a chance, since there's something they call an appeal."

"Tomorrow I'll go see him myself."

"I wouldn't have expected less."

And she rose to leave.

"But how can you leave before we've done our duty by you!"

"There's a car waiting for me, and it's very late."

❋

It was the intensity of people's suffering that created the rebels. Yes, it was! And don't forget the sense of humiliation and defeat that came over people after Shaykh Izz al-Din al-Qassam and his comrades were martyred. Who could forget the day of his funeral? Who? The funeral procession went from the mosque out to the large square in front of it. There were thousands of people in the procession, and the bodies of al-Qassam and his comrades were being carried on people's shoulders. The women were ululating from the roofs, the balconies, and the windows, and the Boy Scouts were singing anthems that aroused a sense of honor and patriotism. When the procession reached the police station, some people in the crowd started pelting it with bricks and stones. Some policemen who were there ran away, and three police cars parked in front of the station were demolished by the crowd. When we caught sight of a British soldier who was directing traffic, some of us attacked him and he ran away. We started marching again, and kept going till we reached the railroad station. The crowds attacked it with more rocks. A battalion of British soldiers wearing steel helmets and armed to the teeth came out, led by Officer James. At that point, the people who had been carrying the bodies on their shoulders put them down and got ready for a confrontation with the British, who had come to stop the procession, and I saw Officer James fall to the ground. Seeing that it was no match for the crowd, the British force quickly withdrew. It had been decided that the biers would be sent to the Baldat al-Shaykh cemetery. To the sound of music that would have made you cry, some people came forward to put the biers in the cars, but the crowd prevented them, and resumed its march on foot to the cemetery five kilometers away. The march from the big mosque in al-Jurayna Square to the Yajur Cemetery took three and a half hours. I saw delegations from Nablus, Acre, Jenin, Bisan, Tulkarm, Safad and Zahufa—all the villages around Haifa. But I didn't see the party leaders. In a comment on the invitation that had been issued for people to take part in the funeral procession that morning, the al-Jami'a al-Islamiya newspaper wrote, "As for the practice of escorting funeral processions, this is a religious matter that is not subject to political considerations or legal texts. Rather, it is subject only to the rule of religion, which makes no distinction between one deceased person and another and which goes beyond political circumstances and the pettiness of this earthly realm!"

When Hajj Khaled, Rayhana, and her two brothers Jamil and Hafiz reached the train station, Mahmud was waiting for them in his gray suit and his red fez.

"The only person we can depend on in this case is Sulayman al-Marzuqi."*

Not long afterward they were in his office next to the French Hospital in the old city of Jaffa.

They explained to the lawyer the details of the case.

"Simple!" he said. "However, I'll need to review all the official files."

Turning to Rayhana, he said, "Don't worry."

"What mother could help but worry when a noose is about to go around her son's neck?"

"God help us."

The first thing he did was file for an appeal before the verdict was ratified. Before the date set for the trial, he had found out the name of the judge—a military man with the rank of lieutenant colonel—who was to preside over the case.

The events that followed were recounted in awe by Hajj Khaled to the men who had gathered in the guesthouse, and even though not a single person had been absent from the first telling, he had to repeat the story over and over on subsequent nights. They were as much in awe as he was.

He said, "When we got to the courtroom, we found no lawyer there. The clerk called his name once, then twice, but there was no answer! But before the clerk had had a chance to pronounce him absent, he walked into the courtroom accompanied by one of his assistants.

---

* Sulayman al-Marzuqi was one of the most famed lawyers of his day. After losing his sight as a child, he was sent by his father to al-Azhar, where he studied under Shaykh Muhammad Abduh. As a lawyer he was subjected to numerous penalties by the British judicial authorities, and was exiled by Jamal Pasha "al-Saffah" to Anatolia during the Second World War due to his opposition to the seizure of peasants' crops in order to feed the Turkish army. His office was relocated next to the Sports Club on Jamal Pasha Street after the part of old Jaffa in which it had been located originally was destroyed. The British forces had lost control over this part of the city due to the presence of rebels there. On 18 June 1936 the city woke at 4:30 a.m. to the drone of airplanes in its skies as British military forces surrounded it. At 6:00, soldiers began blowing warning horns, and shortly thereafter, crews of British army engineers began placing trunks of dynamite at the bases of the houses and blowing them up one after another. Within two hours, most of old Jaffa was in ruins, including its houses, baths, schools, bakeries, coffee shops, factories, and saints' tombs. More than six thousand

366

"'How can you be late to a court hearing when your client is threatened with death?' the British judge demanded angrily, as though it wasn't he who had issued the death sentence!

"'Necessities, Your Honor.'

"'And what necessities do you have that are more important than your client's life?'

"'I'm late, Your Honor, because I have a girlfriend, and I needed to spend as much time with her as I could.'

"'And would someone like you have a girlfriend?' asked the judge with a smirk.

"'And why shouldn't I, Your Honor?'

"'Is your girlfriend more important than the person who's placed his life in your hands?'

"'This person has special importance, and so does my girlfriend! But don't you want to know where I've just come from?'

"'That doesn't matter to me,' replied the judge.

"'But it matters to me that you know, since I want you to be sure that my girlfriend deserves a great deal as well.' Then, before the judge had a chance to respond, he went on, 'I've just come from my girlfriend's house, which is located between the Palestine newspaper and the Collège des Frères. And I'll tell you honestly that she's the wife of a high-ranking official.'

"The judge nearly jumped out of his seat, at which point al-Marzuqi's escort squeezed his hand. (This was what al-Marzuqi had instructed him to do whenever he saw that the judge was agitated.)

"'I was in Building No. 3, and when I went up to the second floor, I had to come back down again, since her maid Suzanne was there.'

"The escort squeezed his hand again.

Palestinians were made homeless. The British colonial secretary announced that the government of Palestine had taken advantage of the presence of the royal engineers' team to open up two streets leading to the port. On this pretext, it had evacuated and blown up this area, which was crowded with dirty buildings, and which had been a gathering place for people being kept under surveillance and a refuge for outlaws from the police, who had been unable to enter the neighborhood.

"'It was hard to find a chance to be alone with her on account of her maid, so I waited in the street until my escort saw the maid leaving, since my girlfriend had managed to think up an errand she needed her to go on.'

"The escort squeezed his hand again.

"'Haylana! She's the most beautiful woman a man could hope to win! If you put her in this courtroom among all these people without telling me where she was, I could still find her easily even though I'm blind. She used to tell me, "I think this red couch was made just for us!"'

"At that point the judge screamed, 'Shut up!' and brandished his revolver in al-Marzuqi's face.

"The people in the courtroom were in an uproar, and panic-stricken screams rang out. Many of them hid behind their seats.

"'A revolver is being pointed at you,' his escort told him.

"Then al-Marzuqi let out a booming laugh that shook the courtroom. He said to the judge, 'If you're willing to commit murder for your wife's sake, then how can you sentence a man to death for defending his homeland?'

"The judge suddenly realized the predicament he was in. So, in order to disappear from sight as quickly as possible, he said, 'The court sentences the accused to ten years in prison, and forbids you to appear in court for six months.'

"He said to the judge, 'I've done my duty, and beyond that, nothing matters to me.'

"The judge said to him, 'If you had your sight, you'd ruin the country!'

"He said to the judge, 'Thank God I'm blind, since I can't see the crimes Britain is committing against my people.'"

Whenever Hajj Khaled got to this place in the story, the place would be so quiet you could have heard a pin drop.

"But how did he know all those things about the judge?" Muhammad Shahada wanted to know.

"Do you really think it would be difficult for a man like Sulayman al-Marzuqi to find out this sort of thing? He'd sent someone there to ask around and get the details about everything."

368

This was the first time they had met al-Marzuqi. However, it wasn't to be the last, and the surprise that awaited them in the future would be beyond description.

Rayhana hadn't expected more than this. In fact, for a moment she'd been certain that the sentence would be harsher.

When she came out of the courtroom, she saw him there. She recognized him: Sayf al-Din, her husband. He signaled to her, then disappeared around a corner.

"Wait for me," she said to the others.

"Sayf al-Din! How are you?"

"Tell me how things went."

"Praise God, praise God, the danger's passed! He was sentenced to ten years."

"It's all right. He's my son, and I know him as well as I know you. And always remember: if men believe that they'll outlive an empire, they will."

That Peasant!

Salim Bek al-Hashemi arrived at his country mansion. He was angry. The days that had passed had been too cruel to bear. Everything was going against his wishes, and the streets were being pulled out from under his feet. In an attempt to calm himself, he contemplated all the objects that surrounded him with their varying shades of blue, from the curtains to the chairs to his employees' uniforms. But he discovered that he needed some deep sea to drown in, not just these colors, which now seemed as miserable and silly to him as the idea that had once popped into his head, then drawn him after it.*

---

* The following description is the most precise I've found: "a calm, sedate man, soft to the touch, with a smile on his lips, reticent and secretive, who counts his words as though they were gold pieces." He completed his education in British universities, and when he returned, he decided to be an entrepreneur. It wasn't long before he had become a man of note in this area, and in 1933 he established the first model Arab farm for cattle, poultry, and rabbit husbandry. He employed new methods of vegetable and fruit agriculture and concluded an agreement with the British army on the basis of which he would supply it with vegetables, cartons of pasteurized milk, and packaged cheese. He was also able to conclude an agreement to supply British hospitals with the farm's produce. As for his marketing strategy, it was the same as that

After finding himself obliged to attend al-Qassam's memorial service, al-Hashemi tried to get away to the extent that he was able.

"As far as I'm concerned, it's a tragedy that I'm being forced to attend this peasant's memorial service!" he shouted in his wife's and son's faces. "We thought that once someone like this was dead, we'd be rid of him once and for all, but here he is dragging the entire population along behind him, and we've got no choice but to go along with the crowd. He's defeated everybody and turned into a national symbol even though he was killed in the first battle he entered. Does that make sense?"

He wasn't the only one feeling this way. On the contrary, there were scores of political leaders in the cities who were equally shaken. They realized that if they didn't move quickly they would lose their legitimacy, and they had to find a solution.

The secret meeting that was arranged with the High Commissioner hadn't been enough to reassure them. They informed him that the anger that had filled the streets since al-Qassam's death threatened them just as it did Britain itself, and they asked him to understand why they had not absented themselves from the memorial service: "If we hadn't attended, our legitimacy would have been on the line."

They also demanded that the British authorities be more resolute, since there was no telling where these early developments might lead.

Al-Hashemi sent for Abd al-Latif al-Hamdi. When he arrived, he was still so angry, he didn't invite him to sit down.

"What's going on right under your nose? A boy from one of the villages I put you in charge of has gone and shot a British officer in broad daylight!"

"He shot him in the city, Bek, and not here."

"But he came from here, you moron! The root of the problem is here. The viper's head is here, and what's happened means that its tail moved over there. And what about Hadiya, where they had the audacity to go

_____

employed by the Jewish Tenufa Company. Toward the end of September 1936 he became one of the most enthusiastic supporters of attempts to thwart the uprising and the general strike that was being called due to the approach of the orange season.

371

looking for someone to free that boy from the gallows after the noose was already around his neck?"

"As you know, Bek, Hadiya has never been under our control. And although it's under the protection of the Greek Orthodox monastery there, we've always done the best we could."

"The things happening now mean that you've got to do more than you have in the past. Otherwise, everything's going to come down on our heads. Do you understand?"

"I understand."

"Tell those 'women' of yours that you're always so proud of to get moving, or else."

"For heaven's sake, don't swear, Bek! Everything will be just the way you want it to be."

"I want you to move fast, and to do what you've got to do."

"And what's that, Bek?"

"Do you also want me to tell what you've got to do?"

Abd al-Latif al-Hamdi left feeling more confused than he had been before he went in: What does he want of me, exactly? The ax falls on their heads there, and they come and rake us over the coals for it here!

He sent word to Mayor Sabri al-Najjar to come right away. When he arrived, he was still so angry that he didn't invite him to sit down.

"What's going on in Hadiya right under your nose? They're going to hire a lawyer to defend that boy who shot the British officer in the city!"

"The boy came from one of the villages that are answerable to you, Bek."

"But the head of the viper that moved to rescue him, Hajj Khaled himself, was in your village."

"You know, Bek, that I've done more than anybody else in this region, and I regret to tell you that I was the only one who suffered the consequences when I was caught between the British and the people of the village."

"But we rewarded you for it by making sure that you'd be the village's mayor for life."

"I don't deny the kindness you've shown me, Bek."

"I want you to move fast and to do what you've got to do!"

"What is it that I've got to do, Bek?"

"And now you want me to tell you what it is you've got to do!"

Mayor Sabri al-Najjar left angry: If there's somebody that's able to do something, then he is welcome to do it!

Al-Najjar realized that he had been done for from the day he walked into that square with his revolver hanging from his neck. However, the good thing was that the British hadn't forgotten his sacrifice, and had rejected all attempts to deprive him of this honorary post. Consequently, he had continued to feel that Hajj Khaled's position was no better than his, since the people of the village had to come to him for his stamp of approval on every little thing.

The Slap

Realizing that the old days would never return, Hajj Khaled sent for Fayez. When he arrived, he said to him, "We need you now."

"I'm at your service, Uncle."

He was sure that the rifles that were brought out now would never go back into hiding. At the same time, though, he was thinking in a different way: We'll hit and run. We'll strike as far away as we can, then sneak back into the village without anybody noticing. And when we agree with somebody to come and attack here or there, we'll do everything necessary to prove that we'd never left the village.

"You know the people in the neighboring villages. But I don't want many, not more than two or three from every village," he instructed Fayez. "That way we won't attract anyone's attention."

"Don't worry, Uncle. Your being in the mountains will mean a lot to the young men."

Those who left Hadiya with him were Fayez, Iliya Radhi, and Sa'd Saleh, and from the five neighboring villages under Abd al-Latif al-Hamdi's authority he chose ten men, including Adel Abu Mamduh, whose story everyone knew by now. Adel was the man who, as soon as he heard of al-Qassam's martyrdom, went and stood on the side of the road. When a British jeep came along, he killed the three soldiers that were in it, seized their weapons, and disappeared into the mountains.

"Adel will join us in the mountains as soon as he hears you're there."

Their operations would take place far from Hadiya: setting a settlement on fire, sabotaging railroad tracks by tying them to camels and dragging them away or by greasing the tracks to hinder the movement of the trains and make them easier to attack, and firing at cars belonging to the British and the Jews in order to seize their weapons.

Seeing that the operations they had carried out thus far had been successful, Hajj Khaled decided to divide his forces into four groups. He sent one of them north, one south and one to the coast, which left his own group room to maneuver in the central region.

The harsh provisions of the emergency law that had been passed by the British came as no surprise to them. It called for

the death penalty or life imprisonment for anyone who attacks any telephone line or apparatus, airport, port, railroad, public fountain, corridor, or power-generating station. The governor shall have the right to impose a collective fine on the residents of any city, village, or encampment in the form of cash, cattle, sheep, goats, camels, or crops; to impound and sell property in order to pay the aforementioned fine if they fail to provide assistance by reporting the crime or identifying the perpetrators; and to confiscate or destroy any home, building, or installation without compensation . . . ; to arrest anyone who carries a stick, a club, an iron bar, a rock, or any sharp instrument of any kind or description. . . . The law authorizes the chief of police to arrest without a warrant any person who sings a patriotic anthem or uses words or gestures that might lead to a breach of security.

Within three weeks, Hajj Khaled realized that he urgently needed more men if the operations were to continue and expand. Meanwhile, the British were furious, and the commander of the Jerusalem region announced a reward of five thousand Palestinian pounds for anyone who provided information that would lead to the arrest of the ringleader of these 'criminals.'

However, this didn't change a thing. Sa'd Saleh managed to steal into the house of the British commander himself one night, where he shot him in bed. When he tried to flee, he found scores of rifles pointed at him in a single moment, and he was killed instantly. When they searched the body, they found nothing to indicate who he was or where he was from. So the next day they put him in the trunk of a car and began making the rounds of the villages, one after another. However, they got nowhere, since the single ready answer they received in every village they entered was: "We don't know him."

They handed the body over to other patrols, which made the rounds of still other villages, but to no avail, until the car stopped one day at Edward Peterson's door.

Peterson had become even bloodier since the attempt on his life, and he had come to be ruled by a single certainty, which was: at any moment any one of these people might shoot you.*

Peterson came out, and the first thing he did was remove the blanket from the body and take a look at it. He'd been hoping he would be lucky enough to recognize the person.

He said, "Now I know how much they all look alike when they're dead." But none of the soldiers or officers laughed. Nor was the stench emanating from the corpse the only reason.

The corpse was so full of holes and the temperature—which had been rising steadily since nine o'clock on that Tuesday morning—was so high, it had begun to decompose by the time the car finally reached Hadiya.

---

* That night Peterson wrote: Through the darkness of the centuries your apparition travels: White as snow, / Blue as tragedy. / For a long time I haven't heard your steps in the hallway / Or seen your face in the mirror. / I turn my spirit over like a dead cat with your fingers, which used to be mine, / And I gaze at the sparrow napping on the windowsill.

Even so, the face was clearly recognizable despite the dried blood that covered large parts of it.

They recognized him. It was Sa'd Saleh. They turned their faces away from the corpse. Peterson noticed.

"So you know him, then?"

They shook their heads as if to say a collective "No."

He ordered the soldiers to bring all the women of the village.

They came. He told them to form a long line so that every one of them could take a look at the corpse. After this, they were all to stand in the square facing the car.

They did so, one by one. But, to his consternation, he saw no tears in their eyes.

He was about to give up, about to throw the body in their faces and leave, when he heard a sob coming from where the women stood.

He came up to the woman who had sobbed. She was his mother. "So you know him? Is he your son?"

Everyone knew that if it was determined that he had come from this village, it would mean, first of all, that the house he had come out of would be blown up, and that a number of men—how many, it was impossible to predict—would be arrested.

"So you know him?"

"No, I don't know him."

"Why are you crying over him, then?"

"I'm crying over his lost youth. I'm crying for his mother, hoping she won't have to see him this way. That's why I'm crying."

Peterson took a few steps back and said, "Do you think a criminal like this deserves the tears that are being shed over him?"

He fell silent for a little while and stared at the toes of his shoes, then said, "I don't think they killed him completely." As if the corpse had moved!

Then he opened fire and pumped three bullets into the corpse's chest.

Loud weeping and cries of protest went up: "Fear God!"

"What's to be upset about if you don't know him?"

They made no reply.

He saw a little girl hiding fearfully behind her mother. He walked toward her, then grabbed her by one hand, his revolver aimed at the onlookers' faces. The mother tried to hold on to her little girl, but he struck her with the butt of his revolver and she fell to the ground.

"Don't be afraid! Don't be afraid!" the mother kept saying, her voice filled with terror.

He stood with the little girl in front of the trunk of the jeep.

"Do you know this person?"

She was crying, but she found the strength to shake her head and say, "No."

He brought her head closer to the corpse, and at that moment she fainted. He looked at her, then let her fall to the ground at his feet.

Her mother rushed over to her. The soldiers tried to prevent her, but she managed to get to her before them. As she bent to pick her up, she received a sudden kick from Peterson's foot, and fell on her back.

He retreated: "You don't want to confess. So then, you won't know where he is. You'll never know. I'll torture you with this all your lives."

And these were the words he repeated in every village.

The vehicles drove away, and as soon as they got out to the road, the sound of wailing filled the air.

As I see it, the second event that shook the government was the death of the secret officer Ahmad Nayef in Haifa. He was the one who had helped discover al-Qassam's gang and went after al-Qassam's followers.

But the piece of news that settled the matter and nearly drove Edward Peterson out of his mind was one that arrived too late. It said, "Khaled al-Hajj Mahmud is actually the one who's behind many of the operations against the British."

When he heard this, he gave himself a hard slap on the forehead and said, "What an idiot I was not to kill him when I had the chance!"*

---

* That night Peterson wrote: When the open country is your arms, / Where does the sun hide? / When the sun is your forehead, / Where can I sleep? / When the day slips away before my very eyes like an adder into a cave, / What can I do with all this night?

Face to Face

There wasn't a mountain left in all of Palestine but that Hajj Khaled had made it his home. Or at least that's how it seemed to people. He was more than fifty-five years old. However, what he hadn't been prepared for was the illness that had come to threaten his life: diabetes. Yet he managed to cope with it through insulin injections, which he learned to administer to himself. The coolness of the mountains in those days and the fact that he was able to protect the syringes from high temperatures by carrying them in a special case of the sort that the British used had been a great help to him.

As the days passed, the British got a clearer picture of this mysterious figure. In order to make sure they were targeting the right man, they carried out several surprise inspection campaigns, which confirmed to them that Hajj Khaled was no longer present in the village. This was followed by a small incident in the mountains that told them their hunch had been correct.

Peterson decided to appoint a Palestinian officer by the name of Sanad Rajab to head a British force whose job would be to go after Hajj Khaled and arrest him at any price. Peterson had chosen him for this mission due to the fact that he had met Hajj Khaled more than once when he was a sergeant. Sanad's mission was to move about however he liked, traveling whichever roads he thought Hajj Khaled might take. Thus it was that, along with his ten-man force, he came to live a life that was no different from that of the rebels themselves, and there were many moments when he was closer to them than he could ever have imagined.

Sanad became interested in all of the settlements, police stations, and British institutions that might be tempting targets for the rebels, and the only thing he lacked in order to become just like them would have been to attack the sites he thought they were going to attack.

Three times he nearly died because he and those with him were such easy, isolated targets. He had been attacked by men fighting under the command of Hajj Khaled, Hajj Yusuf Abu Durra, Abd al-Rahim al-Hajj Muhammad, and Farhan al-Sa'di, and every time he had lost some of his men. At Bab al-Wad, he was surrounded by a force led by Muhammad Saleh Abu Khaled that finished off his ten soldiers. However, he survived thanks to a British caravan that happened to pass by.

So he chose ten more men, and with them began wandering the valleys and foothills once again.

Little did he know the extent to which the uprising would escalate. During his moments of reflection, he suddenly began to wonder how he could possibly carry out a successful military operation when all the British forces put together had been unable to achieve any decisive victory. And it was through this tiny hole that Hajj Khaled was able to slip.

When Hajj Khaled was moving from one area to another, he would send one of his men to the nearest village, and from there he would bring him a horse from one of the men he knew there. If he wanted something from his own village or its men, he would send a homing pigeon that would land in Sumayya's dovecote. She would take the message and give it to Naji, who would do whatever his father asked, and when someone left the village with whatever it was that Hajj Khaled wanted, the pigeon would be with him, waiting for its next assignment.

One time he sent to the mayor of Kazaza, Mahmud Abdallah Jarwan, asking him to send him his mare because he would be moving to another location. When the mare arrived, he mounted it and headed for Mighlis. At a bend in a certain mountain pass, he suddenly found himself face to face with a British cavalry patrol under the command of none other than Sanad Rajab.

One of Hajj Khaled's men had seen the patrol from the mountaintop. He had called out, trying to warn him, but to no avail. There wasn't so much as a handspan through which Hajj Khaled could have passed, since the corridor was so narrow that there was hardly enough room for four horses to pass through it.

Their eyes met. Sanad recognized him.

"Where are you headed, man?"

"I'm going to Mighlis. I sell oil, and was coming from Kazaza. I left some oil with its mayor, Mahmud Jarwan, and I'm going now to Mighlis to see if anyone there needs some. If so, I'll go back and get what people have ordered rather than carry the oil with me to all the villages."

Sanad thought fast. He knew that any attempt to arrest Hajj Khaled would mean the total annihilation of his force. He was sure that there were rifles in the mountains pointed at him from all directions.

"Don't you have a weapon?"

"What do I need with a weapon, when all I'm doing is selling oil to people rather than fighting them?"

Of course he didn't carry a weapon during the day, since, if a dagger had been found on him, that would have been the end of him.

"What's that bag you're carrying?" Sanad asked him.

"I'm sick, and I give myself injections." He took out a syringe and showed it to them.

"We're looking for rebels around here. You shouldn't be going around by yourself, since that's dangerous for you, too. They might kill you!"

"I'm nothing but an oil vendor, and I have to sell it for a living. But if you don't want us to travel through the countryside, we won't."

"There's no need for such talk. But as I told you, don't go around by yourself." Then he said dryly, "Goodbye."

The news that no one had wanted to hear arrived: They've arrested Hajj Khaled!

Everyone—men, women, and children—began crying, certain that the British would take him straight to the gallows.

The British heard people sobbing in the villages before they heard the news itself. They looked for Hajj Khaled in their hands, and found them empty. They circled Hadiya and searched it, but found nothing. There was nothing but weeping and wailing.

"It's him, then," said Edward Peterson. "The fox has fallen into the trap, even if we haven't caught him!"

An hour after entering the village, Peterson gave orders for Hajj Khaled's house to be mined and blown up. When people tried to bring some necessary items out of the house, Peterson fired warning shots in the air with his revolver.

"Let us bring the horses out, at least."

"Just the horses!"

Peterson's weak point was Arabian horses, which, as far as he was concerned, were the most beautiful creatures on earth. Once he had even gone so far as to say, "The only thing that makes life here bearable is the presence of these enchanting animals."

When he saw those horses before him, he nearly forgot why he had come to the village. He went up to one of them, patted its back, and circled around it, eyeing it contemplatively. Then, in a flash, he jumped on its back and began riding down toward the plain as everyone looked on in stupefied amazement. He crossed the plain twice, back and forth, as people's eyes followed the dust that ascended heavenward. Then, before any of them could utter a word, they saw him heading back. When he arrived, he jumped off the horse's back with the agility of a true equestrian. He patted its back in a rare show of affection, turned to his soldiers, and said, "When we've finished with all this shit, I'm going to buy a horse like this and take it back to England."

No sooner had he finished his sentence than he raised his hand as a signal to blow up the house.

Within moments the house had been transformed into a cloud of dust.

This didn't mean much to the people of Hadiya or even to the owners of the house. After all, houses were being blown up every day. But it isn't every day that time blesses us with men like Hajj Khaled.

A few nights later, Hajj Khaled himself arrived in Hadiya. As he entered the village, there was nothing but silence, a silence so suspicious that it nearly caused him to turn back. He proceeded, but with caution. Although he had received news that his house had been destroyed, he still headed toward it as he usually did, and for a moment he thought he would actually find it there. He reached the spot where the house had once stood, but the place was completely vacant. It had turned into a miserable heap of rubble. Nothing suggested its former existence but the dovecote, now in pieces, and the evergreen oak that stood in the center of the yard. As for the orange tree, it seemed to have evaporated into thin air.

Less than a week later, he was sentenced to death in absentia.

That Evening

Rafiqa heard a knock on the door. Hamdan got up to open it.

"Wait," she said. "Who is it?"

"It's Amin."

"Amin who?"

"Amin, your son!"

"What are you doing here, you who say you're my son?"

"That's it! I've had it. Here's the rifle. If somebody else can benefit from it more, let him take it."

"Do you really think I'm going to fall for a trick like this? You've got to be a spy, and you've only brought the rifle you're talking about because the British are with you."

"But I really am Amin. I swear to God, I'm your son, Amin! Al-Far!"

"I don't have a son named Amin. Amin, the son I know, would never leave men fighting and dying in the mountains so that he could come and live under his mother's protection."

Suddenly there was silence, and on both sides of the door copious tears fell. Umm al-Far buried her head in Hamdan's chest and wept bitterly.

"I sold my gold to buy him a rifle, and now he comes to tell me, 'Let somebody else take it, somebody else who could benefit more from it!'"

Looking up at the ceiling as if the sky were there, she said, "O God, why are you tormenting me with this?"

Some time later, she heard her son's footsteps as he walked away.

Battlement of Fire

From north to south, the country was jubilant over the news of General Andrews' assassination.* Our spirits were so high, we felt well-nigh invincible.

Two days after the assassination, we heard the sound of gunfire coming from somewhere. It was morning. As usual, people tried to determine which area the sounds were coming from. Some said there was a battle going on in Sajad, while others said it was in Kazaza. The people of Hadiya gathered, then rushed off in the direction of Sajad. When they got there, they found people hurrying away from Sajad to Khalda. "Where's the battle?" we asked, and they said, "In Khalda."

---

* General Andrews had come from England seething and threatening to discipline the Palestinian rebels who had risen up against his country. Muhammad Abu Ja'b related to me more than once the way General Andews had been killed. He said, "The rebels learned that General Andrews would be attending a mass next day at the Church of the Annunciation in Nazareth. So we went early the next morning and lay in ambush for him there. Preparations were being made to receive the general, and as people were standing there, a mentally deranged person came up, followed by some young boy, and pointed to a spot on the ground, saying, 'Blood will flow here! Blood will flow here!'" Abu Ja'b told me that the general had, in fact, fallen in the very place the mentally deranged man had pointed to. The general arrived in a Rolls Royce, and Abu Ja'b drew his revolver. Then, overcome with fright, he hesitated before firing. Meanwhile, Andrews continued on his way to the

We reached Khalda's high hills. Beneath them there were broad lowlands with a road running down the center, and to their left were the quarries located adjacent to Khalda. The area where we were located was planted in wheat, but it was high as well. Some people were carrying weapons, and some of them were completely unarmed. If you asked one of the people who were unarmed, "Why are you here?" he would say, "To treat the wounded, and to take martyrs back to their families." However, their hands weren't completely empty, since they always had something with them: a stick, an ax, a dagger.

We were all tormented by the same realization, namely, that if the Jews lost, they would go back to the countries they'd come from. But if we lost, we would lose everything.

When we got closer to the place, we saw the Palestinian flag. In the center of its triangle, the revolution had added the image of a crescent embracing a cross. We could see by this time that there were more than five hundred armed rebels, as well as reinforcements from among the villagers.

This was what always happened at times like this: all anyone had to say was, "Your brothers in Sajad need you," or "Your brothers in al-Duwayma or Fallujah need your help," and people would rush out to lend a hand to the rebels and the villages that were under attack.

When we got there, we found the rebels surrounding a Jewish caravan that had stopped in the middle of the road. It was being guarded by the British army, and the Jews were trying to break the siege and firing from the elevated areas of the quarries at anyone who tried to approach.

We said, "What are you waiting for, men?"

They said, "We're exposed, and if we try to go down, we'll be killed."

We said, "And is everyone down on the plain either a Jew or a Briton?"

They said, "In fact, there are some rebels surrounding the caravan, too."

---

door of the church. When Abu Ja'b saw that the general was about to get away from him, he took off his shoes and ran after him. He shot him three times in the back, and he fell to the ground dead. Afterward, a British officer came out of the church, and he and Abu Ja'b stood there pointing their revolvers in each other's faces. The following moments were filled with tense anticipation, since it wasn't clear which of the two would fire. But then the British officer turned around and retreated, and so did Abu Ja'b. Two of Abu Ja'b's companions were arrested and later executed by the British. As for Abu Ja'b himself, he was pursued by the British until the end of the uprising, at which point he left with the rebels for Syria.

In a rush of enthusiasm, a large number of young men decided to go down to the plain, but at the last moment they heard the voice of Hajj Khaled, who had tied his keffiyeh* tightly around his head.

"You're not going anywhere," he said. "I'm not going to risk everybody's lives. I want just one or two volunteers to go check out the area."

A young man from Mighlis whom I didn't recognize said, "I'll go."

"Who else?" asked Hajj Khaled, looking in our direction.

"I'll go," I said.

"With God's blessing," he replied.

So we went down without a single shot being fired at us.

We said, "Maybe the men who are here are on our side."

I took my white keffiyeh and raised it up on my rifle, shouting, "Arabs! Arabs!"

Then things got even quieter than before.

Behind us, everyone wanted to rush down to the plain. But Hajj Khaled prevented them, saying, "Nobody's going anywhere until we know what's happening down there. It might be an ambush. I'm not going to gamble with hundreds of people's lives with all those machine guns on the other side."

We advanced farther, and the situation stayed the way it was. There was no gunfire or anything. Suddenly, after we'd come closer and were running across a small waterfall, bullets started to whiz past us again. My buddy from Mighlis jumped and fell, and when I tried to jump over him, I fell into a muddy puddle facedown.

I laughed. "Why did you trip me?" I asked.

He was lying in the waterfall, which couldn't have been more than a meter high.

I looked at him, only to find his blood trickling into the water. I turned him over.

He said, "I've been wounded, brother."

---

* It was a known fact that the rebels in Palestine wore a keffiyeh and camel-hair headband on their heads, which was also the customary head attire for men in the villages, whereas men who lived in the cities generally wore the fez. Since the British authorities had no way of distinguishing the rebels in the cities from regular villagers, they thus considered everyone who wore the keffiyeh and the headband to be a rebel. The leaders of the revolution then issued a statement in which they urged Palestinian city dwellers to remove their fezzes, and in this way they erased the distinction between rebels and others. Senior officials, magistrates, and qa'imaqams wrote to the British authorites telling them that they couldn't leave home for their jobs unless they wore the keffiyeh and the headband (the symbol of the revolution), so the British authorities gave them permission to do so. Some British people and foreign journalists also began wearing them.

I tried to give him first aid, but I had nothing with me but my keffiyeh, and I couldn't tell where the blood was coming from. He was bleeding all over, as though every part of him had been wounded. I began by bringing him out of the water, being careful not to raise my head higher than the waterfall.

Suddenly, he said, "Leave me here. The Jews have arrived."

I looked up, and sure enough, there they were, fifty meters away. Letting him fall, I began shooting at random. By the time I'd fired all the bullets in my rifle, he would have his rifle loaded and hand it to me, and so on.

The British rifle of the type we were using took five rounds from the top. To load it, you pulled the bolt handle back, put the bullet in, and pressed on it, and it would go down into the magazine.

I said to him, "They're coming closer and closer."

I had a bag with me that held three Mills grenades that I'd bought for a dinar apiece. He handed me the bag and I took out a grenade. I pulled out the safety pin and threw it as far as I could. It went off. I took the second and threw it, then the third, and threw it, too. After that, no more shots were fired in our direction. We looked up at the foothill and saw the men pouring down in our direction. At the same time, I heard Hajj Khaled shout, "Not now!" But the chaos, the lack of discipline, and the fact that the villagers were together with the rebels mixed everything up into a royal jumble!

There were men running out unprotected, and on the other side, untold numbers of machine guns mowing people down right and left. May you never have to see what I saw that day! Fortunately for us, though, the number of our men was so large that they threw the ambushers and the men in the caravan into confusion. I saw Hajj Khaled leaping from place to place like a tiger. Never in my life have I seen anybody as nimble or strong as he was. He disappeared for a little while, and I started looking around to see where he had gone. All of a sudden, I saw him right over me at the waterfall. He asked me how my buddy was, since he had seen him bleeding.

I said, "We won't know until we treat his wounds."

One of the men said, "I'll take the wounded man back, since I don't have a weapon with me."

I said to Hajj Khaled, "No, I'll take him back. I've done all I can in this battle, and I've been through plenty!"

I picked him up with the help of another man, and together we got him out of the waterfall. Then I carried him the rest of the way.

A few meters farther along, I found a man with a wounded foot. I recognized him: he was Hannuk the gypsy. I tried to take him along with me as well, since he was a slight man, but he said, "Leave me here. The one you're carrying is hurt more badly than I am."

"I'm not going to leave you behind," I told him.

"There's nothing even wrong with me," he said. "Look!" Then he took hold of his broken leg and moved it back into place without screaming in agony! He really did!

"You've got to do your duty," he told me. "Those who are in danger of not making it you try to save, and as you can see, I'm not going to die just because a bullet or two shattered my leg."

So I left him and went on up. At first the battle was ahead of me. Then I found myself in the middle of it, and then I came out on the other side. If you ask me how it happened without my being hit, all I can say is, "I don't know!"

When I got him onto higher ground, there were men waiting to take the wounded away. As I began to leave, he said to me, "You still don't know who I am!"

"There was no chance for us to introduce ourselves," I told him. "But we can do that now."

"I'm Fawzi Mahmud from Mighlis, the mayor's son," he said.

"And I'm so-and-so from Hadiya," I told him.

"You're our family, then, and I want you to complete the favor you've done for me by telling my brothers and the rest of my family what's happened to me."

"If I get back alive, I'll go see your family right away," I assured him.

By this time a car had arrived to take the wounded to Ramla.

"Here's my rifle," he said. "And here are my revolver and my bullet belt. Take these to them, too."

"OK," I agreed. "Don't worry about a thing."

There were twenty-four other men with me from our village, and I said to him, "All the guys who are with me will help get your things to them."

I wanted to sit down and catch my breath. But then I remembered Hannuk the gypsy, and I said, "It won't do for me to leave him there alone. I'll go back and get him." I remembered how, in more than one battle, he had said to the other men, "I don't want a rifle. I can help you more with a dagger."

I went back to him. On my way, I met up with three men hiding behind a large boulder.

One of them said to me, "Where are you going? This whole area is full of British and Jews." As he spoke, he raised his hand to point, and a bullet went through his palm. I hid behind the boulder with them. It wouldn't have been possible for anybody to go on attacking even if he'd been crawling on his belly. A British war plane appeared in the sky, circled overhead, and left.

The battle was like an ammunitions depot in the middle of a blaze: you couldn't tell where the bullets were coming from, or where a shell might land.

Still, I kept remembering the way Hannuk had put his broken leg back in place, and I couldn't get the image out of my mind! His clan had passed through Hadiya's territory a couple of years earlier, and had then gone on to the 'fifth column' villages next to us. When Abd al-Latif al-Hamdi saw a certain gypsy girl dancing, he was so smitten with her beauty that he paid five gold pounds to the head of the clan for her. When the clan moved on, Hannuk, who was love in her, didn't move on with them. Instead he pitched a small tent nearby. Al-Hamdi's armed men set it on fire, so he brought another one, and they set that one on fire, too. But he refused to budge. When al-Hamdi began harassing Hadiya, Hannuk sided with Hadiya. And when he realized that al-Hamdi was with the British and the Jews, he was against them both. He would hover around al-Hamdi's house every night, saying over and over, "My heart is naked without her!"

Hajj Khaled instructed the force in the vanguard to begin firing while the men began withdrawing toward higher areas, so that's what they did. However, instead of retreating with them, I advanced in search of Hannuk. I was sure I'd find him in the spot where I'd left him. After all, where could a man with a broken leg like his go? But I didn't find him. Where on earth had the darned guy disappeared to? I wondered. Then, fifteen meters away, I glimpsed a dead body. I recognized him. I went crawling toward him until I reached him. I didn't need to turn him over to know what had happened to him. A bullet had gone through his forehead and come out through the top of his neck. Bullets were coming down on us like rain. In his hand I saw a rifle for the first time, a rifle he must have taken out of the hands of some martyr or wounded man.

I said, "God have mercy on Hannuk. He died at the moment when he exchanged his dagger for a rifle."

A Bullet in the Heart

The presence of that many men created indescribable chaos. The battle had begun with fifty men, and suddenly they'd become five hundred!

Once again, Hajj Khaled organized the fighters after most of them had withdrawn to the wheat fields.

The temperature had risen, and we were expecting the British forces to close in on us from three directions. Instead, though, an airplane approached. Some of us knew what to do, while others thought it would be better to flee. However, everyone who had fled during our first raid had died or been wounded.

"Weapons!" Hajj Khaled cried.

He instructed us to lie on our stomachs and point our rifles toward the sky, then shoot when he gave the order. We were like a long wall of rifles. And when the airplane came back again, we heard him shout, "Fire!"

The rifles went off at that same moment. The sounds of the guns' reports fused into a clap of thunder the likes of which we'd never heard before. I closed my eyes without knowing the reason, and when I opened them to the sound of the men's elated cheers and looked where they were looking, I saw a long cloud of smoke trailing behind the airplane.

A few moments later, I saw it crashing into the ground. We figured it had landed somewhere between the villages of Saydun and Abu Shusha.

Seeing that plane go down was great for our morale.

Suddenly, we saw a young man with skin lighter than any we had ever seen before standing next to Hajj Khaled. Tall and skinny as a rail, his eyes were small, and as blue as the sea.

The two of them spoke for a few minutes, then came toward us.

"We could have all died on account of the chaos. You saw it with your own eyes. What happened at the start of the battle mustn't happen again. Whoever wants to fight the British and the Jews has to fight them the right way, not be the cause of the death of those he's fighting with. And now Sava will explain the plan to you."

Sava had a distinctive, powerful presence the likes of which I'd never encountered before, even in Hajj Mahmud, may he rest in peace. And when he opened his mouth to speak, we were astounded by his ability to speak Arabic. As if to interrupt the train of questions in our minds, he said, "I'm Sava from Yugoslavia, and I'm a volunteer from the revolution. I entered the First World War when I was a little boy and served in the army for fifteen years.

"We're going to break up into units. Every offensive unit will be made up of ten men, and behind each one there will be another unit of ten men for protection that will cover the offensive unit's advance. When the front unit advances, it will cover for the unit behind it, and so on."

It was a nice organization.

The battle had subsided on the plain, but the caravan was still unable to move. Those of its soldiers who were still alive were outside the jeeps, and at the rear of the caravan there were rebels that no one could get past. As for the road ahead, it was blocked by rocks and tree branches.

Hajj Khaled and the Yugoslavian led two offensive units that crawled ahead. When they had reached a place they could fire from easily, the battle started up again, and at that point the rear units advanced.

We weren't afraid at all. You ask me why? Because we knew that the spirit God had given us could be taken by Him alone, and at the time of His choosing, not at the time chosen by the British or any other creature on the face of the earth.

When I left the house that morning, my wife Safiya asked me, "Where are you going? What can you do with this puny stick of yours in the face of the British and their tanks?"

I said to her, "Don't insist on hearing my answer now. That way, if I come out of the battle alive, there'll be a reason for me to come home to you again!"

The advance was successful and we'd gotten close to the enemy in spite of the fact that our legs were bleeding from all the crawling and bumping up against rocks, and in spite of the net of fire through whose holes we were passing.

"Advance!" shouted the Yugoslavian.

We advanced. Suddenly, I saw the armored car's turret open and bullets being fired. I saw everybody in front of me falling down dead. I went down on my belly. A man in front of me was breathing his last. His legs were convulsing and kept hitting me in the face. With some difficulty, I reached out and took hold of his feet in an attempt to steady him, but it was no use. He kept on convulsing until, in the end, he died a martyr.

We went back to Plan A, namely, for a unit to advance, and for another to protect its advance from the rear. The turret closed in the face of our gunfire. When we reached the armored car, I heard the Yugoslavian shouting to those inside it: "Surrender!" as he pounded on its metal walls.

One of our men went up and tried to fire on those inside the armored car through an opening where the glass had been shattered. But someone inside it shot him and he fell down dead beside it.

What stupidity!

I heard somebody say to somebody else, "Go, kill the one who killed your father!" But the boy refused. I heard the first voice saying to him, "Coward." Then he moved forward. But as he climbed up the armored car to do what the boy had been unable to do, he was thrust by the force of more gunfire on top of the dead body of the man who'd been killed a little while earlier.

Man, war isn't our thing!

We pulled the two men back a few meters, as if we were afraid the armored car would suddenly start to move and crush them as well.

Not long after this, a British armored vehicle came along raising a white flag.

"Unbelievable!" we said. "We've lived to see the British raise the white flag!"

They asked us to lift our siege of the caravan in return for their allowing our men to withdraw. The Yugoslavian turned to Hajj Khaled, who said to them, "Look at our dead. After all we've lost, we'll never retreat. And if you don't go back to where you came from right this minute, we'll blow up the caravan and everyone in it."

The white flag went back to where it had come from.

The sun grew hotter. I looked at the water that flowed next to the road, and it was running red.

The Yugoslavian said, "Every one of you hide behind whatever he can find."

Those inside the armored car had gone completely quiet. They must have been scared to death when they heard all that pounding on the metal walls of their machine.

"What are you thinking?" Hajj Khaled asked him.

"I'm going to blow it up," he said, and took a mine out of his bag.

We got away.

At the moment when the Yugoslavian came up next to the armored car, its turret opened and rifles peered out alone. We didn't see a single soldier. Then shots were fired in all directions. They must have thought there were a lot of men around their armored car. Taken by surprise, the Yugoslavian left the mine only two meters away, then hurriedly moved back. But before he could get away, a bullet hit the mine and it exploded. The armored car went flying into the air, and the Yugoslavian was hit by a piece of shrapnel that split his right shoulder open down to the middle of his chest.

Never in my life had I seen a wound like that. But I was going to see plenty more later on, on the night of the massacre!

Then there was chaos all over again, as people went rushing out to the Yugoslavian. If there had been a single machine gun it could have killed scores of us in a single moment. But, thank God, the armored car's explosion had been the end of everything, and we saw the British soldiers and officers on the other side of the caravan raising their hands in surrender. Then, much to our surprise, Hajj Khaled found himself face to face with the Palestinian officer Sanad Rajab.

Now that the British had surrendered, the Jews stationed at the top of the quarries couldn't fire, since they were waiting to see what would happen.

As I was trying to apply pressure to the Yugoslavian's wound in order to stop the bleeding, my hand slipped inside the wound. For months thereafter I couldn't eat with that hand, since every time I saw it come toward my mouth, I would see it dripping with blood.

I started to cry. Yeah, I cried.

The Yugoslavian turned to me and said, "What are you all crying about?"

I looked around me, and sure enough, all the men were crying, including Hajj Khaled.

The Yugoslavian said, "You're crying over a person in your ranks who's fallen. But nobody who cries over a young man who dies a martyr's death will be able to stop the Jews' immigration to Palestine or drive the British out!"

So then and there, we dried our tears.

Those were his last words. However, he wasn't the last man to be martyred in that battle. Suddenly, we saw a wounded British soldier lying in the back of a jeep draw his rifle. The moment he fired, Hajj Khaled moved to block the path of the bullet, which was heading for Qasem Aliyan's chest. The bullet went through Hajj Khaled's shoulder, then continued on its way toward Qasem, who fell a martyr in that instant. At the same time, we saw Hajj Khaled lean over, bleeding.

We gathered around Hajj Khaled to protect him, while some of our men began raining bullets on the back of the jeep. One of them went up and fired three rounds from his revolver into the back of the jeep, then came back.

Many of the men felt that Hajj Khaled had gone too far in what he had done. At the same time, they realized that a man like this was somebody you could storm hell itself with. However, the matter went a lot deeper. It was a secret that would come to light little by little as we got closer to Qasem's village, then to his house.

The men fighting under Fawzi al-Qawuqji, the leader of the uprising, arrived. As we worked hurriedly to bandage his wound, Hajj Khaled said, "They'll take the cars and the weapons." As for the ammunition, it had been placed in the road. There was a lot of it. Crates full.

He said, "Whoever has shot a bullet should take two bullets in its place, and whoever has thrown a grenade should take two grenades."

We started checking on everyone who had been killed, both British and Arabs. I came to a person lying on the ground. He wasn't dressed like us. I saw no blood around him, and he wasn't bleeding. I stuck my rifle in his face and ordered him to raise his hands. He didn't understand. I placed the rifle on his right arm, and he stretched it out, then on his left, and he stretched that one out, too. I poked him in the side and he turned over, and what should I find but that he was a Jew.

"A Jew!" I yelled.

There was a British volunteer with us named Jack. He was one of a small number of British soldiers who were against Britain's crimes and the idea of imperialism. These soldiers had decided to stay with the rebels when the revolution helped a number of them flee to Syria, and from there to wherever they wanted to go.

Jack, who was holding a British Vickers machine gun, said, "Please, let me kill him!"

Hajj Khaled shook his head, struggling to manage his pain. "Nobody is going to be killed here. We'll withdraw with the captives, since they'll be our protection if we're intercepted by any British force, or if we're pursued by British aircraft."

It was around noon. We picked up the Yugoslavian, Qasem Aliyan, and the rest of the wounded and martyred and began ascending the foothill toward the wheat field, whose stalks were so stiff and hard that all the winds of the world would have been unable to shake them.

When we'd gotten some distance away we dug a grave for the Yugoslavian. The men stood in a single row, more than four hundred fifty men, I tell you, and we fired our guns in a salute to him.

Everybody was thinking about what would happen to the captives: eleven officers and soldiers, in addition to the Jew and Sanad Rajab.

The men had dispersed, carrying the martyred and wounded back to the villages they'd come from. I was carrying a rifle and Fawzi Mahmud's revolver, the one I'd promised to deliver to his family in Mighlis.

As soon as we reached a safe area, Hajj Khaled went off to be alone with some of his men. When he came back, he turned to the captives and said a word that floored us all: "Goodbye!"

He exchanged a glance with the Palestinian officer, Sanad Rajab, and we felt as though we could hear Hajj Khaled's eyes saying, "One good turn deserves another."

"Let's kill them!" said one of the men angrily.

Without looking at him, Hajj Khaled shouted in reply, "We're rebels, not murderers!" Then there was silence again.

The captives took off, and we continued to hear the sound of their footsteps until they disappeared completely in the direction of the road that ran through the hills overlooking Bayt Mahsir.

Hajj Khaled said, "There's a mission that only I will be able to carry out. But I want some men to come with me."

I heard a voice saying, "I'm with you." Then I heard another and another and another and another, until Hajj Khaled said, "That's enough."

When I looked into his face, it was completely different than I'd ever seen it before: he looked pale, sorrowful, and anxious.

As the men carried the martyr Qasem Aliyan away on their shoulders, we watched them until they turned in the direction of his village, which was opposite Hadiya.

As if I'd been unconscious and had suddenly come to again, I said, "How could I have forgotten?" And a horrified shudder went through me.

The Flower of the Past

The day he had been fearing arrived.

Ever since Qasem's arrival, Hajj Khaled had realized that it was an unbearable responsibility. Although he concealed the unease he felt when he heard the name 'Qasem Aliyan,' he decided to decline his offer even before he knew whether or not the name belonged to the man he had in mind. He ruled out the possibility that, given the fact that it was common throughout Palestine for more than one person to bear the same name, he might be someone else, since his gut told him that there could only be one Qasem Aliyan, and that this was the Qasem who was standing before him.

When Qasem had come to him, carrying a rifle so old it must have gone through half Turkey's wars, he said to him, "We have a lot of men here, and our movement has become more complicated. So maybe it would be better for you and for us if you joined some other rebel unit."

"If I'm not with you, I don't want to be with anybody. Give this old gun a chance to fight for you. Maybe it will make up for what it did to us when it was in the hands of the Turks."

Suddenly, Hajj Khaled felt a painful throbbing in his heart. He reached down and squeezed his trousers pocket, terrified that the cream-colored handkerchief inside it might be visible, and that Qasem might recognize it if he caught a glimpse of it. Hajj Khaled left his place and walked to the end of the wood, where he could be alone. He felt his pocket again and was reassured. He stood there near the ravine that ran parallel to the mountain forest, kneading his brow with the fingers of his left hand. He gazed for a long time into the ravine, and as he did so, it seemed to him that the earth was nothing but a deep ravine in the universe, a ravine hard for human beings to climb out of. Some of us manage to get as far as a treetop. Some of us make it halfway up. Some of us get to the top of the mountain. Some of us try to get out by riding in an airplane, or on a fast horse, or by car or train. But nothing comes of any of our attempts. We're in the ravine, at the bottom of this universe, and we have to make the decisions that make us feel that we've risen higher than an airplane or become faster than a horse, a car, or a train, that we're about to reach the edge and ascend into the heavens.

He took a deep breath and wondered: Where did this Qasem come from? What brought him here? I thought I'd left the past behind me, that I'd left it and everything in it, only to find it standing in front of me. Did it have to appear now? And now what? Does he have to join me? What curse is this that's on your trail, Khaled? What have you done? What can you do if you're marching side by side with this man? Attack the British and the Jews, and protect him at the same time? If this isn't a curse, then what is?

When he came back to Qasem, he said, "As I've said, there's no place for you. You're sure to have more to offer somewhere else."

"You don't know. I've come here for one reason, and that's not to go back. As you can see, I'm not a little boy that you could convince with a word here or a word there. See? My head's full of gray hair!"

He lifted the edge of his keffiyyeh, and his white head shone in the sunlight filtering through the branches.

"Besides, you won't have to worry about me! I don't have any children who would be orphaned if God chose martyrdom for me. It's just me and my wife, and nobody else," said Qasem.

Hajj Khaled's heart quaked. He turned his face away. When he looked at Qasem again, he said, "Frankly, I can't bear responsibility for your presence with us."

The men were following the conversation without realizing what lay behind it

"I didn't come here to be a burden to you. I came to help you, and if I felt I were going to do anything else, I'd kill myself right now."

Hajj Khaled walked back over to the edge of the ravine. Looking into the distance, he saw smoke rising from the bread ovens in more than one village. He heard the cries of shepherds and the yelping of dogs as they herded their cows, sheep, and goats back home.

When once again he stood before Qasem, he said to him, "Welcome, then. May God lead us aright."

In every battle Qasem fought with him, Hajj Khaled watched him like a hawk. It wasn't that he was a child who needed to be taken care of. In fact, he was as old as Hajj Khaled himself. However, this didn't prevent Hajj Khaled from holding his breath for fear that some harm might unexpectedly come to Qasem.

And now here he was, marching in front of the men who were carrying Qasem's corpse: down into the valleys, over the foothills, and through the fields.

When they reached the hills overlooking the village, he sensed the enormity of the catastrophe even more.

"I'll wait for you here!" he said to them.

"How can you wait for us here?" they wanted to know. "We're not leaving you alone, and we're not going alone. We need you down there! The person we're carrying on our shoulders is somebody they expect to come back alive, not a martyr. We need you, and his family needs you. It will mean a lot to them that you've come personally. It's a way of showing respect for them and the person they've lost."

"Shouldn't I have delivered the other martyrs to their doorsteps too, then?"

"Every one of them deserved that. But you're the one who said you had to deliver Qasem's body to his family in person."

Hajj Khaled knew all this, and he knew it was the proper thing to do. He also knew that his men knew, and that the people of the village and everyone in the country knew. He knew that the opening he was trying to slip through would have been too narrow even for one of his fingers. So how did he expect it to be wide enough for his entire body, his entire spirit?

He shook his head, thinking: Since I was willing to escort his body all the way here, it seems I've got no choice but to keep going no matter what happens.

Despite all these irrefutable arguments, he wasn't sure whether he should continue on his way or stop. Nevertheless, he found himself continuing on his way, following the people as they sang,

Tell us where your house is, pretty Yasmin
We're ready to follow you wherever you go!

Tell us where your house is, sweet Yasmin,
We'll follow you to Jerusalem, to Jericho!

Your long raven hair reaches from Acre to Jaffa,
From Gaza to Majdal, from Haifa to Safafa!

Then, as though the father of the bride were coming to greet the delegation, the women sang on his behalf:

A loving welcome to those whose coming
Is like abundant showers after dearth!

Suddenly Hajj Khaled came to a halt. The men behind him ran into him, and he felt the martyr's skull colliding with his head. It was then that he knew he was about to face a test that was beyond a human being's capacity to endure.

402

From a distance the village glimpsed the five men, and all its senses went on high alert. With every step the men took toward the houses on its periphery, the hotter the minutes blazed.

People working in the olive groves saw them and came running toward them from a distance. When they reached them, their cries went up: "God is greatest! There is no god but God!"

Many of the villagers rushed out toward them. They met. One of the men of the village came up and uncovered the martyr's face. He took two steps back.

"Who is it?" asked those who hadn't been able to see the face.

"Qasem. Qasem Aliyan. He was martyred for your sakes, for Palestine's sake."

Some of them wept, and some said, "God is greatest!" They headed down toward his house.

Many of the men recognized Hajj Khaled and came up and walked with him, flanking him on either side. He looked at his arm. Blood was seeping out of the wound and falling drop by drop.

From a distance he saw her look out, then advance toward them with timorous steps like the scores of other women who were there. When the funeral procession turned and marched toward the house, led by a little boy who acted as though he was the only one who knew where the martyr had lived, she trembled, then froze. Her eyes stopped blinking.

She whispered to herself: "So his guilty conscience finally killed him!"

Emptiness

Y ou couldn't exactly say he'd been an informer. However, he had prattled too much, and he knew the reason why. It was the hole that had opened up deep in Qasem's soul, then grown larger and larger when he wasn't able to have a single child by Yasmin.

"I've got her now, and that's all that matters," he had said to himself in the beginning. But after she'd become his, he felt as though she was completely empty—empty in every sense of the word. There was nothing inside: no heart, no viscera, no womb, no compassion. She was like a beautiful edifice that had been abandoned, with nothing in it but the spiders that kept multiplying to fill the corners. Yasmin herself didn't understand what had happened. Suddenly, after Khaled recovered Hamama and everything that had been stolen from the village, he had turned into an outlaw on the Turks' wanted list.

Qasem would whisper to everyone he met, "I tell you, there's no one else that could have done it. He's the hero. Khaled is the hero who did all that to the Turks."

Then the whispers spread from one person to another, the way rain spreads through the soil.

Those who loved Khaled would deny it, saying, "No, it isn't him. It couldn't be. There's no single human being who could do all that." But their denials did no good.

The winds carried the whispers to neighboring villages, making the rounds with them until, along with other whispers that were even clearer, they settled in the ears of the Turkish military police.

When Qasem heard that Khaled was being pursued, he couldn't specify exactly how he felt. Sometimes he would whisper to himself: I've really made him into a hero, so he should thank me! Other times, he would doubt everything he had done, and would think out loud, "How can Yasmin agree to marry me now that I've turned Khaled into a hero with my own hands?"

But in the end, Yasmin did agree. She agreed because she had no choice but to agree. She went to her husband's house like a ewe being led to slaughter. She was haunted by her father's words, "Empires survive longer than people do. And this empire is here to stay. No one who's fled from the Ottoman state has survived to tell the story unless he disappeared forever. And in this case, too, the state has been the victor. We really do love him. At the same time, though, there's something being woven by fate. In fact, it's already been woven, and it goes beyond our own hopes and dreams. So you need to think carefully about what I'm saying."

After she was married, she said to her father, "But he *has* survived! He's lived longer than the empire itself. The empire has died, and he's still alive."

"This topic is closed," he said, "and it's not proper for you ever to talk about it."

"No, Baba. The topic isn't closed, at least as long as we're alive. When we die, maybe it will be. But as long as people remember him, he'll live forever, as a curse. Everything dies except this type of curse."

"Time will erase everything."

"Time does erase things, Baba. But not everything."

When Yasmin's mother came to visit her two months later, she whispered in her ear, "Tell me some good news! Is there something on the way?"

"No, Mama. There isn't anything, and there never will be."

"Qasem isn't 'of no use,' is he—God forbid?"

"It's got nothing to do with Qasem. It's got to do with me."

"We'll take you to a doctor tomorrow morning. Your father will come and take you to a doctor. To Ramla, to Jaffa, to Jerusalem, to Haifa."

"The doctor's got nothing to do with what's happening with me, either. I've made a decision. I'm not going to have any children by Qasem."

"How can you say such a thing? You're a young girl, and your husband's in the prime of his youth! This is something neither the woman nor the man has any control over. As long as everything is normal, there have to be children."

"No, Mama. I know myself. My body's not going to conceive or give birth, since it's my soul that conceives, and my soul that gives birth."

And in fact, Yasmin didn't conceive. Three years went by, and she didn't conceive. Four. Five. Twenty. And she didn't conceive.

Qasem didn't dare say to her, "If that's the way things are, then I'll take another wife."

Instead he said, "I'm going to enlist in Hajj Khaled's army."

"I'm afraid you'll be the cause of his death this time," she said, and as usual, she didn't look at him.

"What do you mean?"

"In any case, it's too late. It's too late for you to do anything for me."

"What I'm doing now is only for me. The only thing I could have done for you, I should have done a long time ago."

When Hajj Khaled stood face to face with Yasmin, those who knew he had been her fiancé once upon a time and that she'd given him up for Qasem the blabbermouth felt a shiver go down their spines.

Even though Hajj Khaled knew her father had passed away some time before, for some strange reason he began looking for his face in the crowd.

Looking over at Qasem's lifeless body, he said to her, "May the years he was deprived of be added to yours."

"And to yours," she replied. Then she began to cry.

The sun was going down, and some of the men pointed out the importance of burying him that same day: "A prompt burial is the best way to honor a martyr."

The funeral procession, whose numbers continued to grow, then continued on its way.

"We'll take him to his house so that his family can say goodbye to him. Then we'll take him to the cemetery."

They took him to his house. His sisters and his mother came. The sound of weeping filled the air. A moment later, his father came in and said, "Don't contaminate his wound with tears. This is a martyr."

"He doesn't belong just to God!" the mother shouted in his face. "He's mine, too. He's my son!"

Qasem had been her eldest son, and from the time he had snatched Yasmin out of Khaled's hands, she had been aware of the curse that had afflicted him to the core. She said, "I'm afraid God will never forgive you for what you've done. No matter what you do, it can't change the fact that you've separated two hearts in love and deprived them of each other."

Her prediction had been fulfilled. Even so, he had surprised her by coming home a martyr. She looked into his face. There was the hint of a smile on his lips. She looked over at Yasmin. Then, gazing heavenward, she cried from the depths of her being, "Your mercy, Lord!"

When people learned the details of what had happened at the moment he was martyred, and how Hajj Khaled had wanted to die in his stead, they felt more ambivalent than ever. They talked about destiny, divine wisdom, and how God has foreordained how long each person will live from the time he's born.

As for Yasmin, she was more lost than ever. She was doubly tormented, now that she knew that Khaled had still been prepared to give his life for her even after all that had happened. It tormented her to think that he might have died for *her* sake at that moment, and not for the sake of Palestine, not realizing that if he had been martyred and Qasem had come home alive, his revenge against her would have been all the more complete.

"Your mercy, Lord!" she wailed. "What's happening to me?"

It was the last time she would see Hajj Khaled before her: the final meeting, baptized in blood, that opened out onto the unknown. It was the final meeting, which had been necessary in order for her to realize that she had lost Khaled forever, just as he realized that he had lost her forever.

As he looked at her, he saw the martyr's blood pouring forth in a stream between them, a stream that no human being could ford.

Hamama's Return

ajj Khaled peered into the distance and saw seven horses crossing the plain. His heart skipped a beat. As they drew nearer, he saw her more clearly among them. That is, he saw Hamama. The horsemen ascended the foothill and disappeared among its trees. For some reason, none of them was riding the white mare. When he noticed this, his heart skipped a beat again, just as it had at the moment when he had seen her beside him that night so many years before, not knowing whether what he was seeing was real or just a dream.

He tried his best to see through the trees, but to no avail. Realizing that the mare had to be Hamama herself, he suddenly lost all his reserve.

Perturbed, he said to himself, "What Hamama? She must have died by now, or at least gotten old like you!"

To his dismay, he found himself standing alone and exposed, far from his army, as though he weren't living under a death sentence. What an irony it would be if Hamama were now being used as bait! Yet still he didn't budge.

Suddenly, her head popped out from among the trees, alone. It *was* her. But who were the horsemen with her? He tried to retreat, to disappear behind a tree, but his feet only planted themselves more firmly on the ground.

"There's nothing you need more than a mare like this," came a voice to his right.

He turned, and who should he find before him but Tariq, the son of Shaykh Muhammad al-Sa'adat. He had grown a lot older, and had come to resemble his father, Shaykh Muhammad, quite a bit. Hajj Khaled saw Iliya Radhi, who had come with them, looking on with tears in his eyes.

Suddenly, time turned back, and Hajj Khaled saw himself as he was returning her to her original owners.

"I'm afraid time will treat your beloved badly if she stays with me," he said.

They made no reply.

"I'm leaving her here," he added, "and when things get a bit better, I'll come back for her."

"You know that the mare that's brought back won't leave again."

"But I'll lose her if she stays with me. I'm a hunted man, and what has she done to deserve such a fate?"

"A horse with a free spirit can bear it."

The words cut him like a knife.

"But I can't bear it."

They kept approaching as he stood there, unable to move. When Tariq wrapped him in a tight embrace, he lifted his arms and embraced him in return.

"This is Hamama. There's no one who deserves a mare like her as much as you do."

Hajj Khaled tried to open his mouth to say he couldn't take her, but Tariq clapped his hand over his mouth to prevent him. "We've brought you our daughter for a second time because you mean so much to us."

Hajj Khaled's army gathered around them, listening intently to a conversation that had begun before their time.

Looking over at Hamama, Hajj Khaled said, "It seems it really is her."

"She's her granddaughter," said Tariq.

"And Hamama herself? How is she?"

"Like us, she's gotten older, but she's as feisty as ever."

"I'm afraid you're saying that just to be polite."

"Do you mean what I said about her, or what I said about us?"

They laughed.

Then, suddenly, they fell silent.

Hajj Khaled gazed at her, and when he found the strength to move, he walked toward her. One of Tariq's men had tied her to a stone pine tree. Hajj Khaled took her face in his hands. A tear escaped, in spite of his efforts to prevent it, and flowed down until it reached his right moustache. However, a tear from his other eye didn't manage to cover half the distance the first tear had gone.

To the amazement of many of the men in his army, he kissed her forehead. Then he knelt until his knees touched the ground. He took her right hoof, raised it to his lips, and kissed it, then gently lowered it again. Then he took her left hoof and did the same thing.

With the return of Hamama, the spirit within Hajj Khaled that had been torn mercilessly apart by that moment when he found himself face to face with Yasmin returned to him as well.

When he was told, "You should rest until your wound has healed," he didn't repeat the words he had been saying over and over during previous days: "As long as it's just a wound, it will heal sooner or later."

Instead he said, "The wound? Are you still thinking about that?"

He took hold of Hamama's halter and led her some distance away. When he was sure no one would hear them, he said to her, "My only condition is that you not remind me of her."

Hamama nodded her head.

He was prepared for anything except for her to go back to her old whispering, the whispering with which she used to fill his ears both waking and sleeping, saying, "It's her, it's her, it's her."

There, out on the open plain, he had nearly lost his mind. "How could a mare be talking?" he screamed.

411

When he could bear it no longer, he had decided to return her to her original owners. He had understood the deeper significance of what he was doing. At the same time, he had known that he would also lose her if she kept on whispering in his ear. He would lose her because he would go mad, and lose himself along with her.

Hajj Khaled tried to banish the image of Yasmin standing before him, looking at him and at her husband's dead body. He tried to banish the image of the woman in her. He didn't even dare whisper to himself: "It's her, just the way she always was. She hasn't changed. It's her."

But in the end, he did whisper it: "It's her." He said it out loud to Hamama: "It's her. And from now on, I'm the only one who can say it, not you or anybody else on earth. Understood?"

Hamama nodded her head again. He reached into his pocket and fingered the cream-colored handkerchief. He started to raise it to his nostrils to sniff it, the way he had always done before. However, his hand stopped in midair. He looked at the handkerchief again. He thought of casting it to the wind so that it could carry it wherever it wished, or maybe even return it to her. "Maybe it never belonged to me from the start," he whispered to himself. "Maybe it belongs only to Hamama." He reached over and tied it to her halter, in the place where Yasmin had put it that day so long before. He looked at the handkerchief, but couldn't identify the feelings that had started churning inside him.

For a long time, Hajj Khaled had tried to escape from the voice that kept haunting him wherever he went, saying: "It's her. It's her."

He would awaken and not find Hamama at his side. He would look around, and her voice would continue even in his waking hours. It would come whispering from afar, "It's her. It's her."

He left the mountains that he had known, and that had known him. He went to the cities on the coast, and in their streets' loud hubbub he managed to sleep peacefully for the first time, far from the curse of that haunting voice.

Iliya Radhi, who found him there, didn't say a word to him about anything. However, his silence said more than words ever could have. As for

Muhammad Shahada, he talked later about a German woman, then fell silent. He knew for certain that the Khaled that was there wasn't the Khaled he had known, or would know later.

Muhammad Shahada, who was ten years younger than Khaled, stood before him as a grown man and said, "We're going back to Hadiya together. Now."

"And what about the Turks?"

"There are fewer Turks there than there are here. Lots of us have gone back."

As though Khaled had been waiting for this for a long time, he got up, leaving behind all his meager possessions in that room overlooking the Haifa sea, and went with him.

Muhammad Shahada said, "Khaled looked behind him twice. When I tried to look where he was looking, he grabbed me by the head and, with a resolve that alarmed me, said, 'Muhammad, if you look behind you, I'll go back to what you'll see.'"

Muhammad Shahada froze as though his neck had turned to a block of ice. Then, with difficulty, he said, "I won't look."

The gallows with which the Turks had filled the country filled the streets and the surrounding hills. They loomed up in the wind like ravenous scarecrows ogling people's necks. It wouldn't be long before the British brought them the prey they needed.

Fog

One cold dawn, one of al-Qawuqji's men emerged from the fog and, without saying a word, handed Hajj Khaled a proclamation calling for an end to the revolution.

Hajj Khaled took it and read:

Proclamation No. 16

In response to calls being made by our Arab kings and princes, and at the request of the Higher Arab Committee, we ask you to cease all acts of violence and not to engage in any provocation that would spoil the atmosphere of the negotiations, which the Arab nation hopes will yield good and through which it hopes to obtain the Arab countries' full rights. We should avoid any action that might be looked upon as an excuse to cut off the negotiations. . . . We welcome honorable peace and will do nothing to violate it, although, when necessary, we will defend ourselves, and we will not lay down our arms.

General Commander Fawzi al-Din Qawuqji, 12
October 1936

No one had ever seen Hajj Khaled as furious as they saw him that day.
He crumpled the proclamation and hurled it away. It fell near Hamama,
who lowered her head and was about to devour the piece of paper that
had landed in front of her when he shouted at the top of his lungs, "No!"
Startled, the mare took a few steps back.

He walked over and picked it up. Then he asked for a match. After
unfolding the piece of paper so that it would burn more easily, he lit the
match and stared at the small flame as it began descending to where the
paper met his thumb and forefinger. At that point it went out, and he
handed the remains of the proclamation to Iliya Radhi.

He walked over to Hamama and took her head between his hands to
calm her. Then, kneading his brow with the fingers of his left hand, he
turned to his men and said, "What does he want? Does he think the British
will allow us to go back to our homes and farms? Would it even be possible
for us to go back with the steady stream of Jewish immigrants that are landing on our shores? And what are these negotiations he refers to? We've
been negotiating for the last twenty years. A decision like this will doom
us to go on negotiating forever.

"In any case," he continued, "it's up to you now. The decision belongs
to each one of you, since the proclamation says nothing about an amnesty
for any of the rebels. Rather, it tells us that whoever has been sentenced
to death will have to head straight for the gallows, and whoever has been
given a prison sentence will have to go knock on the prison door and say
to the British, 'I'm back!'"*

The days that followed were darker than any eye could bear. A thick
fog descended over the mountains and everything suddenly fell silent: the

---

* During that time, the British sentenced approximately two thousand Palestinians to lengthy
prison terms and destroyed more than five thousand homes. In Acre Prison, 148 Palestinians
were hanged, and the number of those serving shorter prison sentences of varying lengths
came to more than fifty thousand.

415

sparrows stopped chirping, the tracks of the gazelles that used to cross from time to time disappeared, and if hadn't been for the soft, monotonous sound of her breathing, you would have thought Hamama had melted away. Hajj Khaled didn't look around him to see how many of his men had stayed with him and how many had left. The fog was a blessing at that moment, since no one could look deeply into the eyes of anyone else, or bid him farewell as he penetrated the wall of cold white darkness.

Hajj Khaled knew that people had 'gotten tired.' But that phrase, as far as he was concerned, meant only one thing: that they'd been defeated.

When the fog finally lifted, he found no one around him but Iliya Radhi and Hamama.

He said to Iliya, "I think you can go back. As for me, I won't go to the gallows of my own accord. Since all our leaders are in Damascus now, I'm going there, and maybe we can reach a solution. I'm going to think about our next step. It seems everybody's against us now. All that's left in this country is illusion."

"When I went up to the mountains with you, I never imagined coming back to Hadiya without you."

"But I want you there. You aren't known to the British, and when I need you, I'll send for you. Or I may come for you myself. Don't worry."

Hajj Khaled brought the homing pigeon out of its cage and set it free. Then he added, "May her wings protect you."

He watched it as it took off in flight. It made a half-circle, cast a glance at the two of them, then decided which way it needed to go and flew into the distance.

On the hills surrounding the village of Kawkab al-Hawa, Hajj Khaled saw a piece of paper dancing in the wind. He stopped Hamama, dismounted, and picked it up. He wanted to read anything that might give an indication of the direction things were headed.

It said:

I hereby call upon the great Arab people to abide by the following instructions: not to retaliate in kind against the Jews, who have begun committing acts of aggression not out of courage or gallantry, but rather in a scheme to bring about division between the revolutionary army and the British army in order to stir up conflict and unrest, and in order to sabotage the negotiations and prevent the country from obtaining its rights. I expect the noble Arab people to endure patiently and wait to see what the British powers will do with regard to the Arabs' rights. The revolutionary army is proud to have done its duty just as it pledged to do, and to have completed its mission and brought the country nearer to the fulfillment of its hopes and rights, which are now entrusted to kings, princes, and the entire Arab nation. Therefore—trusting in the pledge given by kings and princes, wishing to protect the well-being of the negotiations, and unwilling to give our opponents any excuse for tampering with guaranteed rights—the leadership of the revolution thinks it best for the revolutionary army to leave the field now that it has nothing left to do. Nevertheless, it pledges that the revolutionary army will be in the vanguard of the Arab forces that rush to Palestine's rescue!

General Commander Fawzi al-Din Qawuqji,
20 October 1936

He rolled it into a ball and was about to throw it away, then thought better of it. He reached into Hamama's saddlebag and brought out a box of matches. He took out a match and nearly lit it, then threw the paper forcefully to the ground instead. Bending down, he grabbed a rock and pounded it till it was nothing but tiny pieces.

He started to get up, but as he did so he felt his head, the sky, and the earth spinning. Even Hamama wouldn't stop spinning. He quickly realized that he had to hold himself together, get to the syringe in the saddlebag, and give himself an injection, since otherwise he would die right there in the open country. With difficulty, he began to rise, his head still spinning about in the whirlwind that had plucked his feet off the ground, then flung him simultaneously up into the heavens and down into the depths of the earth. He grabbed the edge of the saddlebag and, although he was on his knees, the presence of the saddlebag right in front of him made him feel as though he were standing on his feet. He reached in, got the syringe, and gave himself an injection. As he slowly regained his lucidity, he saw that Hamama had knelt down to help him, and that she was on the ground beside him.

The first thing he did was to look at the shreds that remained of that piece of paper. Nothing was left of it but a single piece that clung to the rock he had used to pulverize it, and with difficulty he managed to make out the phrase, "Proclamation No. . . ."

Within half an hour, he began to feel life flowing through his veins again. He was still on his knees, but his chest was up against Hamama's body.

As he walked alongside her, he saw Lake Tiberias in the distance. It was incredibly still, as was everything around it: the trees, the birds, the steps of the gazelles. He felt as though he were walking along in silence. But why was this feeling coming back again?*

---

* News arrived to the effect that the Saudi king had allowed al-Qawuqji and his fellow freedom fighters to take up residence in al-Qariyyat within his kingdom's borders. According to another report, the Iraqi government had agreed to host him. He was given a national hero's farewell in the Transjordan, and newspapers mentioned that a delegation from Jordan had accompanied him with Prince Abdallah's approval and support. It had been rumored that the British mandate authorities in the Transjordan would hinder his departure, but nothing of the sort occurred!

Aziza's Sorrows

Not more than five months after Hajj Khaled went to Syria, the people of Hadiya learned that Aziza's sons Fayez and Zayd had been arrested on charges of murdering a British officer and three British soldiers on the road between the villages of Lafta and Quluniya.

They took them right away to al-Maskubiya Prison.

Hajj Salem, Aziza, and Muhammad Shahada went to Jerusalem, but the British wouldn't allow them to see Fayez and Zayd.

"I'm staying put until I see them," said Aziza.

"We'll go back to Hadiya today, and tomorrow morning we'll be here. Where would you sleep here in Jerusalem?"

"The only place I know of is the house of Hajj Abu Salim."

"But . . . !"

"He's an honorable man, and if God hadn't taken his daughter Amal, he might have been my children's grandfather."

"Whatever you think is best," Hajj Salem said to her.

※

What I'm going to tell you is something I saw with my own two eyes and heard with my own two ears. Aziza got to our house a little after noon. Hajj Salem, Hajj Khaled's brother, was with her, as well as another person from their village by the name of Muhammad Shahada. My father wasn't at home. My mother invited them in, and they said, "We'll go back to Hadiya, but Aziza will stay. She'll explain everything to you."

My mother said, "Welcome, Aziza. All your life, you and your family have been dear to us."

I went and made tea, then we sat together. She was so tired, it was as if she hadn't slept for ten nights straight.

"What's wrong?" my mother asked her.

So she told us the whole story from A to Z. We were so sad for her. Then she looked into our eyes and said, "It seems I'm going to suffer the same fate my mother did when they executed two of her sons in a single day."

"God forbid!" my mother exclaimed. "The last thing the British would do would be to hang anybody these days, since, now that the uprising is over, there's nothing they want more than to please the Palestinians."

The next day she went with my father, Hajj Salem, and Muhammad Shahada to al-Maskubiya Prison, but they wouldn't let them in. They said, "They're being interrogated, and their case will take a long time."

Aziza came back to our house with my father. My mother asked him about Hajj Salem and Muhammad Shahada, and he said, "They've gone back to Hadiya because they want to go see al-Marzuqi, the lawyer."

Aziza, my mother, my sister Su'ad, and I sat down in one of the rooms and started to eat lunch. We were listening to the news broadcast on the radio, and after we'd all taken a bite or two, we heard horrible news: "This morning, brothers Fayez Abd al-Majid and Zayd Abd al-Majid were executed after being convicted by a military court of murdering an officer and three British soldiers."

Everything froze at that moment. We looked over at Aziza, but she was in another world. She was calm as though she were sitting all alone. A few moments later, she looked at us and said, "What's happened?! Why aren't you eating?"

When we heard what she'd said, we started to cry. My mother got up to leave. I said, "Where are you going, Mama?"

"I can't take it! I can't take it!" she said, hiding her face.

But *Aziza just went back to chewing the bite that was in her mouth. Then she reached out for some more food, and went on eating! That just made us cry all the more. But in the end, we had no choice but to go on eating ourselves, with tears streaming down our faces and mixing with our food.*

Never in my life will I eat food as bitter as the food I ate that day.

After the midafternoon call to prayer, she performed her ablutions and said to my mother, "Take me to the Aqsa Mosque."

Su'ad and I went with her. We went in through the Hebron Gate, and when we got to the mosque, she started slapping her cheeks as she screamed at the top of her lungs and writhed on the carpet.

We let her do whatever she wanted. Half an hour later, she came back to us and said calmly, "Take me to the house." So we took her back.

The people in Hadiya also heard the news, and Hajj Salem, Iliya Radhi, Muhammad Shahada, and Abu Sunbul came back to Jerusalem. What can I say? Lots of people went to the prison, but they told them, "We'll give you the bodies tomorrow."

So they came to our house. Aziza came in to see them and greeted everyone. Then she sat down and didn't say another word, and they couldn't say anything either.

Everybody spent that night at our house, and the next morning we all went to the prison. On the way there, my father bought a copy of the Palestine *newspaper, and their pictures were on the front page. Aziza took the newspaper out of my father's hand. When she saw her sons' faces, she stared at the pictures, then folded up the newspaper and put it in her breast pocket.*

The British officer said to them, "We won't hand them over to anybody. They'll be placed in front of Bab al-Amud so that everybody can see what happened to the wretches!"

Again, Aziza said to us, "Take me to the Aqsa Mosque." So we took her there, and she did what she'd done the day before: she screamed and cried and writhed on the mosque carpet until she was all worn out. Then she said, "Take me back to the house." And she did the same thing for the next four days.

In the afternoon a jeep arrived. They unloaded the two corpses and put them on the ground. There were more than one hundred British soldiers poised to fire on anybody who approached.

The soldiers knew that putting them on the ground that way would cause problems, but the British commanders insisted. The people raised a ruckus, but it didn't do any good. They tried to grab the bodies, but shots were fired from all directions, and the people ran away.

For four days they left them there, until they stank to high heaven and the soldiers themselves couldn't stand to stay in their positions any more. On the morning of the fifth day, a British officer arrived. He looked at the two bodies, then turned to the people and said, "You can take the bodies now."

Return from Syria

A year later, Hajj Khaled returned from Syria, pained by people's complacency,* and more hopeless than someone looking for a rain cloud in the dry season.

He said, "For a year we've been waiting, and nothing has changed. Things keep getting harder, and all we gain by waiting is rusty bodies and spirits."

---

* ". . . and I admit to Your Honor's cunning. In my view, you're both a sly old fox and a catastrophe of the first order who puts his talents and intelligence to use in the service of British imperialism. You have appointed notables' sons to government positions and placed aristocrats in seats of power. Hence, they are now your pawns, having become bound materially to authority and power. You will make mention of all the good things you did for the state, its motto always being: 'one good work will be rewarded tenfold, and if someone greets you kindly, return him a greeting that is kinder still.' You have been able to make many Arabs believe that they need British protection from aggression by the Jews, just as you have made many Jews believe that they need British protection from aggression by the Arabs. I feel insulted, and that my dignity has been wounded, since I belong to a people by whom you put no store and for whose wishes you have no respect. Even after all their many sacrifices, revolutions and efforts, all you have offered them is a lame, defective legislative council that lacks both authority and will." (An excerpt from a letter to the British High Commissioner)

"But you have to wait!" they told him. "Any move on our part at this point would turn the whole world against us."

There were many leaders who had sought refuge from the British in Damascus, and he came back without even saying goodbye to them.

In the place where he had stood a year earlier tearing up the proclamation sent out by the leaders of the revolution, he now stood again. Hamama had grown closer to him, and he'd begun to feel that she was all he had left.

While in Damascus, he had continued exchanging messages with his family, and the messages that couldn't be delivered through the mail were delivered by other people.

It was night when he arrived in Hadiya, and the first thing he did was to go to his sister Aziza's house. He knocked on the door, and when she came out, the surprise nearly bowled her over. Taking a couple of steps toward her, he took her into his arms and she began weeping silently on his chest. Whenever he tried to look at her face, she would bury it even deeper in his chest, and he felt the heat of her tears burning his body. Her son Husayn came out, and he, too, froze in place.

A long time passed before she looked up at him. By this time, the tears had disappeared from her face, and, as if nothing had happened, she said to him, "We missed you!"

He took her by the hand and headed for his house, and Husayn followed them. When he arrived, he didn't recognize the house. There was a new house in its place that looked nothing like the old one. It was lower and smaller. For a moment he thought he'd come to the wrong place. He looked around. Then he remembered that the old house had been blown up. He looked up toward the hill where the graves of his two brothers and his father lay, as well as his own empty grave. In the sky he saw some distant lightning, which was followed by a muffled roll of thunder. He pulled his woolen cloak more tightly around his body, and, as though he were a stranger paying a visit, he knocked on the door. He heard the sound of the doves awakening in their dovecote.

Daybreak was still three hours away.

He knocked on the door again. He heard the fluttering of wings coming from the dovecote, while a voice came from inside, saying, "Who is it?"

He didn't reply. He was afraid his voice would waken the people of the village, but he wasn't afraid that the sound of knocking on the door might do the same!

"Who is it?" came Sumayya's voice again. But he didn't answer.

By the time she opened the door, Naji and Musa had joined her. Something unexplained had moved inside of them, causing them to follow their mother to the door. She had warned them, "It might be the British, and maybe the Jews. I'll go by myself, and you stay here." But they'd followed her anyway.

Sumayya didn't need to light a lamp to see his features and recognize him. His form filled the doorway. Aziza stood beside him, and behind them, Husayn held Hamama's halter. Meanwhile, the mare looked about her as though the memory of the first Hamama had awakened within her.

He hugged them one by one. He kissed Sumayya's forehead. Without saying a word, Musa and Naji put their arms around him. Then Naji reached out and took his father's rifle and headed up to the roof of the house.

Hajj Khaled leaned down and kissed his daughter Tamam on the forehead.

"You've grown up!" he said.

No one said a word. She opened her eyes, and once she had, she couldn't close them again.

"Baba!" she whispered, and like a light dream, she sat up and hugged him.

"I'll go wake my aunt Munira up," said Sumayya.

"No, I'll wake her up myself." After asking Musa to go get Fatima, he headed upstairs without letting go of Aziza's hand.

Hajj Khaled heard the dawn call to prayer. He got up to perform his ablutions, and was followed by Sumayya.

"Don't forget to give my greetings of peace to Shaykh Husni," he said to her.

"May God give you peace," she replied. As she said it, she discovered new meaning in that wish of hers, an entirely different meaning. It was as if, at long last, she had found the true meaning of this wish that people repeated every day so many times over.

"Be careful. There are spies everywhere."*

"God's in control of everything, including our lifespans."

He prayed inside the house. A little while later Naji came in.

Looking this way and that, he whispered, "The sun's up."

"Why do you tell me in such a low voice? Nobody's going to hear you between these four walls!"

They gathered around him the way they would have gathered around a wood stove.

"You'll go today to Iliya Radhi's house and tell him, 'My father's waiting for you.'"

"Where?" Naji asked.

"He'll know. Just tell him, 'My father's waiting for you.'"

He and Hamama headed for the guesthouse. Hamdan came out, dragging his leg, having heard the sound of hooves on the ground outside. He looked

---

* Fakhri al-Nashashibi had organized public meetings in support of the 'peace squadrons' that opposed the revolution and went in pursuit of its forces' scattered remnants. The most important of these meetings were the one he organized in his home in September 1938, and another that he organized in the village of Yatta in the Hebron district in December of the same year. The latter meeting was attended by the British General O'Connor, the general military commander for the central region.

The 'peace squadron' phenomenon spread to include the regions of Nablus, Hebron, Jenin, Rawha, Marj ibn Amir, Acre, and West Galilee. It later reached its peak through the assistance given to the British by one of these squadrons in the defeat of the revolution's general commander, Abd al-Rahim al-Hajj Muhammad. The revolution then issued a death sentence against al-Nashashibi, and continued to pursue him until he was killed two years later in Baghdad.

The British decided to consider Transjordan a contiguous warfront against the Palestinian rebels, and barbed-wire fences were erected along Palestine's northern borders. A people's popular conference was then convened under the leadership of Mithqal al-Fa'iz in the village of Umm al-Amad in order to support the Palestinian revolution with manpower and ammunition. The Transjordan regime crowned its anti-revolutionary activity with the arrest in 1939 of two Palestinian leaders, one of whom was Yusuf Abu Durra, and both of whom it turned over to the British. They were executed a few months later.

toward the gate and saw her there before he saw Hajj Khaled. She was like a piece of the mid-month moon. In the translucent darkness he saw the figure that was so familiar from days gone by, from the time he was a little boy. He ran toward Hajj Khaled, and before he reached him, tears had filled his eyes. He embraced him, but couldn't get a word out of his mouth. Hajj Khaled asked him how he was. Hamdan nodded his head. About his health and his wife. He nodded his head again. He was weeping silently. Then he broke into violent sobs.

"I said to myself: I couldn't pass through Hadiya without drinking Hamdan's coffee!"

Hamdan nodded his head. Then he finally found his tongue.

"It's ready," he said.

He poured him the first cup. Hajj Khaled drank it. Then he poured him the second, and Hajj Khaled said to Hamdan, "It seems you've turned stingy since the last time I saw you. Fill the cup, man!"

He filled it.

Calmly, Hajj Khaled drank his coffee, pondering the guesthouse court-yard and the naked mulberry tree. He gazed out at the distant plain as though he expected Hamama to appear.

The mare murmured. He looked back at her.

"I know. You're here!"

He climbed the hill to the graves of his father, his two brothers, and his two nephews. He looked over at his empty grave. It was filled with water. The grave's being filled with water aroused a feeling in him that he tried get hold of, but he couldn't put his finger on exactly what it was. He recited the Fatiha, then jumped on his horse. He cast a glance at Hadiya, where people had begun leaving their houses.

In the distance, more than one person saw Hamama's white form. But when she suddenly disappeared from view, they concluded that what they'd seen must have been nothing but an apparition.

The Trap

Edward Peterson, who had been quite disturbed by the resumption of military operations, didn't believe his ears when he got the news: "Hajj Khaled is back, and he's preparing to ambush a British force that will be leaving Jenin and crossing the road between the villages of Burqa and Sabsatiya."

He quickly made a number of contacts and, together with the regional commander, decided that the force would set out at the scheduled time and take the same route in order not to arouse suspicions. At six-thirty on Tuesday morning the truck engines roared, drowning out the sounds from any other vehicles. Rather than filling their trunks with weapons and ammunition as he had planned to do, Peterson affixed a number of heavy machine guns to the vehicles, then concealed everything under thick green military tarpaulins that could easily be removed as soon as the first shot was fired in the direction of the caravan. And in order to ensure that the plan didn't fail due to the fact that the bend was located in a low spot surrounded on three sides by mountains, he decided to use aircraft to take the ambushers by surprise.

Hajj Khaled and those with him had not been expecting this. After a long wait that had yielded no results on the ground, the rebels were eager for a big operation that would be nothing like the small ones they had carried out in the past.*

"Where are you going?" Fatima asked her husband Nuh.

"To him, to Hajj Khaled. Do you mind?"

"If I mind, then Kahila will mind," she replied.

What Nuh had just heard was nothing new. He knew she didn't need to tell him what she thought of anything he did. All he had to do was jump on Kahila's back. If she moved, this meant that Fatima approved, and if she dug her hooves into the ground, he knew he would have to get off, since no force in the world would be able to make her budge from her place as long as Fatima didn't want her to.

Taking hold of Kahila's reins in the dissipating darkness, he didn't know whether she would move or not. However, she did move. So he went back and hugged his wife. In fact, he hugged her so tightly, Fatima got the feeling he didn't want to leave. Lifting her head off his shoulder, she patted him on the back and whispered, "Give him my greetings. God be with you."

An early morning haze filled the valley, and the foothills had begun to light up with the cool March sun. The task before them wouldn't be an easy one, and they had begun gathering in the agreed-upon place since two o'clock in the morning. Nuh, brother of Khadra, stood before Hajj Khaled holding Kahila's reins.

---

* Jewish immigration had not stopped, Palestine's leaders had not returned from exile in the Seychelles, the committees assigned to investigate what was happening in the country had gotten nowhere, and arrests and executions were still ongoing. Abd al-Salam al-Badri of the village of Burqa, a laborer who worked in the city of Haifa, had been hanged by the British in Acre Prison. When he was found carrying a box of small nails that he had purchased for two piasters to fix a pair of wooden bathroom clogs in his house, he was arrested because a bomb that had gone off in Haifa contained nails that were similar to the ones he was carrying, and he was accused of planning the operation or taking part in its planning. A military court sentenced him to death by hanging without taking his testimony into account, even though the man had had no part in any acts of violence. His story is familiar to most people from Burqa of my generation.

"I've come," he said.

Hajj Khaled hugged him. "What are you doing here?" he asked. "Didn't I say I'd send for you if I needed you?"

"I think you do need me, and others, too."

"How would you know that I need men?"

"Since you're back, it means you need them."

Kneading his brow with the fingers of his left hand, Hajj Khaled gave Iliya Radhi that look that they'd all come to know.

"I didn't need to say anything to him," Iliya explained. "The minute he realized that you were going to start fighting again, he said to me, 'I'm coming with you.'"

A passenger bus, several civilian cars, and a military jeep crossed safely. They had specified the moment when the road would be blocked. In the distance were two fighters who had been assigned the task of signaling by turns. They were hiding five hundred meters apart.

All eyes were on the road, and all ears were listening for the roar of the caravan's motors in that isolated place. It was distant and faint in the beginning, but now grew louder and louder. Their gazes shifted skyward, and at that moment they heard the signal that announced the caravan's arrival. Movement at that moment would have been a fatal gamble, despite the fact that they didn't know whether the three airplanes that were flying low overhead had come to attack them, or whether they just happened to be passing through.

Peterson knew that as long as their target was the caravan, they wouldn't fire at the airplanes even if they flew low enough to graze their heads.

In the small thicket where they had hidden the horses, the airplanes passing overhead caused a huge stir. The horses were trying to break loose from their reins, which had been wrapped around tree branches.

The rebels stuck close to the ground, insinuating themselves into any shady place that might afford protection. However, the pilots had seen them. Hearing the sound of hoofbeats, the men who were lying in ambush turned and saw a horse galloping away from the thicket. One of the airplanes flew lower until it was directly over it. The horse stumbled, then gained its footing again. However, the sound of the airplanes, which had now passed the horse, caused it suddenly to backtrack and start running in the direction it had come from as though it were heading back into the thicket. When the other horses saw it coming alongside them, they whinnied and tried again to break loose, but to no avail, and before long they saw it galloping away again.

At that moment the airplanes returned from the direction they had come from the first time. Taken by surprise, the horse was confused, and before deciding which direction it would go, the airplanes' machine guns began firing at the ground where the rebels were hiding in the shadows of boulders and wild shrubs.

Retreat would have been impossible in the face of the storm of fire that broke from the sky, mowing down everything in its path. By the time they saw the caravan arrive, there was nothing they could do. They were totally surrounded. Fortunately, however, the fighters who had been assigned to block the road in front of the caravan managed to carry out their task successfully thanks to their distance from the cluster of hills and the fact that the pilots had not discovered their presence.

The caravan found itself in front of the stone barrier, and before a single shot had been fired at it, its machine guns had appeared.

As the military aircraft came around for their third foray, the fighters began to realize that they had fallen into a trap. Their plan had been exposed. Hajj Khaled gave orders to form a firewall to confront the three airplanes, which had returned more confident than before, as though the whole thing were no more than a game to them. The airplanes continued to approach, firing their machine guns until they were directly overhead, at which point Hajj Khaled gave orders to fire. The men's guns all went off in a single moment. They looked behind them to see whether any of the airplanes had been hit, but could see no smoke coming out of any of them. They knew then that the next foray was just minutes away.

❀

In those pregnant moments, Hajj Khaled got the strange feeling that the sun was shining with a mad intensity the likes of which he had never seen before, that the humidity was so thick that he couldn't penetrate it, and that the air was so heavy that his lungs couldn't bear for it to pass through them.

A sense of defeat and frustration pressed in upon him as he wondered how his plan had been discovered. He took a deep breath. Over and over, he tried to calm himself, to forget the airplanes that hovered over them and the military vehicles that would soon be advancing in pursuit of them. Yet he could bear anything but an episode of insulin shock. He cast a glance at the small thicket where the horses were being kept, and Hamama looked farther away than she ever had.

In the valley, the force that had been assigned to block the road was able to divert the caravan, but it wasn't easy, since the gunfire had opened the gates of hell. Everything around the rebels was flying in all directions: rocks, tree branches, dirt, grass. It was as though the earth had turned into countless little volcanoes. The rebels discovered there that the few shots they had fired were the last ammunition they had, and that if any part of their bodies became visible, it would mean instant death. At the same time, they had become increasingly aware of the fragility of the boulders they were hiding behind. In what seemed like a miraculous moment, one of them was able to throw a hand grenade in the direction of the caravan. Suddenly, everything went silent. But the grenade didn't go off. It settled under one of the trucks as though it were nothing but a rock. However, this didn't prevent those inside, once they had seen the grenade coming toward them, from jumping out the back and getting away as fast as they could.

Just as the airplanes returned, three men managed to withdraw to the top of the hill. They were now easy targets, and before they could aim their weapons skyward, they had been mowed down.

So, for the second time, the firewall was unable to accomplish anything to speak of.

To everyone's surprise, the grenade finally exploded. The British soldiers didn't know what to do now. They could no longer go back to the truck, nor could they fire at the grenade, since this might have meant burning up a number of the vehicles in the caravan. The bus behind the caravan had also been emptied of soldiers.

At that moment, Hajj Khaled realized that they would have to withdraw quickly before the airplanes returned again, and that before long the soldiers would advance toward the now-exposed ambush.

He instructed them to split up as soon as they got to the thicket so that they wouldn't be easy prey for the airplanes. By the time the airplanes returned, they had reached the thicket and disappeared inside. As far as the pilots were concerned, it was as though the earth had opened up and swallowed them all. A number of the rebels had found small hiding places, their mission being to prevent the advance of the soldiers in the caravan so as to give the others a chance to withdraw.

The horses came rushing out of the thicket, their aim being to reach the forest that lay three kilometers away. Once there, they would be well hidden and could fight if necessary.

However, the presence of three enemy aircraft made their escape no easy task. Although the horses had scattered far from one another, they were still easy targets. A horse might escape harm while its rider was shot, or a rider might escape harm while his horse was wounded. The men's eyes were on a terrified Hamama as she traversed the short but potentially fatal distance. She would dodge right and left, then stop suddenly, then break into a run once again, or run in circles, then charge ahead. The airplanes could still have made two more rounds before the horses reached the outskirts of the forest. However, a large number were able to get there at last and disappear inside.

The sound of gunfire rent the blood-drenched morning, and the moments that followed were pregnant with infinite possibilities.

The battle had been one-sided from within minutes of the time it began, since the rebels had been deprived of the element of surprise. Indeed, the element of surprise had been turned against them.*

---

* Oral accounts, confirmed by British archival documents from the same period, unanimously affirm that the reason for the Palestinians' defeat in this battle lay in the fact that

433

Finding themselves surrounded on all sides, the men who remained of the ambush party couldn't do much. But little by little, the sound of gunfire faded until at last silence reigned.

Edward Peterson stood pondering the bloodied corpses. He cast a glance at the woods in the distance, and seemed so gleeful you would have thought he was about to achieve all his life's dreams in a single moment.

However, as the jeep he was riding in began crossing the plain in pursuit of the fleeing rebels, his smile gradually faded until it turned into a matchless fit of rage. When he saw the first horse prostrate on the ground, trying in vain to get to its feet, Peterson's body quaked. As the car passed the horse, he kept staring at the mass of pain as it writhed in agony behind him. He commanded the driver to stop. He got out of the car and went back to the horse. He drew his revolver and aimed at the wounded creature. Turning his face away, he fired a shot, then came back to the car without looking back at the slain animal. When they'd gone another two hundred meters, he saw a slain gray filly under whose body lay a wounded young man no more than twenty-five years old. Peterson stopped. The young man's rifle was five meters away from him. Near it lay his yellow keffiyeh and his headband. Peterson planted a bullet in the rebel's head, and watched him until he was certain that his spirit had departed completely.

Seven horses had been killed. However, he found no trace of their riders. The jeep moved on. Spotting a trail of blood, he instructed the driver to follow it cautiously. The jeep stopped in front of a steep slope. Peterson and the soldiers with him got out of the jeep. They saw the vehicles behind them heading straight for the forest. As they advanced toward the edge of

---

the British knew of the ambush prior to its occurrence. They learned of it through one of the thieves and criminals who had been released or whose flight had been facilitated by the British mandate authorities in return for their willingness to join the revolution as spies. These spies had been promised amnesty and material rewards for whatever successes they achieved. The man who supplied the British with information on this particular operation, and who was later executed, confessed the names of the remaining spies. He also confessed to having collected twenty-five pounds for engaging in espionage and, if possible, assassinations, and to having received promises of larger sums depending on the magnitude of the successes he achieved.

the slope they heard a faint sound, and there they found themselves face to face with a thoroughbred mare. It was none other than the mare that belonged to Nuh, brother of Khadra.

They searched the area, but found no one. Peterson aimed his revolver at Kahila's head, and for a moment their eyes met. In her he saw an indescribable beauty, and his hand froze. The soldiers stood there, waiting to see what the next moment would bring. Suddenly he fired a shot in the air, then turned to come back.

Peterson knew that storming the forest would be no easy task, and that it would cost him a great deal. Up to that point in the battle, his losses had amounted to no more than two soldiers dead and three wounded.

The military vehicles stopped at a safe distance from the forest. He surveyed the ghostly, dark verdure with piercing eyes that had lost none of their gleam despite the long night he had spent waiting for the dawn. Then he issued his instructions: "We'll strafe the forest with artillery and aircraft fire. After that, all we'll have to do is comb the area."

The airplanes were gone for a long time before they came back. The pilots saw a horse standing beside its rider's dead body, after which they counted the bodies of seven horses that lay dead on the plain.

No one could see what was happening in the forest. No one could be certain that those who had sought refuge among the trees were still there. Nevertheless, the airplanes quickly got to work. The explosions sent trees flying high into the air, and the branches as they fell looked like human beings dying on their feet. More than one fire broke out, and the sky was filled with clouds of black smoke. After six successive sorties, the artillery began to fire.

At exactly ten o'clock, about two hours after all hell had broken loose, Peterson raised his hand in a signal to begin advancing on the forest.

The armored cars moved forward, followed by the jeeps and a large number of soldiers who had gotten out of the trucks. Every minute was laden with countless possibilities. However, what amazed Peterson was that not a single shot was fired at the advancing force.

"Given the force of the attack we've launched, no one could have survived," he whispered to himself.

The armored cars went through the forest, making their way around the shattered trees, while the jeeps stopped at its edge.

Nothing.

In the moments that followed they realized that the trees were so dense it would be impossible for the vehicles to advance. The soldiers advanced on foot, penetrating deep into the small forest with Peterson in the lead.

Nothing.

Shortly thereafter, they saw a horse's dead body. Its head had been nearly cut off, and there was a large pool of blood around it. It seemed to Peterson that it was still warm. Ten meters farther on, they found another horse, then another. There was nothing but slain horses. Ten of them. And some of them had been completely incinerated.

Peterson nearly turned back, since he couldn't bear to see any more dead horses. However, he wanted to know what had become of that white mare, Hamama, that he had heard so much about but had yet to see. He knew that getting to her would mean getting to Hajj Khaled. He only hoped he wouldn't find her dead.

By the time they were about to reach the other side, he was certain that the hours of strafing had given the men they were pursuing a chance to escape.

The Spartan

They had to split up again . . .

Hajj Khaled headed to the far north with his son-in-law Nuh, brother of Khadra.

A heavy rain descended, washing away the pebbles in the foothills and valleys. Never in his life had Nuh been as sorrowful as he was on that day. With every step, he looked back, hoping to see Kahila breaking through the thick wall of rain and whinnying for him to stop.

He knew she had been wounded, but he didn't know what her wound would do to her. He was afraid she might be taken captive, or be an easy target for a shot that would end her life.

The bay mare beneath him had belonged to Jamil al-Sirhan, whose skull had been shattered so badly by a bullet that it had looked as though he was headless. When Nuh had seen him, the mare had been galloping along with Jamil on her back, clinging to her reins as though he didn't yet realize he had been killed.

The airplanes had circled yet again, and Nuh had been sure he would never make it to the forest, which by that time was only three hundred meters away. A distance that short had never been anything to a filly like Kahila. However, the airplane had been close on his heels, and he had known that he was no match for this mad metallic bird that was roaring and plowing the earth with its machine-gun fire.

He could tell that he'd been wounded. Blood gushed out hot between his leg and Kahila's right side. Then one of the airplanes came from a place he hadn't expected. It was on his right, while another was behind him and still another to his left. The pilots were trying to deprive the horsemen crossing the plain of any chance to maneuver. When he saw another airplane coming at him from the left, he pressed Kahila's body in an attempt to turn, and realized that his foot was unharmed. He veered, and for a moment felt that the wound had stopped bleeding, since he was closing it off by the force of his leg. However, Kahila had painfully, slowly begun to pant and lose strength beneath him. At that same moment, he saw Jamil al-Sirhan riding away without a head. Urging Kahila on, he followed him. It wasn't easy to catch up with that bay mare, whose neck and ears were covered with blood. Yet he followed her, since she had become his only hope of survival before the airplanes came around once more. At last he came up behind her, then alongside her.

In the twinkling of an eye, he jumped off Kahila's back and onto the back of the bay mare. Jamil was still holding onto the reins as though he intended to ride all the way home. Nuh tried to wrest the reins from Jamil's grip, but couldn't. So instead he took hold of the stiffened hands and clung to Jamil's body. He knew that two riders on a single horse would mean certain death. At the same time, a strange thought occurred to him: Since Jamil insists on staying on the back of his horse, he must want to reach a certain place, a place that no one but the bay mare knows.

By the time the airplanes returned, he had made it to the outermost tree of the forest. That tree meant a great deal to him. It was the most beautiful tree in the world. It was the tree of the whole universe: the tree of life.

Hamama was circling wildly around the trunk of a cypress. Hajj Khaled wasn't there. Nuh looked around from his refuge next to the body of the horse and rider. He didn't see him. Hearing the sound of the airplanes passing overhead, he looked up at the sky, but didn't see them. The trees were so dense they concealed everything above them.

Then came Hajj Khaled's voice. "The worst beast God created was the human being, and the worst beast human beings have created is war," he said as he looked at what remained of the rider's head.

Then he said to Nuh, "Take him down off his mare. You're in need of her."

Nuh turned to look behind him. Hajj Khaled was holding his rifle, and had hidden for protection behind a large tree trunk.

"They're going to surround us and burn everything. We've got to withdraw before they get here."

He knew it wouldn't be long before the bombing began on land and from the air. He knew the airplanes would be going back to refuel and be loaded with fresh ammunition. If, on the other hand, their day ended worse than it had begun, other airplanes would be arriving before the departure of the airplanes that were hovering overhead.

In the distance he saw the fronts of the British armored cars. He looked up at the sky even though he knew that, under the circumstances, he needed his ears more than he needed his eyes.

The sound of the airplanes grew more distant, and when they were late in returning, Hajj Khaled ordered the twenty men who were with him to move quickly. However, before they could budge, shells began raining down on that small spot, and as though the British forces knew that destroying the horses would destroy their riders as well, a blind shell fell and killed four horses. Hajj Khaled took off running toward Hamama, shouting to his men, "Quick!" He told Nuh to jump on the bay mare's back. However, Nuh still hadn't dared bring Jamil down off his mare's back. The thought of it struck him with such terror that he couldn't bring himself to do it.

"We'll divide into two groups," Hajj Khaled told them. "Some of us will go down and escape across the valleys on foot, and whoever still has a horse will ride it out the other end."

However, the shells began falling more thickly. At that point, Nuh came up to Jamil's body. He took his hand and kissed it, saying, "Forgive me." Then he lowered him gently off the mare, as though he were afraid his wounds would cause him pain if he moved him the wrong way.

This was their only way of escape. But fortunately for them on that bloody day, the rebels on horseback were able to reach places of safety before the airplanes' return, while those who had gone down into the valleys managed to disappear easily, then come out and head back to their villages.

With them there was a young man from Haifa by the name of Sami al-Asmar, for whom Hajj Khaled had developed a special fondness. He had spent two years in Cairo studying drawing, and over time, the pleasure he took in drawing faces became a source of delight for everyone. In the end, though, they were forced to tear up the pictures he had drawn of them lest they fall into the hands of the British, a fact that saddened them terribly. It saddened him, too, and to make them feel better he promised, "Some day I'll draw all of you. I'll draw both those still living and the martyrs. Then, when there are no more British here and no more Jewish settlers, I'll stage an exhibition and take it around to all the cities in Palestine."

Sami had interrupted his studies and joined the revolution. However, his nostalgia for Cairo was overwhelming. He never stopped talking about it, and he never talked about anything else. He would say to them, "It's enough for me just to sit in front of the paintings of Mahmud Sa'id and the statues of Mahmud Mukhtar. God, if you could only see his statue 'Egypt's Renaissance'! God, if you could only see the statue of 'The Peasant Woman' or 'The Khamasin.' God, if you could only hear Umm Kulthum and Abd al-Wahhab!" He would talk to them about all this as though he were telling the stories of *The Arabian Nights*, and when some of the men expressed their desire to visit Cairo he would say, "Lots of things from there you can see here! The films are here, and so is Umm Kulthum. Rayhani and his band are here. The only thing you can't see unless you go to Cairo is the Nile."

Sami stopped and said, "I don't think I can go any farther."

"We'll carry you."

"No, you need me here now more than you'll need me later on. The British will get here, and you'll need someone to keep them busy."

"You won't be able to do it alone."

"I know. I won't be able to do anything with this rifle. Take it!"

They had reached a paved road.

"I'll wait for you here," he said.

"They'll kill you."

"They've already killed me. There's no way I'll survive this wound. I know my body. Believe me. I'll be happy if they get here before I die. All I want is for you to bandage my wound and give me another cloak, since this cloak of mine is dripping with blood."

He sat down on a large rock, wrapped in a cloak that Iliya Radhi had draped over him after they'd bandaged his wound with his keffiyeh.

By the time the British arrived, the other men had gotten a good distance away. A jeep drove up to him with rifles aimed in his direction. He sat with his hands exposed so as not to arouse the soldiers' suspicions.

They made a circle around him.

"Where are you from?" they asked.

"From that village over there," he replied.

"And what are you doing here?"

"I'm waiting for a car to take me to Jenin."

"Have you seen anyone pass by here?"

"Half an hour ago ten men passed by, and they were armed."

"What did you say?" Peterson demanded.

"I said I'd seen ten armed men."

"Which way did they go?"

"Toward that valley."

"Are you trying to trick us? Do you want to lead us into an ambush the way they do with us when they send us false reports?"

"If I wanted to trick you, I wouldn't have even told you I'd seen them. I could have just kept quiet and left it at that."

"What would make you want to lead us to them?"

"It's a long story. It was people like them who caused my father's death a couple of years ago. They accused him of selling land to the Jews!"

"And was he really doing that?"

"No. He never would have been capable of such a thing. But they killed him. It was a rumor, just like all sorts of other rumors that are circulated as a way of settling scores between one person and another, or one clan and another. But you all know more about these things than I do!"

"There's one way we can be sure you're not trying to deceive us."

"And what's that?"

"For you to go ahead of us."

"I don't mind. There's nothing I'd love more than to see their dead bodies after you've killed them."*

The exhausted British force left Sami al-Asmar where he had fallen. Letting forth a torrent of abuse the likes of which the soldiers had never heard before, Peterson raised his hand in a signal for them to turn back.

Two days later a shepherd from the village of Jabaʻ stumbled across Sami's body. He carried him back to the village on the back of his donkey. The villagers met to consult about the matter. Having seen the deep wound, it wasn't difficult for them to realize that he had been one of the rebels. They searched him for evidence of his identity, but all they found in his pocket was a chunk of bread and three dates. Raising their find high in the air, one of them said, "Look! This was his entire fortune!"

Then he headed for the door of the mosque, hung the items there, and wrote beneath it, "Let it be known to the people of Jabaʻ: this is all the rebels have to eat!"

---

* A few days later, the Jewish newspaper *The Palestine Post* published a news item entitled "The Spartan Arab," in which it said, "A member of one of the Arab gangs that had fired at the soldiers posed as a guide. After marching two kilometers with the soldiers over rugged mountain passes, he collapsed and fell down dead. When his body was examined, it was found that he had been wounded by a bullet that had gone through his stomach and come out his back. They discovered belatedly that he had deceived them."

The Campaign

I t would be necessary to do something bigger in order to get decisive
results. This was the feeling of both Peterson and the British command. They hadn't forgotten the failure of the huge campaign the
British forces had launched in July 1936, in which a search force of four
thousand soldiers had left no stone unturned and no village unransacked
under a scorching red sun. Nevertheless, Peterson was in favor of moving
quickly and resorting to the same methods that had been employed before,
even if it required the use of larger forces.

At six o'clock the next morning, two forces of five thousand soldiers
each moved out. They were reinforced by tanks and armored cars, along
with an air force sufficient to cover two fronts, each of which was at least
twenty kilometers in length.

Peterson spent the night with Colonel Lammie, who had taken part in
the first campaign, in preparation for the largest mission the British forces
had ever undertaken in Palestine. They were busy all night transferring
soldiers in the trucks, with all estimates indicating that the rebels had
moved southwest.

The forces gathered along the Jerusalem–Nablus road to the east, and the railroad connecting Tulkarm and Lod to the west. By sunrise the soldiers had occupied their positions all along the railway between Qalqilya and Ra's al-Ayn.

The night's bitter cold wasn't in their favor this time, just as the July sun hadn't been in their favor the time before. At five o'clock in the morning, the advance began on the two parallel fronts, the aim being for the two forces to come together in a single line after having trapped any rebel elements between them.

According to Peterson's estimates, there were three hundred rebels in the area.

Their task promised to be difficult in those rugged valleys and mountains filled with caves and wild shrubs, and in fact, it wasn't long before it had turned into a mission impossible, as clouds gathered and merged with the fog in the valleys. When the first drops of rain began to fall, the forces' leaders realized that the situation would get increasingly difficult. However, the fog then dissipated and it became possible for the soldiers to communicate by signaling with flags and by using the wireless devices in the cars.

Fear of surprises prevented the soldiers from advancing rapidly, as did the mud, which had not been there when they had first set out. The days previous had been partly sunny. After all, it was March, which people described by saying, "March's bane: sometimes sun, sometimes rain!"

From time to time the sound of gunfire would fill the valleys, echoing off the surrounding heights in such a way that it could be heard by all. Even so, no one knew exactly what was happening. The soldiers had to fire inside every cave or old well, and into every stand of trees that might have offered the rebels a place to hide. They also had to frighten the shepherds by firing into the air, then seize them and interrogate them to make sure they were innocent before letting them go.

As for the sky, it had become a playing field for the airplanes, which were keeping watch over every movement on the ground and making certain that the valleys and plains were devoid of any potential dangers. They would even fly as low as thirty or forty meters aboveground in order to check out anything that looked suspicious.

By two o'clock in the afternoon nothing had changed, though it looked to all of them as though their mission was about to begin in earnest. The fact that the rain had stopped facilitated somewhat the movement of the foot soldiers. They hopped from rock to rock in order to stay out of the mud that filled the valleys and red plains, which had now become traps for the jeeps. The mud closed in on their wheels like pincers, obliging the armored cars to go back and pull them out.

Peterson realized, as had Lammie before him, that the mission would be exceedingly difficult. They had searched Sabsatiya, Kafr Qaddum, Kafr Sur, Ramin, Anbata, Burqa, Bayt Umrin, Siris, and Dayr al-Ghusun, but to no avail. They had found nothing there, nor would they be able to find anything, since the minute the rebels put their rifles away, they looked like any ordinary peasant, and no one would be able to prove that they had ever borne arms in their lives. Entering one village was no different from entering any other.

The soldiers knew exactly what they had to do: surround the village and order the villagers over loudspeakers to leave their houses and gather in the courtyards, since everyone who hid in his house would be killed. Then they were to storm the houses and break down any closed doors by opening fire on them, gather the men on one side and the women and children on the other, then break all the containers in the houses and pour out whatever they contained by way of grains, oils, and other foodstuffs. They were to rip through blankets, mattresses, and pillows with spears, fire into wells or set off bombs, bring sheep, goats, horses, and cattle out of their enclosures and search them, and brutally interrogate anyone suspected of being a rebel. If the village was lucky, Peterson would be the one to carry out the interrogation. He would try without success to extract confessions from the men and boys by forcing them to walk barefoot over cactuses, since confessing to anything would have meant dying in ignominy, and once they had finished with all of that, they would start firing in the air right over people's heads.

At six o'clock in the evening of that long day, the two British forces met at the place agreed upon. They had achieved nothing.

Realizing this, Peterson stamped the ground with his feet and screamed, "Fuckin' Arabs! Fuckin', fuckin' . . . !"

The Week of Torment

All Edward Peterson needed was a single shot to be fired from Hadiya at a British patrol.

Then one evening, there was a half-stray bullet that hardly wounded the air. Lots of people swore they hadn't heard it. Others swore they hadn't seen a patrol. Still others said it was nothing but an excuse to punish the village.

In keeping with his usual custom, he had the British forces surround the village.

He searched the village house by house, but came up with nothing. He looked over and saw seven men in front of a wall. He ordered his soldiers to fire on them, and when it was over he said to them, "But why did they all line up in front of this wall?"

He fell silent for a moment, then said, "I hadn't been intending to kill them, but they stood in front of that wall. Fuckin' Arabs."

Then he bellowed, "If you don't cooperate with us, all of you will be suspects in this case!"

His losses in the most recent battle had been unbearable. "How could he have gotten away when I had him in my grasp?" he kept saying night and day. Then things had turned catastrophic with the trick that 'the Spartan' had played on his forces and the publication of his story in the newspapers.

"I know you're stubborn. I know nobody is going to cooperate with us so that we can make things easier for everyone. So my first decision is that you're all going to spend the night in the square, right where you are."

The punishment was more than cruel. No one was spared: not children, women, or the elderly. Not even Sabri al-Najjar himself, whom Peterson would have loved to shoot like some worn-out old horse.

With the absence of the sun, the night chill became unbearable. The soldiers sat inside the vehicles with their weapons drawn. As the hours passed, people began edging closer to one another in an attempt to keep warm. By midnight they were packed so close together that not a bit of air could have passed between them. Children's crying could be heard, and in vain their mothers tried to quiet them.

By the time two more hours had passed, they were thoroughly frozen, and the soldiers could hear people's teeth chattering and the rasping of their lungs as they struggled to keep functioning. As the first light of dawn appeared, many of them had taken ill. Coughing could be heard everywhere, bodies were shivering violently, and eyes were open wide and watering uncontrollably.

Never before had Hadiya endured such a night. People wished it would end or that they would die. One or the other, it made no difference. All they wanted was to escape forever from the agony of those moments.*

---

* The British response to the outbreak of the Palestinian uprising between 1936 and 1939 was devastating. Britain stormed all of Palestine once more, killing more than five thousand Palestinians and wounding more than fifteen thousand others. It exiled and executed the Palestinian leadership. In addition, it organized death squads made up of British soldiers and Zionist forces known as 'special night forces,' which attacked Palestinian villages by night and killed many Palestinians.

As drops of rain began to fall at nine o'clock the following morning, Peterson came back and stood before them.

"Is anybody willing to relieve everyone and talk?" he asked.

Here and there, children could be heard crying, and more than one elderly woman called down curses on Satan's soldiers. When Peterson saw them this way, he realized that they were ready for the next step, which had occurred to him the previous night not long before he'd drifted off to sleep. He'd gotten up and written it down on a piece of paper beside his bed so that he wouldn't forget it the way he usually did.

He had once read about authors and poets who had developed the habit of recording inspirations that came to them either before or during sleep. He had been quite impressed with the idea, since, like most people, he suffered from a peculiar tendency to forget the flashes of genius that would cross his mind with the speed of shooting stars.

The next morning he reached out for the paper to read what he'd written the night before, and he was astounded when he realized what an ingenious idea it was.

Peterson held up a white piece of paper. He unfolded it, then said, "Before I read it, I would like you to know that, as of this morning, the reward for the arrest of Khaled al-Hajj Mahmud is ten thousand pounds."

After a pause, he continued, "Which of you is the lucky one who'll win it?"

Gazing out at the weary mass of humanity before him, he said, "Nobody. It's your loss, then!"

He then proceeded to read what was written on the paper in his hand:

In view of the fact that the people of the village of Hadiya colluded with those who fired in the direction of a British patrol on the evening of 13 March 1939, the court has determined that all of its residents will be required, beginning today, 14 March 1939, to confirm their presence every evening for the period of one week at the British police station closest to their village.

Signed, Military Judge Carl Newman

The people of Hadiya could see that the journey of anguish hadn't even begun yet, and that the hellish night they had just endured had been nothing but a way station. The police station nearest to their village was five kilometers away, which meant that they would have to walk ten kilometers every day.

Hajj Salem stood at the front of the long line, and Muhammad Shahada at its end. Heading the line for his clan, Sabri al-Najjar moved ahead with pride in his gait and cast Hajj Salem a glance that said, "Khaled al-Hajj Mahmud is no better than I am!"

At four o'clock that afternoon, the first journey of anguish began. The sky was giving notice of a heavy rain to come, and the illnesses that had begun invading before now began occupying their entire bodies. Fortunately, though, it didn't rain.

Peterson stood there waiting for them. They arrived in a state of total exhaustion, as though they had crossed ten deserts on their way. When he saw them, he suspected that those who had come were far fewer than their actual numbers, so he insisted that they pass one by one in front of the police station entrance before returning to Hadiya.

At the end of the trip back, Hajj Salem searched for Hadiya in the darkness that had descended over the earth, but he saw nothing. It was so dark, it was as if there were nothing there. But they found it at last, and as soon as they reached its outskirts, they silently parted ways, each of them heading to his own house.

The minute they reached their doorsteps, curses went up. They discovered that the soldiers had plundered and destroyed whatever they wanted.

They slept like the slain, and woke as captives.

At the same time, they knew they were slaying Peterson by their endurance just as he was slaying them with his cruelty.

Next morning the streets of the village were completely empty, and over the course of the following six days, the hellish journey was repeated over and over. Suns blazed, rains fell, and springs erupted beneath their feet. They lost two children—Nur, Taha Sa'ada's little boy, and Samih, Adib Nasir's young son—and three elderly people, Fahmi Abu Sunbul, Faruq al-Nashif, and Kamal Sa'id al-Sharif. Meanwhile, illness ate away at the bodies of many others.

They slept like the slain, and woke as captives.

"I know you've done what you had to do. But I'm sure I've done what I had to do, and I hope you'll always remember this pleasant visit of mine!"

Many things would happen after this. Some of them they would forget, but that week of torment was something they would always remember, and when, years later, they had the opportunity to erase it forever, they did so without hesitation.*

---

* That night Peterson wrote: That which I have yet to dream of / I haven't experienced before. / That which once belonged to me / wasn't near my pillow in the morning. / Your sweet name, it's you, / Yet it's empty as a dried-up well when you're not here.

The Red Flower's Secret

Three days after the great week of torment, Hajj Khaled passed through Hadiya. After leaving Hamama in the olive groves behind the graveyard, he stole into the village. The echoes of that battle were still shaking his spirit and leaving it naked: the battle that had turned against him and his men, and in which their rifles had found themselves powerless in the face of the airplanes and armored cars that had closed in on them from all sides.

When he got to the house, he surprised Sumayya with a pair of white pigeons of the fantail variety that she had long wished to have.

This pigeon's features made it more like a horse than anything else, and like Hamama herself in particular: the petite, proudly raised head, the puffed-out chest, and the tail that, as soon as it began to shake, would begin spreading until it was the size of her entire body.

Some years earlier Sumayya had seen pigeons of this variety in Jerusalem, and how she had wished she could have some like them! Indeed, she seemed so delighted with the gift that she nearly forgot that the person who had brought it would only be able to stay a few hours before going away again!

In his mother's room Hajj Khaled sat surrounded by his aunt Anisa, his sister Aziza, his wife Sumayya, his daughter Fatima, and the rest of the family.

Then suddenly his mother asked him a question he hadn't been expecting: "Was her husband really martyred?"

As soon as Sumayya heard it, her delight in the gift vanished.

"Whose husband?"

"Yasmin's."

Suddenly everyone went mute. He looked over at Sumayya. He could see her color changing and her features tightening up in the dim lamplight.

"Yes, he was."

"Is it true what people are saying, that you tried to shield him with your own body, and that the bullet that passed through your shoulder was the one that killed him? Why?"

"I didn't think a bullet could go through two bodies!"

"Was it for her sake or for his sake that you did that?"

"For all our sakes, Mama. For all our sakes. He was one of my men."

"Did you really go there?"

"I had to do my duty."

"And did you see her?"

"Yes, I did, just the way anybody else would have seen her."

"And her children?"

"She doesn't have any children."

"Did you—?"

"I think we've said enough."

Hajj Khaled got up, took Sumayya by the hand, and left the room. Out in the courtyard, Hamdan's eyes glistened as they surveyed the vast expanse beyond the village. His ears were wide open, and his hands clutched the mortar and pestle as though they were holding a rifle.

"It seems you haven't gotten her out of your system!"

"That part of the past is over, Umm Mahmud. It's over completely, and for good."

"For sure?"

"For sure!"

"But you say it with sadness in your voice."

"I'd be betraying your trust if I told you I wasn't sad. But I don't know why exactly. I promise you, though, that if I figure out the reason some day, I'll tell you what it is."

"That's a promise from Hajj Khaled."

"No, that's a promise from Abu Mahmud."

Sumayya had been about to ask him, "And the handkerchief that flutters on Hamama's harness—isn't it hers?"

But at the last moment she held her tongue.

Beneath a woolen cloak, Naji sat on the roof looking out in all directions. Meanwhile, Hamdan was watching for any move on Naji's part that would tell him to get to work. Since the beginning of the uprising some time earlier, his job had developed into a good deal more than just preparing coffee. In short, he'd become the early warning man. If danger was approaching, all he had to do was to start pounding with his mortar and pestle in a rhythm that had become known to the whole village. That night, Hamdan heard what Naji had been unable to see from his perch on the roof. So he started grinding coffee in his copper mortar, which could produce a sound as loud as that of a small church bell.

Naji looked at him and whispered, "What are you doing? I don't see anything."

"I hear something you don't see."

Hajj Khaled squeezed Sumayya's hand and said to her, "It's time." She clung to his hand, not wanting to let go.

"Be calm," he said, "and let your heart be with me."

"My heart *is* with you, and with all your men. May God protect you."

Hamdan's pounding with that particular rhythm was sufficient to waken everyone. People began stirring in the dissipating darkness, and within moments everyone who had come with Hajj Khaled had gathered with him in front of his house. Naji threw a rifle down off the roof—a new rifle that Hajj Khaled had seized from a British patrol, and that had yet to fire a single shot. Hajj Khaled caught it, then gave everybody quick hugs. He planted kisses on his mother's and Aunt Anisa's hands, and on Aziza's and Sumayya's heads. Then he bent down, lifted Tamam up and hugged her, causing one of her lily-white arms to be exposed. After setting her down again, he took hold of her wrist with one hand and her elbow with the other. He lowered his white teeth toward her forearm.

"Is this tender-looking meat edible?" he asked.

"No, no!" she cried, pulling her arm away and giggling as though she were still the little girl she'd been so long ago.

He waved to them, his bullet holsters forming a cross over his chest. He pulled his heavy coat tightly around him and went up the hill. He passed by the graves of his two brothers, his father, and his two nephews, and began to move on. But then, for some mysterious reason, he went back and stared inside his grave, which, the last time he had seen it, had been filled with water. He peered inside it and saw some green grass, in the middle of which was a budding red anemone. The darkness was striving in vain to swallow up the flower's bright red hue. The flower's stem had grown so tall that it was four or five times higher than the grasses around it. He didn't have to think long to discover its secret, since he had always known that whenever a plant or tree was in shade, any shade, it would grow faster than plants or trees that were in direct light, for the simple reason that it was trying to reach the sun.

A strange feeling came over him, as though the flower that had budded before its time were part of his own body.

"We've got to hurry," Nuh said to him.

"It's trying to reach the sun," he said.

"What's trying to reach the sun?"

"The red anemone. Look."

"And the British armored cars are trying to reach *us!*"

The pounding noise produced by Hamdan's mortar and pestle grew louder, and for the first time Edward Peterson realized what it meant. He thought back on the previous times he had raided the village and had heard the same rhythm. His ears couldn't be deceiving him: it was the same rhythm. Never, for as long as he could remember, had Peterson been deceived the way he had been by these rap-a-tap-taps concealed behind a façade of innocence and indifference. By the time he reached the village, he was certain that his intended prey had managed to escape.

Peterson kept going until he reached Hamdan, who kept on working as though the soldiers who had gathered around him were in another country, on another continent, in another world. Sensing a peculiar movement around him, he looked up and saw the barrel of a revolver right between his eyes. He heard Peterson say, "The last stroke is mine." Then he fired.

However, Hamdan's hand, which had frozen in mid-air when he saw the revolver, brought the pestle he was holding down into the mortar, and Peterson heard a sound that was even louder than the report of his gun.

"Fuckin' Arabs!" he screamed, realizing that Hamdan had deprived him of the final stroke he had promised himself.

Peterson stood gazing at Hamdan's dead body. After a long silence, he took a piece of paper out of his pocket and, contrary to his usual custom, wrote,

Your face, blue as the sea,
contains nothing but sharks.
Your arms, open as the sky,
anticipate the next step like fate.
And your conversation, flowing like a waterfall,
Divulges nothing to me but silence.

The Will

Hajj Khaled clung to his rifle. He looked at Hamama through the crack in the door. He pondered her in those inscrutable moments, those moments open to all possibilities.

The owner of the house said to him, "You still have a chance to withdraw. Behind us there are lots of houses you could slip out through, and right beyond them are orchards and olive groves."

The dawn, whose sun had yet to rise, was filled with the roar of the military vehicles and the rattling of armored cars. It wasn't difficult for the people of the village to realize what was happening.

A boy came in a panic and said, "The British are at the entrance to the village!"

Hajj Khaled kneaded his brow with the fingers of his left hand. Turning to his travel companion and son-in-law, Nuh brother of Khadra, he said, "Let's do our best not to let Khadra and Aziza down."

Then he said to Iliya Radhi, "Today is your day!"

Hajj Khaled looked again at Hamama on the far side of the courtyard. He wanted to say something to her, something he was feeling, but he couldn't put it into words.

"I still think you ought to retreat from the back," said the owner of the house.

"Don't worry. We've been through days more difficult than this one. This moment has always been waiting for us, and we've always been waiting for it. However, I'm going to say something I've been thinking about for a long time. Nuh and Iliya, there's something I want you to say to the people of Hadiya if I'm not able to tell them myself."

Nuh nodded his head in mute sorrow.

"My father, may he rest in peace, always used to say, 'No one can go on winning forever. No nation has ever been a permanent victor.' I've always remembered what he said. But today I feel that something else can also be said, which is that I'm not afraid of their winning and our losing once, or about our winning and their losing once. There's only one thing I'm afraid of—that we'll be broken forever, since someone who's been broken forever will never rise again. So tell them: 'Beware of losing forever.'"

Standing there with grave faces, Nuh and Iliya felt that his words were turning into a farewell.

Then Hajj Khaled's voice came again: "Nuh, do you remember that day, after you and Fatima were engaged, when you told me you had been defeated in your battle for your cows? And I said to you, 'No, you weren't defeated, because when you attacked, you didn't want to win. You only wanted to take back what was rightfully yours.' Never in my life have I had the thought that I was going out to fight in order to inflict defeat on somebody. Rather, I've always gone out to protect what was rightfully mine. And now, I don't want to run away. All I want to say to them is, 'I'm not fighting to win. I'm fighting to preserve what's rightfully mine.'"

Hajj Khaled looked up at the sky. He reached out for his yellow keffiyeh and wrapped it around his neck. He placed his coat in Hamama's saddlebag. He looked at his two companions, and in his olive-green eyes they saw a mysterious gleam. He smiled.

※

The news had reached Edward Peterson the evening before: "Hajj Khaled will be in one of two villages." After doing a few calculations, he decided to form two forces. One of them would go to Meithalun, and the other to Sanur. Once again he found himself unable to decide which direction to go. Should he head the force that would surround the first village, or the one that would surround the second? He finally decided to go to Meithalun and storm it quickly. If he didn't find Hajj Khaled there, he would go back to Sanur and join the two forces.

On that calm, cold dawn in late March, it wasn't difficult for the people of Sanur to hear the sounds of gunfire and bombs coming from the direction of Meithalun. For years they had been able to hear the voices of wedding songs wafting on the winds blowing from the other village. So why wouldn't they be able to hear the sound of gunfire?

Peterson combed the entire village, but didn't find a thing. So he ordered his troops to retreat toward Sanur.

Peterson rushed back to Sanur before the other force began storming the village. When he finally got there, he divided the two forces into three lines one hundred meters apart. He chose the force that would launch the surprise attack on the village without forgetting to send thirty soldiers to the other side so that they could close off any escape routes that might open in that direction.

Hajj Khaled walked toward Hamama. He had never seen her looking as far away as she did on that day, and this in spite of the fact that the distance that separated them was no more than thirty meters.

He wasn't certain she was really there until he had placed his hand gently on her forehead. She shook her head as though she wanted to say something. He took her face in his hands. Then he bent down, gently kissed her right foot, and placed it back on the ground. He did the same with her left foot. He stood up. He looked straight into her eyes and said, "Today is your day."

Then he jumped on her back. He looked over at Nuh, who had already jumped on the bay mare's back, and at Iliya Radhi, who had mounted the gray mare.

He placed a cartridge in the chamber, as did Nuh. He drew his rifle, saying, "If God loves us a lot, then maybe we'll be able to pass through their forces. If He loves us less, then, at the very least, He won't let them capture us alive and lead us away to be hanged on their gallows."

The owner of the house opened the enclosure gate. Hajj Khaled shot out, with Nuh and Iliya close on his heals. Before long, they were speeding along side by side. Then, little by little, the distance between them began to widen.

They didn't see the soldiers who lay in wait for them. They heard bullets whizzing around them. They rode faster. Hajj Khaled was in the center, with Nuh to his right and Iliya to his left. They managed to get past the first line. But before they had reached the second, they were confronted unexpectedly by half the soldiers, who stood with their rifles expertly aimed. At that point the three horsemen began firing. Feeling a sting in his right side, Hajj Khaled charged ahead with even greater fervor. As they came up against a wall of soldiers with their bayonets at the ready, Nuh received a stab wound that went through his thigh. It was delivered with such force that it pulled the rifle out of the hand of the soldier who had struck him, and the gun swung from his thigh until he managed to lean down and pull it out.

Another bullet went through Hajj Khaled's shoulder. However, he knew he had to reach the third barrier, which suddenly appeared with three armored cars and a number of jeeps in the middle of it. Suddenly, Iliya Radhi made his mare swerve to the right. Seeing what Iliya had done, Nuh swerved to the left, their aim being to disperse the enemy gunfire and give Hajj Khaled a chance to clear the third line of British soldiers.

At that moment, Edward Peterson saw the white mare coming toward him.

"Hold your fire! Hold your fire!" he shouted.

Some of the soldiers obeyed the order, which allowed Nuh and Iliya to get away. However, the soldiers hunched inside the armored cars kept firing. Then, in a bizarre occurrence, they saw Hajj Khaled's body fly into the air as Hamama continued charging forward without noticing that he was no longer on her back.

He fell to the ground, his revolver in his hand. As for his rifle, it wasn't there. It may have fallen before he reached the ground. He fired several shots right at the soldiers, who were no more than twenty meters away. He saw one of them fall before a sudden fog descended and filled his eyes. However, he was still able to hear the shout of a military man barking out his orders: "Don't shoot! Don't shoot!" The sound of Hamama's hoofbeats grew fainter, and he could see the off-white handkerchief fluttering alongside her face.

Their rifles had turned in Hamama's direction, and they had been about to kill her as she passed through their line. However, they found Peterson himself standing between them and her, raising his hand and saying again, "Don't shoot! Don't shoot!"

Suddenly, everything grew still. Peterson turned toward Hamama and saw drops of blood following her.

"Fuckin' Arabs. Fuckin' British. Fuckin' world. Fuckin' . . . !"

Peterson approached Hajj Khaled's body with a heaviness in his step that bewildered his soldiers. He saw him supine, his face to the sky, his hand clutching his revolver, his body riddled with bullets, and his clothes soaked in blood. One of his soldiers aimed his rifle and was about to fire a last shot at the lifeless body.

Peterson reached out and lowered the soldier's rifle. "He's dead."

"Congratulations!" he heard one of them say.

Without turning to see who had been speaking, Peterson said, "This was a courageous man, and it's shameful to congratulate each other on his death."

Then, looking into the soldiers' faces, he said, "He was an honorable man. Where will I ever find another opponent like him?"

Peterson instructed his soldiers to dig a grave so that they could bury Hajj Khaled's body. His eyes were fixed on the hole as it grew larger and larger. Before they had finished digging, Major General Bernard Montgomery, commander of the British forces in northern Palestine, arrived.* He stood silently beside Peterson. Peterson signaled to his troops to carry Hajj Khaled to the grave. When they placed him inside it, a number of the soldiers formed a queue and fired in the air in a gesture of respect, while Peterson and Montgomery and the senior officers saluted the deceased.†

Wounded in several places, Nuh and Iliya reached safety at last. They didn't have to think long to understand why the British had not come after them. After all, they had bagged their prize, and this or that minor victory was no longer of any concern to them.

Sumayya saw Hamama approaching in the distance, galloping madly. She didn't need to look very closely to see that she was returning alone. Sumayya froze in her tracks. As the moments passed, a number of the members of the household gathered around her, and for a moment it seemed to them that, despite the mad pace at which she was approaching, Hamama would never arrive.

However, she did arrive finally. In her right thigh, a bullet had caused a transverse wound that was bleeding so badly that one hind leg was red. Her tail was also covered with blood, which was flying in all directions. When at last she halted in front of Sumayya, she seemed to be waiting for Hajj Khaled to get down off her back, and when he didn't, Hamama began to weep. At that point Sumayya broke down.

"What are you doing here?" she cried.

Flustered, Hamama took two steps back. Then she began walking eastward with heavy steps, looking behind her every few seconds, so that, even an hour later, she hadn't yet disappeared.

Sumayya sat down and wept. "What have I done? Bring her here!" Fatima went running after her and asked her to come back. However, Hamama continued on her way with heavy, broken steps. She called her by name, but Hamama didn't turn her head. It was the first time an animal

---

* After the Second Battle of El Alamein in Egypt's Western Desert, he was to become one of the most prominent heroes of the Second World War.

† That night he wrote: Did I need you, O feet, / In order to reach that distant place? / I ask everyone I happen to see there, "Have I really arrived?" / Did I need you, O heart, in order to hate and love? / My father always said to me, "If you want to make it home alive, hate your enemy."

462

had failed to respond to Fatima. It was then that they realized that Hamama's wound was too deep to heal. When the other horses took off running after her, she broke into a wild gallop, as though she wanted to catch up with her rider.

A little after noon, everyone was able to hear the news directly on the radio broadcasts.

"We're lost!" cried Muhammad Shahada, Shakir Muhanna, and many others.*

For five days, Nuh was suspended between life and death. As for Iliya Radhi, he and a number of other men made their way stealthily to the grave the British had dug for Hajj Khaled. They dug up the grave and removed the body, then took it to Hadiya.

When they stopped there, Iliya Radhi and Nuh saw it. The red anemone, which had now blossomed, had grown so tall that it rose above the edge of the grave. One of the men was about to get down in the grave to remove the grass when Iliya shouted, "Leave it alone!"

They placed the body beside the flower and began throwing dirt in from both sides.

"Don't let the dirt cover the blossom," Iliya instructed them.

The next morning Iliya returned alone. He looked at the flower. It had grown taller. He gathered up some dirt in his hands and placed it on the grave. He went on doing this every day. Meanwhile, the flower grew higher and higher. Seven days later, he arrived at the grave in the morning and saw one of its petals falling. When that happened, he burst into tears and wept more bitterly than any man has ever wept.

That year was the year of death. They lost many. Every woman and girl twelve years of age or older who had lost a relative was to remain for forty days in the dress she had been wearing when she received the news. Then

---

* Movement in Palestinian cities came to a halt: businesses closed, students in public, private, and foreign schools went on strike, transport services were immobilized, and cars and other vehicles disappeared from the streets. The Muslims announced his death from the minarets, the Christians rang church bells in mourning for the martyr, and people carried wreaths of flowers and black flags through the streets. The Greek Orthodox Church even canceled all celebrations that had been scheduled from Palm Sunday until noon on the day after Easter.

she was to take it off, bathe, and don black attire. All the families were wearing black. When the holiday arrived and Hajj Salem still saw all the women in black, he shouted, "By God, if any of you goes on wearing those black things, I'll break her legs!" So they took off all their black clothes. Then he doused the clothes with kerosene and set them on fire.

The mystery that robbed them of sleep for years to come was how Hajj Khaled's whereabouts had been discovered.

Then one day Iliya Radhi asked Sumayya, "Didn't you get the homing pigeon?"

With tears in her eyes Sumayya said, "The last time we saw her was the day you took her with you!"

The Spittle

H e turned in the direction of the cloud and spat. The spittle came
back toward him, carried by the wind. Turning, he saw it fly past
his shoulder and land on Salim Bek al-Hashemi's shoe.
Salim looked at his shoe, then at the officer.

Their dry eyes froze, searching for something to say about this wet mess.

Salim Bek al-Hashemi was about to open his mouth when, without
warning, he received a blow from Peterson's cudgel. It was a violent, lightning-quick blow, which might have sent his head flying had he not leaned
sideways at the last moment and taken it on his arm. He fell, the world
spinning around him.

Rashid Adnan, a man in his seventies, roared at Peterson. "What are
you doing? Don't you know who you're dealing with?"

Then Rashid received a blow on his head. Blood spattered in all directions, staining Salim Bek al-Hashemi's clothes. As for Peterson, he managed to avoid the flying drops of blood, which he had seen coming toward
him with astounding slowness.

Leaving the two men, he went on his way. When he heard insults and cries of condemnation coming from behind him, he stopped and looked back at the black cloud again. He thought of spitting. But instead, he turned back to them, then charged like a raging bull, scattering the crowd and striking out every which way. He ran after them, and when he saw them falling like dominoes and heard the wailing of the wounded behind him, he was filled with peculiar sensations. When at last he stopped, a good distance away from the people, he spat, knowing full well that the wind would carry his spittle in their direction this time and not miss its mark.

On his way back, not one of those who had fallen was spared a second or third blow that glued him to the ground. And when he got to Salim Bek al-Hashemi, he stopped and spat again.

The ten days that followed Hajj Khaled's martyrdom were the worst of Peterson's entire life. The whole country went on strike, and wherever he turned, he found Hajj Khaled: a picture of him here, an article about him there. The radio stations spoke nonstop about the details of his life, and about his integrity and impeccable morals. And one of the newspapers talked about the white mare's mysterious disappearance.

Everything seemed to Peterson to have become so meaningless that he wondered: What can I do now? When he got to the region's central command, he said, "I want to get away from here."

No one had expected him to go back to the city that had nearly snatched his life away. But he did go back, and the first thing he did was to go to the coffee shop where someone had tried to assassinate him. In fact, he made a point of sitting at the very same table. In a bizarre moment, he found himself looking at the floor, and what should he see there but his blood, which was still fresh. He stood up in a fright, took a deep breath, then sat down again, unfazed.

In the days that followed, Salim Bek al-Hashemi continued to take pride in his wounded arm, which was bandaged and in a sling. People gathered around him with words of condemnation for Peterson's crime. It served as a remarkable occasion for him to write letters of protest to the High

466

Commissioner as well as fiery articles, the most famous of which bore the title, "The Beast Is Back in the Streets."

The doctor did his best to convince Salim Bek al-Hashemi of the need to take the bandage off. When he finally did so, he said to him, "But it still hurts!" So the doctor wrapped it in a new white dressing.

The murder of the German Stephen Shaefer, who owned Stephen Press, at the hands of a group of Jews, released a torrent of rage among members of the German community, who demonstrated in the streets and raised protest banners in front of the British police headquarters, demanding that they find the murderers before he was buried.[*]

Edward Peterson came out and said, "If you don't leave now and take him to the cemetery, you won't find any place to bury him at all."

But they refused to back down.

He said, "Don't say later that I didn't warn you."

In the end, they were all obliged to go home.

Next morning, however, they were back. They demonstrated for three days, and were joined by groups of Germans who had come from Jerusalem and Haifa. However, Edward Peterson paid no attention to them. Everything he could say to them, he had already said.

Eventually, they headed for the hospital and took Stephen's body to the church. And because the matter had become the talk of the town, Palestinians came streaming to the church to escort the funeral procession.

It was a rainy day. I remember it so clearly, I can almost feel the raindrops falling on me as I speak to you!

When the funeral procession reached the courtyard of the German church, Peterson was standing at its door, surrounded by a large group of policemen. He was oblivious to the rain, which was pouring down as though the sky were trying to empty itself of everything at once. The people

---

[*] With the start of the Second World War, Jews began harassing all the German communities in Palestine, forcing them to leave the villages, cooperatives, farms, and factories. By 1948, all Germans had left Palestine, most of them for Australia.

approached, carrying the bier. Peterson drew his revolver and raised it skyward. A shot rang out, mingled with the sound of a clap of thunder. The people backed away somewhat, and for a few moments the bier rocked in their hands.

The people found themselves on the verge of a bloodbath.

They jeered, they hurled insults. Yet they had no choice but to retreat.

"I warned you, but you didn't listen."

The people consulted among themselves, then decided to go straight to the cemetery and conduct the funeral there before burying him. However, on the way there they found Peterson blocking the road.

When they tried to get past the police force, shots were fired at them from all directions: "You want more people dead, it seems. If so, I'll be happy to oblige."

They stepped back a short distance.

"If you want to bury him, then look for a place outside this city."

So the funeral procession went back to where it had come from, to the hospital, and as evening approached, Stephen's family came back alone, picked up the bier, and headed for the port.

Roseline's Night

efore the day was half over, news of the previous night's dinner
party had become the talk of the town. When newspapers came
out two days later, more than one article made clear references to
the soiree, though none of them named names.

The district governor had heard about what happened to Salim Bek al-
Hashemi, so he sent him a bouquet of flowers, together with an apology
and wishes for a quick recovery. The flowers' arrival awakened all sorts
of conflicting thoughts in al-Hashemi's head. The most important of these
ideas was to send an angry, reproachful letter to the district governor,
who received it quickly and decided to host a soiree in al-Hashemi's
honor, to which he would invite a number of political leaders, notables,
and public figures.[*]

---

[*] Quite regrettably, some of those working in the nationalist movement, including prominent
members of the executive committee with their varying partisan leanings, went along with
the practice of hosting banquets and parties that brought Jews and Arabs together. The
British authorities began inventing occasions for gatherings of this type, and such individuals

Al-Hashemi gave some thought to how he should present himself when he went to the district governor's home. Should he remove the white bandages from his arm and free his neck from their weight, or should he go with them still on? He chose the latter course of action, and as he had expected, his appearance with his arm in a sling exerted a special charm, and he for his part felt that he was entering that spacious hall like a warrior returning from battle. He had managed to kill two birds with one stone, since in this way he was making it clear to those in attendance, friends and foes alike, that he was coming to the governor's home with his head held high. At the same time, he was making it clear to the governor that he accorded him such respect that he was willing to overlook the insult to which he had been subjected.

Conversations during the first hour of the party centered around the arm, the pain resulting from the injury, when the bandage was due to come off, whether al-Hashemi had gotten more than one medical opinion so as to set his mind at rest, and whether—God forbid—there might be any future complications.

As al-Hashemi fielded all these questions, he had his eye on the other guests. He was thinking about who had attended and who hadn't, and was making quick calculations as to the reasons for their coming, the excuses for their not coming, and the real reasons for their not coming.

As for the district governor, never in his life had he been as gracious and jovial as he was on that night. He flitted about with obvious pleasure, his beady eyes illumined by a weird gleam. He gazed about at those in attendance and listened to their laughter with a sense of euphoria, since, like many of his guests, both Arabs and Jews, he could see that the four gloomy years of 'unrest' had come to an end and that he, like them, could breathe a bit more easily.

---

responded to the High Commissioner's invitations to banquets and parties where they would sometimes mix freely with Jews. They also accepted his appointments to mixed Jewish–Arab consultative committees dealing with issues pertaining to labor, roads, commerce, and agriculture. Hence, as a result of Palestine's double affliction with, on one hand, the British and the Jews and, on the other hand, the weakness of its nationalist movement, there emerged what might be termed a dual, or 'hermaphrodite,' nationalism. No one could fail to note the weakness and apathy that came over the independent nationalist movement, or the disunity and chaos into which it fell.

The full program, which had opened with impromptu encounters inter-spersed with countless toasts, was summed up in a brief speech delivered in Arabic, in which the host welcomed those who had come, as well as the guest of honor. He concluded his speech with a joke, saying, "I'm not a physician, but I promise you that Mr. Hashemi will leave here tonight with an arm that's perfectly sound!"

Everyone laughed, including the one with the suspended arm. A few moments later, however, he began to turn the joke over in his mind in search of ulterior meanings.

The orchestra that had been brought in by the district governor began playing a number of pieces, and when it was halfway through "Les Drag-ons d'Alcala," a totally unexpected event took place: Madame Roseline arrived. She entered arm in arm with the district governor, who had been waiting for her at the door. The moment the rhythm of her steps mingled with the strains of Bizet, the meaning of the piece was transformed, since Roseline herself appeared to be the musical instrument the orchestra needed in order to perform Bizet perfectly on that particular evening.

Madame Roseline was the talk of the upper classes in the city, and, in al-Hashemi's opinion, she was the most beautiful woman ever to have set foot on the country's shores. She was the woman who, if she had become queen of England rather than the king, "we'd take to the streets and demand that we be annexed to Britain," as Rashid Adnan, a septuagenar-ian notable, used to tell the district governor whenever they met at gath-erings of this kind. As for the district governor himself, he would say to them, "If she were appointed in my place, I don't suppose you would ever leave the governor's office!"

For a long time, Salim Bek al-Hashemi had aspired to more than a mere meeting with her. He had made earnest efforts, but every time he did so, he had been obliged to stop at that subtle boundary that separated him from Madame Roseline.

By the time the orchestra had finished playing, al-Hashemi had downed his fifth glass. More than once, he forgot what had prompted him

471

to attend the party with his arm still in a sling, and he would periodically lift it to scratch his chin.

The district governor had made plans for a lengthy soiree and had, accordingly, made a point of postponing the dinner till a late hour of the night. He had postponed it so much, in fact, that Mr. Fakhri Salman commented to him with a guffaw, "We didn't know you'd invited us to a pre-dawn meal!"

Everyone laughed.

"My apologies," said the district governor. "Isn't this the month of Ramadan?" And they laughed some more.

Salim Bek al-Hashemi realized that this was his night, and that he was free to conduct himself more or less however he pleased. He walked over to Madame Roseline. When he was four steps away from her, the district governor blocked his path. "Allow me to introduce you to Madame Roseline," he said. "After all, you're the groom tonight."

"If only she were the bride!" replied Salim Bek with a chuckle.

"There should be no difficulty here! What could Madame Roseline possibly want in a man that you don't have?"

To Salim Bek al-Hashemi's surprise, she leaned into him with a warm embrace. Then she took a couple of steps back and said, "I hope your arm isn't injured so badly that you can't do everything you need to!"

"No, no! In a few days I'll be rid of these bandages."

"But I'd promised to rid him of them tonight!" laughed the district governor.

"In this house, miracles are performed. Just ask me. I ought to know!" Madame Roseline let forth a resounding laugh that shook Salim Bek al-Hashemi to the core.

By eleven-thirty that evening the food had still not arrived. However, Madame Roseline's presence had made them forget all about it.

She sat on a chaise longue, flanked by Salim Bek al-Hashemi and the district governor, and the heat emanating from her body seared everyone, setting the March night on fire. Everyone felt merry and ready for anything.

At the same time, they envied al-Hashemi for having had her all to himself the entire evening. However, the beginnings of what transpired later had been a mere game, or words that hadn't been entirely sincere. For when al-Hashemi leaned into Roseline and she became aware of it, she turned to him and said in a voice everyone could hear, "Mr. Hashemi, you're not a young man any more! Aren't you over seventy?"

"I'm not even sixty yet."

"That's impossible. Show me your identity card."

He produced his identity card, being careful not to move his injured arm, and handed it to her. She looked at it intently.

"It's true. You're still a young man!"

Those words were enough to pump new life into him again.

"What do you say we play a game, then? If you win, I promise you in front of everyone that tonight will be your night. Ready?"

Al-Hashemi looked into the faces of those present. They had suddenly fallen silent, as though they were standing in front of a death squad. Every one of them was thinking: Will al-Hashemi really be the first of us to have her?

He could see with his alcohol-dimmed eyes that all the envy of the world had been packed into that hall.

"What do you say? Are you ready?"

Al-Hashemi looked at her and said, "Ready!"

She took his identity card and threw it to the other end of the hall.

"What are you doing?"

"If you can pick it up with your teeth, bring it back here, and hand it to me, I'll be yours."

"That's not fair!" shouted Mr. Aziz Pasha, who appeared to be the drunkest one in the room.

"What do you suggest?"

"I suggest that anybody who wants to should be allowed to join the contest."

"No, that's not possible," Madame Roseline said. "This way, you'll deprive me of the chance to choose the person that I want to be my prize, too."

"Well, then, let's specify the age range of the people who can participate. Does that meet with your approval?" asked the district governor.

"Let me think," Roseline replied as she pondered the guests' faces. Then she nodded her head. "Don't you say in Arabic, 'amri lillah', 'I commit my concern to God'?"

They nodded their heads. Her way of speaking Arabic had its own special charm.

"All right, then: 'amri lillah' However, I won't accept anybody who's a day older than Mr. Hashemi. Agreed?"

"Agreed."

All the identity cards then appeared.

Salim Bek al-Hashemi had been born on 16 October 1882. The district governor, who had been made the referee, disqualified everyone who had been born before that date. Cries of protest went up when it became apparent that only four of them were younger than al-Hashemi.

"I promise you," said the district governor, "I promise you that next time, the contest will include people who are a little older. Now, then, let's see who the winner will be on this memorable night!"

Roseline looked thoughtfully at the contestants. Al-Hashemi really was the most handsome one among them. He was the tallest and the most fair-skinned, and no one who looked at him could help but fall under the spell of his marvelous long moustache.

She said, "But I have one condition, which is that we have to tie participants' hands behind their backs."

"I can't do that, and you know it," al-Hashemi said angrily.

"You're exempt. But the rest have to do it."

"Why don't you turn out the lights, too? The contest will be more exciting that way," said Hasan Pasha.

"Whoever wants to dance in the dark, let him dance alone," said Rashid Adnan, as though he wanted to get revenge on the contestants.

"You're right. Aren't we here to have a good time?"

"But you've got to set a time limit for the contest. Otherwise it will be meaningless," said Aziz Pasha, half of whose inebriation seemed to have worn off.

"That's an excellent idea," said Roseline.

"Let's put the other identity cards next to al-Hashemi's, then," said the district governor.

"Just a minute. Just a minute. There's got to be another condition. If they all lose, we have to be allowed to join the contest after them," said Zahir Effendi.

"We'll leave that till another occasion," the district governor replied. "After all, I think we'll need to eat tonight. Aren't you hungry?"

"No! No!" they cried in unison.

The district governor took a seat directly across from the identity cards. The race began with an extraordinary push-and-shove, and they got there quickly. The sound of muttering and of heads colliding grew steadily louder, while the other guests began rooting for one or another of the contenders. Taking advantage of his free hand, Salim Bek al-Hashemi bent down and, after three attempts, managed to get hold of the identity card by the use of his tongue. When, huffing and puffing, he beat everyone else to the finish line, he'd totally forgotten that his injured arm had come loose from the sling.

The other contestants objected when they saw his free hand. Feigning a wince, al-Hashemi took hold of it with his right hand and put it back in the sling.

As they stood at the door, the district governor put his mouth to al-Hashemi's ear. "I think you're going to have to get rid of her completely if you want to accomplish anything worthy of this evening."

"Get rid of Roseline?" he asked, seeming thoroughly intoxicated.

"No. The bandage on your arm."

"OK, OK."

They then made their way down the stairs to her car, which stood waiting.

Shortly after noon, Salim Bek al-Hashemi received a telephone call from the district governor.

"Tell me how it went!"

"It was great. She's a tigress. When I woke up, I found a different piece of my clothing in every room!"

He hung up and called Roseline. "How did things go?"

"He chased me from room to room, and in every room he would take off a piece of his clothing. By the time we finally made it to the bed, he'd forgotten why he was chasing me, and fell asleep!"

A Shot after
the Dawn Prayer

H adiya awoke to the sound of shouting and wailing. It was coming from the direction of al-Najjar's neighborhood, and it filled the village's sky.

"Sabri al-Najjar has been murdered!"

The chaos then spread.

Before anyone knew who had killed him, his clansmen went rushing in the direction of Hajj Salem's neighborhood. But before any of them got there, Karim, Sabri al-Najjar's son, shouted, "I'm the one who killed him!"

They didn't believe it.

He drew his revolver and fired a shot into the sky, saying, "With this revolver."

Everyone froze in their tracks. No one knew any more what he was supposed to do.

Karim had never accompanied his father on any of his errands outside the village. He hadn't liked anyone to see him walking beside him, whether he was known to the person or not.

On the other hand, al-Najjar was constantly being embarrassed by his son Karim. Whenever he disappeared, news would come saying that he was in prison for taking part in a demonstration here or a demonstration there. Whenever Karim heard or read about a demonstration in Ramla, Jaffa, or Jerusalem, he would sneak off to march in it. One time, after Karim had gotten out of prison, Hajj Sabri swore that he would divorce his wife if he didn't manage to marry his son off, and Karim agreed to it in order to prevent his mother from being divorced. Al-Najjar thought marriage would make his son 'come to his senses,' and in fact, there was a quiet period, after he had had two children, when it seemed as though Karim had become another person. Al-Najjar said, "I should have married him off five years ago!" Then one day al-Najjar saw his daughter-in-law walking down a street full of British soldiers. He called out to her from the window to come in, but she paid no attention. He went out after her, and when he got to the place where she was, he grabbed her and screamed, "What is this? You come out with your newborn child without feeling afraid?" He reached out to snatch the child away from her, only to find that what she was carrying was a weapon. He grabbed her by the hand and started dragging her toward the house right in front of all the soldiers, and once they were inside with the door closed, he started screaming at her, "I married him off so he'd come to his senses, and here you are two years later going crazy just like him!"

After Hajj Khaled's martyrdom, Karim felt more ashamed than ever. Whenever he found himself looking at his father, a strange thought would come to him: never in his life was my father opposed to Khaled, the former pilgrim to Mecca. Rather, he was opposed to Khaled the martyr.

That morning Hajj Sabri had been strangely insistent. He said to Karim, "You're going with me. That means you're going with me."

When he found out, halfway there, that they would be passing by Abd al-Latif al-Hamdi's house first, Karim said, "I'm going back." Hajj Sabri swore that if he did, he would divorce his mother.

"You're going with me. That means you're going with me."

Karim tried to figure out why his father was insisting so forcefully. Unable to solve the riddle, he continued on the journey with him without saying a word.

Nevertheless, Karim refused to go inside al-Hamdi's house. "I'll wait for you here in the car," he said to his father. Less than fifteen minutes later, Hajj Sabri came out and said to his son, "Now we'll finish our errand."

The car, which he had hired specifically for this trip, headed out for its next destination.

"Where are we going?"

"To Jaffa."

"To Jaffa?"

"Yes, to Jaffa."

When they reached the city's Clock Square, he said to his son, "I'll let you out here. Wait for me in that coffee shop. I'll be back in half an hour."

The square, which was actually rectangular in shape, had been the city's main square since the beginning of the twentieth century: a hub of social, economic, and tourist activity, and a meeting place for all social classes thanks to its numerous coffee shops and restaurants. It had also come to be known as 'Carriage Square,' because for a long time it had been the place where horse-drawn carriages would gather and wait for passengers who wanted to be taken to various other parts of the city. Not long thereafter, however, its name was changed to 'Martyrs' Square,' since the demonstrations against Britain would generally begin at the large mosque after the Friday prayer, and many martyrs had fallen in this very square.

Twenty-five minutes later, the car pulled up in front of the coffee shop. His father gestured for him to get in quickly. He got in. Karim looked over and saw a peculiar-looking bundle, which his father was clutching with both hands.

They didn't talk the entire way back.

Before they arrived in Hadiya, the car pulled up again in front of al-Hamdi's house. However, al-Najjar didn't ask his son to accompany him inside. He was gone for ten minutes, then came back.

Karim looked at the bundle, which had shrunk to half its original size. The matter might have ended there if it hadn't been for a raging curiosity that got the better of him, impelling him to investigate the mystery that lay behind that bundle.

※

The first, and easiest, step was to seek out the driver, whom everyone knew. He went to see him. After a shrill exchange, the driver admitted that his father might have gone to the British governor's headquarters, since he had asked him to stop the car on a side street not far from there, and had told him not to budge from the spot until he got back.

Karim came back to the house in search of the bundle itself. Two nights later he glimpsed a string hanging from a small nail over the back of the wardrobe in his parents' room. He tugged on the string. Suspecting that he had found what he was looking for, he pulled on it gently so as not to make a racket. However, he couldn't break it. He went and got a knife, cut the string and brought the bundle outside. Out in the courtyard, he opened it up and saw a sum of money the likes of which no one in Hadiya had ever laid eyes on before.

Suddenly he was gripped by the strange sensation that he knew exactly how many pounds it contained: five thousand. He said to himself, "It's five thousand." In order to make certain, he counted the money, and as he had suspected, it was five thousand, not a piaster less.

He got up and headed for the place where he knew his father kept his revolver. He took the revolver out and sat down at the courtyard entrance to wait for his father's return.

Not long before his father came back from the dawn prayer, Karim set fire to the five thousand, which, after he had strewn it about, formed a gigantic pile of bills. Before the father had said a word or done anything to rescue whatever he could of the money, Karim took the revolver out and aimed it at him. The surprise alone would have been enough to kill Hajj Sabri. Even so, Karim needed to fire as well.

The shot settled right in the heart. Karim turned and closed the courtyard gate, leaving his father to wallow in his blood three meters away from the entrance.

Nobody could say anything. They froze. And when they saw the remains of the incinerated money, the matter grew even more mysterious.

Shaking him, Karim's mother screamed in her son's face: "Why?"
Her question at that moment was the question everyone was asking.
"Some day you'll know," he replied.*

---

* No one knew how the secret of the homing pigeon Hajj Khaled used to send messages to
his family and his men in Hadiya had reached Sabri al-Najjar. But as soon as he learned of
it, he knew that Hajj Khaled's days were numbered, since not long thereafter, he replaced
Hajj Khaled's homing pigeon with another that looked exactly like it.

Some of his assistants kept an eye on things until, one day, they saw the pigeon in a cage
on the back of Iliya Radhi's mare. They attacked him shortly before sunrise. He managed
to flee and hide in a distant spot. When he returned to the place where he had been attacked,
he expected them to have taken Shahba, his gray mare, only to find, to his surprise, that
she was still there, as was the pigeon. He continued on his way at top speed to the place
where he was to meet Hajj Khaled. Several days later, the pigeon returned with a new message, in which Hajj Khaled asked Hashem Shahada to meet them between Sanur and Meithalun. He hadn't specified the location, for fear that the message might fall into the wrong
hands. However, they knew that in such cases, it was always the first place that was meant.
And, since it was in Sabri al-Najjar's house that this pigeon had hatched, grown up, and
hatched her own young, it was there that she landed. And with her arrival, it was all over.

Book Three
Humankind

The Manuli Era

When Muhammad Shahada, whom Hajj Khaled had dubbed "the sage of Hadiya," opened his mouth, he said one thing: "Listen, everybody. No offense, but we didn't need to go all the way to Ramla to find out that we've been a bunch of donkeys!"

The arrival of the black Pontiac that brought Father Manuli to town had turned the lives of the people of Hadiya upside down. Father Manuli's arrival had come as no surprise to Father Theodorus. However, like Father Georgiou before him, he hadn't informed anyone that he would be leaving, not even Hajj Salem, who had become the village elder after his brother, Hajj Khaled, was martyred.

Theodorus had packed his bag and his big wooden chest, and once the newcomer arrived, he was content simply to shake his hand at the door of the monastery as though he didn't want both of them to be in the same place at once.

The people watched the car as it drove away. Like the carriage that had brought him to the village once upon a time, it reached the eastern edge of Hadiya's plain without stirring up a cloud of dust. Then it stopped.

There followed a heavy silence that made some people think the car was going to turn around and come back. But that didn't happen.

As the car continued to stand there, more than one man thought of getting on his horse and riding out to see what the matter was. As the people of the village stood there wondering what to do, they saw the car door open and Father Theodorus get out.

He turned and gazed at Hadiya from a distance. He pondered the plain's expanse and its olive trees. He gazed at the parts of the village that had expanded across the valley, such that the houses on the hill were no longer anything but a small part of it.

Father Theodorus was saying goodbye to a cherished part of his life, and he wondered: Was it necessary for me to leave it in order to see it from this new perspective?

A long time passed as he stood there—so long that people began to conclude that standing at that particular spot was a rite that one had no choice but to perform. When he got back into the car, nothing remained in the distance but the car's mirage.

People anticipated the appearance of the new abbot. However, he didn't appear, while what remained of the sisters Mary and Sarah—who had grown emaciated, with bowed backs, noses that were longer than ever, and eyes that were sunken and lackluster—had disappeared as well.

Then, on the fourth day, he swung the monastery door wide open.

Father Manuli was the tallest, skinniest man they had ever seen. His eyes were as small as a cat's and protruded in a strange way that gave one the impression that he could see what was behind him. As for his hands, they were longer than any hands they had seen before, even if they were measured in proportion to the rest of his body. The loose-fitting black robe he wore couldn't conceal the length of his shoes, which resembled a couple of small boats. And the first expression they saw on his face—an expression they would never forget—was a strange smile as broad as the prairies, which he scanned the way a person scans the pages of a book.

Hajj Salem wondered what it was that would cause people to stay such a long time in the village and then, when it came time to go, not say goodbye to a soul and not leave anything in the distance but glances suspended in space, like a cloud whose contents one could only guess at.

His first impulse was to treat Father Manuli as the village's guest for at least three days. "That's what Hajj Khaled, may God have mercy on him, would have done if he were here," he whispered to himself. However, the beginning of the visit didn't leave pleasant memories.

Rashid, who had taken Hamdan's place, poured the old coffee onto the ground and began roasting new coffee. When he started to grind it, it became apparent that his mortar and pestle weren't of the kind they had been familiar with. That is to say, they weren't Hamdan's mortar and pestle. Nor was their rhythm the one people had been accustomed to. There was a strange melancholy to it, a melancholy that was profound and nameless. In fact, one might say that Rashid's mortar and pestle were closer to a reed flute than to anything else.

Where did all that sorrow come from? Was it on account of having had to part with Hamdan? Of all people, Rashid had always been the keenest to watch Hamdan as he ground the coffee, and the keenest to listen to the sighs that wafted on the echo of his mortar and pestle to some distant, unknown place.

No one knew.

When Hajj Salem handed Father Manuli the cup of coffee, he thanked him, then added, "I don't drink coffee." When he asked him, "Can we offer you tea?" he said, "That would be fine." When they brought him the tea, his hand didn't touch the glass until the steam that rose from it had disappeared. And when they brought the dinner, he said, "I don't eat meat." So Hajj Salem gave instructions for them to take the food back to where it had come from.

By this time, Hajj Salem was about to explode, and it amazed him that he was still able to control himself so well. The men pondered the newcomer in silence. However, it wasn't language that stood between them, since Father Manuli spoke Arabic like someone from Damascus, and anyone who spoke with a person from Damascus was bound to discover the precision with which he enunciated every word.

All of his questions were about the village, agriculture, recent seasons, the land, the area that was now taken up by the Jewish settlement, the area that al-Hamdi had taken over and annexed to the neighboring village, and the tithe that was no longer a tithe. He said, "People who prefer to leave the land and become laborers will never be able to offer anything either to the land or to the government."

At that point, Hajj Salem found himself obliged to disregard the rules of etiquette and hospitality, and pretend to forget that he was in the presence of a man of the cloth. He said, "The only service Great Britain offers people is its attempt to turn them into slaves who work on their lands in order to go on paying the taxes that pay for the bullets that kill them, the nooses that are wrapped around their necks, and the truncheons that consume their flesh without mercy. You say that people have left their land? No, people haven't left their land. People return from their misery elsewhere to work here on the vacations, during which they're supposed to see their children, and all the government does in the end is to take newborns from the doors of their mothers' wombs, leaving the mothers nothing but the remains of the blood that soils them. Yes, people leave because they're forced to go elsewhere for the water they need to wash off the remains of their blood here!"

Hajj Salem's voice had reached such a fever pitch that everyone in the guesthouse was sure he was going to grab Manuli by the neck and throw him out.

Then Father Manuli stood and uttered the words that would echo mercilessly in people's ears and hearts for years to come: "If they were really the owners of this land, we wouldn't be suffering the things we're suffering now!"

Hajj Salem jumped to his feet and looked him in the eye: "What do you mean, Manuli, by what you just said?"

"In any case, it was Father Theodorus' responsibility. That's why he had to pay the price he did, after his lenience turned the lush garden he'd received into a desert!"

These last words were no less cruel than the ones that had preceded them.

"Will you insult us in our own house?" Hajj Salem screamed.

The first encounter left more than one question hanging in the village's sky. Consequently, the few people who had deeds that proved their ownership of the land began coming to the monastery and asking for them to be returned. But the only answer they received to their question was another question: "What deeds?"

When they came pouring out of the guesthouse one evening, after a large meeting that had been called to discuss the issue, Father Manuli came out and said to them, "Father Theodorus said nothing to me about this before he left!"

A group of people decided to go down to the city of Ramla in the hopes of unraveling the mystery. But when they came back that evening, they didn't say a word. They came back in silence. No one could find out what they had seen there, or what had been said to them. And when Muhammad Shahada, whom Hajj Salem had dubbed "the sage of Hadiya," said, "Listen, everybody. No offense, but we didn't need to go all the way to Ramla to find out that we've been a bunch of donkeys!" he was inundated with questions from all sides.

He went on: "The tax department says it has no record of land in our names! It says that this land is the property of the monastery, and that its ownership of the land is proved by the taxes it's been paying on it since the days of the Turks."

Before they had decided what to do, they received a strange warning demanding that, as 'laborers,' they vacate their houses and the land they were working on, since the monastery wanted to reclaim its land and cultivate it by modern methods.

They looked around them. There was nothing but open country.

They looked for each other, but they weren't there.

"We'd been expecting the storm to come from somewhere far away, only to find that it's blowing up right under our feet," said Hajj Salem.

"The only thing we can do is to go see Salim Bek al-Hashemi," said Iliya Radhi. "He's the only one who can help us. Everybody knows he's a great freedom fighter and that he spends his money on our national cause. More than once the British have put him in prison for it. Besides, you know what's said about his generosity. When some needy person comes to him, he passes him the money under the door so that whoever it is won't have to feel embarrassed, and so that if they happen to see each other somewhere, he won't feel he's obliged to pay him back for the kindness he showed him."

"A person would think you'd never fought with Hajj Khaled, Iliya," Anisa interjected. "You're still as good-hearted and gullible as ever! What's this you're saying about Salim Bek al-Hashemi and others of his ilk? That they're defending the homeland? Everybody who's defended the homeland has either died on the gallows or been shot by the Jews and the British. As for these 'leaders,' they only die of natural causes! How amazing!"

Then she added, "What's wrong with you men? What's happened to you? Have you gone blind? What on earth does a person like him have to offer you? If he had a lick of goodness in him, he wouldn't come here and build a mansion that everybody says is bigger than the one he's got in the city. Haven't you heard people say that whenever he changes the color of the furniture in his house, he forces everybody who works there to wear that same color? Haven't you noticed that the people who work for him sometimes wear green, sometimes yellow, sometimes red, sometimes black? And here you are saying he spends his money on Palestine. No offense, but if he were really spending his money on Palestine, he wouldn't have all that money left for himself!"

But they insisted. "What he does in his own house is none of our business. All we care about is what he does for the country," said Iliya Radhi.

"If he could have taken Hadiya away from you, he would have done it years ago. He's one of the biggest usurers around. What are you talking about, Iliya?"*

"Anisa is right," Hajj Salem said. "Someone who humiliates people can only be working for his own personal interests. But if you want to give it a try, go ahead. I don't want it to be said that I closed a door that you thought might lead somewhere useful."

They wouldn't have to wait long, since they knew that he came on the last Thursday of every month and stayed in his mansion till Saturday morning. There were ten days left before they would be able to meet with him.

Manuli left the monastery on Wednesday morning and headed for the village's plains. To everyone's surprise, he had the two sisters Sarah and Mary in tow. Pitifully old and decrepit, they would lean on each other for support, trying together to avoid a fall that would send both of them sprawling. The way they moved, you would have thought they shared a single body. Father Manuli would talk and they would listen in silence, and when he pointed in this or that direction, they would raise their eyes languidly and look without seeing a thing.

After a while, he looked at them and said something that no one could hear. They sat down on a large rock while he kept on going. He bent over and filled his hands with soil, then watched it sift through his fingers. When he reached the first olive grove, he broke off a branch and looked at its end to see how much life it had in it.

---

* "Hardly would you pass through a district of Palestine without hearing reports of 'Palestine's Balfours': people who were working to fulfill Balfour's promise to establish a national homeland for the Jews. Among these were the usurers who benefited from other people's financial woes. They would lend people money at 30 percent interest, sometimes for a year, sometimes for eight months, sometimes for six. Some of us were salesmen and some of us were brokers. We were told that people were bargaining over the sale of the lands in Zayta and Kfar Saba. Some of these lands were the property of the second head of the Farmers' Party who, when we asked him for clarifications concerning the sale, said, 'I'm two thousand pounds in debt to usurers who are "nationalist leaders." I offered to pay off the debt by selling them land for half a pound less than the price Jews were paying for it, but they refused. Then I asked them to bring the interest rate down from 30 percent to 12 percent, but they refused.'"

He returned to the monastery two hours later. On his way back he passed by shepherds and farmers, women working the fields and men repairing the low stone walls separating the fields or tying up sagging branches. But none of them looked his way, while he for his part passed by them as though they weren't there. When he got back to the rock where Mary and Sarah were sitting, he beckoned to them with his forefinger. They rose with difficulty, as though their bodies had become part of the rock.

Once back in the monastery, he closed the door himself, and didn't appear again until Friday evening.

Salim Bek al-Hashemi always enjoyed the times he spent in his country mansion, which was only seven kilometers west of Hadiya. He would invite his Arab and British friends there on the last Thursday of every month, and when he reached the place where the road curved up toward the mansion, he would find the elders and mayors of the villages under his jurisdiction lined up and waiting for him just as he'd planned for them to be. As for his paved driveway, it would be decorated with pictures of Hajj Amin al-Husayni, while the villagers would be assigned the task of sweeping it and spraying it with water from the well in the village of Ayn al-Nakhil.*

"The Bek is here, but he's still asleep," said one of the 'blue' men to the men of Hadiya who had arrived at the gate to his mansion at midmorning on Friday.

They had decided not to go back to Hadiya without answers. "We'll wait till he wakes up," replied Iliya Radhi.

Rather reluctantly, al-Hashemi's men allowed the visitors inside the mansion's walls.

One look around was enough to tell them that al-Hashemi lived in another world altogether. They saw marble pillars with capitals and archways,

---

* Less than a year later, he hosted a wedding party for his son Anas that would be attended by the British High Commissioner and senior British government officials. The celebration would be legendary in proportion, with a guest list that included thousands, all of them notables and men of influence in Palestine. Five hundred sheep and thousands of peacocks, turkeys, and chickens would be slaughtered for the wedding feast.

fountains, flowers of a thousand and one colors, and exotic birds in cages that were miniature replicas of the mansion itself.

"If we want to preserve our dignity we'd better leave right now," said Abd al-Rahim Salman. "It isn't right for us to put ourselves in a position like this."

Realizing now that hearing is one thing and seeing is another, Iliya Radhi said, "I'm afraid we won't have anything to say to people when we get back other than what Muhammad Shahada said when he got back from Ramla."

"Anisa was right," Nimr Abbas added.

Iliya Radhi was about to speak again when he heard the mansion door open. Salim Bek al-Hashemi emerged clad in a black silk robe adorned with tiny red, white, and blue flowers.

"Pardon me," he said. "We got in late last night, then we got to bed late. So, as you can see, we needed to sleep in."

The men of Hadiya exchanged glances, turning his words over in their minds.

"What can I do for you?"

"Well," Iliya Radhi began, "no doubt you've heard about what's happening in Hadiya with the monastery."

"And who hasn't heard?"

"But nobody's done anything," said Hajj Jum'a Abu Sunbul. "That's why we had to come see you."

"You all know that when it comes to issues of national pride and dignity, I'm at your service."

"We've been warned that we have to evacuate the village," Hajj Jum'a Abu Sunbul went on.

Salim Bek al-Hashemi nodded his head.

"What this means—and you would know better than anybody else— is that the monastery has already settled the matter in its own favor," said Hajj Jum'a.

"And what are we supposed to do?"

"As you know, the British authorities are going to side with the monastery, since they won't come to the defense of someone who's been accused of stealing land. But in fact, all they do is steal our land, or help others to steal it. So we need somebody powerful to stand by us on this issue."

"Don't worry. We'll do all we can."

"If we lose the village, six thousand acres of Palestinian land will be gone in a flash. That's four thousand five hundred acres of agricultural land, and fifteen hundred acres of woodland."

"As I told you, your case is no secret, and we're just as concerned about it as you are. So don't worry. We'll do all we can."

For a moment, Hajj Jum'a Abu Sunbul got the feeling that Salim Bek al-Hashemi was just humoring them the way he would a little boy who's pestering him for something he wants. He felt angry. Jumping to his feet, he said, "Salim! If people have agreed for you to be their leader, and if you're not willing to stand by an entire village, we'll fend for ourselves and do what we want."

Turning to the men with him, he said, "Come on, men."

At that moment a servant arrived, carrying coffee on a silver tray with gilt edges.

"Surely you won't leave without drinking your coffee!" protested Salim Bek al-Hashemi.

"We drank it without sugar in the village before we came," retorted Jum'a Abu Sunbul.

They jumped on their horses without a word and began heading back to the village.

"Go after them and see what they want," he said to one of his men.

"What can I tell them that you haven't already told them, sir?"

"Tell them we'll hire a lawyer to defend their case."

They hadn't gotten very far when they heard someone shouting after them, "Wait!"

They listened to the Bek's message without making any reply. Meanwhile, they kept going.

Hadiya was waiting for them with bated breath.

When they appeared in the distance, their horses were about to collapse under the weight of those on their backs. Anisa turned around and headed back to her house, saying, "What are you all waiting for? You can tell what a book is going to say by looking at its title. What a shame! We don't know where we stand any more. We're lost. The British are tearing us to pieces, the Jews are tearing us to pieces, our own leaders are tearing us to pieces. They say, 'Jump!' and we jump."

Peterson's Wisdom

wo successive pieces of news, neither of them pleasant, had reached Peterson only one week apart. The first said: "The person who once tried to kill you has managed to escape with two others from Acre Prison."

"Khaled?" he asked.

"That's the one."

Peterson was troubled, not only because he was hearing the news of the escape, but because he was hearing the name 'Khaled' once again, after he had thought he was rid of that name forever.

He was still pondering this peculiar irony when he got the second piece of news: "Someone is planning to kill you."

"So what's new?" he asked dismissively. "It's just that I do my job right. As for the outcomes, that's another matter. Outcomes belong to the future, and there's no way we can know the future by dragging it into the present. In any case, I've always carried out what's in here." And he pointed to his head.*

---

* That night he wrote: The one who comes in the end / You don't wait for. / The one you can catch up with on foot / You don't run after.

"There's somebody who's going to strike today. They're going to take advantage of your return to the city and carry out the operation."

"They're really close, then, and that's what I want."

"Let's look for some bait that will whet their appetite!"

But he insisted: "Some birds will only stick their heads out if the bait is the real thing."

Although he didn't know why, a strange feeling came over Peterson, and he found himself recalling the way stations in his journey through Palestine as though he were watching a motion picture.

He recalled the image of Hajj Khaled as the soil was being shoveled over his body. He recalled the image of Hamama as she galloped away. He recalled the fruitless attempt to find her. He recalled the image of the young man he had stopped a few days after that, who had been riding an exquisite mare the likes of which Peterson had never seen before. He recalled the young man's discomfiture, and how the soldiers had searched him and found that he was carrying a dagger.

"What is this?" he had asked him.

"It's a dagger," the young man replied, realizing the seriousness of the trouble he was in.

"Why are you carrying it?"

"To protect myself from the bandits in these valleys."

"Do you realize that this dagger of yours would be sufficient cause for me to kill you on the spot?" said Peterson.

The young man made no reply.

However, Peterson didn't take his eyes off the mare for a second.

"Does she belong to you?" he asked him.

The young man nodded.

Peterson walked over to the mare and patted her on the back. He gazed at her lovingly. Then he ordered the young man off the mare and jumped on her back himself. He rode such a distance that they could no longer see anything but the cloud of dust that had been stirred up when he took off. When he came back, he dismounted slowly and, as though he were talking to himself rather than to the men who stood looking on in amazement, he said, "When all this shit's over, I'm going to buy myself a mare like this and take it back to England."

Then he turned to the young man and said, "It's an unforgivable crime for you to have this dagger. And your problem is that I'm your enemy. However, you own a beautiful mare, and for this reason I'm going to give you a chance that I've never given anyone before."

Then he took a bullet out of his revolver.

"If you can guess which hand I have the bullet in," he said, "it will be yours. Otherwise I'll shoot you with it."

He put his hands behind his back, then asked the young man, who now teetered on the brink of death, "Are you ready to choose?"

At exactly six o'clock that evening, while he was in the same coffee shop in which he had suffered his first assassination attempt, a masked man appeared on the street corner. He walked directly toward Peterson. With that sense of his that he trusted as he trusted nothing else, Peterson realized that this was the bird he had been wanting to snare. Within moments he was certain that this was the same Khaled who had tried to assassinate him before. Quickly, Peterson drew his revolver and fired a shot that struck the masked man in the forehead. He followed it with two more bullets in his body before he saw him fall. However, he suspected he had been mistaken when another person, who resembled the first, suddenly appeared. Peterson fired three shots, all of which hit their target. When he pulled the trigger to fire another shot, he realized that the gun was empty. By this time, the square had descended into a hellish chaos. Before Peterson had managed to reload his revolver, a third masked man appeared and walked toward him steadily, unfazed by the bullets the soldiers had begun firing into the air. Although his hand was busy loading the revolver, Peterson kept his eyes on him. The man came closer: five meters, four meters, three. Then, in a flash, the man drew a revolver out of his pocket and fired at Peterson from that fatally close range.

The surprise descended on the soldiers' heads like a thunderbolt. For here was their leader, dying as they looked on, despite their awareness of what had been happening.

The shot that pierced Peterson's head left part of his brain clinging to the restaurant's front window. As the chaos escalated, the assailant managed to disappear into the crowd. However, one of the soldiers had seen him. So, even as targets were moving every which way, the soldier's eyes were fixed upon one target and no other. He began running after him, and within less than two minutes, he was holding his revolver to Khaled's head and ordering him to stop. Khaled stopped.

At that frenzied moment, another shot rang out, shattering the soldier's skull.

Khaled Sayf al-Din ran his hands over his head. He looked back. "Come on!" shouted his companion.

Jaffa's Seas

When Mahmud went to Jaffa, there was nothing he looked forward to more than living with the sea. He rose at dawn, hurriedly put on his clothes, and went out across the Manshiya neighborhood, which was awash in silence. He passed alongside the Marwaniya School, then the Abbasiya School. He turned in the direction of Manshiya Street, and as he headed for the beach he could see the Hasan Bek al-Kabir Mosque.

When he was almost there, he felt he was hearing something more than the sound of the waves. He quickened his pace, and found long nets that were like walls full of trapped birds too exhausted to move their wings.

This wasn't the kind of scene with which he would have wanted to commence his life in Jaffa. But this was what had happened. He didn't know whether he ought to go back to his small apartment, or try to get past the nets. He looked for an opening, and when he found it, he was surprised by an even crueler scene: several birds collided with him and fell to the ground half-dead.

He decided to get back home fast, and for a long time he couldn't bear to go down to the sea, the sea that he hadn't really seen, the ashen sea covered with wings so easily broken. Although quails were a common, inexpensive meal in the autumn months—he could buy fifteen birds for five piasters—he couldn't bear the thought of eating them after what he had seen.

In the end, he replaced the sea with the fragrance of Jaffa's orange trees—the fragrance that would waft out and envelop the city as though it were another sea, her own special sea. He began going for a walk past the orchards every evening, as though he were strolling along the seashore.

"I'll take you to the sea," Layla said to him.

He hesitated. She sensed his hesitation. She asked him, "Are you afraid of the sea? Or are you afraid of me?"

He told her about his first encounter with the sea. He told her about the scare he'd gotten, and about birds bumping into him every night in his dreams and falling half-dead on the ground in front of him.

She said, "You yourself are a walking story!" And she laughed.

But he didn't laugh.

She took him to the sea. She said, "There isn't just one sea in Jaffa. There are lots of them. That's what I always say. The sea off al-Manshiya is different from the one off al-Barriya, which is different from the beach off the old town. And the sea off al-Ajami is different from all the others. I'll take you to al-Ajami. What do you say?"

He said nothing. He had been hoping to see something else, something that would help to erase that sad memory.

They left from Clock Square for Ajami Street. They passed the Arab Club, the Orthodox School, the British Girls' School, the Frères School, and the Armenian Cemetery before turning and heading toward the sea alongside the British Hospital.

He was recording everything in his head. This was what he'd been used to doing in little Ramallah, in sprawling Jerusalem, and in Jaffa with its beehive-like bustle. There was nothing he feared more than getting lost.

As a result, he was constantly in search of landmarks that would get him back easily to his own doorstep.

She asked him, "Do you see what I mean now about Jaffa's seas being different from each other?"

He nodded his head. The sea he had seen now was different from the one he had seen that early dawn: a sea dark and filled with death. However, it wasn't just that the sea itself was different. It was also the fact that Layla had been there.

The season when quails would arrive exhausted on Jaffa's shores was no longer anything new. Mahmud had been through it one autumn after another since that first memory: thousands of spent quails would arrive to find nothing but fishing nets waiting for them, just like the sardines that would come pouring onto the beach in early September in schools hundreds of meters long. And the fishermen would be waiting for them.

He had lots to do: he needed to go to his job at the newspaper, and meet Layla after that. However, the quails' fates took him by surprise once again, and in an even crueler way. For when he opened the door, he found hundreds of them on the doorstep. Before he could decide what to do, several birds rolled inside like balls and landed at his feet. He leaned over, picked them up, and placed them outside the house again. With great caution, he managed to get past the mound of worn-out birds. Before he turned in the direction of the main street, he saw boys gathering the quail. Some of them placed the birds in bags, some in cages, and some in their pockets or inside their clothes.

He couldn't go on. He rushed home, fearful that a bird might bump into him and fall half-dead in front of him again. He could bear anything but a surprise like that! Surprises, as he was always telling Layla, were "the end of all ends."

Shortly after midafternoon he dared again to open the door. He looked down at the doorstep. There was no sign of the birds. When he looked up, he found himself face to face with Layla.

"Where have you been? I've been looking everywhere for you! And when I called the newspaper, they said you hadn't come to work!"

Tillers, Plowers,
and Shepherds

I t wouldn't have required much intelligence for them to realize that they had lost the case even before the hearing was over. The lawyer Salim Bek had sent them was none other than his son Anas.

Salim Bek had said to him, "I don't think they could find anyone better than you!"

"But I don't have any experience with this kind of case."

"And who ever said that people are born with experience in law, medicine, or whatever else? This is your chance to get training in this type of small case until bigger cases come along that will make a name for you."

"But this isn't an easy case."

"I know it isn't. But if you win it, it will be proof of your competence and it will go down on your record as a nationalist. If, on the other hand, you lose it, people will blame the biased British judicial system. I've given it a lot of thought. So don't worry!"

The monastery was backed up by a wooden chest filled to the brim with documents demonstrating that it had never been remiss in paying taxes, whether under the Turks or the British, and that the entire case had to do with a group of laborers who, now that they had finished the work required of them, had nothing more to do but leave. They were nothing but laborers who came and went. One of them might have come once or twice, or possibly even three years in a row. However, as soon as they collected their wages, they went back to their own villages. When the British military judge asked the village's lawyer to produce evidence confirming that 'these laborers' owned the land, he didn't find a single piece of paper in his hand.

In no time, the judge had ruled in favor of the monastery, and the ruling was viewed as still one more document proving the monastery's ownership of Hadiya's lands.

They walked out of the courtyard that noontide as though they had been hit with sunstroke. Their cries of protest had done no good, and the only thing they knew for certain was that they owned nothing—not their land, not their houses, not their fields, not their vineyards. The court's ruling told them that their memories were nothing but dreams, that their dreams were illusions, and that the afflictions they had suffered and the sacrifices they had made in order to keep this land had all been in vain. They realized that they were being stripped of the shovels with which they had dug, the scythes with which they had harvested, the horses they had lived with through the bitter and the sweet, the cows they had milked, and the flocks they had kept vigil over in the open fields to protect them from death and the jaundice of the dry seasons.

Suddenly, nothing in Hadiya was theirs any more.

They were laborers: tillers, plowers, and shepherds who owned nothing but the shirts on their backs.

Half an hour later you could hear a man cursing or shouting, or see someone turning his head away so that no one would see the tears that filled his eyes.

"Where are you going?"

The question was biting and full of reproach. Hajj Salem turned and looked behind him. He knew it was the voice of Hajj Khaled.

"Back to Hadiya."

"What will you say to your mother? To Aunt Anisa, to Aziza, to the people of the town? That you've lost Hadiya? What are you doing, man?"

Hajj Salem's feet were pinned to the ground. He couldn't take another step forward.

Hajj Abu Sunbul shook him. "What's wrong?" he demanded.

Hajj Salem realized that death would be preferable to returning to the village in defeat.

"There's only one place we can go now," said Hajj Salem.

"To hell. Is there anywhere else left for us?"

"Yes, plenty. We've fought the Turks, we've fought the British, we've fought the Jewish colonists, we've fought hunger, we've fought poverty. And now it's time for us to fight this unjust verdict."

"So what do you suggest?"

"That we not go back to Hadiya until we've gone to see the lawyer Sulayman al-Marzuqi."

No one objected.

They arrived at his office on Jamal Pasha Street in Jaffa a little after midafternoon. He wasn't there. They waited for him.

"It's all right," his legal trainee said to them. "He'll be here at exactly three-thirty. All you have to do is watch the hands of this clock. The only thing in the world that he can never do is be late for work."

Despite all these reassurances, watching the wall clock turned into a veritable torment. Never since the invention of the clock with its tick-tock, tick-tock, even when people had been in a state of anxious anticipation, had that faint sound, usually forgotten, turned into such terrible drumbeats. The rhythm grew louder and louder until the drum was about to explode. How had the clock turned into a bomb that, in their desperation, they had no choice but to cling to?

None of them was immune to this miserable feeling. Suddenly, Iliya Radhi got up and said, "I'm about to suffocate. I'm going to wait outside."

He was followed by Muhammad Shahada and Hajj Abu Sunbul, who said, "You all will know when the hands reach three-thirty. But I won't. So I'm not to go on sitting here, tortured by the racket they're making!"

At exactly three-thirty, the door opened. Al-Marzuqi walked in, and with him those who had been outside.

They explained the case to him from beginning to end, and told him about the judge's decision.

He didn't say anything. In fact, he kept quiet for so long they began to think he hadn't heard them. Or maybe he was asleep. Who could tell? He was staring at the clock as though he were counting the seconds. When they had finished with everything they had to say, he said, "The first time you came to see me, I was banned from the courtroom for six months. As for this case, it might cause me to be banned from the courtroom for the rest of my life. Do you realize that?"

"We've got nobody else to turn to," said Hajj Salem.

"You should have come to me before, instead of going first to the Right Honorable Anas, son of Salim Bek al-Hashemi!"

"We didn't go to him. We went to Salim Bek, who, as you know, is a prominent nationalist leader."

"You know, the greatest threat to this whole country is the fact that you all are too kindhearted for your own good. In fact, your kindhearted-ness is liable to be the death of you. It's as if Hajj Khaled wasn't one of you, and that you didn't really know him!"

His words were distressing and full of sorrow.

"Please, don't let Hadiya be lost so easily," Hajj Salem said. For the first time in his life he seemed like a different person, someone who would do anything, even beg. He turned to Mahmud, who was amazed at what he was hearing. With that, Hajj Salim's deep sense of himself returned, and he added, "I swear to God, if this verdict could be wiped out with blood, we would have done it ourselves. And if it could be done by setting Manuli on fire, we wouldn't hesitate to do it. But it's a decision that can't be overturned in these ways."

"You know this case could cost me my future as a lawyer."

"We're willing to do whatever you ask."

"Do you love your village?"

"How could we not love it? It's our life!"

"Since this is what you say, and I see clearly that you mean it, I tell you: your right will be restored to you whether the judge is British or even a devil. But in return, you'll pay me fifty pounds for every word I utter in the courtroom!"

"Fifty pounds for every word! Isn't that an awful lot?"

"That's my condition. And if you can't accept it, you're free to leave."

"But you know that's more than we can afford," said Hajj Salem.

"Can you afford to lose your village?"

"No, no, we can't," said Hajj Abu Sunbul.

"Are we agreed, then?" He looked into their faces so intently, they were sure their features must have been imprinted forever in his eyes.

"Agreed," said Hajj Salem, reaching into his pocket.

Noticing what Hajj Salem was doing, al-Marzuqi said, "I don't want anything from you now. Once I've restored your rights to you in full, you'll pay me in full. But not a minute earlier."

"If he gets the town back for you, you'll have to sell it in order to pay his fees," al-Barmaki remarked.

"The river of words that's going to come gushing out of his mouth will cost us a river of money. And to my knowledge, there's no river like that in Hadiya," seconded Hajj Abu Sunbul.

"You were with us, and you heard with your own ears every word he said, but you didn't object," said Hajj Salem.

"Because I was crazy just like you were! Who in the world would agree to a condition like that?"

"You would. Didn't you agree?" Muhammad Shahada asked him.

"If your people go crazy, your own sanity will do you no good! I had to go crazy along with you."

"Listen, everybody. Anything on the face of the earth would be more merciful than to have Hadiya taken from us unjustly right before our very eyes. Remember that if the monastery wins, you won't find a square inch of land where you can live with dignity, or even where you can die and be buried with dignity."

Then he added, "What do you think, Mahmud?"

"I don't know. There are always surprises!"

"But I'm asking you so that we can know, since the only thing we can't take any more is surprises!"

There was nothing Mahmud feared more than surprises. Surprises were the end of all ends.

The showing of *Another Thin Man*, starring Myrna Loy, was over. At the door to the movie theater, he was surprised to find demonstrators marching through the streets of Jaffa. It was the loudest, most boisterous demonstration he had ever seen.

"What's going on?"

"It's a demonstration. Everything comes to an end in this country except demonstrations," one of the theater employees said to him.

He went back to his room in the Manshiya neighborhood. It occurred to him to try to find out the reason for the demonstration he had seen less than an hour earlier. He turned on the radio and waited for the news broadcast to come on. Asmahan sang, but he didn't hear her. Saleh Abd al-Hayy sang, but he didn't hear him. When it was time for the six o'clock news, he dropped everything he was doing and stared at the big radio before him as he had never done before. Suddenly, the unexpected news came: "Arab crowds came out today in large demonstrations in all the cities of Palestine when they learned of the martyrdom of their leader Khaled al-Hajj Mahmud. Palestinian political parties have issued a statement calling for the nation to observe a three-day period of mourning . . ."

The Master of Finales

Mahmud was enthralled with Layla's punctuality, for the simple reason that he feared that even a minute's delay might strip him of a piece of his clothing in that large square. How he detested standing alone! The first time they met, he had chosen a place that nobody could miss: Clock Square. How happy that had made him. Finding a place that everyone knew had been one of his greatest triumphs. This, at least, was what he had always thought. There was no place in the city more famous than the Old Saray, and it was in front of it that he waited for her.

"I'm here, sir. Where are you?" Layla said with a laugh. Then she added, "Amazing. Every time I find you, you're lost!"

"Sorry. My mind was somewhere else."

"Stay with us, sir. You don't want to get lost again."

Mahmud couldn't deny that she was unusually witty. But Afaf was prettier and taller. If only she didn't have that one problem: she was uneducated!

The first time he had met Layla had been unforgettable, just like the endings he was always talking about. He had reached out for a copy of Dante's *Inferno*, translated into Arabic by Amin Abul Sha'r. However, as he was trying to read the headlines of the newspapers arranged on the pavement, she snatched the book.

When his hand finally reached the place where the book had been, it was empty. Completely empty. He turned and saw it in her hand. He said to her, "But I wanted to buy it."

"What?"

"That book. I wanted to buy it."

"Of course you can buy it. Here!"

"Sorry. I didn't mean . . ."

"What do you mean, then? You want it. So take it. There's no problem. I've got enough books to last me ten more years. I don't need one more!"

"Is that right?"

"Yes."

"I'm sorry."

"Never mind. You need it more than I do." She handed it to him, her features softening.

He quickly paid for the book and, wanting to catch up with her before she got away, he shot out of the bookstore like an arrow. Then a most unexpected thing happened: he ran into her, and she nearly fell. A second problem in less than three minutes!

"Sorry! I'm so sorry!" He was terribly flustered. He broke into a sweat, his face turned red, and the book nearly fell out of his hand.

"It's all right. Why are you in such a hurry? Do you have a train to catch?"

"No, no, not at all!" he replied, as though he were denying an accusation!

"I was just asking, that's all."

She studied him from head to foot. Then she asked a question he would never have expected. "Would you like to go walking for a bit?"

He began walking with her without even answering. Fortunately for him, he knew a lot about these things in Ramallah. However, what amazed her most was the fact that he worked for a newspaper.

She said to him, "I write as well."

"Have you ever published anything?" he wanted to know.

"No," she said.

It would have been a natural thing to say to her, "Why don't you give me something I could publish for you?" However, he didn't dare make such a bold offer. He knew himself, and he knew he wouldn't be able to do more than read what was presented to him.

After years of journalistic work, the power of endings was the theme that most preoccupied him. However, when he met her, he knew little about beginnings. For him, the most successful approach was to let the beginning come and take him by the hand, then proceed to the place where it wanted so that it could choose the end that suited it. However, he was a good reader, and thus it might be said that he had become educated. In addition, the fact that over the years he had translated quite a number of Oscar Wilde's stories, as well as stories by de Maupassant and Chekhov—which he published under the initials 'M.K.'—had left a deep impression that for a long time he hadn't been aware of.

When, two years after meeting her, he confided to Layla that he had translated and published stories in the newspaper, she asked, "Whose works have you translated?"

"De Maupassant, Chekhov, and Wilde."

"So you're 'Brain,' then!" she cried happily. "Why hadn't that ever occurred to me?"*

"What do you mean by 'Brain'?"

"Don't you sign your translations with the initials 'M.K.'?* You're 'Brain,' then."

He finally caught on to what she was saying. "You know, I'd never thought about that before!"

A little while later, he said, "Anyway, thank God!"

"What do you mean?"

"Thank God my name wasn't Taysir, or my initials would spell takhkh!"†

---

* Mahmud's initials in Arabic—mim, kha'—spell the Arabic word for 'brain.'
† The verb takhkh means 'to be flimsy and dilapidated.'

512

Caught up on a wave of euphoria, she said, "Or something lots worse than that!"

"Like what?"

"It wouldn't be proper for a girl to say it."

He dropped the subject right away. However, he started racking his brain in search of a letter that, if he put it together with his last initial, would spell something scandalous. When he figured out what it was, he said, "You're right. It could have been a disaster if my first name had been Shukri, or Shakir, or Sharif!"*

Meanwhile, on the other side of his world, Afaf was following the last parts of the story in silence, since Layla wouldn't let him go back to Hadiya without placing a letter in his hand—a letter that he would read at least ten times on the train, then five times more after getting to Hadiya. Sometimes she would include a new story she had penned, which lacked nothing but an ending. Hadn't she told him: "Endings are your specialty"?

"And beginnings: whose specialty are they?"

"They're my specialty. Wasn't I the one who took the initiative in getting to know you?"

But he was always bewildered by the fact that she never gave any indication of where their relationship—which had never reached the point of his touching her hand, or her touching his, not even in the dark—was headed.

---

* The letters shin and kha' spell the Arabic word for 'urinate.'

The Broker, the Buyer, and the Seller

A jeep drove up and three men got out: a broker by the name of As'ad Nasnas,* a Jew by the name of Levi, and Father Manuli. They stood together examining a piece of land to the west of the wall of the settlement that had been erected on the outskirts of Hadiya and on part of its land.

---

* As'ad Nasnas, a native of the village, had fallen in love with Muhammad Shahada's daughter Salma. However, her paternal cousin said he wanted her to be his wife, so he married her. As'ad then went and asked for the hand of a very pretty girl and brought her back to Hadiya. He wanted to make Salma and her family angry, so every day he went out walking with her to show her off. One day, as he was out walking with his wife, he found himself face to face with Salma in the street and shouted, "I swear to God, a hundred wives couldn't make me forget Salma!" "And what's wrong with me?" his wife asked angrily. Wanting to placate her, he told her that, whereas he and she had never met alone before marriage, he and Salma used to go out the woods together. "All right, then," his wife said. "Let's go out to the woods." When they got there, he took off her clothes. "Did you used to do this with Salma?" "This and more," he replied. Then, with the speed of lightning, he sank a knife into her chest. After dumping her onto Salma's husband's property, he went to the police and turned himself in. He said, "I found Salma's husband on top of my wife, so I killed her," since he knew this would lighten his sentence. What he didn't know, however, was that his wife hadn't died. When they found her and carried her back to the village, she told them

The matter needed no explanation. Hence, the whole town came rushing out to where they were. Whoever found a horse or donkey jumped on its back, and everyone else came running, barefoot if need be. Women, young children, elders, and youths came running from both neighborhoods. It was the first time in a long time that such a thing had happened, since the court's ruling in favor of the monastery had left everyone feeling vulnerable in that great expanse, which was open to countless dangers. The three besieged men sensed what was happening. The broker and the buyer tried to get in the car, but Father Manuli wouldn't let them: "This land belongs to the monastery, and nobody can tell us who we can and can't sell it to!"

They took a few steps back, but their nearness to the car made them feel a bit safer.

From all sides the people surrounded them.

Hajj Salem stepped forward, nearly mad with rage. His eyes red and his pole-like frame fully upright, he demanded, "What are you doing here?"

"It's none of your business. This land belongs to the monastery, and it has the right to dispose of it however it chooses. In the end, you all are just a bunch of hirelings," retorted Manuli.

"Hirelings, you say!"

"If you didn't realize this before, it isn't your fault. It's the fault of Father Theodorus for not telling you."

"So that's how it is!" Hajj Salem replied. Then he added, "We'll see who the hirelings are around here."

He turned to the people, then pointed at the car.

The broker and the buyer, who had thought that their proximity to the car afforded them some protection, suddenly felt it would be better to get away from it. They moved away, but again their senses deceived them.

Like an overwhelming tempest, some of the people rushed toward the car, while others went for the broker and the buyer.

---

everything, and he was sentenced to fifteen years in prison. He got out of prison when the British released thieves and other criminals during the 1936–39 uprising, and never went back to Hadiya.

515

The car rocked from side to side, and within moments it had turned over. One more push turned it completely upside down. They gave it another push, and another, until it reached the edge of a small downward slope. Then came the most forceful push of all. The car swayed slightly, then flipped three times, and landed at last on one of its sides. Behind the people who had been rolling the car, clubs were descending from all directions on the two men, who found no place to hide. They fled for refuge to Father Manuli, who met them with a look that cast them into the unknown. Meanwhile, Hajj Salem and Father Manuli stood face to face no more than five steps apart, each glaring into the other's eyes with mad defiance.

The settlement dwellers, visible to all, watched the scene from a distance.

As soon as the broker and the buyer got some distance away from their pursuers, bullets began raining down on the townspeople.

Turning toward the settlement, Father Manuli screeched, "Are you insane?" As though they could hear him!

"It's your own insanity," replied Hajj Salem.

When Shams, Jamal Ribhi's daughter, cried out, "Baba! Blood!" the people realized that the shots that were being fired had one aim only: to kill.

She was no more than ten years old. Not long afterward, Hatem Abu Umayra cried in a strained voice, "Help me!" Blood was gushing out of his neck.

When the people saw what had happened, a group of the men went running after As'ad Nasnas and Levi, who had begun dragging themselves with difficulty toward the settlement's barbed-wire fence. Bullets rained down on their pursuers to prevent them from reaching their target. This made it possible for the people at the other end to get away and hide behind the stone walls between the fields and among the olive trees, carrying Shams and Hatem, the latter of whom had breathed his last.

The men were running madly, oblivious to the bullets that were mowing down everything in their path. Imad al-Akhras and Husayn al-Sa'ub fell, but no one stopped. The intensity of the gunfire began gradually subsiding as the distance between those fleeing and their pursuers became smaller and smaller. And as soon as they caught up with them and began beating them with the sticks in their hands, the firing stopped altogether.

"Don't kill them!" shouted Ziyad Najm.

"What are you saying?" came the voice of Hasan Barakat.

"If we kill them, we'll be killed ourselves on the spot. Instead, we should withdraw with them still alive."

Why hadn't they thought of that? How had they failed to notice that they were in the middle of a trap?

"If I survive, I'll say it was Ziyad who saved me and these other men," said Hasan Barakat.

"If we survive, it will be because it was God's will to give us a new lease on life," Ziyad replied.

They retreated, dragging Nasnas and Levi along with them. They got to Imad al-Akhras, who was bleeding profusely. One bullet had gone through his right shoulder, and another his left side.

"Kill them!" Imad shouted.

They carried him away, and by the time they got to Husayn al-Sa'ub, he had died.

The people peeked out of their hiding places, and when they realized that no more shots would be fired their way, they went running toward the village, where the men had arrived with Nasnas and Levi.

No one saw Father Manuli after that. He had disappeared completely. Hajj Salem tried to find out where he had headed, but to no avail. He had disappeared in less than a moment.

"He disappeared while I was looking straight at him!" These were the words Hajj Salem went on repeating during the difficult days that followed.

A few minutes after everyone had reached the outskirts of the village, a huge explosion rang out. They ducked, but before they raised their heads again to find out what was happening, a bomb went off. They realized that it had fallen some distance away, and they saw smoke rising near the overturned car.

A second bomb went off, closer to them. Then a third. The car blew up and was transformed into a mass of fire from which a column of smoke rose.

The people stared into each other's faces. The biggest surprise was their realization that the weapons that had been aimed at them from the settlement were more powerful than any weapon they had expected to find there.

The British force that arrived less than an hour later saw nothing in the place but the remains of a column of smoke, the dead bodies of Hatem Abu Umayra and Husayn al-Sa'ub, a wounded Imad al-Akhras and a wounded Shams, and the fury of the people. It was a fury that exploded in the soldiers' faces against Great Britain, which was willing to hang one of them for possessing a knife, but couldn't hear the sound of bombs falling on them in broad daylight.

However, this did nothing to deter Lieutenant Jack Edmund from questioning the villagers about what had happened to Nasnas, Levi, and Father Manuli.

"If you find Father Manuli, you'll find Nasnas and Levi too. As soon as the firing began, the earth opened up and swallowed them. Where did they disappear to? Only God knows," Hajj Salem said.

Lieutenant Edmund was twenty-six or twenty-seven years old. Everything about him suggested that it was the first time he had been confronted with such a situation.

"The people in the settlement say you captured them."

"And we say we haven't seen them since the firing started. If you're going to accuse us of killing people because you don't know where they are, why don't you accuse the settlement, which, as you can see, has left people dead and wounded here?"

"The settlement was defending itself."

"By shooting us and throwing bombs at us even though we're unarmed?"

"Unfortunately, I'm going to have to search the entire village!" replied Edmund, who was the politest British soldier they had ever met.

"Search all you like, but you won't find anything, since both they and Father Manuli are on the other side by now. Yes, we stood up to them and refused to allow them to see our land, which they want to capitalize on.

However, that's all we did. And we'd do it again if we had to. As for you, what you need to do now is help us save these two people who are wounded so that you won't have been the cause of their deaths."

Lieutenant Jack Edmund didn't find what he had been looking for. When he got to the door of the monastery, Sister Sarah came out and said, "Father Manuli isn't here." Taking her at her word, he helped her close the heavy door. Then he went back to the village, where people were crying uncontrollably and trying in vain to administer first aid to the wounded.

Before he had a chance to tell them he was going back to the settlement to get more information, Shams' mother cried out over her daughter's body, and they realized that she had died.

Turning to Lieutenant Edmund, they said, "You killed her."

"I am sorry," he said over and over, clearly in genuine distress. Then he instructed the soldiers to carry the wounded man to the car.

The soldiers seemed surprised at such an order. When he saw them hesitate, all signs of his innocence suddenly disappeared and his face clouded over. "Now!" he bellowed.

Manuli didn't reappear until the morning of the trial. As for Nasnas and Levi, all Lieutenant Edmund's attempts to locate them came to nothing, even after he took Imad al-Akhras away in his car as a goodwill gesture.

"They claim we took them away, and we claim they fled to the settlement. We're the ones with three dead and one wounded. So what are they saying?"

Eventually the investigation was closed due to insufficient evidence and the impossibility of leveling an accusation at any particular person or persons.

Greta Garbo's Arrival

She approached from a distance. He gazed at her childlike face and her hair, which covered part of her shoulders. He thought about the happiness that constantly filled her features, causing her lips to be all the rosier, and the exuberance that made it seem as though she was coming to embrace the whole world.

She lacked nothing. Perhaps she had deliberately begun walking this way after he had invited her four times to see *Grand Hotel,* and twice to see *Anna Karenina.* He had kept on repeating a certain line to her until she knew it by heart: "You know . . ." Before he had a chance to finish, she would interrupt him and finish it herself, saying, ". . . that Greta Garbo is the most beautiful woman on the face of the earth, and that she walks more beautifully than any creature on earth."

Layla saw it as an enjoyable adventure that a writer like her had to experience without denying that she also liked it, and that, although it had been a long time since their first meeting, she still didn't dare look straight into his eyes. She had tried it once, and had realized that if she did it again, she was bound to fall in love with him. Whenever he tried to look straight at her, she would let out a sweet little laugh, avert her gaze, and start looking at anything else she happened to see around her at that moment. The thing that charmed her most about him was his amazing ability to invent unusual endings to her stories. He would say to her, "What matters isn't the beginning, but the ending. Tell me what the ending is, and I'll tell you how much attention your story deserves."

For every story she had written, including even the ones she had written before she knew him, he had come up with a new ending. On the few occasions when she hadn't taken his advice, she had regretted it later when there was talk of this or that story's weak finale. However, she didn't venture out of her own world in order to write about his. As far as she was concerned, his world was a lovely, pleasant thing (too lovely and pleasant), and even a 'new' Layla wouldn't be able to risk writing about it. Of course, she hadn't told him so. For her, the level of the story depended on how sophisticated its topic was. A readable story was one that could be read by people who knew how to read. She thought: Why should I write about people who don't know how to read in the first place? And why should I drag readers who have read and learned about everything into stories that are of no concern to them?

From the time she met him, he had spared her having to answer a certain question: "Why don't you write about anything but life in Jaffa?" Even so, she had long ago memorized the line she would use to answer him if he did ever ask, which was, "I only write about what I know." It was a relief to her that he had never asked. However, she had begun thinking of a series of questions that he would be likely to ask her when he heard this reply of hers. He might ask, for example, "Is it necessary for you to die in order for you to write about somebody who dies? Is it necessary for you to live to be seventy years old in order to write about a woman that age? Is it necessary for you to be an engineer, a doctor, a teacher, or even a woman of the night who works in one of Jaffa's bars, in order to write about people like these?"

However, he had only said one thing to her: "The ending. What matters is the ending, Layla."

Oddly, she had never gone in search of an ending for their relationship. Consequently, she couldn't say whether it was worth it or not. She wasn't concerned about the fact that he had a wife, since it would have been shameful to descend to the level of being a peasant woman—an uneducated one, no doubt, and part of what disturbed the tranquility of her life. Yet, in spite of it all, and without her realizing it, she found herself imitating Greta Garbo's gait, her hairstyle, the masterfully studied side glances she cast every time she turned to look at anyone, and the way her eyes would wander off to look at something on top of his head that neither he nor she could see.

Mahmud noticed these things, and it made him happy.

The new thing that he hadn't noticed was that she had begun urging him to write, and not to content himself with editing articles and news items. "You've got to get your talent out in the open, let people know you!"

"I don't want anybody to know me. The more anonymous I am, the better. This way, nobody points to me, and nobody stops me to ask what I think about what's going on. Imagine somebody coming up and asking me, 'Mr. Mahmud, what do you think of what's happening? Where are things in Palestine headed in your estimation?' I'd go crazy. Who could possibly solve an equation whose elements are the Palestinian villagers, their leaders in the cities, their leaders in the countryside, the poverty there in the villages and the wealth here in the city, the European industrial superiority that the Jews have brought with them, and the backwardness the Turks left us all over this country? Who can solve an equation that consists, on one side, of the chaos of the countless parties here, with their confused, inconsistent aims and their never-ending disputes, and on the other, of the Jewish organizations with their methodical approach and their focus on a single goal—to occupy Palestine and drive its people out? Who can solve an equation that consists of us, the Arabs, the British, and the Jews?"

"But you know, since you're such a master of finales, I should have asked you this question before: How *do* you think things will end up in Palestine?"

"Are you serious? Or will you take what I say as some sort of novelty?"

"No, I'm really asking you, seriously."

"And who told you I could answer a question like that?"

"Since you raised the question yourself, it means you're thinking about it."

"I would think about it if I were a writer. But I'm not a writer, so I haven't thought about it."

"I'll ask you another question, then. What do you want?"

"What do I want? Do you want the truth? I think it's there in the film *Grand Hotel*. I've thought a lot about why I like to keep going to see it. I think there are three reasons. The first reason is what the phony count says to the heroine: 'I've got no character at all. When I was a little boy, they taught me to ride horses and to act nobly. In school they taught me to pray and lie. Then in war they taught me to kill and hide.' It's true, of course, that I haven't killed, but I do hide."

"But you're not like that."

"The person you know, then, and who goes by my name, isn't me."

"I won't argue with you. So what's the second reason?"

"It's something else the phony count says to the heroine."

"And what's that?"

"He says to her, 'I like to be in your room so that I can breathe the same air you breathe.' That's what I always think when I'm with you!"

"Is that right? And the third reason . . . ?"

"I'd expected you to say more than that about the second reason. In any case, I'll tell you the third reason. It's the ending."

"That's something I can't talk about, since you're the teacher. But what do you mean?"

"The end of the film has no end. That's what I discovered recently. I think this is the greatest kind of ending, since it's an ending and a beginning at the same time."

"I don't understand!"

"After the phony count is killed, the maimed doctor says, 'What do you do at the hotel? You eat, you sleep, you lounge around, you flirt with the women a little, you dance a little. A hundred doors lead to the same room. Nobody knows anything about the person next to him, and when you leave, somebody else occupies your room and sleeps in your bed.' For the first time he realized that the grand hotel wasn't just a hotel. It was a lot more than that. Didn't you notice new people coming in and others leaving right after their stories were over, and through doors that kept revolving nonstop? That's what life is like. Can you give me an ending without an ending? An ending that's a beginning? A beginning whose ending is a beginning?"

"I don't know."

"It stumps me, too. I've got lots of beginnings, but they're insipid."

"And what about your ending? I mean, can you imagine an ending to your journey in this life?"

He kept quiet for such a long time that she thought he would never say anything, and she regretted having raised such a thorny question. But before she could open her rosy little mouth to apologize, he said, "I belong to a family whose menfolk's fates are decided by horses."

At that point, she mustered the courage to say in a sad voice, "But I'm talking about you."

"Me? I've never had a horse!"

"I don't think you're normal today!"

"You're right, I'm sick. Haven't you noticed? Have you forgotten what the doctor in the movie says: 'When I see someone whose clothes are big on him, I know he's sick.' My clothes are big on me. Hadn't you noticed?"

"No, they fit just fine!"

The Step and Time

The thing Hajj Salem hadn't anticipated was that time would always outrun him.

He looked at his nephew Naji and his son Ali and said, "When we get bullets, we don't find rifles. When we get rifles, we don't find training, and if we get bombs, it's only the lucky ones among us who don't fall on their heads when they try to throw one. I've thought about this for a long time, and I've decided there's something the two of you could do that the country would never forget."

It didn't occur to either of them to ask, "And what might that be?" Instead, they just went on listening.

He said, "You could join the British police force."

"The British police?"

"Yes, the British police. You could go there and learn, then come back and teach the people."

Naji had never felt so responsible before, even when he had been blessed with his first son. Suddenly, he had become responsible for the fate of the country, the people, and their military training!

So off to the city of Lod he went with Ali.

"If you don't make it, Ali will. And if Ali doesn't make it, you will," said Hajj Salem.

They both submitted applications.

The interviews would be in two days' time, they were told.

They arrived two hours early for the interview. The applicants stood in a long line. A British lieutenant came and examined them all, down to the end of the line, then went back to the beginning.

He gestured to Naji to step forward. Then, after looking them all over again, he chose Ali, who was standing next to him.

"You're dismissed!" he shouted, and the line dispersed.

The British lieutenant's assistant, who was related to Ali by marriage from his mother's side, gestured to them to follow him. When they had gotten some distance away, he asked them for twenty dinars. He said he would give the money to the British officer, who had agreed with him on this arrangement.

Ali turned to him and said, "You want twenty dinars? I don't want to join the police force to begin with!"

Before reaching the door, the assistant said to him, "I was only talking about you, since they won't accept Naji into the force when they find out who he is."

"Why?"

"Because he's the son of Hajj Khaled Mahmud. Have you forgotten?"

"I'm leaving anyway," said Ali.

The assistant stopped him again. Naji said, "You know we haven't even got twenty piasters, and here you are asking us for twenty dinars. So I'm leaving with him."

"No, please! I know," said the assistant. "You'll embarrass me back in the village. Stay. I'll pay it out of my own pocket, and God will make it up to me!" He turned to Ali and Naji and looked at them for a long time.

Then he said to them, "Give me your identity cards."

After scrutinizing the identity cards, he said, "I think I've got the solution. You look a lot alike."

"What are you thinking?" Naji wanted to know.

The assistant then gave Ali's identity card to Naji and Naji's to Ali.

"This is what I'm thinking," he said.

"Do you think this will work?"

"I've done what I can, and the rest is up to Naji, who has to remember from here on out that his name is Ali Salem Hajj Mahmud."

Two hours later, a military vehicle drove up. They told Naji to get in. It then proceeded on its way to al-Bassa in Jaffa. When he arrived, he found hundreds of men waiting on the sand to find out who would be chosen.

"Did the damned guy want twenty dinars just so he could send us off to another test?" Naji wondered to himself.

As had happened the first time, they asked everyone to line up in four rows. Before they had chosen anyone, they asked those who had served in the British army during the Second World War to take three steps forward. There were fifteen of them.

From the first row the lieutenant in charge chose two, from the second row he chose four, from the third row he chose one, and when he got to the fourth row, he chose Naji and two other young men.

Naji then remembered something he shouldn't have forgotten—that he was ill, and that his back was covered with red circles thanks to the cupping (a folk remedy used to draw out 'bad blood') that he had undergone. At the same time, he knew what a serious matter it would be if he had to go back to the village now that Ali had left.

The men who had been chosen gathered in a small courtyard in the rear, while the others looked on from a distance. However, Naji felt dejected, since he knew he would be disqualified the minute he took his shirt off.

One of the other young men saw that he was worried.

"What's bothering you?" he asked.

Naji explained the situation.

"Don't worry. I can solve your problem without any difficulty."

He beckoned to a young man standing some distance away. He came over to where they stood.

"This is my brother, and as you can see, he's got a strong constitution. He'll go in when they call your name and he'll be examined in your place. That's all there is to it!"

"Can something like this really work?"

"Don't worry. We've done it a lot."

He wondered how on earth he could be yet another person, now that his name was officially Ali!

However, things went in the opposite direction. Everyone was told to stand in a line, then the soldiers were bound together in pairs to prevent any attempts at trickery!

The car took them on to Na'ana. When they got there, Naji lost all hope, and he anticipated the shame he would feel when he stood in front of Hajj Salem when he went back to the village without having managed to join the British police.

The examination began with an eye test. The nurse inspected his picture on the identity card, then turned to scrutinize his face, and his color changed for a few moments. However, remembering the responsibility he bore, he held himself together.

"Can you see the symbols on the chart well, Ali?" she asked.

"Of course," he replied, happy that she hadn't discovered anything.

"Sit on this chair, then," she said to him.

He took hold of the chair and picked it up, then began heading out of the room.

"What are you doing?"

"I'm going to show you that I can see the symbols even from this distance."

Naji was his old self again. She laughed. "You're not going to see anything when you're that far away!"

But, to her surprise, he passed with 20/20 vision.

"I've never seen anything like this before," she said. "Your name is Ali, right?"

"Yes."

"I'm not going to forget that name!"

He still needed another miracle, and he got it.

They brought the conscripts one by one into a large hall in order to conduct the examination.

The first surprise to hit them was that they would have to strip down to nothing, which caused some of them to flee! As for Naji, he felt that he was the only one who couldn't afford to run away from a test like this, no matter what they did to him. He had to do what he had to do. As for the outcome, it would determine his fate, which he had no way of knowing in those moments.

There was only one conscript ahead of him in line. He started thinking about how he would take off his clothes. Should he start with the trousers, which he had worn specially for this occasion? Or should he start with the shirt? I'll start with the shirt, he decided. This way, at least, I won't have to take the trousers off for nothing!

Just then, someone started beating on the door.

"Doctor!" the voice came urgently. "An army vehicle has hit a little girl, and they need you right away."

The doctor got up quickly and left the room. They gestured to the conscripts who had passed the test to follow them. As for those who had failed, they had already been asked to leave. And since Naji was inside, he went with those who had passed. It was that easy.

What he couldn't get off his mind was that accidents of this sort were extremely rare. He spent the following three days trying in vain to find out what had happened to the little girl who had been the reason for his success.

The conscript at the head of the line placed his hand on the Qur'an. The conscript behind him placed his hand on the first one's shoulder, and so on until the end of the line: "I swear that I will not betray the British government, that I will serve it loyally, be faithful in my work and truthful in my duty, and not be partial to anything but the truth."

After taking the oath, they picked up their military uniforms, which had been distributed to them out of a large trunk. Each was given two pairs of summer trousers, two shirts, a pair of winter trousers and a shirt to go with it, an overcoat, and a pair of military boots.

Naji went into the barracks, only to discover that he would be the sole Arab among thirty-one Indian conscripts. The situation alarmed him. A little while later, a young Palestinian man came in. Overjoyed, he began getting to know him. His name was Sami Atiya. He asked him where he was from, and he said he was from Shu'fat.

"I'm Ali," he said, "but the people in my village call me Naji!" This was what he would say to anyone who wanted to know his name.

Even so, he and Sami felt lonely in the midst of all these people they didn't know, and whom they couldn't talk to.

They'd just gotten settled on their cots when they were approached by a tall, broad-shouldered man who looked the size of a mountain. He bent down and took Sami's pack of cigarettes. He lit a cigarette. Then he left, carrying the whole pack with him, and started passing out its contents to his fellow conscripts.

In the following days, they were astounded by this same man's ability to play an instrument that looked something like a reed pipe. They were so impressed with his abilities that they forgot he had taken the pack of cigarettes. However, their admiration began gradually diminishing when he began harassing them again.

Then one day he pointed at them and said, "From now on you two will be responsible for cleaning the barracks and its bathrooms."

At noon they asked the Palestinian trainees to begin attending an English class. They gathered in a large lecture hall, and before long an Armenian instructor came in. The purpose of the course was to teach them the vocabulary they would need in order to deal with simple, necessary situations such as receiving orders and doing guard duty.

Naji sat next to Sami Atiya. The instructor wrote the word "photograph" on the board. Sami, who had picked up a bit of English here and there, whispered, "What is this? They're starting out at a really simple level. That's the word 'photograph'!"

"Who can read this word?" the instructor asked.

"Don't raise your hand," Naji said to Sami. However, before the instructor had called on him, he answered, "Photograph!"

"Does anyone else know how to read this word?"

"This is too simple. You should teach better things than this!" Naji told him.

"You be quiet," the instructor commanded.

And thus the lessons went. Whenever the instructor wrote down a word or a phrase, Naji would raise his hand, and the instructor would say, "You be quiet."

The course would come to an end and Naji would pass. In the meantime, however, the instructor's words, "You be quiet!" would be repeated countless times a day.

They got back to the barracks to find that the Indians had prepared everything they would need for their cleaning detail.

"If we keep quiet about this, they'll take advantage of us from here on out," he said to Sami Atiya.

"But what can we do?"

"We'll wait till they've all gone inside the barracks. Then I'll tell you."

When the Indian conscripts had all gone inside, Naji came out and told Sami to follow him.

"Do you see the bricks around those flower beds?" he asked him. "When I give you the signal, I want you to hand them to me one at a time. Then leave the rest to me."

Grabbing a broomstick, Naji held it behind him against the wall near the door. He gestured to the tall, broad man to come out. When he had gotten close enough, Naji pulled the broomstick out and hit him on the head with it. The man began to bleed. Then, before the big man knew what was happening, he hit him again and the broomstick broke. Raging like a bull, the man lunged toward Naji, who took five steps back. "Sami!" he shouted. "Give me the bricks!"

As soon as he had taken hold of the first brick, the big man fled inside. He threw the brick at him, and kept pelting the other soldiers with bricks until there were none left and they'd been obliged to take refuge in the far corners of the barracks.

Feeling the earthquake, other soldiers and trainees came running. The scene required no explanation. A ruling was issued requiring them all to stand trial. The camp was divided into two factions—the Indians on one side, the Palestinians on the other—and tension rose to the point where the British demanded that a solution to the problem be found.

Mr. Kemen, the camp director, wasn't satisfied with the ruling that had been issued. Nevertheless, he needed to close the door to further disturbances. Consequently, he issued orders for everyone to clean the camp over a period of two weeks. In addition, it was decided that Sami would be punished by having ten days' pay docked from the wages he had yet to receive, and that Naji would be assigned to guard the camp gate for ten nights in a row.

On the following day, Lieutenant Abd al-Mun'im, the Palestinian trainer, intervened by mediating a truce between the Indians and Sami and Naji.

However, Mr. Kemen's decision would open a door through which would blow dusty winds, the likes of which he had never anticipated!

Afaf's Sorrow

A few months before the birth of his first daughter, Mahmud arrived in Hadiya on one of his bimonthly visits—visits that within two years had become monthly, within three years had become once a season, and after five more years, had become biannual. His visits were no different than some government official's periodic inspections of the region under his jurisdiction. From the time his father was martyred, he had begun to feel that nothing tied him to Hadiya any more, and he paid no attention to anyone's words of reproach or anger. He was like a bird that had been tied down by a string, a string that had now been broken.

Afaf had been wanting to surprise him with the fact that she had learned to read properly. She wanted to show him that she had learned because she wanted to learn, not because she had to. She wanted to tell him she loved him, and that she was up to the challenge of being a respected journalist's wife.

One day, as she was about to hang up his clothes, she felt something in his trousers pocket. It pricked her, but she didn't know whether she'd felt it in her hand, or in some unnamable part of her soul. She reached into his pocket and took it out. It was a piece of paper that had been carefully folded. She unfolded it and read its contents. It was a letter from a woman in Jaffa. Afaf could see from the letter that the woman was a writer, too, since she talked about a book of hers that she wanted to publish soon, and she was asking her "beloved" Mahmud to choose a title for it, since he had "already read everything in it."

Afaf was beside herself. She nearly shouted in his face, "Who is this Layla, anyway?" But she managed to rein in her fury. However, she suddenly lost the enthusiasm she had felt to say to him, "Look! I've learned to read!" Instead, she held her peace, and decided to go on with her life with him, an ignoramus who had forgotten everything she had learned before, a blind ignoramus with an empty head. She thought of throwing the letter in his face. In the end, though, she decided that the best way to let him know that she knew was to say, "Since God's given us a daughter, let's name her Layla."

Taken off guard, Mahmud exclaimed, "And why Layla?"

"Because I like that name," she said.

"Any name but that!"

"You'll have to choose, then: either this name and me, or somebody else!"

He realized that Afaf was onto his story. Even so, he kept saying to himself: Maybe it was just a coincidence. After all, since she doesn't know how to read properly, how could she know?

The White Night

A white car stopped two hundred meters from Hajj Salem's house. One person got out. He asked the first person he saw for directions to the house of Hajj Salem. When he had come to offer condolences on the death of Hajj Khaled, he had learned that Hajj Salem was now the village elder. He approached the house with heavy steps. He knocked on the door, and Hajj Salem came out. He recognized him.

"Father Elias!"

"Lower your voice. All these things belong to you. I heard about what the monastery did. I'm sorry I didn't find out about it until recently. But what I've brought you will solve your problem completely. These are your deeds and other documents. Father Theodorus was supposed to have destroyed them two or three years after people had stopped asking about them, but for some reason he didn't."

"But why did they do this to us when we'd trusted them with our lives?" Hajj Salem asked bitterly.

"Like a lot of other monasteries here in our country, and in other countries from Africa to India, this monastery has nothing to do with religion.

They're like tanks or machine guns, which, when they fire, have only one aim: to mow down everything around them. I hope I can pull out the dagger they've plunged into your backs without causing too much bleeding. As for Manuli, don't underestimate the harm he can do. I knew him before I came here, as I'd met him at quite a number of meetings. He's the most fanatic creature I've ever known in my life. When they said he was coming here, I thought: God have mercy on Hadiya. Hell itself is headed their way!"

The Black Night

L ittle did Naji know that for ten nights he would be living inside a trap. No one before him had escaped from Mr. Kemen, who was a master of inventing ways to catch guards dozing off, or even sound asleep.

Ribhi Mahmud, who had come to the camp two months before him, said, "Now you're doomed to having ten days' pay docked from your wages over and above your first punishment."

"Why's that?"

"Everybody who's done night guard duty has fallen into Mr. Kemen's trap. Nobody has ever escaped."

The night guard's shift was from midnight until six o'clock in the morning.

Naji made up his mind: Mr. Kemen won't have anything to gloat over this time!

Two hours into his shift, he began to feel that it was his duty to restore the honor of all those who had suffered on account of this director.

✳

Moonless darkness, the sounds of nocturnal insects, motors roaring in the distance, the rustling of the tall dry grasses, the hand of the wind wending its way through the open spaces: all these were inviting him to rest, rocking him to sleep.

He would hear Mr. Kemen's door open, and his body would jump to attention. He pricked his ears and listened for the pulse of the darkness, and his eyes strained to penetrate its fearsome black wall. All the senses he knew, and the senses he had possessed thousands of years earlier, were jarred awake.

"So here's Mr. Kemen," he whispered to himself. He drew his weapon and asked for the password, only to find that it was nothing but Mr. Kemen's dog.

On the third night things took a different turn. At four a.m. the door opened, and Naji saw Mr. Kemen bent over and stealing toward him. However, instead of continuing in his direction, he went around the house, his dog in the lead. Then he disappeared, and when he appeared again from the other direction, he was down on all fours.

Naji was on the alert, and when Mr. Kemen came closer, he shouted, "Stay where you are! The password!"

He shouted again, but no one answered.

He placed a cartridge in the chamber. Then a voice came across the dry grasses: "Don't fire. I'm Mr. Kemen."

"Hands up!"

He put his hands up.

"To the left," Naji commanded him to march. So he marched.

"To the right," he commanded. So he marched until he came to a briar patch.

Mr. Kemen stopped at the edge of the patch and refused to go any farther. "I'm Mr. Kemen!" he bellowed.

"Fucking Kemen! Damn Kemen! At night I don't know Mr. Kemen from anybody else! I only know people who've memorized the password!"

Mr. Kemen let forth a torrent of curses. Naji hurled insults back at him, using all the Arabic curse words he knew. It was the first time he had ever had a chance to berate a British army man, so he took full advantage of it!

"You're coming to catch me off guard here. Well, I'll show you!"

"I'm Kemen."

"No, you're a thief. Now down on the ground. Crawl!"

He got down on the ground and crawled.

"Turn over on your back."

He turned over.

After he'd had enough, Naji shouted, "Idiot guards! Get over here!"

Within moments the other guards and their commander had come running.

Mr. Kemen was on the ground, trembling and cursing hysterically.

"Put your rifle down. That's Mr. Kemen," the guard commander told Naji.

"I'm sorry! But I'm not going to put my weapon away until I see him in the light. I've got to be sure it's really Mr. Kemen. Mr. Kemen is a military man, and this is no military man."

The white jersey he was wearing had turned the color of dirt, and so had his shorts and his light running shoes.

In vain, they tried to convince Naji that he was who they said he was.

"If I can't confirm that that's who he is, I'll kill him right here."

At that point, of course, everybody had to go along with him, since the guard on duty had the right to conduct himself however he saw fit!

Mr. Kemen stood up and marched with Naji's rifle at his back. They got to the barracks, where the lights were on.

"Turn your face this way now so I can see you."

Mr. Kemen turned around, his face purple with rage.

Naji lowered the rifle, stood at perfect attention, and raised his hand in a salute. "I am sorry, Mr. Kemen."

"What? You're sorry? Fuck you, Naji!"

Then he turned to the guard commander and said, "Take him to lock-up."

Naji began marching in front of the guard commander. But halfway between the barracks and the building where the prison cells were, he stopped. The guard commander ordered him to move. He refused.

"I'm not a criminal who deserves to be led away to some jail cell. I refuse this order. Either I go to my own barracks, or I go back to finish my guard shift. And in the morning, if he wants to try me, then let him try me!"

The guard commander went back to Mr. Kemen and told him what Naji had said.

"Leave him be. He's stubborn. He could have really killed me. Let him finish his shift, and in the morning we'll see," said Mr. Kemen.

At noon of that same day, they informed Naji that he would be tried the next morning. He told his Indian buddies in the barracks. The big man, who still had a scar on his forehead, said to him, "Don't worry. We know Mr. Kemen."

"So what should I do?"

"We know what to do."

One of them took Naji's army boots and polished them till you could see your reflection in them. Then he ironed his khaki uniform, making his shirt collar stiff as a board. They had him shave his beard three times, and shave off his pubic hair. They even told him to remove the hair on his buttocks. He changed his underwear. They cut his fingernails and toenails. They cleaned his ears. Then they dressed him in his uniform. When he was about to sit down, they all shouted, "No! You've got to be neat as a pin when you get there!"

So he remained standing until the military vehicle arrived. After he had gotten to the door of the barracks and was about to step outside, they shouted, "No!"

He stopped in his tracks.

They carried him from the door of the barracks to the car so that his boots wouldn't get dirty.

"We'll feel better this way," they said.

When they arrived at the place where he would be tried, they carried him from the car to the doorstep.

Once inside, he stood waiting. Not long thereafter, a number of officers walked in and took their places. Among them sat Mr. Kemen.

Naji removed his beret and military belt and saluted.

The simple words he knew in English weren't enough for him to understand what was going on, so they assigned Lieutenant Abd al-Mun'im as his interpreter.

"Why did you do that to me?" Mr. Kemen demanded.

"Tell Mr. Kemen that this soldier says: God must have wanted you to live, since if it weren't for God's mercy, I would have killed you. If somebody comes along in his underwear and crawls around on all fours in the middle of the night, and then doesn't tell me the password, this can only mean one thing—that he's a trespasser who's come to blow up the camp! For all I know, he might be coming to murder Mr. Kemen himself! How can I allow such a thing when I've been assigned to guard Mr. Kemen?"

The minute he heard the translation of what Naji had said, Mr. Kemen's whole demeanor changed. He sat back in his chair and said, "Really, this guard was a potential killer at that moment, and I knew there was nothing between me and his bullet but the sound of the gun's report."

"Tell Mr. Kemen that I was about to kill him at that moment. However, if I'd done so, I wouldn't have been breaking the law. I would have been enforcing it."

Mr. Kemen got up from where he sat. He walked up to Naji, looked him in the face and said, "What did you use to do in your village?"

"When a boy from our village is seven years old, he takes the cows, sheep, and goats out into the plains and foothills and stays there with the herds for days on end. We aren't afraid of the dark. I'm prepared to stay up all night, every night, on your doorstep, and you'll never catch me sleeping."

Mr. Kemen took two steps back. He looked at Naji's boots, and found them shining.

Naji knew that the personal inspection had now begun.

Mr. Kemen walked in a circle around him. He looked at him from behind. He put on his glasses. He came up to his face. He reached up and ran his hand over Naji's chin to see how smooth it was. He nodded. He unbuttoned Naji's trousers and they fell in a heap on top of his shiny boots. He unbuttoned his shirt and checked to see how clean his undershirt was.

He took hold of his right ear, tugged on it a bit, and looked behind it and inside it. He turned to his left ear and did the same thing. He nodded again. He took a step back. He took a good look at his boxer shorts. He grabbed the top of them and pulled them out, then peered inside, where his pubic hair would have been. He nodded a third time. Then he took Naji's hand and checked his nails. He nodded his head.

After telling him to put his clothes back in place, Mr. Kemen went back to where he had been sitting. He sat back in his chair and said, "You deserve fourteen days."

Disconcerted at what he had heard, Naji objected, "What fourteen days are you talking about?!"

"Vacation," replied Mr. Kemen. "In spite of the hell you put me through, you're the type of man I take pride in."

The Indian soldiers in the barracks were even more ecstatic than he was. Naji was the team they had been rooting for, and their team had won.

Not many days would pass before another surprise was waiting for them all.

A New Day

The editor-in-chief asked to see Mahmud. He went to his office. The editor-in-chief said, "Mr. Mahmud, I think you've done quite a bit since you first joined us, and that you've proved through your efforts that you're capable of taking on bigger responsibilities. Consequently, I've decided to appoint you as the newspaper's editorial secretary, and to increase your salary by twenty pounds. What do you say?"

"Thank you!" Mahmud said excitedly, and left.

"Where are you going?" The editor-in-chief's voice followed him out the door.

"To my office!"

"Your office isn't on the left any more. It's on the right. Over there."

The new office wasn't unfamiliar to him. If it had been up to him, he would have preferred to go back to the room where he had always worked. The new office was dark all the time, and its window, the view from which was blocked by a cement wall just two meters away, made it a miserable place to stay for very long, especially in the summer, when the heat and humidity rose unbearably and getting a breath of fresh air was a challenge unequaled even by the position of editorial secretary.

The editor-in-chief had realized instinctively that having the name of Mahmud Khaled al-Hajj Mahmud on the newspaper's front page would be tantamount to a badge of honor. It would be like a journalistic scoop that would go on renewing itself every day, a journalistic scoop that no one would be able to take away from him. It wouldn't be long before the newspaper would begin to reap the benefits of this name to a degree that far surpassed the twenty-pound raise he had given Mahmud.

Many things changed after that day.

The first thing Mahmud did was to begin frequenting more upscale kinds of places. He began spending his time at the Lyons Café and the Bristol Café, both of which were gathering places for merchants and businessmen. He felt self-conscious in the beginning. But as the days passed, he began to feel more confident, especially as word spread about his new position, and his obvious generosity caused the employees at both establishments to give him attention that was more than special.

Anything could be bought in Jaffa, even respect.

He began going on some nights to the Ghantus, Lawrence, and Abd al-Masih Nightclub, which was a cross between a nightclub and a coffee shop, and more European than Middle Eastern. When he heard that some well-known Egyptian artist had come to the city to perform or for a stopover on his or her way to Lebanon, he would go to the hotel or the coffee shop where they might be just to get a glimpse of them.

He also began to feel that Layla was closer to him than before. As soon she heard about his new position, she invited him enthusiastically, and for the first time, to visit her family.

But he refused. What would he say to them when he met them: that he had a wife and children?

"I'll go to the cinema," he told her.

She was angry. "I invite you visit my family, and you say you're going to the cinema instead?"

When he came out of the cinema after seeing *For Whom the Bell Tolls*, he was certain that Ingrid Bergman had dethroned Greta Garbo. She had the sweetest, most serene face he had ever seen on the screen. However, the strange feeling suddenly came over him that Layla had never looked like Greta Garbo, since the person she really looked like was Ingrid Bergman.

Five Stars

Salim Bek al-Hashemi had been trying to think of a way out of the scandals that had been closing in on him from all sides. People were still talking about that dinner party, where many of his enemies and rivals had been in attendance. Then, after al-Marzuqi took on Hadiya's case, the story about how he had assigned his son to the same case earlier began coming to light. The newspapers talked about people who were nationalists by day, and land brokers and merchants at the High Commissioner's home by night.

He decided to contact the provincial governor. His wife said to him, "What you're thinking of is sheer madness," and his son Anas agreed with her.

"Your problem is that you don't look far enough ahead."

"I'm in desperate need of Your Excellency's help these days," he said to the provincial governor.

"And what have we failed to offer you so far?"

"You know that officials in my position need people's trust, and I think that when we do win their trust, this makes you happy as well."

"And how can I do what you should do yourself, Mr. Hashemi?"

"By putting me in jail for a few days!"

"Pardon me, Mr. Hashemi? I don't understand!"

"I want you to issue orders for me to be put in prison for a week or two."

"Is that all? You just say the word, Mr. Hashemi. Do you prefer any particular prison?"

"I think a prison that's some distance away might be better."

"Would al-Maskubiya Prison in Jerusalem be good?"

"No. I'd prefer something farther away. As you know, Jerusalem is full of people I know!"

"Then the best place for you would the Awja al-Hafir Prison in the Negev Desert. There's nobody around there!"

"It's true that I asked you to have me locked up. But I didn't mean for the prison to be quite that real."

"You're wearing me out, Mr. Hashemi. Do you have a particular prison in mind?"

"The Acre Prison might be suitable. What do you think?"

"You be the one to decide, Mr. Hashemi. When do you want us to take you there? And from where?"

"Tomorrow after the Friday noon prayer. I think the best thing would be for me to be arrested in front of the big mosque."

"You know I prefer to steer clear of places of worship, since sensitivities run high there. But since you're the one that wants it that way, then so be it!"

"I thank you, Your Excellency."

"Will two weeks be enough for you? Or shall we make it three?"

"Three weeks would be better. As you know, even three months wouldn't erase the things that have happened recently."

After being arrested quietly, without anyone raising any objection, he asked the officer who had been assigned to him to take him to his house. He had stuffed a suitcase with clothes before going to prayer. He passed by the house and grabbed it in a hurry. The car then headed for the train station. As soon as they had taken their seats on the train, he asked the sergeant who was escorting him to release him from his shackles, and the sergeant did as he had requested. When they got to Acre, he asked the sergeant to let him hire a porter. His suitcase was heavy, he said, and the prison was quite a distance from the station and one could only get there by passing through the city's marketplaces. The sergeant agreed, saying, "But you'll have to pay him yourself."

One of the officers escorted him to the door of his room, which had been prepared for him before his arrival. Hashemi cast a glance around the room. It was truly ideal. It lacked nothing. They had even remembered to provide him with a radio and telephone. The officer asked him to pass by to see the prison warden after he'd rested for a while, since he would be waiting for him.

When he arrived to see the prison warden, he squeezed his hand warmly and wished him a pleasant stay. He said, "Telephone service here hasn't been cut off, and the provincial governor has told me to provide you with everything you need. Remember that my office is at your disposal at all times!"

The thing that bothered him most during his incarceration was thinking about his arrest, which had taken place all too quietly: Not one of those bastards made a move, not even the ones I thought were my friends!

Many times he would find himself thinking out loud: "The bastards don't believe that somebody like me might be wanted by the government. And the ones that say they're my friends know that the badge of honor I won when I was arrested was taken off their own chests."

However, he discovered during his jail time that he had needed to get away from everything for a while.

During the first few days of his stay, he ate at the prison warden's own table. After that they would play chess till a late hour, and then he would go to the comfortable quarters they had assigned him. By the fourth day, however, he realized that three days in prison is no small thing, even if you're having your meals with the prison warden himself.

On the third day, the prison warden surprised him by saying, "Tomorrow morning we're going to be executing a couple of 'insubordinates.' If you're interested in watching it, let me know now, and I'll send someone to wake you up early."

"I'd really like to, but I don't like to start my day with a scene like that. If the executions were going to be in the afternoon, I might attend."

"All I have to do is reschedule it to a time that would be convenient for you."

"I really appreciate that. In any case, you do what you have to do, and I'll do what I have to do, which is to rest."

"I never knew your heart was so weak!"

"Is that a dare?"

"No, not at all."

"Well, so that you'll know what kind of heart I've got in this chest, I'll attend the execution, and in the morning to boot!"

"Now that's the Mr. Hashemi we know!"

An hour after the execution had been carried out, he said to the prison warden, "I'll be leaving today!"

"Do you want to go home?"

"No, I just want to go into town, walk around a bit, then come back."

"I have to warn you, Mr. Hashemi, there are a lot of people who might recognize you. I want you to be careful."

"Not to worry. I'll keep a low profile. I'll do the same when I go to the airport and come back from there."

"Are you intending to take a trip, too?"

"For just a few hours. Less than half a day. I'll fly to Jerusalem and Tel Aviv, then come back."

"There was no reason for you to come to the prison if your schedule is this full!"

The Apparition

T he training period passed quite quickly. Meanwhile, time outside was going by with such speed that the days didn't have a chance to catch their breath. Then, a few weeks before the training course was to end, a small incident nearly changed the course of Naji's life.

As the trainees were heading to the mess hall for breakfast after their morning calisthenics, Naji went into the bathroom. The faucets were spaced only half a meter apart. He turned one on and began washing his hands and face. He noticed that the water was collecting in the narrow cement trough that ran along the floor under the faucets. As he tried to get the water to run out, he discovered that it was being blocked by a small wallet. Bending down, he picked the wallet up. He shook the water off of it, then looked around. There was no one there. He opened it. He saw the identity card of his trainer, Abd al-Mun'im, in one of its pockets, and in the other, some cash. He took it out. There were twenty-two pounds.

Naji put the wallet in his pocket and started to leave. As he got to the door, it occurred to him to keep it. He opened the wallet again. He went into one of the stalls and closed the door, which consisted of a piece of burlap, behind him. He looked intently at the sum of money. Then he heard a voice. Putting the wallet back into his pocket, he pushed the piece of burlap aside and looked around to see who was there. Suddenly, he received a hard slap. His father, Hajj Khaled, was standing in front of him. Before Naji could say a word, his father had disappeared.

He began to tremble. He left the bathroom quickly and headed for the mess hall.

Lieutenant Abd al-Mun'im planted love and respect for him deep in everyone's hearts. The British found him to be an excellent trainer, and had once promoted him by awarding him an extra star. However, he refused the promotion, saying, "Either two stars, or none at all." After lengthy consultations, they'd given him what he wanted.

Two hundred forty conscripts would march to the rhythm of his steps and respond to the ring of his stentorian voice.

Ten minutes later, Lieutenant Abd al-Muni'm came into the mess hall and stood in a place where everyone could see him. He said, "I have something to say, although I'm not sure it will do any good!"

Everyone listened attentively.

"I want to say that I've lost my military ID, and I'm asking whoever found it to throw it into the street. I don't want him to return it to me directly, and I hope the good soul who found it is listening to me now. You all know that Abd al-Mun'im, who made the British award him two stars at once, deserves to have his ID returned to him. It would be a shame for it to be lost among you when he loves you all the way he does."

Silence reigned. They sat there looking at each other. Naji got up. He took a few steps forward, to a place where he could be seen by all the other trainees.

"Abd al-Muni'm, sir!" Naji called out.

"Yes?"

"Could you please describe the wallet you lost?"

"Turn to face the other men," he said to Naji.

He turned to face them.

"What did you just ask me to do?"

"I asked you to describe your wallet to me."

"All I asked for was an ID, and you're talking about a wallet. As you all just heard, this young man is asking me about a wallet. Did you hear? So I say to him: It's got three snaps, and one of them is missing."

"And what's inside the wallet? Cash, or other things?" asked Naji.

"Listen to this, guys! He's talking about money, and asking me about it. Inside the wallet there are twenty-two pounds: a ten, two fives, and two ones."

"This is your wallet, then, and your ID, and your money inside it," said Naji.

"I thank you for your honesty. You know, I've never asked what village you're from."

"I'm from Hadiya."

"I salute you, and I salute your integrity. I salute your village, and the mother who nursed you."

He fell silent for a few moments. He looked around at the faces of the other trainees, then said to Naji, "From now on you'll be eating in the officers' mess hall. And beginning tomorrow, you'll have the rank of trainer. You'll wear two stripes for the time being, until you're officially promoted. My barracks and my tent are over there, and you're welcome there whenever you like!"

When the other trainers heard what he had said, they broke into applause.

Everything in Naji's life changed. The food served in the officers' mess hall was something altogether different from what was served to the trainees, and the atmosphere that reigned there was like another world. In the wave of euphoria over what he had done, they made an appointment for him to meet with the camp director. When Naji went in to see him, Mr. Kemen smiled, stood up, and shook his hand heartily, saying, "Vigilant and dependable! I'm going to write you a letter of promotion as Mr. Abd al-Mun'im has recommended."

Then he turned to Abd al-Mun'im and asked him, "Have you given him a vacation? He deserves that, too."

"No, we haven't."

"All right, then, let him have one week's vacation, and after he graduates he'll be a trainer for one of the new groups."

His return to the village was an occasion they had all been waiting for. Once there, he started passing on to them the things he had been learning, point by point, and they started to realize the huge difference this would make in the course of their lives and in the life of the village in the future.

His uncle Salem said to him, "You haven't told me: how are things for you there?"

"They're tops!"

"You can't imagine how happy I am that you're going to learn everything and come back to us soon."

Naji was about to tell his uncle everything that had happened, but suddenly he decided not to.

That night he laid his head on the pillow, and no sooner had he fallen asleep than he heard a voice saying, "So, you're going to become a drill sergeant for the British police?"

Naji was flustered. "But how did you know, Baba?"

Hajj Khaled was in front of him.

"There are people who are prepared to pay two hundred pounds to become drill sergeants, and the only people who make that rank have finished three years of high school!" Naji protested. Then he began telling him excitedly about all the things that had happened.

Hajj Khaled made no reply. Then he began shaking his head sorrowfully.

Even more flustered now, Naji asked, "What's the matter, Baba?"

"Son, a drill sergeant has to be shameless. Consequently, he can't be a nice person! If he has a sense of shame and wants to be well-mannered the way his mother and father taught him to be, he won't be able to train anybody. What the drill sergeant has to do is forget morals altogether. The drill sergeant insults and curses people's fathers and grandfathers. He might even go so far as to slap his trainees. Could you do all that to decent folks? If you tell me you can, then I'm telling you now: you're not my son, and I don't even know you. Go back to them as some ordinary person. If you've forgotten what we sent you there for, they may send you to hell. But in that hell you'll at least still be a human being. If, on the other hand, you start vilifying people and trampling on their dignity, that's something we can't accept in any way, shape, or form."

In a single moment, everything was turned on its head, and the castles Naji had been building in the air came crashing to the ground. He woke up in a fright and looked around him. There was nothing but darkness.

Naji brought some kunafa in Ramla, which he had reached by train, then headed for the camp.

He was received back with great enthusiasm.

That same day, they went out for training in how to shoot from moving cars. The training went on till noon. When he went to the officers' mess hall, he sat down across from Lieutenant Abd al-Mun'im. After they had eaten the kunafa with hot tea, Naji turned to his trainer and said, "Abd al-Mun'im, sir."

"Yes?"

"My father sends you greetings of peace!"

"And peace be to him. I hope all is well?"

"My father greets you, and wants me to tell you that he doesn't approve of my being a drill sergeant."

"My goodness!" Abd al-Mun'im said with a start. "That's incredible! There are people who would be willing to pay two hundred pounds in order to be a drill sergeant."

"My father says that if a drill sergeant wants to teach people, he might have to hit them and call them names, and he says we're from a family that refuses to insult anyone."

Touched deeply by Naji's words, Abd al-Mun'im sat there for a long time without saying a word. Then he said, "I'll take you to see Mr. Kemen."

They went to see him. Mr. Kemen got up with a smile, shook Naji's hand warmly, and asked how his vacation had gone.

"It was great, Mr. Kemen."

"But he's come back with a new surprise for us," added Abd al-Mun'im.

"A new surprise? What might that be?"

Abd al-Mun'im explained the situation from beginning to end. As he spoke, Naji's eyes were fixed on Mr. Kemen's face and on his head, which he shook every time he heard a new sentence. When Abd al-Muni'm had finished, Mr. Kemen turned to Naji, clearly moved, and said to him, "You're decent folks, brave and honest, and I have more love for you in my heart than ever before. Tell your father when you see him on your next vacation that Mr. Kemen hopes to see him and get to know him!"

Meanwhile, outside, time's wheel was spinning ever faster.

Wadi al-Sarar

The Wadi al-Sarar camp was the most extensive off-limits area they had ever seen, with countless guarded gates at three-hundred-meter intervals, a paved road that was flanked on one side by the barbed-wire fence that surrounded the camp and on the other by another barbed-wire fence farther to the inside, buildings and warehouses, and railroad cars that would steal deep inside toward its well-fortified underground arms depots, above which rose four meters of soil for further protection.

"It's got everything," said Aziza's son Husayn, "from cartridges to heavy artillery."

The British forces had not constructed the camp in connection with their mandate over Palestine, but, rather, in preparation for the surprises the Second World War might have in store for them.

The men of Hadiya and other villages who worked at the camp would see trucks arrive empty from the Jewish settlements, then depart filled with all manner of weapons, ammunition, bombs, and mines.

"Listen, everybody. You're just sitting there while the Jews take British weapons off to their settlements."

"And what solution do you propose?" asked Hajj Salem.

"You know that if even so much as a cartridge is found on any of us, it's sufficient reason for him to be hanged. So, if you want my advice, there's only one solution. The Jews aren't worried about anything. They take weapons away before our very eyes and deal with us as though we were blind. We know when they come and when they leave. We also know how heavily they're guarded every time they come."

"So what do you think?"

As they sensed danger approaching, they began arming themselves again. There was no one more capable of providing leadership in this endeavor than Iliya Radhi and Nuh the brother of Khadra, who formed two groups for this purpose. The beginnings were more than successful, since the element of surprise was in the rebels' favor. Just as they had been accustomed to doing years earlier, they would set up an ambush here and an ambush there along sharp bends in the roads or in narrow valleys, and the caravans that had been ambushed had no choice but to surrender or be wiped out. All they wanted, however, was arms, and on many occasions they would release the Jews they knew—the Jews who had lived with them for many years without any problems between them.

From time to time, one of these Jews would be taken captive.

"We don't like problems," they would say. "But the Jews coming from abroad force us to work with them."

So they would let them go.

It wasn't long before the British began providing their arms caravans with guards that were virtually impenetrable. However, this didn't prevent the occasional caravan from being attacked in this or that valley or near this or that forest.

When the British began withdrawing from Palestine and leaving a small number of their soldiers behind, they sent a guard from the Arab army that had been under the command of the British commander Glubb Pasha to fill the vacuum.

Then, with the appointment of Shawkat Mukhtar as director of the Wadi Sarar camp, the winds began to blow in a slightly new direction.

From the time Shawkat Mukhtar was appointed, not a day passed but that the Jewish trucks took more arms away. Ali Salem, Hashem Shahada, and Husayn, who had all been working at the camp, decided to speak with him come what may.

"Mr. Shawkat, you're responsible for guarding the camp, and you see the Jews filling their trucks with arms and ammunition. So we're asking you to let us carry some away ourselves. We need them. You know this. After all, you're an Arab, too!"

"I can't. You see the British army patrols all around us."

Indeed, the patrols, with their motorcycle and jeeps, were in constant motion.

"What matters is for us to reach an agreement with you first. You tell us what you want from us, and then we'll find the solution. We know the camp like the back of our hand, and whatever happens, we guarantee that you won't be held responsible."

"Can you really manage that?"

"Definitely."

"Don't you know that the patrols hover around the camp until midnight?"

"Yes, we do. So we could come at one or two in the morning."

"But I couldn't be with you."

"No problem. Leave the door to the warehouse we've agreed on open, and we'll take care of the rest."

The bullets glistened like gold nuggets in their chests, bullets the likes of which we could never have gotten our hands on before. There were also a lot of Mills grenades and artillery shells of the type required by cannons that we didn't have.

"I'll let a soldier I trust open the door for you, and the rest is up to you, as you were saying."

No one could believe that an agreement of this sort had actually been made. Many hesitated to go. But when they later saw that the results were guaranteed, they all started coming: men young and old, women, and boys. They would muzzle the camels and horses to keep them quiet, then tie them some distance away and start advancing stealthily toward the camp.

In every chest there were around a thousand bullets.

Shawkat Mukhtar made it quite clear: one chest would be sold for ten pounds.

The soldier would stand at the gate and count the chests. When they had finished, they would go to him, and every time they found him wringing his hands with his eyes on the door.

Under the small searchlight, the payment would begin. He would take the money and hide it in his pocket, and every night when they got to the door he would say the same thing: "Remember: if you make it out of here without getting caught, I'm with you. Otherwise, I'm against you!"

It was difficult for him not to be anxious, despite the fact that the operation had been going on night after night, and he was always nervous when they brought him his money.

"I don't want it in one-pound notes! I want it in tens," he would say to Ali, who had become the official go-between.

He started to get really scared, and he couldn't bear to waste a single second during those critical moments.

To make him feel better, a number of the men started paying him right away, while the others were making their way to the depots.

"Whenever he sees our pounds, he seems more agreeable," remarked Husayn. However, Hajj Salem instructed them to be on their guard.

Shawkat Mukhtar sent word to them that he wouldn't be able to see them at night because a number of British officers and soldiers had come back to the camp.

One day, Aziza's son Husayn, Sulayman Sammur, and Hashem Shahada went to see him. To their surprise, however, things took a different turn this time.

They went to one of the guard posts and asked the soldier for permission to meet with the camp commander. "We're his relatives," they told him, "and we've come to visit him."

The soldier retorted, "I'll show you who's going to come now!"

He picked up the receiver, made a call, and before they knew it, they were surrounded by British military police on motorcycles with red berets on their heads.

"What are you doing here?" one of the soldiers barked. Before anyone replied, they told them to get behind them on the motorcycles. Hashem held on tightly to the soldier in front of him, fearful of falling off, only to get badly elbowed.

The motorcycles stopped in front of the residence camp.

"What brings you here?" asked a British soldier whose shoulder was decorated with three stars.

"We don't know! We were on our way to Yibna to buy livestock, and these soldiers brought us here!"

They had a lot of money with them. Each of them had sixty pounds in his pocket.

A short while later, Shawkat Mukhtar arrived and shouted at them, "What are you doing here, you thieves?"

The British officer spoke Arabic as well as they did.

"We were going to a village by the name of Yibna to buy livestock the way we always do. But then a soldier stopped us and called the patrol, and they brought us here," Husayn replied.

"You must have been too close to the camp's barbed-wire fence!" fumed Shawkat Mukhtar, who seemed to be trying to find excuses for them.

"We don't know if we were too close or not, since we don't know how close we're allowed to get."

The British officer ordered the soldiers who had brought them to search them, and they found the money.

"What's all this money for?" demanded the officer.

"We told you, it's so we can buy livestock!"

"No, it's so you can buy a 'bang bang'!"

"Leave them to me. I'll interrogate them myself," said Shawkat Mukhtar.

When the officer and soldiers were some distance away, he asked them, "Who's the soldier who made you come here?"

"The one at Gate 12."

The British officer came back. "I've got to turn them in at the Qatra police station."

※

The military's orders were clear to everyone in that region: civilians were to stay at least fifty meters away from the camp regardless of whether they were grazing animals, sowing and reaping, or just passing by. Anyone who got closer than this was to be treated as suspect.

The three men tried to act as though they were offended at the decision. But on the inside they were pleased, since they knew the police chief there, and he was a sympathizer. He was a Palestinian officer working with the British, a top-notch young man by the name of Abd al-Fattah Milhim. Unlike the security men, tax collectors, and government employees who were nothing but spongers, people loved him and treated him as an important guest when he visited the villages.

The jeep brought them to the door of the military police station. One of the soldiers who had accompanied them explained the case to the police chief. He waved three envelopes in front of him, then placed the money in them, and they wrote on each envelope the name of the person it belonged to.

The police chief asked the soldier, "How much money is in these envelopes?"

"There are sixty pounds in each one."

"Sixty, you robbers! What were you planning to do? What were you going to do with this money?" the police chief demanded angrily.

"We were going to buy livestock. That's all," Husayn replied.

But, contrary to all expectations, the soldier did not turn the money over to the chief of police.

"Their money will be kept in Ramla until they've been thoroughly investigated," he said.

No sooner had the jeep driven away than the police chief began embracing them one after the other, saying reproachfully, "How did you manage to get yourselves into this?"

They explained everything to him, although he wasn't unaware of what had been going on.

"Come on now, I'll take you back to Hadiya myself," he said.

"No, no, it's all right. We can spend the night in this cell. We wouldn't want anybody to notice. Then tomorrow you can be our guest."

"I didn't know you'd gotten so stingy. I tell you I'm going to be your guest tonight, and you say, 'No, you'll be our guest tomorrow!'"

"You'll be criticized for doing this kind of thing."

"Not to worry. The British won't be here forever, but all we've got is each other."

"All right, then," they replied in unison. "Damn the British!"

Even before he left Hadiya, the police chief had written a report in which he stated that after hearing the testimony of witnesses, including that of the town's mayor, it had become apparent that the suspects had not been intending to buy weapons, but only livestock. He went on to affirm that he had released them after keeping them in custody for two weeks. In order not to arouse suspicions, he told Hajj Salem that he wouldn't send the report to the British until two weeks had passed.

One morning not long afterwards, a British car stopped in the village and asked them for their names one by one. Then they gave them the money they had in their hands after the men had signed papers confirming its receipt.

See? It was only in this one case that the British were good to us!

As for the soldier who had been the cause of the commotion, Shawkat Mukhtar had him sent back to where he came from before the men's money was returned to them. At the same time, however, what had happened caused him to be more careful. After that he began inventing excuses for his soldiers to fire on this or that, in order to justify the reduction in the supply of bullets in the arms depots. In that frenzied atmosphere, there was no better type of justification. And by having his soldiers shoot, he was killing two birds with one stone: he was gaining the trust of the British, who could see how vigilant he was, and he was selling the ammunition without attracting anyone's attention. Things even got to the point where he would send word to this or that village, saying, "Don't come tonight. There's shooting going on."

The only thing Shawkat Mukhtar couldn't figure out was how, despite all the burdens they were laboring under, these villagers managed to organize their activity on their own without a central command.

A Belated Victory

Newspapers ignored Hashemi's arrest for an entire week, which worried him. If things went on this way, everything would have been in vain. He called his son Anas and told him to get the papers moving on the story.

"I want articles, respectable articles, impeccable articles. And work on getting Mahmud al-Hajj Khaled to write one of them."

"But he doesn't write."

"Well, it's high time he started, then. Tell the editor-in-chief so. After all, we're his biggest advertisers. And later on I want Mahmud for something bigger."

"Tomorrow you'll be reading news that's to your liking."

"I think we need to see you start demonstrating your talents," said the editor-in-chief to Mahmud. "And there's no better place to begin than with an article on the arrest of Salim Bek al-Hashemi. As far as I know, all the newspapers are going to be working on it over the next few days."

"What should I write?

"Write whatever you want. Lambaste the British and their policies. Besides, what do you need me to tell you after what they did to you, your family, and all of us by killing your father, Everyman's martyr!"

As if he had been imprisoned inside himself and had suddenly seen the light of his spirit, Mahmud wrote an article that was the most forceful and most important imaginable, because it was the most honest imaginable. And despite the fact that Hashemi's name appeared only once in the entire piece as an example of the injustice of the British authorities, that was more than enough as far as Hashemi was concerned.

Articles appeared in three newspapers, and before long 'Hashemi fever' had spread to other newspapers that felt they should be in the vanguard on nationalist issues. When Mahmud saw this, he felt as though all the little doubts that had assailed him had been baseless, and that the words he had written were things that needed to be said not only for Hashemi's sake, but for his father's sake as well.

The fact that there was now so much news coverage prompted Hashemi to conduct himself more responsibly, particularly after the papers were filled with pictures of him. He stopped leaving the prison, and thought it best to have his favorite foods brought to him. Hence, the prison administration made a deal with a well-known restaurant in Acre to send food to him twice a day, at noon and in the evening. The food that arrived was enough to feed him, the prison warden, and all the prison's senior officers, and he made sure to pay for it all out of his own pocket.

One important development was that the prison administration started getting calls nonstop. Numerous political leaders from various cities called to demand that Hashemi receive VIP treatment. After all, they pointed out, he was a major nationalist figure and industrialist, and one of the most prominent thinkers in the whole country.

As he began to taste the sweetness of his victory, he felt more self-assured and comfortable. He spoke with his son and told him that, after clearing it with the provincial governor, he should leak the news that his imprisonment had been extended for two additional weeks.

The news was published the next morning, and people were in an uproar. More than one article was published on the need for him to be released as soon as possible. Article after article continued to appear, until his last night in prison. He called his son Anas and asked him to go personally to the provincial governor and show him the news item that he would dictate to him shortly. He stressed the importance of securing his agreement. Otherwise, he said, the prison issue was going to turn into something serious.

The provincial governor had no objections. "But," he said to Anas, "let him remember that this is all I'll be able to give him!"

On the day before he was to be released, headlines read: "Mandate Authorities Decide to Release Hashemi after a Wave of Popular Protests."

When he read the newspapers that had been brought to him, he said, "It's time to go home."

He called his son. "You should be here tomorrow morning, and Mahmud al-Hajj Khaled should be with you. I want him to be by my side when I get off the train."

The reception that had been prepared for him at the train station was a major affair. The crowds picked him up and carried him, and did the same to Mahmud, whose appearance was quite unexpected. They took them all the way to the town square, where a large rally was held. The rally was concluded with a moving speech by Mahmud, which, in actuality, was none other than the article he had written. Anas had brought it and given it to him, thereby preventing any attempt he might make to refrain from participating on the pretext that he wasn't prepared. This was followed by a speech by Hashemi that was no less moving. It was a speech he had thought about before he went to prison, and which he had written down and memorized during his stay there.

After the rally was over, the crowds scattered and a car came and took Hashemi and his son away. As they rode away, Hashemi waved goodbye to Mahmud from the window.

"Let's offer to take him wherever he'd like to go, provided it's far away from this square," Anas said to his father.

"Why?"

"His role is over now."

In that empty square, Mahmud felt as though he was waiting, and that what he was waiting for wasn't going to come. The minutes passed. No one. As soon as he'd taken off his fez, his clothes began to fall off his body the way the leaves fall off a tree in the autumn chill. He looked at himself. He was completely naked. Everything around him seemed darkened like the windows in Jaffa during the war days, the windows that would be blacked out, their black curtains drawn, so as to block any light that might escape and cause the city to be bombed while Italian aircraft attacked the oil refinery in Haifa.

Darkened like people's eyes, which looked on, unable to see anything clearly, as the countries fell like dominoes before the German armies. When Romania, Yugoslavia, and Greece fell, and the German forces leapt over to the island of Crete, things became more complicated, and the sounding of warning sirens in Jaffa became an almost daily affair, causing darkness upon darkness to fall.

It was as though warning sirens were going off in Mahmud's ears, and he could hear the sound of them coming from all directions.

Darkened like the quails that would fall exhausted onto the autumn shores, like those fleeing from the war who had fallen on the Palestinian shores. And like them, Mahmud was falling. 'Ladies of the night' had became a familiar, ubiquitous sight on the streets of Jaffa, Haifa, and Jerusalem.

He felt like nothing but a lady of the night in front of some nightclub.

Within weeks, the winds had begun blowing in another direction, and with a speed that Hashemi could never have anticipated. In fact, he began to wonder what good had come of the time he had spent in prison. He realized instinctively, and based on the information that was being leaked to him, that he needed to end everything quickly, since the country was going to hell in a handbasket, and any delay on his part could cost him dearly.*

---

* When sparks began to fly throughout the length and breadth of Palestine, sending everything up in flames, when the shrapnel from mines and other explosives mowed down the innocent in hotels and cars, in vegetable markets, schools, and other gathering places, he started a rumor, which was then spread by his men in the city and the countryside, to the effect that revolutionary elements had advised him to leave the country for fear that he might be assassinated in the course of his comings and goings because of the Jews' and the Britons' intense hatred for him! Before the catastrophe of 1948, he sold his factories, houses, lands, camels, and horses and relocated to Lebanon. He took up residence in Beirut, where he continued to oversee the affairs of the city's residents from the office of the Arab Higher Committee there!

The Flood

When al-Marzuqi rose to deliver his defense, he took five steps in the direction of the judge, then deliberately dropped his cane. He bent down to look for it. He ran his hands over the floor, right and left, in front of him and behind him. At last he found it.

The judge watched him, waiting for him to stand up again. Instead, however, he continued his search.

"You were looking for your cane. Haven't you found it?"

"Yes, I've found it."

"What are you looking for, then?"

"For Great Britain's justice, Your Honor," he said in reply as he went on looking.

"Stand up, then. You're not going to find it this way!"

He stood up.

"But would you allow me, Your Honor, to say one thing that has nothing to do with this trial?"

The judge took a deep breath, then said, "Very well, provided you don't go on too long."

"Don't worry, I'll make it short."

"Go ahead."

"Your Honor, might I ask you when you're from?"

"From Britain, of course!"

"What city in Britain do you come from?"

"Manchester."

"Do you belong to a family there?"

"Of course. The Johnson family."

"If someone were to come and take your house from you by force or deceitful means, would you allow him to have it?"

"Never."

"But this, Your Honor, is exactly what has been done to the people of Hadiya."

"Hadiya isn't a village. As was demonstrated in an earlier trial, Hadiya is a name used to refer to lands owned by the monastery. Farmers come from a number of villages to work the land and receive wages for their labor."

"What you're saying is fine, Your Honor. However, I would like to ask: when a farmer comes to work on someone else's land, does he build a village and raise livestock? Does he keep dogs there and build two schools, one for boys and the other for girls, as well as a place of worship? As Your Honor knows, a farmer who works someone else's land will bring nothing but his plow at best, and in most cases the plow will be the property of the landowner."

While this conversation was going on, Hashem Shahada was sitting in the corner counting al-Marzuqi's words as the men of the village had told him to do. His heart was racing, and when the word count passed the one hundred mark, his head started to spin so badly he lost track. The sum involved had gone beyond anything he could imagine.

"Your Honor, Hadiya is indeed a village, and is a known entity in the district. It's a village with a history. It existed before the country was divided into districts, and continued to exist thereafter. It existed before the first British soldier arrived in this country. It existed before the first Jewish settler emigrated here. And as proof of what I am saying, I present you with these supporting documents."

Al-Marzuqi then produced the deeds and other papers that Father Elias had returned to Hajj Salem.

It was a bombshell, and by means of it al-Marzuqi was able to cover half the distance to his intended destination. He had demolished the plaintiff's case, leaving the monastery's lawyer so befuddled he couldn't do a thing. As for Father Manuli, he sat at the back of the courtroom following the proceedings with a glassy-eyed stare, his thoughts roaming far and wide in search of an explanation for this utterly unexpected development.

Before those in the courtroom had recovered from the shock, al-Marzuqi asked the judge to allow him to examine witnesses for the defense.

Based on birth certificates that had been brought in, Anisa confirmed that she, her brothers and sisters, and her father and her grandfather had been born in Hadiya. A group of people living in neighboring villages testified that Hadiya had been in existence in their grandfathers' day, and that they had intermarried with the people of Hadiya and shared in their joys and sorrows. Similarly, al-Barmaki was able to show that his son had gone to war on behalf of the Ottoman Empire based on the official documents specifying what village he was from.

They also produced a large number of marriage certificates. As for divorce certificates, they weren't easy to come by, since divorce was rare in those days.

The judge asked the monastery's lawyer to present his case, but he asked for it to be postponed. The judge then issued an order for an inquiry commission to be formed for the purpose of verifying the claims made by the defense.

At the courtroom entrance, Hajj Salem stepped aside with Hashem Shahada.

"Do you know how many words the lawyer has said so far?" he asked.

"Well, Hajj," he stammered, "when I'd counted a hundred words, I started to get dizzy."

"This way we're not going to be giving the man his due. Can't you estimate how many words he said after that?"

"I'd be lying if I said I could."

"Listen, we've still got a long way to go. So pay closer attention next time."

Two nights before the commission's arrival in Hadiya, Shaykh Husni stood on the roof of the mosque and cried, "People of the village! Let those who are present inform those who are absent, and let those who hear this inform those who haven't heard: none of you are allowed to leave the village on Tuesday, the day after tomorrow. Gather your children here. If anyone has a son outside the village, let him send him word to come. And gather all your horses, cattle, camels, sheep, goats, dogs, donkeys, mules, chickens, and even your cats inside your houses."

When Tuesday rolled around, not a soul was left outside of Hadiya, not even Mahmud al-Hajj Khaled, who had come from Jaffa. Like the others, he stood waiting, holding the hands of his son Samir and his daughter Layla, while his wife Afaf stood behind them observing the scene with a look of sorrow on her face.

When the car appeared transporting the commission members, who had been assigned to present a report to the government, Shaykh Husni shouted, "To your houses! We don't want anybody outside his gate! Wait for my signal!"

Within three minutes the car had reached the edge of the village. It came to a halt in the center of the town square.

Three men got out and looked around at the lifeless scene.

"There's nothing but houses," one of them said.

"Where are the people?" another wondered.

The third got out his papers and, leaning against the side of the car, said, "The lawyer's deception has been exposed." But before his pen had touched the blank page before him, Shaykh Husni's voice rang out, "People of Hadiya, open the doors!"

The silence that followed was deafening.

Suddenly, a stream of camels, cattle, horses, sheep, dogs, cats, and chickens came stampeding out, followed by people urging them along. The living torrent roared, sweeping away everything in its path. Realizing that the animals were heading their way, the commission members jumped into the car for refuge. Nevertheless, the torrent overturned it, then went rushing out in all directions. As for the people, they stopped in the square around the car, one of whose wheels was still spinning.

The commission members were in a terrible fright. With difficulty, they managed to climb out through the door on the side of the car, which was now its 'roof.' The first thing they saw was the sky, and when they jumped out with the people's help, the only thing they could say was, "What is this? What is this?"

Hajj Salem replied, "This is Hadiya."

"These cows and horses . . . do they live here?"

"As you can see. They belong to the people of the town."

Many of the young men had gone rushing out to bring the agitated herds back in, and when they brought them back, the commission members were shaking the dust out of their clothes.

"Who does this herd belong to?"

"This one belongs to Iliya Radhi."

"And this one?"

"And this one?"

"And this one?"

The men gathered around and set the car upright again. As it fell onto its wheels, it made an extraordinary racket, as though the torrent were coming through again.

"Couldn't you have found a gentler way to tell us you were here?"

The hearing was scheduled for a week later. Battles were raging all over Palestine, and just getting to the courtroom promised to be a huge adventure. Nevertheless, they decided to go. Al-Marzuqi was waiting for them when they got there.

"We were afraid you might not make it."

"Don't worry about me. In a crisis this dire, nobody finds his way around more easily than a blind man!"

The session was convened hurriedly. The judge ruled that Hadiya belonged to its people and rejected the monastery's claim. When they heard the verdict, the people starting jumping up and down and dancing about.

"Order in the court!" shouted the judge.

They quieted down.

"Your Honor, will you allow me to say one thing about this case?"

"The case has been closed in your favor. What more do you want to say?"

"I wish, Your Honor, that Mr. James Arthur Balfour, who promised the Jews a national homeland in Palestine, could have been here in this courtroom now to hear your ruling, which confirms that Hadiya belongs to its own people. Thank you, Your Honor."

"Court is adjourned."

At the courtroom entrance, Hajj Salem stepped aside with Hashem Shahada and said to him, "Do you know how many words the lawyer spoke in the courtroom this time?"

He replied with a stammer, "I was so worried about what the verdict would be, I forgot to count at all!"

"This way we're not going to be giving the man his due. Can't you estimate how many words he said?"

"I'd be lying if I said I could. But I'll bet it was more than a thousand."

"More than a thousand!"

Hajj Salem went back to the lawyer and said to him, "Things are still in an incredible mess, but since we agreed to a certain condition in the beginning, we're determined to follow through. So I think the time has come for us to pay you your fees."

"It isn't proper to discuss such things in public."

"Where would you be comfortable discussing them?"

"In my office. There's no better place than my office."

"Are you going there when the country's in such chaos?"

"Where else can I go? Home? What's the difference?"

"And now!" said Hajj Salem, "Forgive us for having to ask the question, sir, but how many words did you say in the courtroom?"

"That's a difficult question. In fact, I can't answer it, since I can't talk and count words at the same time! Didn't you assign someone to do that?"

"Yes, we did. But when the number went past a hundred during the first hearing, he got dizzy and couldn't go on. Then, in the second hearing, he was so worried about the verdict, he forgot to count at all!"

"What happened to him during the first hearing is understandable, since it comes out to be quite a large sum. And what happened to him during the second hearing was understandable as well, since I was just as worried as he was. So what if I told you that I'd said a thousand words?"

The men exchanged stunned looks. Then Hajj Salem replied, "You'd be right."

"So then, you would owe me fifty thousand pounds."

"Fifty thousand," repeated more than one voice in muted alarm.

"That's all. Just fifty thousand."

When he noticed the pall of silence that had suddenly descended on them, al-Marzuqi smiled and said, "But given the fact that you supplied many of the deeds and other documents, I'll consider your contribution equal to half the fees due."

"God bless you," said Hajj Salem.

"But I haven't heard anyone else say anything," al-Marzuqi replied. "I'm afraid the others might not be satisfied with this solution!" He was still smiling.

"We won't say no, sir."

Al-Marzuqi took a deep breath, then sat back in his chair. "It seems you still haven't figured out the secret behind the request I made. When I told you I wanted fifty pounds for every word I'd say in the courtroom, I only wanted one thing, namely, to find out whether you were willing to do absolutely anything for your village. True, I restored Hadiya to you. But I also restored it to myself. Or do you think it only belongs to you?"

At that moment the men got tears in their eyes.

The monastery door didn't open for a full ten days. Then a black car drove up. Its driver went hurriedly up to the large gate and knocked five times. Sister Sarah poked her head out, followed by Sister Mary. The driver stepped across the threshold, and when he reappeared, he was carrying two shabby brown suitcases, which he thrust into the trunk of the car. As the car passed through the village, it was easy to see that the two sisters had no desire to look at anyone. And when the car reached that spot where Father Georgiou and Father Theodorus had stopped before, it kept on going till it was out of sight.

Some of the people timorously approached the monastery gate.

But when they heard Hajj Salem's voice saying, "Where are you going?" they came back.

You're asking me about Manuli? No one ever saw him again. And the monastery? It remained closed until it burned down!

A Shell or Two

In the final days of the chaos that was shaking everything to the core, a Jewish convoy drove up, loaded up with arms, and left.

Shawkat Mukhtar was present, and if they had asked him about the matter this time the way they had asked him about it some time earlier, he would have said, "The British are in charge, and this is their property!"

The convoy was heading for Jaffa. As soon as the news got out, men on horseback set off in all directions to inform the neighboring villages. Every village that got the news spread it to the villages next to it, and before long everyone in the region had learned of the matter. Before the convoy had gotten very far, it sensed the danger that surrounded it and headed for protection to the Khalda settlement, which overlooked Wadi al-Sarar and Bayt Mahsir and bordered on the lands belonging to Na'ana, Saydun, Shahma, and Aqir.

A few weeks later, Ali would confide in his father, Hajj Salem, saying, "I can't take the credit this time. It was Shawkat Mukhtar who sent us word that they were coming. He said, "In two days a convoy will be leaving here. So do what you need to do!"*

By eight o'clock in the morning the battle was on, and it lasted until eight o'clock that evening. However, the settlement possessed all the arms that the villagers did not.

Mortar shells began raining down on the attackers, paralyzing their movement.

Ali, Abd al-Jawwad, Salah, and Iliya Radhi decided to approach the driver of an armored car belonging to the Arab army that was standing some distance away and convince him to intervene.

They implored him to fire a shell or two at least.

He refused, saying, "I have no orders." It was a phrase the Palestinians would hear countless times in the days to come on the lips of the soldiers and officers of the Arab Rescue Army.

"Do you need orders in order to do what your conscience dictates, namely, come to this land's defense against the settlers that are threatening it?"

The armored car driver hung his head in shame.

"At the very least you could let one of us use the armored car, and you could teach him how to fire the shells."

"Do you think you can learn how to fire shells and drive an armored car in just a few seconds?"

"All right, then," offered Abd al-Jawwad, "just show me how to fire, and I'll be the one responsible if Shawkat Mukhtar court-martials you later for acting without orders."

"This armored car doesn't belong to Shawkat Mukhtar. It belongs to Glubb Pasha. He's the one who'll court-martial me!"

After half an hour of this sort of back and forth, the driver finally agreed to a solution he found convincing: he would bring the armored car close to the battlefield and aim the cannon at the settlement, then Abd al-Jawwad would be the one to fire. In this way, the armored car driver could swear if he was court-martialed that he hadn't fired!

---

* Shawkat Mukhtar was later to take part in a number of battles in defense of Bab al-Wad, in which units of the Arab army under the command of Field Marshal Habis al-Majali also fought. He lived a long life and was awarded numerous badges of honor.

The armored car driver loaded the cannon and Abd al-Jawwad fired. He reloaded it, Abd al-Jawwad fired again, and so on.

It came as a huge surprise to the other side when the shells began raining down on the settlement from weaponry they hadn't known was there. When one of the shells destroyed the water tank, the attackers, to their amazement, saw a white flag go up.

With the firing of those shells the tide began gradually to turn, and the attackers were infused with fervor. Rushing toward the settlement from all directions, they stormed it and seized its weapons after those who were inside it had withdrawn.

The night before the battle, four men carrying rifles arrived in Hadiya. They asked where the guesthouse was, and people gave them directions. They were received by Hajj Salem. The hour was late. Supper was prepared for them. Hajj Salem brought them some things of his own to put on, then we lit a fire and dried their rain-drenched clothes. When they'd finished their supper, Hajj Salem asked them, "And who might our guests be?" One of them said, "I'm Harun bin Jazi," who was a renowned fighter. "And this is Muhammad al-Fayez." I don't recall the names of the two other men. Hajj Salem asked them what had brought them to Hadiya in such rainy weather, and Harun replied, "We've come from the Transjordan to take part in the fighting." This caused us to feel a lot of respect for them. The next morning we slaughtered a sheep for them, but when they learned of the convoy headed for Jaffa, they exclaimed, "How can we sit here eating when others are dying?" Then they went with us to where the battle was going on. When the battle was over, I pointed to the rifles, bullets, and other weapons we had taken as booty and said to them, "These are yours. Take whatever you want." Harun replied, "All we wanted was to help you." I said, "Let's go back to the house so that you can eat. Your food is still waiting for you there." But Harun said, "We'll go look for some other area in Palestine that might need us." Just then they heard the sound of gunfire in the distance. "We know where to head now," said Muhammad Fayez. And we watched them until they disappeared.

It was a battle the likes of which they'd never experienced before. Abd al-Fattah Milhim, Muhammad As'ad, Hashem Shahada, and Iliya Radhi were wounded, and a number of the men who had come from other villages were martyred.

"That battle was history," Hajj Salem kept saying. For until that time, all the battles had been waged in secret.

"I've Found It!" He Cried

The news was late in arriving: "A British convey will be passing through Hadiya tomorrow morning to supply the settlement on the eastern hills with weapons."

Like many others, this settlement had endured successive night raids, as a result of which some of its residents had fled to Tel Aviv.

Of course, in a case like this, mines could easily have solved the problem of the convoy. However, getting hold of a single mine was a major challenge. As for getting hold of several of them, it was an impossibility.

They tried to think of a way to destroy the convoy and everyone in it. They thought of sending news to the rebels, but they knew how dangerous it was to move around in the mountains by night. Consequently, whoever went to deliver the news was bound to run into either a patrol, a British or Jewish ambush, or the rebels themselves.

Muhammad Shahada hesitated for quite a while before saying what he was thinking. However, it had taken them so long to arrive at a solution that he finally felt compelled to speak his mind.

Their first reaction was to say, "And who could possibly carry all those ashes there?"

His response was: "Everybody could. Wasn't everybody punished once on account of a single bullet that was fired from the village onto a British patrol? Or have you forgotten?"

They began by deciding where they would surround the convoy. The spot they chose was no more than three kilometers from the houses on the outskirts of Hadiya. It was a road that ran between two small hills, and its sides were so steep that it would be difficult for the soldiers to climb them if they wanted to go in pursuit of anyone.

Once the initial work was done, all the young men of the village would have to do would be to light the fire.

The first jeep in the convoy stopped before it reached the barrier they had placed on the road. A British officer got out and gestured to the cars behind him to stop as well.

The soldiers got out of the vehicles, their weapons drawn, and examined the sides of the road. They smelled something strange, but to their surprise found no one. There was nothing but a profound silence at that early morning hour. And there was nothing but the wind, which seemed to be blowing from all directions.

When the soldiers began taking down the barrier, they heard a movement behind them. Turning around, they saw rocks rolling down and blocking the road. Then they saw torches falling onto the asphalt from the sides of the road. It was perplexing, since it seemed that whoever was throwing them was blind. Otherwise, why would they be throwing them so far from the vehicles? Nevertheless, the soldiers began firing. In a few moments, they saw the fire creeping toward them. They saw the road itself burning, and were mystified. The fire was advancing rapidly in the direction of the vehicles. Realizing that the fire would soon consume the cars, the soldiers clung to the shoulders of the road. The flames stole under the armored cars, then continued to the first jeep. When the soldiers had reached the peak of their bewilderment, they saw one of the jeeps fly into the air as its fuel tank exploded, and before long the flames were consuming everything they touched. Yet even this wasn't the most difficult thing. They realized that within moments the ammunition would begin exploding. Some of them sprang toward the front of the convoy in an attempt to cross the barrier in front of the leading car, oblivious to any danger that might lie beyond it. The soldiers near the barrier in the rear did the same.

Not a single bullet had been fired in their direction, which made it more nightmarish than real. Screaming at them to flee, their eyes were fixed on those who had been surrounded by the flames.

The sky was ablaze, and the sound of explosions filled the air.

The people who heard and saw what happened that day could hardly believe there were this many bullets and shells in the world!

At last the settlers came to the convoy's rescue with their weapons. But by that time it was too late. They approached with caution, certain that they would surround those who had surrounded the convoy, but they found no one. Thinking the battle must be taking place face to face, they approached with even greater caution. More than one shell fell near them, and they withdrew a short distance. The fire was so intense it was impossible to advance any farther.

When everything finally quieted down, they crawled back, and there was nothing in the small, narrow valley but burning vehicles.

An hour later, a large British force arrived and encircled the area before determining what had happened. Everything that had taken place pointed to a battle like scores of others they had seen. Two airplanes appeared, flying low to the ground, but nothing became clearer. And when they asked the surviving soldiers what had happened, things appeared more mysterious than ever.

One of the soldiers said, "We didn't see anybody. All we saw was the ground burning under us."

Another said, "No, we didn't hear any explosions. There were no mines. Just burning ground."

None of their attempts to dispel the mystery surrounding this battle-that-was-no-battle yielded anything whatsoever.

They raided Hadiya and all the surrounding villages, but to no avail. They arrested scores of men, but found out nothing.

At nightfall, after dragging sixteen incinerated vehicles to one side of the road, the British forces withdrew. However, the echoes and flashes of the explosions would go on filling the dome of sky that curved over that region for a long time to come.

Muhammad Shahada, who had managed to hide some distance away with other men of the village, went back to the spot, incredulous over the outcome of what they had done. As far as he was concerned, it was no less revolutionary than the invention of gunpowder. It had been tantamount to inventing another type of gunpowder that no one had ever thought of before: a type they had been accustomed to casting to the wind to carry it far from the ovens and stoves where, to housewives' dismay, it was constantly accumulating.

On that day, of course, Muhammad Shahada seemed to be the most ingenious person they had ever laid eyes on!

He said to the people of Hadiya, "The convoy will arrive before the rebels do. But there's got to be a solution."

"What sort of solution do you have in mind, O wise one?"

"There's always a solution. The only question is: will we be able to figure it out or not? That's our problem right now."

As he spoke, he looked over and saw Umm al-Far shoveling the ashes out of her bread oven, and suddenly he cried, "I've found it!"

Fortunately, no one raised any objections.

All through the night, the women, men, and children worked to bring ashes from all over the village. They collected them into four small piles along the edge of the road at the specified location. Then they brought all the crude oil they could find and proceeded to knead it into the ashes. Lastly, they spread it all along the area where they expected the convoy to stop in front of the first barrier. By the end of the night, everyone was back home again. They were so black, you couldn't have told them apart. However, some of the men—their features concealed beneath layers of ashes—stayed behind.

All they had to do now was to light the fire. What happened that day, I'll never forget. Never!

Jaffa to Jerusalem

Y ou're putting me in an awkward position," Lieutenant Abd al-Mun'im said to Naji. "How can I transfer you to Jerusalem when it's already been decided to transfer you to Jaffa?"

"I like the city. Besides, I have relatives there that I could stay with," said Naji.

"You like the city. I can understand that. But don't say you have relatives there, since we never send anyone to a place where he has relatives, or to the district where his hometown is located."

Lieutenant Abd al-Mun'im went to Mr. Kemen and said, "To Jaffa. He can't go anywhere else."

The cars headed for Gaza, Hebron, Safad, Nablus, and Haifa had left, and the cars heading for Jerusalem and Jaffa were the only ones still waiting.

Abd al-Mun'im came back. "Mr. Kemen has rejected your request."

"I'd sooner die than get into the car going to Jaffa."

In the face of Naji's insistence, he went back again to Mr. Kemen. "8410 insists on going to Jerusalem."

A short while later, Mr. Kemen and Abd al-Mun'im appeared. "OK. We'll send you to Jerusalem, but you'll be on probation. If it becomes apparent that you're going there for some reason we don't know about, I'll make sure you're transferred to the remotest point in the country, to the Safad district. Understood?"

"Understood, Mr. Kemen. You can be sure I only want to be in that city because I love it, and if I wanted to be in another district, I would have chosen the one my village is in."

"To Jerusalem, then. And while you're there, don't be anything less than what you've been here. The way we've known you. I'm going to recommend that you be awarded two stripes, and until you're officially promoted, you'll have the rank of reserve sergeant."

After he had been working for several days at the Talibiya station, they decided to transfer him to the military court as a guard. Armed clashes were growing steadily worse, and the Jews were spreading terror among the Palestinians in a variety of ways.

Then one day, a certain report began to spread like wildfire: "The Jews have written Hajj Amin al-Husayni's name on a donkey, and they're taking it down one street after another through the Mahane Yehuda Market."

The people were in an uproar. Chaos reigned. The Palestinians began gathering for an attack on the Shamma'a Market, where a good number of Jewish jewelry and woolen-goods shops were located.

The news was quick to reach the British police, who decided to send out a force, of which Naji was a member. Before it moved out, the British lieutenant, Antony, made the following peculiar statement: "If they want to burn the market down, don't intervene! If, on the other hand, they want to loot it, you should prevent them by force."

The people did not, in fact, loot the market. They burned it down. And no one on the British police force intervened to prevent it.

Those were Britain's final days in Palestine, and everybody knew it. All the British cared about any more was to be able to withdraw with minimal losses.

Naji had settled in the home of Hajj Abu Salim (Amal's father) in Montefiore. Hajj Abu Salim occupied one side of the large house, while a Christian family and a Jewish family rented the other. As for Naji, he lived in two rooms that were joined by a stone staircase in the small courtyard, which was divided down the middle by a rickety wooden partition.

Before Naji got to the house, he discovered that Hajj Abu Salim and his wife had been evicted. They were standing in the street, shouting and pleading with people to intervene.

"Where are you going?" they asked him. "They're turning everybody out!"

However, their words didn't prevent him from continuing toward the house. Not long afterward, he saw the Christian Sam'an family dragging their children out of the house with terror etched on their faces.

"Where are you going?" Sam'an asked him. "The Haganah forces have come and taken over the house. No one's left inside but the Jewish family, and they told us, 'If you want to survive, take whatever you can carry of your things and leave. If you stay here, you're dooming yourselves to death.'"

"All my clothes and other things are inside the house. I'm going to get them no matter what happens," said Naji, who was wearing his military uniform.

Before he could get inside, however, one of the Haganah forces looked out the window of Naji's room and recognized him. Suddenly, he drew his weapon and fired. Naji stepped back.

"The bastard was shooting to kill, not just to scare me," muttered Naji, agitated.

"It's all right, we'll get your stuff," Lieutenant Antony replied.

"Do you really think it's just a matter of getting some stuff back? What will I say to Hajj Abu Salim? The Jews have occupied his house, and I promised him you would help him."

"In cases like this we can't do a thing. The orders are clear: that is, there aren't any orders." Turning to a number of the military police, he said, "Get an armored car, then go in with him and get his clothes."

When the armored car arrived, the Haganah forces retreated, and it was as if they weren't there any more.

Naji went into the courtyard, where he saw the Sam'an family's clothing and other belongings thrown outside. The Jewish family removed the wooden partition and observed the scene from both their apartment and that of the Sam'an family. They had occupied the entire place with extraordinary speed.

Sha'ul, the sixty-year-old head of the Jewish family, came out and walked up to Naji. "There's no need for you to go upstairs. We've put your things over in that corner, right behind you."

Naji turned around. They had put his belongings beside the door. "Take them and go in peace. If you want my advice, you'd be better off not stopping till you get to Transjordan."

Naji stooped down to pick up some things belonging to the Sam'an family so as to give them back to them. "No. Leave them where they are," Sha'ul said. "If they want any of it, they'll have to come get it themselves. But believe me, they won't get anything even if they show up in an armored car the way you have. This is the last time anybody comes back here to get something by force!"

On the other side of the house, the Haganah men were waiting for the armored car to withdraw before they reappeared. At the end of the street, Hajj Abu Salim's family stood waiting.

"What happened?"

"They've occupied the house," Naji replied. "They've thrown everything out in the courtyard, and they won't let anybody come back and get anything. I think you should go to Hadiya until the situation becomes clearer."

"If this is happening in Jerusalem, do you think the situation in Hadiya will be any better?"

A few days later, the Haganah forces began harassing the guards. At the same time, the British police began taking weapons away from their Arab personnel and supplying them with nothing but clubs.

Naji refused to perform his duties without a weapon. He was seconded by Sudanese Lieutenant Ahmad Mabruk, who said, "I'm not going out to make myself an easy target for the Jews' bullets."

As far as Naji was concerned, he now had one duty to perform— to make off with the guards' weapons.

They objected, saying, "You're going to get us into trouble that's bigger than we are!"

"Don't worry, I'll find a solution."

At the police station there were fourteen rifles, six revolvers, a Bern machine gun, and a flare gun.

"The revolvers will be yours. As for the Bern, the ammunition, and the rifles, we need them in Hadiya."

He got to Hadiya a little before midnight and explained to Hajj Salem what was going on in Jerusalem. Then he told him about his plan: "These weapons are our only hope," he said to his uncle. "I just need somebody to help me."

The following night, a car pulled up in front of the courtyard and three men from Hadiya got out. They tied up the guards, and Naji along with them. Then they took the weapons and went back to where they'd come from.

At dawn, a British patrol passed by. When they saw that the guards weren't in their places, they were bewildered. The soldiers got out quickly, drawing their weapons. As soon as those inside heard their steps approaching, they began shouting. The soldiers on the patrol came in and found the guards tied up with their faces to the floor.

They weren't able to convince Lieutenant Antony of their story.

"How could anyone have overcome all of you?" he wanted to know. "How is it that not one of you was able to defend himself? There's something fishy going on!"

They led them off to a jail cell: "You'll stay here until the truth comes out."

Two weeks later they released them, then redeployed them to various locations. Thus it was that Naji found himself in the Kashla Prison, looking for a way to escape.

The Tower

The settlement's two towers suddenly disappeared. Everybody noticed it. The two towers had become a part of the settlement, a part nobody could imagine it being without. People didn't understand. How could such a thing happen when gunfire was coming at it from all directions?

"They're leaving. Now that they know the rescue armies are on their way, they must have decided to leave."

"But if they're planning to leave, what do they need with the two towers? People who leave take the things they need. Maybe they'll take those houses of theirs that fell out of the sky all of a sudden. But the towers . . . ?"

Then, in what seemed like a miracle, they saw another tower growing up in place of the northern tower. It was rising from the ground and getting higher and broader before their unbelieving eyes. They didn't see anyone outside the tower, so they concluded that all the work was being done from the inside. Within three days it was higher than any building in the village, and even higher than any of the surrounding hills. From its top, cannon muzzles peered out like someone squinting in an attempt to see more clearly.

"They'll never be able to enjoy anything they build here as long as the rescue armies are coming," said Hajj Salem.

"Your thinking is so strange, nephew," Anisa said to him. "It's as if you haven't learned anything from what happened in 1936. Even though you've vilified them till you're blue in the face, you still relate to Arab leaders like the Bedouin in the story about the basket of figs!"

"What do you mean?" he asked.

"Once upon a time," she said, "a Bedouin went out to the mountains before sunrise with his herd and took a basket of figs with him. As the morning went by, he ate quite a few of the figs, thinking that someone would be bringing his lunch to him at noon. He looked at the figs and started bad-mouthing them: 'Lousy, rotten figs!' He even pissed on them! By noontime he was hungry, but nobody came. He waited a while longer, but still no lunch arrived. He got up and started looking regretfully at the basket of figs. Then he said, 'I'll bet no urine got on this one.' Then he ate it. He did the same with the next one and the next one until they were all gone."

After finishing her story, she fell silent for a while, then added, "If you'd just eaten the figs in the beginning, I would have said, 'It must have been God's will.' But what you're eating now is, if you'll pardon my language, shit!"

Before the sun had risen over the village's squares and the corners of its courtyards, they heard a single shot. A few seconds later, they heard screaming.

No one but those out in the square knew what was happening. They saw a man wallowing in his blood, his face in the dirt. They turned him over. It was Tamim Abu Diyya. A bullet had gone through his heart. They looked around to see where it had come from, but didn't see anything. In the distance the settlement was calm, and the tower's stones were illumined by the morning light.

Next day, the same thing happened. In the other neighborhood, near the entranceway to Abu Ribhi's corner store, a woman screamed, then fell to the ground. They ran over to her. It was Layla Hassan, Umm Nayef. They tried to remember whether they had heard gunfire before she screamed. They looked in all directions, but there was no one to be found. The tower seemed so quiet, and the distance that separated it from the spot where she had fallen was so great, it seemed impossible that it would have had anything to do with what had happened.

On the third day no one was shot. Everything was so calm, they began to think that what had happened on the two previous days had been nothing but a nightmare. But then they remembered that they had marched in the two victims' funeral processions.

On the fourth day, a shot rang out. No one could have helped but hear it, since they were paying closer attention now. Abdallah Rashid fell near the entrance to the wheat mill. His wife, Turkiya Musa, cried out, then burst into sobs over his lifeless body. Then she stood up and began crying for help. But while her cry was still on her lips, another shot came, and she fell on top of her husband's corpse. Everyone in the village went rushing over to them, though they did so warily. They were both dead.

Jabr Darwish confirmed that the shot had been fired from the tower. Yes, from the tower, and nowhere else. He had seen its flash. No one could believe that anybody could hit a target from the distance that separated the settlement's barbed-wire fence from the houses on the outskirts of Hadiya.

He said, "I'll go check it out myself before sunrise. I'll go watch and see."

Abbas Rashid said to him, "I'll go with you. I can't let my brother and his wife die in vain."

When the sun had risen, they heard a shot. Jabr's head had appeared from behind the large boulder he had chosen as his observation post. The bullet passed directly under his right eye. He fell back, and his head dropped on Abbas' shoulder. Spattered with blood and fragments of flesh and bone, Abbas tried to speak, but before he could say a word, the people in the village heard the second shot. The bullet passed directly under his left eye. Blood and fragments of flesh and bone scattered over the dirt behind him.

All signs of movement in the village streets disappeared.

On the seventh day, a force from the rescue army arrived. Its commander, Wasef Bashir, met with Hajj Salem and the village elders.

"From now on there will be no guerrilla warfare," he announced, with a confidence that astounded them. "It's a war between armies, and nothing else."

"But the Jews fight us as gangs more than they do as armies. So why can't we do the same thing? Besides, why are you depriving us of our right to defend our homes?"

"The orders are clear. The only warfare that will be allowed here is between armies."

They gathered all the weapons they could get their hands on and began digging trenches all along the front of the settlement in the area between the borders of the village and the barbed wire. Then they joined the long trench they had dug to the village with a new zigzag trench.

It was a mystery to them all that none of those who had dug the trenches had been fired at.

Nevertheless, death knocked once again at the village's doors when twelve-year-old Yahya Ayyad was killed. They went to Wasef Bashir, but he did nothing, and over a period of four days, the same kind of incident repeated itself.

Hajj Salem stormed in to see him. But before he had uttered a word, he discovered to his alarm that the officer was crying.

"What's the matter?"

"Every day I see someone killed and I can't do anything! What sort of humiliation is this?"

"Let us take care of it. We'll find a solution."

"And what will you do?"

"Leave it to us."

Wasef Bashir said nothing more. As for Hajj Salem, he didn't go back home after their meeting. Instead, he went straight to the house of Aziza's son Husayn.

"Listen, son, we need you," his uncle said to him. "You've got to find us a way to destroy that tower."

"Not to worry. I've been thinking about it myself. We'll blow it up."

"And how will we do that?"

"I have a friend by the name of Isma'il al-Ghalayini who knows how to make mines. I'll go see him and ask him to make me a mine that will take care of our problem once and for all."

"Where does he live?"

"In Hebron."

"And who can get all the way to Hebron these days?"

"I'll manage, then come right back."

That evening, Husayn came back from Hebron accompanied by al-Ghalayini himself.

He told Husayn, "I won't be able to make the mine unless I see the tower myself."

The next morning, he examined the tower from a distance. "Now I can get to work," he said.

Hajj Salem went to Wasef Bashir and announced, "Today we'll relieve everyone of this demon."

"But don't forget that the settlement is under both British and Jewish protection."

"The guys will find a solution."

The mine was ready shortly before dawn. Al-Ghalayini said, "I'll go with you."

"Your job here is finished, and I know this area better than you do," Husayn objected.

"All right, then, I'll escort you as far as I can to make sure things go all right."

They walked inside the tunnels as far as they could. Then they started crawling. Al-Ghalayini hid behind a large boulder and whispered to Husayn, "Don't forget anything I've told you."

"Don't worry."

❀

The tower's entrance was on the other side, and behind it there was a small forest. Husayn crawled around to the entrance. No one was there. Everything was quiet. He went in. As soon as he was inside, the door suddenly closed behind him. He tried to open it, but couldn't. He felt a movement coming from somewhere. Terrified, he looked down and saw a door opening under his feet as a shot was fired. The bullet grazed his cheek and then ricocheted off the stairwell ceiling. He began fleeing up the stairs, the mine in his hand. The trap had closed on him completely. Looking down, he saw a stream of bullets being fired his way. He took one of the grenades he was carrying and pulled out the pin. Then he threw it. He heard it collide with the edges of the stairs, and within moments it exploded.

He kept climbing the stairs with all the strength he could muster. It was a winding staircase that coiled upward along the tower's inner walls. Consequently, he could see the bottom easily if he leaned out over the railing.

He could feel the warmth of the blood gushing out onto his face and neck. When he realized that no one was following him, he decided to turn back. When he was halfway back down, he heard the door opening again and the sound of a shot ringing out. The sound it made was dreadful inside that narrow, closed space.

He threw another grenade, and the blast it produced was no less dreadful.

He placed the mine near the ground-floor entrance and lit the fuse. Then he ran back up as fast as he could. Standing now at the tower's periphery, he had no choice but to jump. The doors of Hell opened as bullets went whizzing through the air all around him. When he landed on the small mound of red dirt at the bottom of the tower, he realized he hadn't died, that he was still alive. Yet it still took him a few moments to believe it.

The sun wasn't up yet, but there was enough light for any movement to be detected.

He kept on crawling till he reached the place where he had left al-Ghalayini waiting for him.

"You need first aid right away."

"What first aid? The mine didn't go off."

"Don't worry. I designed it not to go off right away so that I could make sure you got out of the tower safely."

Husayn was pressing on the wound with his palm, but it was bleeding badly.

"It looks as though the mine's no good."

"I told you not to worry."

Before he'd finished uttering his last word, a tremendous explosion rang out. Rocks began falling everywhere, nearly crushing them.

"Now!" said al-Ghalayini.

They took off running, and kept going till they reached the trenches without a single shot being fired at them. The power of the explosion astounded everyone. Sounds of jubilation could be heard coming from Hadiya, and they kept growing louder until, by sunrise, they had turned into an out-and-out celebration.

People had experienced so much sorrow, they didn't know what to do with all that joy!

Hajj Salem went to see the officer, but before he'd had a chance to say what he'd come for, the officer stood up and said, "Let's go for a little walk."

After a long silence, Hajj Salem asked, "What is it? It seems there's something so big you don't know how to say it!"

The officer still didn't say anything.

Then at last he spoke. "Yesterday we received orders to withdraw, but I don't know when it will be. A truce has been declared."

"A truce? What truce? These armies that have come to fight, what have they done? Have they just come to confiscate our weapons?"

"I'll give you back the weapons we've taken from you. I'll bear responsibility for that. But that's all I can offer."

In the distance, one could hear the sounds of vehicles approaching. They stopped at the edge of the long trench. The vehicles were carrying officers from the rescue army and observers from the United Nations, who went and held a meeting with the Israelis in the settlement. Two hours later they came back.

"From now on, this trench will be the settlement's border!"

It was the first time the villagers had seen the settlers close up. They came out and went into the trenches. The sandbags that had been prepared by the rescue army were at the end of the trench opposite the settlement, and the Jews began moving them to the end opposite the village.

One of the soldiers in the rescue army grabbed his rifle and broke it against a boulder. Then he began to cry.

"Why did you do that?" shouted Wasef Bashir.

"This rifle was broken even before I did anything to it."

Hadiya by Night

aji was the last person to reach Hadiya. As for his brother Mahmud, he found himself naked and alone, just the way they had left him in that square on the day when he had delivered a speech on behalf of Salim Bek al-Hashemi. By this time, the roads had become impassable, and Ramla, Lod, Jaffa, and Haifa had all fallen. When he received a letter from Layla telling him that she would be flying with her family to Beirut, he felt even more naked in the midst of the jostling crowds. Some people were heading for the sea, some for the north, and some for Ramallah and Bethlehem. But before doing any of those things himself, he succumbed to an overwhelming longing to visit Clock Square. There, in front of what remained of the Saray Building where he used to wait for Layla, he stood like a pillar of salt. The building had been destroyed four months earlier by a booby-trapped car the Jews had parked in a nearby alleyway, killing the scores of people who were in it that day.[*]

---

[*] The Zionists had begun resorting to new ways of quelling the Palestinian uprising. Such methods included bombing coffee shops (in Jerusalem, for example, on 17 March 1937)

In front of a demolished building and a no-longer-existent door, he stood waiting.

He took out her letter again and read it more than once. Then he decided to head north.

Naji reached Hadiya that evening, the rifle he had fled with in hand. The battles in Jerusalem were at their height, but everything reeked of defeat.*

When the taxi he had hired reached the hills overlooking the village, the driver said to him, "This is as far as I can go."

"Why?"

"Look over there."

The shock was almost unbearable. Many of the houses in the village were going up in flames.

He got out of the car. There was nothing but silence.

"Lots of things have happened over the past few days," the driver told him. "All I can tell you is: keep away from the paved road, and be careful."

Leaving the road behind him, he headed east, then turned south. Then he turned and headed west again.

---

and planting time bombs in markets crowded with Palestinians (these were used for the first time against the Palestinians of Haifa on 6 July 1938). When the British were obliged to reduce their support for the Zionist enterprise after putting down the Palestinian uprising in 1939, they themselves became targets of Zionist attacks. This was a decisive moment in the history of British-Zionist relations, since the Zionist response was to assassinate British government officials, take British citizens hostage, blow up British government offices and murder government employees and other civilians. They blew up the British Embassy in Rome in 1946 and cars parked near government buildings, killed hostages in retaliation against practices of the British government, and sent booby-trapped letters and parcels to British politicians in London. The mastermind behind these attacks, particularly the bombings of Arabs' markets, coffee shops and cars, was Menahem Begin, who would later become Israeli Prime Minister.

* Lieutenant Ghazi al-Harbi of the Arab (Jordanian) Army led a bold attack from Bab al-Amud on the Notre Dame Building with cover from the forces beyond the wall and a number of armored cars. He successfully occupied the building. However, an order to withdraw was issued by his British commander, Major General Goldie. This was after the detachment had lost nineteen men. The detachment's sergeant, Fayyad Dahilan of the Huwaytat clan, along with eight other soldiers, protested and joined the rebels. Ghazi al-Harbi then received orders to return to Amman. When the Arab army's artillery subjected all the Jewish quarters in New Jerusalem to heavy gunfire, the artillery commander, Lieutenant Colonel Muhammad al-Mu'ayita, was placed under arrest, replaced by Major Pollock, and sent back to Amman to be tried on charges of wasting ammunition.

There was no one. Fire was consuming many of the houses. Dead bodies filled the streets. When he came to the place where his house had been, he didn't find it. It had been blown up. Nothing was left of it but scattered rocks. He began digging with his hands in a search for some clue as to what had happened and what had become of his wife and children.

There was nothing but ruins.

He headed up to his father's house.

The attackers had apparently not managed to get that far. Even so, the dovecote was in a state of bedlam, with birds fretfully landing, then flying away, landing, then flying away.

He made the rounds of the village, but found no sign of life.

He went up to the roof of the school. He was crying. He remembered the rifle in his hand. He looked in the direction of the settlement, and silenty awaited the enemy forces.

The sounds of gunfire and explosions filled the air. What he had thought was coming from the south, moments later he would discover was coming from the east, and from time to time the horizon would be lit up by a mute explosion that would quickly vanish like lightning.

He no longer knew which way to go. There was nothing but the settlement, with its constant stream of cars coming and going.

When it was nearly dawn, he dozed off for a few brief moments. He saw the people of Hadiya rushing out from all directions. He saw the car that the court had sent out with the members of the inquiry commission as it turned over in the middle of the city square. He woke up. He looked around him. No one was there.

He thought of sneaking into the settlement and attacking it, then dying like all the others who had died.

He came down from the roof and walked down the street. Abu Ribhi's corner store was open. He heard a sound, a strange movement. It was the first movement he had encountered since his arrival. He took a few steps back, ready for anything. Then a tired-looking figure appeared.

"Stay where you are!" shouted Naji.

The figure froze in its tracks. "I'm Ribhi!"

"Ribhi! What are you doing here?"

"I'm looking for something we could use to keep the little ones quiet in the vineyards and orchards."

"What's happened?"

"No time to tell you now. Take this bag and follow me."

We went to sleep, sure that there was an army to protect us. The next morning when I went to prayer, I sensed a strange movement. The area where the rescue army had been the night before was completely empty. It was as if the earth had opened up and swallowed them.* There wasn't a soul left. After I got to the mosque, I heard strange sounds. I knew right away it was the Jews. I went into the mosque and said, "Shaykh Husni, go up to the roof of the mosque and warn people. The Jews have arrived. Go up!" But before he could finish saying, "Listen, people! The Jews have entered the village . . . !" he was hit by a bullet. That was the first gunshot. Those who had been killed before that had been killed by axes and cleavers. I think he was still on the roof of the mosque. I fled, and was followed by gunfire. I tried to get to the Bern that I'd brought. When I got there, people in the village were awake and everybody took to the streets, carrying whatever they could get their hands on to ward off the attack. Salim Aql arrived with the rifle, and I said to him, "They're behind me." He stationed himself in the corner of the guesthouse and started firing. As if they'd been taken by surprise, they stopped charging, and there was nothing but gunfire. Two bombs went off. I don't know where. I heard screaming coming from everywhere, as if shrapnel had wounded everybody around. The Bern was in its place, inside the wall, as you know. I removed the layer of mud and pulled on the cloth that was wrapped around it.

The entire village square was before me. There was no light at all, as if the entire night had been concentrated there in the square. But I could still see. Or maybe I wasn't seeing. Maybe I was just hearing, but it seemed as though I could see the sound that was moving from place to place. When I fired the first volley, I realized I'd hit one of them.

---

* Fawzi al-Qawuqji's success in putting an end to the 1936 uprising had a significant part to play in the unanimous decision made later by Arab kings and leaders to appoint him field commander of the rescue army. After this army entered Palestine, King Abdullah of Jordan granted him the title of 'Pasha.' But beginning on 15 May 1948, he withdrew to Syria over a period of three days, leaving the army's positions to the Iraqi and Jordanian armies. Then he returned and amassed his troops in south Lebanon, and entered the region of Galilee in northern Palestine.

I don't know whether I killed him. In any case, I was happy when gunfire came from the other side, since, for a moment, I'd been afraid that the shots I had fired had been directed at the villagers rather than at the Jews. Not long after that, everything got mixed up. The men began clashing with them face to face, but how could anybody tell whether the person in front of him was his son or his enemy? We were fighting the air, fighting everything, fighting ourselves. Then an explosion rang out in the distance, in the other neighborhood, and flames rose toward the sky. I thought to myself: Sabri al-Najjar's livestock pen must be on fire. And it was. Where had the rescue army gone? I don't know. Nobody knows. How could it have withdrawn without our noticing? They'd left like thieves in the night and turned the country over to the Jews as it slept. I came out carrying the Bern and went running after the attackers. I saw them withdrawing. They fired in my direction, but I couldn't feel a thing any more. I was running in order to drive them away, just to drive them away. I was firing as if I wanted to scare them, not to kill them. When I thought back on it later, it was confusing. In any case, I caught up with one of them, and he aimed his rifle at me. At the same time, I felt he was aiming not at me, but at somebody else. He pulled the trigger, but the rifle was empty. He threw it down. It might have shattered my skull if it had hit me. He fled. I stood there watching him run away. A few moments later, I came out of my stupor and fired at him. I killed him. I didn't know whether he was still under the window of Sa'id Muhammad's house or not. I went back and saw five rifles in the men's hands. They weren't our rifles. Suwaylim Abdallah had gotten into an argument with Hasan Shahada and Jamal Ribhi. One of them would say, "This rifle is mine!" and that one would say, "No, it's mine!" I asked them where it had been thrown down. They said, "Over there." I said, "That rifle nearly shattered my head when somebody threw it at me. So it's mine." They didn't say anything. Suwaylim handed the rifle to me. "Who knows how to use it well?" I asked. "I do," replied Hasan. I handed it to him. Hasan asked me, "Have you seen my father?" "No," I said. Suddenly, he started running toward his father's house. "Wait!" I said. "We've got to move out carefully to find out where they've gone. All we have with us are thirteen rifles and this Bern that you see." Whenever we got to a house, we would hear crying and screaming. There were people being killed all over. They had attacked while people were sleeping, whereas we thought we were being protected by the rescue army. But it was our fault, because we'd forgotten—how could we have forgotten?—that they'd deceived us in 1936. How, how could we have forgotten? They'd sent us armies formed and led by the British to fight against the British and Jews who were being protected by the British. So how could we have believed them?*

We went into Muhammad Shahada's house and found him dead on top of the corpse of one of the attackers. We tried to lift him, but we couldn't. His hands were wrapped like a vise around the neck of the Jewish man who lay under him. Apparently, he hadn't had a weapon near at hand when he saw the attacker, so he had thrown himself at him. With difficulty, we pried his hands off the man's neck, and found that the Jew had shot him with the revolver that was in his hand. He'd shot him five times, I swear. We saw the bullet holes in Muhammad Shahada's body. Inside, we found that the whole family had been killed. It was then that we realized that Muhammad hadn't died with him. Maybe he'd been in another room, and when he came back and saw what had happened to his family, he attacked the Jew.

We knew they'd come in from the north, too, and killed Ghazala Nimr and her six children, and her sister Aliya Nimr and her five children. All of them had been killed in their sleep, including Nahar al-Jasem, who was seventy years old, and his younger brother Ahmad al-Jasem. Raja al-Faris, who was blind and didn't know where to go, had been shot in bed, and Yusuf Mahmud couldn't move, since his foot was broken. Then there were Hamed Khalil, Husni, Amsha al-Sa'ub, an elderly lady, Ahmad Ayid, and Adla, Muhammad al-Khalil's wife . . . all of them, all of them . . .

We said: They'll be back. Be careful, people, they'll be back! And next time they'll strike even harder, now that they know we have weapons. I told them to take the children and go out into the hills, the plantations, and the vineyards. "What matters is to get them away from here. They'll be back, and they won't have mercy on anyone."

---

* Throughout the entire year that preceded the Catastrophe of 1948, there were only two members of the Arab Higher Committee in Palestine. The 'leadership' preferred to leave quietly and elegantly before the huge flood hit. Its ringing pronouncements—coming from outside the country—urged people to be calm, and praised the Arabs' 'admirable' efforts. These pronouncements were a prime example of the worst possible type of political subterfuge, since they were at complete odds with the political decisions being made at that time.

War Casualties

The Israeli forces had blocked the progress of an Egyptian detachment from the rescue army between Qabiba and Hadiya. The part east of Qabiba then headed for Hebron, while the part to its west headed for Iraq al-Manshiya. The Israeli forces then attacked between Iraq Suwaydan and Majdal, forcing part of the army to seek refuge in Hadiya.*

There were more than a thousand officers and soldiers, and when they entered the village they started to cry. They helped those who had stayed in the village to bury their slain, and Commander Ayyub Abduh asked the

---

* A memorable event of that time was the decision of one division of the rescue army to bomb another unit from the same army for attacking an Israeli settlement near Gaza without asking for its permission first. The former unit then ordered the latter to retreat! In short, there was no coordination among the Arab armies, and leadership on the highest level was virtually nonexistent. It became apparent in many cases that our weapons were defunct, and at the height of hostilities, the rescue army's corps of engineers received orders to build a chalet in Gaza for King Faruq. At one point I received orders to lead a force from the Sixth Infantry Batallion to Iraq Suwaydan, which was under attack by the Israelis, but before we set out, our movements in full were published in Cairo's newspapers!

men to go get their families and bring them back from the mountains and orchards. Before the first family's arrival, he gave orders for the village to be fortified with two parallel barbed-wire fences, and for the space between them to be mined. New trenches were dug other than those that had been handed over to the Israelis, and in less than two days, sheds for the cannons had been prepared. The front and rear positions were joined with telephone lines, and the soldiers were deployed in the small vegetable gardens and plantations surrounding the village. He also instructed his soldiers not to fire a single shot unless they had seen the enemy at close enough range to guarantee that they could hit their mark.

"If you don't withdraw, we'll consider you war casualties!"

The central command's reply to the besieged forces' request for support had come in loud and clear.*

---

* "You see, the situation in northern Palestine was completely different. The crowds went out to receive the hero Fawzi al-Qawuqji, commander of the rescue army! The person they thought they were receiving was the hero Fawzi al-Qawuqji, whose pictures had hung on their walls since the events of 1936. This time, however, he hunkered down in the village of Jaba', and established his headquarters at the Dubbai Tursalalla Palace near Silat al-Zhahr—a huge, sumptuous mansion, which, at an earlier time, had been a police chief's center of operations. When the people of the region sent delegations to him urging him to fight, his reply was that he would go out and fight after the winter months were over, his argument being that he was 'waiting for better weather, since I need the soil to be dry on account of the fact that I'm going to be using heavy artillery'! Delegations of notables under guard by his men were constantly coming to see him at his headquarters. What people didn't realize until later was that these notables were Zionist leaders! On 1 April 1948, al-Qawuqji met secretly with Josh Palmon, a Haganah leader who would later become the first head of Mossad, concerning how the previously agreed-upon plans would be implemented. This meeting took place in the forests that adjoined the village of Nur Shams. Al-Qawuqji asked Palmon for 'one symbolic victory.' Palmon's response was to say, 'However you attack us, we'll hit you back even harder than you hit us. So don't interfere!' In short, both he and his army engaged in dubious actions in an attempt to give people the false impression that he was actually fighting. In fact, however, he turned the entire region of Galilee over to the Jews, and in the rescue army's presence, sizable Palestinian cities the likes of Haifa, Jaffa, Acre, Nazareth, and Safad fell under Israeli control. No, he wasn't simply careless, as some people suspected in the beginning. Rather, it became clear beyond a shadow of a doubt that he was in cahoots with the Zionists and coordinating his efforts with theirs in the most peculiar way. He left Palestine a condemned man, haunted by curses."

Under Dar al-Umari's olive trees, thirteen officers met with Hajj Salem to consult about the matter. It came as a huge shock to them when the commander informed them of the government's response to their request for support.

"That's the situation these days," the commander said. "I wanted you to be aware of the facts, and to make a decision yourselves."

"We'll do whatever you tell us," said Officer Umar.

"We aren't meeting today for me to give orders. We're meeting in order to consult together and to make a joint decision. Will we withdraw in shame and ignominy, or stand firm and defend these people's lives and their just cause? Who knows? If we abandon them now, it might not be long before we see the Israelis in Cairo."

"We either die or go home to our countries with our heads held high."

"This kind of talk isn't enough," the commander said.

"What do you want, then?"

Hajj Salem got up and brought a copy of the Qur'an. Together they took an oath, saying, "We either die or go home to our countries with our heads held high!"

Turning to Lieutenant Lutfi, the commander said, "You're responsible for the operations. I don't want you to fire a single shot that doesn't hit its mark. All we have is the ammunition in our hands. As for the people of Hadiya, I want them to dig a shelter in every house. This is Hajj Salem's responsibility. The second thing I want to discuss with Hajj Salem is the matter of food supplies. Potentially, at least, we can go on fighting indefinitely, but as you know, food supplies are as important as bullets."

"Don't worry. We have a large supply of wheat. We always keep a reserve, not to cope with war conditions, but to cope with times of drought. I don't think we'll die of thirst, since there's plenty of water. But we need to form a committee of military personnel and civilians to collect food supplies from people in an organized way."

"But we won't be able to eat wheat by itself!"

"There's a lot of livestock, too, and it's better for everyone for the animals to be slaughtered for food than to die under bombardment."

"But we can't take people's animals."

"There's a solution. Whenever we take someone's livestock, we'll give him a receipt signed by you stating what we took from him and what we owe him. Besides, who's going to say no in a situation like this?"

The earth, red and soft, gave way easily under their pickaxes and hoes, and the availability of railroad ties and the grasses used to hold them in place enabled them to build strong, secure roofs for the shelters. Meanwhile, the army's fortifications were nearly complete, and the soldiers could walk back and forth inside them without anyone's being able to detect their presence.

Hadiya was closed off from all sides, and there was no longer any way of communicating with the outside unless someone made his way in and out by stealth.

The speed with which the orders had been carried out astonished everyone, including the Jews, who had never expected to find themselves faced with such sturdy barbed-wire fences and fortifications. Those besieging the village tried to advance, but were taken by surprise by its lines of defense, which were unusually calm. When they came nearer the barbed wire, they discovered that there was an ambush awaiting them and quickly withdrew. Nevertheless, they lost quite a few men.

That evening, a number of Jewish soldiers advanced with white flags raised. They requested permission to remove the corpses of their slain, and they were allowed to do so.

"We won't remove them until we have assurances from the commander that you won't shoot."

"Let them take them away."

Those who were under siege had feared greatly that the bodies might begin to decay, and that the stench they gave off would become a crueler punishment than the gunfire itself, especially in view of the fact that the wind was blowing from the west.

In the second attack, which took place at night, the attackers were able to get across the first barrier. However, they were surprised by the minefields. Flares were launched into the sky, and they were pursued by gunfire until they disappeared completely. The white flags appeared again.

After that, everything changed.

Three war planes passed overhead and flew in circles over the village. The besieged soldiers shouted joyously, "Our planes!"

But before the smiles had faded from their faces, the airplanes returned and launched a lightning-quick attack. They were dropping incendiary bombs that set fire to everything they hit. One of them fell directly on the mulberry tree in the guesthouse courtyard and tore it out by the roots.

"I saw that tree flying through the air like a piece of paper," said Munira.

The people of the village had to sneak out at night to get food for their livestock. As the days passed, however, the siege began to tighten, and the plains surrounding the village turned into ashes with the ongoing bombardment from enemy aircraft and artillery. Consequently, the only food that remained was the meat that they cooked with cracked wheat in large kettles over open fires.

Within three weeks, hygiene had begun to dwindle. The soldiers' beards grew bushy and their hair was long and unkempt. You couldn't tell an officer from a regular any more except by looking at the stars or stripes on his shoulders and arms. The bombardment had become so intense that the cactus plants—which were the only things they had found of late to feed the livestock, after burning off their spines—had turned to charcoal.

Hajj Salem suggested to the commander that some of the men of the village might make their way in secret to Hebron to meet with the army units there and ask for help. "It's true, of course, that the governments have made a clear decision not to support the soldiers who are under siege. But who knows? Maybe the officers could act on their own and go against the decision in secret."

The commander agreed immediately to his suggestion.

"My son Ali will go."

"I'll go, too," Abd al-Fattah chimed in.

Jum'a Salah added, "And so will I."

The eastern side of the village was the least hazardous, since the forces from Israel's army there were less concentrated. After the besieged army forces were informed when they would be leaving, the three men were supplied with a single revolver and a password: "Hamama."

We would always use passwords that had the guttural 'ha' sound in them, since the Jews and the British pronounce it as 'kha.'

Thanks to the Israelis' complacency, given the fact that they were the ones surrounding the village, the men were able to cut a hole in the barbed wire and pass through without difficulty.

With this complacency as their protection, they stole out of the village and set out on foot for Qabiba, Bayt Jibrin, and al-Duwayma. Since these villages had been occupied, they had to make their way around them, then continue on their way through the valleys to Hebron. When they arrived in the city at noon, you would have thought it was Resurrection Day. Destruction filled the streets, and people could find nowhere that was safe. At the same time, there was a continuous stream of newcomers.

Exhausted and famished, they went in search of a restaurant where they could get something to eat. They asked about the Egyptian army and were told, "The army command is in Dar Khamashta now, between Bethlehem and Bayt Jala."

When the soldiers in Hebron learned that the three men had managed to steal out of Hadiya despite the siege, they gave them a hero's welcome and brought them food, which they wolfed down as though they hadn't eaten for months.

"Is it possible that there are really still people alive in your town? We've been hearing shells falling on you for the last two months, and at night we see explosions with our own eyes, but we haven't been able to do anything!"

Before long, the commander came hurrying in. Before saying a word, he began embracing them. When he came at last to Jum'a Salah, he kept saying, "God, how wonderful the earth smells on you!"

"We thought we were stinking to high heaven," Jum'a later commented to Ali. Then he said to him, "Come up close so I can smell you!"

When he'd gotten a whiff of him, he said, "Like I told you, we stink to high heaven!"

Ali produced the letter from Ayyub Abduh and handed it to the commander. He opened it and began reading it.

"Tomorrow I'll supply you with everything I can. Now, though, I think you should rest and go take a bath."

"Didn't I tell you? We're unbearable!" Jum'a Salah told Ali.

The next morning the commander gave them nine thousand pounds. Each one took three thousand. They also supplied them with some basic necessities: tea, cigarettes, coffee, and salt, as they'd begun having to eat their food unsalted in recent days. They were given a ride in an armored car, which let them out as close as it could to Hadiya without entering dangerous territory. They went the rest of the way through the valleys.

The soldiers were more excited about the cigarettes and tea than they were about anything else. For a long time they'd put up with hand-rolled cigarettes that made them cough all the time.

The next morning they decided to distribute the money they had brought among the villagers who had supplied them with livestock for slaughter. At first some of them took the money gladly. However, when they realized that the people they had supplied the animals to were offering their lives in the village's defense, they wondered how they could accept it. When Hashem Shahada returned the money he had received, people came and stood in a long line in front of the commander's trench and, without saying a word, gave back the money they'd been given.

It was a moving scene, and the officers and soldiers had tears in their eyes.

Realizing that they would not be able to occupy Hadiya by force, the Israelis sent word through United Nations workers that they wanted to negotiate a solution. But suddenly, before the commander had responded to this suggestion, an envoy from the Egyptian government arrived.

"How long are you going to go on this way?" the envoy asked the commander.

"What way?"

"This situation can't go on forever. The government's position on the matter is clear, and you know it."

"And you know I can't decide anything without consulting with the other officers first."

"When can I expect your reply?"

"Today is Monday. Let's say Wednesday. Is that all right?"

"That's fine."

The government envoy got into the UN car that had brought him and went back to where he had come from—from beyond the barbed wire.

The bombardment stopped completely in anticipation of the commander's response. Movement returned to the streets and people were able to come and go freely. That evening the commander called an officers' meeting, which was attended by Hajj Salem and a number of other men from the village. He explained to them what was happening. All of them, both the soldiers and the people of the village, needed a period of quiet in which to catch their breath.

"We won't lose anything. We'll gain time, and this is to our advantage."

Three officers were chosen to go meet with the UN officials and the Jews.

The commander made sure that when the officers left Hadiya, they were looking smart as a groom on his wedding day. He wanted their appearance to give a clear, positive impression about conditions inside the village.

Nobody who lived those moments could ever forget them!

"I won't tell you anything, and I won't give you any instructions," the commander said to them.

"Don't worry."

The three officers then went to the tent that had been prepared for the negotiations five kilometers away. They shook hands and everyone sat down.

One of the Israeli officers stood up with a pack of cigarettes in his hand. Lutfi and Kamal each took a cigarette. Umar declined. Not long afterward, they brought the tea. No one said a word.

Then Kamal got up and, to everyone's astonishment, brought out two packs of cigarettes, opened them both and began passing out their contents to everyone there. The Israeli officer took a puff on the cigarette in his hand and asked him in a tone of surprise, "Do you have a lot of this type of tobacco?"

"We've got all we need and more."

"But I don't suppose you've got all the ammunition you need."

"We've got all we need and more."

"Does that mean there's no use negotiating with you?"

"You've asked to meet with us, and we've come to find out what you want."

"We'll consider you prisoners of war. You're no better than Hitler's soldiers who surrendered. But at least this way you'll live rather than die in battle or starve to death!"

"What do we have to do with Hitler's army? You're the ones attacking us and trying to drive people off their land."

"This is our land. The Lord promised it to us."

"But you needed Balfour in order for the promise to be fulfilled."

"I won't argue with you. But I promise you that we'll treat you as citizens of a state, not as 'gang members,' which is how you refer to us. In any case, your cause isn't here, since you're fighting on other people's land. Maybe it would be better for you to go back and fight the British army in your own land—the British army that we managed to get rid of here and declare our independence!"

"I've listened to your demands, and now I'm telling you that we're here to arrive at a cease-fire agreement so that we can take the wounded to our hospitals in preparation for the lifting of the siege of Hadiya. Your situation is undoubtedly better than mine. I'm not deceiving myself. Even with my patient endurance, I won't be able to change the balance of power in a war that's already over. However, I can save one thing: my soldiers' honor. And that's why I'll fight to the last bullet."

"And we can guarantee you one thing if you surrender: that you'll be treated as prisoners of war. I think you'll have to choose between two things: your honor, or your life."

Sensing that war was about to break out under the tent roof, the UN officials intervened at this point and began pushing for a one-month truce.

Before leaving, Kamal took another pack of cigarettes out of his pocket, and to everyone's amazement, left all three packs on the table. Then he and the other two officers got into the UN car and returned to Hadiya.

The truce lasted all of ten hours. That night, an Israeli force sneaked in from the south and silently slaughtered scores of soldiers who had not been on their guard, confident that the mini-truce had gone into effect. The Israeli force then continued on its way into the village and, as they had done the first time, used picks, axes, and knives to kill the largest possible number of people without making a sound. When they reached the heart of al-Najjar's neighborhood, a number of soldiers noticed the suspicious movement and asked for the password. Gunfire came their way, mowing down two of them, and it was then that the whole situation changed.

Naji, who had become a member of the regular forces, was on his way back from his guard duty on the western side of the village. Realizing what was happening, he disappeared into a corner, and when the attackers came closer he threw a hand grenade in their direction. As they tried to retreat he threw another grenade, then went after them, firing at them with his rifle. They disappeared. Their forces were now on the bridge that connected the two halves of the village. The villagers and the besieged army came rushing out from all directions, trying to close the breaches that had so mercilessly shattered the village's defenses.

A few moments later, a huge explosion rang out. They had blown up the bridge.

"What can we do?" was the only question anybody could think to ask.

"Do anything—anything but surrender!"

When the besieged army's tanks managed to cross through the dense gunfire to the place where the battles were taking place, things began to change in Hadiya's favor. The Israeli force that had blown up the bridge was surrounded and completely isolated.

When people realized that the streets were dangerous, they began going from roof to roof. Then, most unexpectedly, the sky thundered and a heavy rain began to pour down. At that point, it was no longer possible to distinguish defenders from attackers.

Morning broke to reveal a horrific scene, reminiscent of the black night when the village had been taken unawares. There were bodies everywhere, and the shelters held scores of corpses torn limb from limb by the bombs that had been thrown inside them. They had turned into veritable tombs, and eventually all people could do was put more bodies inside them, then close their doors.

Seeing that things were going from bad to worse, Ayyub Abduh said, "We don't have much ammunition left. We'll send them word that we want to surrender."

"What?" shouted more than one officer.

"They deceived us, so now they need to get a taste of their own medicine. I'm going to give them the surprise of their lives."

He then explained his simple plan to them.

Before the commander had sent a message to the truce observers, they came to apologize, accompanied by the government envoy.

Then, to their surprise, he said, "We want to surrender, provided that they'll consider us prisoners of war, as they promised."

"You're surrendering?"

"Yes. Three days from now, at ten o'clock in the morning. There's a large square in the northern part of the village. We'll go out there with white flags."

Looks of relief spread over the faces of the truce observers and the government envoy. After all, they wanted to get out of the situation they were in at any cost, and the only thing that had prevented them from doing so thus far was this stubborn village known as Hadiya. As for the Israelis, they were beside themselves with glee when they heard the news.

At 10:00 on Monday morning, the large square was filled with those who had come to witness the moment of surrender that they had hardly dared dream of.

At 10:01 silence hung over the square, and people's eyes were wide with anticipation as they waited for the white flags to appear.

At 10:02 necks were craned and hearts were beating wildly.

Ayyub Abduh made the rounds of the trenches. "Are you ready?" he asked.

"We're ready."

"Now, then."

Then everything exploded, and the silence vanished, never to return. The cannons fired mercilessly, the armored cars opened fire with their machine guns, and screams filled the air. It was an excruciating blow, and the Israelis knew now with certainty that Hadiya would never fall by force.

Three days later, the truce observers came back. They were furious.

The response: "A ruse for a ruse, and the one who initiated is the worst offender."

Over a period of weeks they shuttled back and forth between the two sides, until at last they reached an agreement: the besieged army was to be allowed to leave with all its weapons, and without being attacked by anyone. Those villagers who wished to stay and live the life they had lived before would be entitled to do so, and those who wished to leave would have the option of accompanying the retreating forces.

They all decided to stay.

"Is there any country anywhere that would have room for us?" they kept saying.

"We didn't let war drive us out. So why should we leave on our own now that the war is over?" reasoned Hajj Salem.

"They'll pour out their hatred and bitterness on us, and they'll never allow us to live in peace."

"But we're staying all the same."

There wasn't a gathering place but that the departing commander visited it, and over a period of two weeks, he explained to everyone in the village the details of the next step. Even so, his mind wasn't at rest. "I'm afraid this whole thing might just be another ruse. But you all know that if we don't accept this agreement, they'll slaughter everyone."

The people of the village, chief among them Hajj Salem, understood that some of its men would have to leave with the army whether they wanted to or not, since the Jews would cut them to pieces if they captured them.

As the forces set out, people lined the streets bidding the soldiers farewell. There wasn't a single villager who didn't receive a hug from the commander.

"If it weren't for you, the army wouldn't have been able to hold out this long," he kept saying.

As the armored vehicles stood waiting up and down the main street, there wasn't a dry eye. Meanwhile, the sky was threatening to rain.

The commander thought back on all the nights he had spent there. As he did so, he found himself recalling the statement that had changed the course of his life forever: "We'll consider you war casualties!"

The convoy set out with the five captives in its last car.

"If they behave well I'll restore their captives to them. Otherwise, I won't."

The Israelis tried over a period of weeks to reach an agreement concerning them. However, the commander saw them as a bargaining chip that shouldn't be wasted before a clear solution had been arrived at.

In front of a police station that had once been used by the British army, the Israeli forces waited for the retreating force to arrive. The convoy came up and stopped for a few moments. The Arab commander was standing up. The Israeli commander waited for him to get out of the car, but he didn't.

The Israeli commander took a few steps forward and invited him to get out.

He refused.

Ayyub gestured to the soldiers to release the captives.

When the force reached the new international borders, the convoy halted. The commander got out of his car, and immediately got into an armored car that stood waiting for him.

And no one ever saw him again. I assure you!

The Portals of Hell

The tower whose stones had been scattered in all directions began growing again. As soon as people saw what was happening, they realized what awaited them in the days to come.

After a quiet week a jeep passed by carrying four armed Jewish men. It did nothing. They cast a glance at the fields, then left.

Two days later the jeep returned in silence, then left in silence. On the third day, a single bullet was fired. It lodged in the head of Ali al-A'raj as he plowed his land. Then the jeep left.

On the fourth day it came back again. It stopped, and two soldiers got out. Rashid Saleh was plowing his land.

"What are you doing here? Don't you people ever learn?"

"I'm plowing my land. It's planting season."

"Don't trouble yourself, since nothing will come of it. Go tell the people that this is our land, not yours."

The village closed in on itself even more then. The village elders gathered to discuss what was happening, and before their meeting was over, a jeep made the rounds of the village, ordering people over loudspeakers to stay in their houses because of a curfew that was in effect from two p.m. to six p.m.

The people didn't obey the order.

At two-thirty p.m. a single shot rang out. People realized it had come from the tower. 'Adel al-Hilw fell right outside his front gate. For seventeen days the sniping continued nonstop. A shot here, a death there. Consequently, people no longer dared appear during the day.

On the eighteenth day they stopped contenting themselves with the occasional shot. Jewish armored cars and jeeps tore like mad through the village, shooting heavily into the air. Then they left without wounding anyone.

The truce observers had established their headquarters in the girls' school. Hashem Shahada, Isma'il Radhi, and Taysir Jum'a sneaked out to see the truce observers one night.

"We'll do what we can," they promised.

Before sundown the following day, the armored cars and jeeps were back. But this time bullets rained on the doors and windows of the houses.

Hashem Shahada, Isma'il Radhi, and Aziza's son Husayn stole out to see the truce observers, and the answer came louder and clearer than they could ever have imagined: "The agreement you've made is meaningless, since they don't recognize it, and we can't do anything for you. All we can do is ask them to stop harassing you. But as you can see, what we say doesn't mean anything to them."

Life's doors closed completely. The remaining livestock died from lack of food and it became impossible to go out for any reason, whether to tend to their fields, bring food, or even pray. The pigeons alone were able to fly out in search of food. In the beginning they would come back quickly. But when the siege began to take its toll, their absences grew longer, since it was no longer possible for them to find sustenance on the nearby plains.

Sumayya would gaze tearfully up at the cubbyholes, and whenever one of the fantail pigeons, whose numbers had grown because she had never slaughtered any of them, came down into the courtyard and strutted proudly about before her, she would weep in bitter silence.

The truce observers told us, "You have two choices: to go to Gaza, or to Hebron."

Clouds appeared high in the sky. Then piercing, sword-like streaks of lightning flashed and deafening thunder rolled. It was as though the earth was in a rage. Suddenly, it began pouring down rain, a rain they were certain would never stop. But, as suddenly as it had begun, it stopped, leaving behind it an eerie, death-like silence.

After gloomy conversations and discussions that led nowhere, people began gathering their things in front of their houses in preparation for the day of departure, and another group of truce observers came to coordinate the exodus.

"UN trucks will come and take everyone. Meanwhile, you have to leave your houses and wait on the main road."

Five hours went by, but no truck arrived. Night fell, and some families tried to go back to their houses.

"That's not allowed!"

"What's not allowed?"

"For you to go back to your houses again."

"But we can't spend the night here."

"The trucks will be here any minute now."

They went back to their places on the roadside, surrounded by their bundles of clothing and a few sacks of wheat they had thought they might need.

At four o'clock in the morning, a drop of water fell from the sky, and in a few moments it was followed by a heavy downpour more violent than the one that had torn the village apart a few days earlier.

By the time morning peeked over the horizon, they were in the most pitiful condition anyone can imagine: mud-spattered, sopping wet, and chilled to the bone.

"We'll go back to our houses."

"Nobody's going back."

※

Small tents were pitched, and blankets were turned into more tents. Meanwhile, shells began falling on the village until the people were afraid even to think about their houses, since the minute anyone said, "I'm going back to my house," a shell would fall on it and destroy it, or a mine would rip it off its foundations.

Hadiya began growing smaller with every passing day, disappearing before their very eyes. The monastery went up in a cloud of smoke, and when that happened, they realized that the attackers wanted to wipe the village off the face of the earth.

Eleven days later a hot sun rose. Over the following four days it continued to grow hotter until it was an utter blaze. Another morning dawned, and another night fell.

Still another day ended and another night fell, and a night, and a night, and a night, and a night, and a night, and a night.

Then another day began.

They looked over at the sacks of wheat, only to find that the grains had sprouted and broken through the pores in the burlap. The people gathered firewood and began roasting the grains of wheat, which were the only food they had. What with the little ones' screams, which were now unending, it was an alarming scene.

The weeks we spent on that roadside were crueler than the days of the siege. Believe me.

When at last the trucks arrived one afternoon, the people couldn't even climb up into them. The long wait had left them totally enervated. With difficulty Sumayya found her legs, which she couldn't even feel any more. She got up and looked at the hill where her husband's grave lay. She closed her eyes, then opened them again, not believing what she saw. Then she took off running toward Hadiya.

They ran after her and brought her back.

"Let me go!" she cried. "Don't you see her? She's there!"

"See who?"

"Hamama! Don't you see her over there?"

"Where?"

"At his grave. On the hill. She's there. Don't you see her? Let me go! I want to see her, just once. I want to apologize to her, ask her to forgive me. Let me go!"

They held on to her. She struggled to break loose.

In the end the only solution they found was to carry her to the truck.

Suddenly, she grew calm.

She curled up into a ball like an unclaimed bundle of clothes, a bundle that had found itself in a truck whose destination no one knew.

Shortly after sundown the trucks were on their way.

They heard Sumayya's voice, a voice that seemed to well up from the deep darkness inside her. She was singing:

Bring a lantern, friend,
And light the darkness for me.
I'm afraid there's a long road ahead,
And that you'll be burdened with me for a long time,
You'll be burdened with me for a long time.

Tears cascaded down the faces of Munira and her grandchildren, Afaf and her children, Husayn and his children, and Umm al-Far, who were all gathered in the back of that white truck.

Several explosions rang out. They turned and saw fire consuming a number of the houses in the village. Aziza, who had been weeping quietly, resting her face on the truckbed's iron railing, stared blankly. One of the bombs had fallen on her father's house. It caught fire. Then another bomb fell, and the dovecote went up in flames.

The doves were flying away, covering distances she never thought a bird whose wings were on fire could cover. By the time they began falling in the surrounding orchards, vineyards, and plains, a new fire was ablaze. And when the trucks reached an elevated spot from which the people could see Hadiya for the last time, tongues of fire were consuming it from all directions.

"If I was an Arab leader I would never make terms with Israel. That is natural: we have taken their country. Sure, God promised it to us, but what does that matter to them? There has been anti-Semitism, the Nazis, Hitler, Auschwitz, but was that their fault? They only see one thing: we have come here and stolen their country. Why should they accept that?"

David Ben Gurion, quoted by Nahum Goldmann (former president of the World Zionist Organization) in *The Jewish Paradox* (New York: Fred Jordan Books, 1978), p. 99.

This novel incorporates material derived from numerous memoirs and other writings. These include:

Abu Ghurayba, Bahjat. *Fi khidamm al-nidal al-'arabi al-filistini*. Beirut: Mu'assasat al-Dirasat al-Filistiniya, 1993.

Abu Khadra, Kan'an. *Sahafi min Filastin yatadhakkar*. N.p., 1985.

al-'Arif, 'Arif. *al-Qada' 'ind al-Badw*. Beirut: al-Mu'assasa al-'Arabiya li-l-Dirasat wa-l-Nashr, 2004.

'Awda, Ziyad. *'Abd al-Rahim al-Hajj Muhammad*. al-Zarqa': al-Wikala al-'Arabiya, 1984.

Ben-Gurion, David, and Thomas R. Bransten. *Memoirs: David Ben-Gurion*. New York: World Publishing Company, 1970.

Darraj, Faysal. *Dhakirat al-maghlubin*. Beirut: al-Markaz al-Thaqafi al-'Arabi, 2001.

Darwaza, Muhammad 'Izzat. *Mudhakkirat Muhammad 'Izzat Darwaza*. Beirut: Dar al-Gharb al-Islami, 1993.

———. *al-Qadiya al-filistiniya fi mukhtalif marahiliha*. Beirut: al-Maktaba al-'Asriya, 1959.

Fadhl, Yusuf. *Istidaratal-zill*. http://www.grenc.com/a/yFadel/show_Myarticle.cfm?id=436.

Haykal, Muhammad Hasanayn. *al-'Urush wa-l-juyush*. Cairo: Dar al-Shuruq, 1998.

al-Hut, Bayan Nuwayhid. *al-Qiyadat wa-l-mu'assasat al-siyasiya fi Filistin 1917–1948*. Beirut: Mu'assasat al-Dirasat al-Filistiniya, 1991.

Ibrahim, Hanna. *Hanna Naqqara: muhami al-ard wa-l-insan*. Acre: Manshurat al-Aswar, 1985.

Ibrahim, Rashid al-Hajj. *al-Difaʿ ʿan Hayfa: mudhakkirat Rashid al-Hajj Ibrahim*. Beirut: Muʾassasat al-Dirasat al-Filistiniya, 2005.

al-Khalidi, Walid Raghib. *Ramlah tatakallam*. Amman, 1990.

Khalifah, Ahmad. *The Great Arab Revolt in Palestine, 1936–1939: The Official Israeli Narrative*. Beirut: Muʾassasat al-Dirasat al-Filistiniya, 1989.

al-Mawsuʿa al-filistiniya. Damascus: Hayʾat al-Mawsuʿa al-Filistiniya, 1984.

Misʿad, Joseph. *Daymumat al-qadiya al-Filistiniya*. Beirut: Dar al-Adab.

Morgan, David. "An Interview with President Gamal Abdel Nasser." *The Sunday Times*, 18 June 1962.

Nassar, Najib. *Riwayat Muflih al-Ghassani wa-l-masirah al-maydaniya fi arjaʾ Filastin wa Sharq al-Urdun*. Nazareth: Dar al-Sawt, 1981.

al-Qalyubi, Tahir Adib. *Risalat ʿishq ila Yafa*. Amman, 2002.

al-Qawuqji, Fawzi. *Mudhakkirat Fawzi al-Qawuqji, 1914–1932*. Beirut: Dar al-Quds, 1975.

Rabiʿ, Walid, ʿAbd al-ʿAziz Abu Hadba, ʿUmar Hamdan, and Muhammad ʿAli Ahmad. *Dirasah fi-l-mujtamaʿ wa-l-turath al-shaʿbi al-filistini*. Ramallah: Muʾassasat Inʿash al-Usra, 1987.

al-Sakakini, Khalil. *Mudhakkirat Khalil al-Sakakini*. Ramallah: Manshurat Muʾassasat Inʿash al-Usra, 2003.

al-Sarisi, 'Umar 'Abd al-Rahman. *al-Hikaya al-sha'biya fi-l-mujtama' al-filistini*. Beirut: al-Mu'assasa al-'Arabiya li-l-Dirasat wa-l-Nashr, 1985.

al-Tarawina, Muhammad Salem. *Qada' Yafa fi-l-'ahd al-'uthmani*. Amman: Jordan Ministry of Culture, 2000.

Zu'aytir, Akram. *Yawmiyat Akram Zu'aytir*. Beirut: Mu'assasat al-Dirasat al-Filistiniya, 1980.

The works of Palestinian researcher Nimr Sirhan.

The writings of Ghassan Kanafani on the 1936 Palestinian Uprising (http://www.newjerseysolidarity.org/resources/kanafani/kanafani4.html)
.

Numerous other newspaper and magazine articles.

Glossary and Notes

Bashlak: An Ottoman coin that was equal to one-eighth of an Ottoman piaster.

Bekbashi: The term used in Ottoman times for the military rank of major.

'Bridal exchange': In a bridal exchange, or badal arrangement, a man would take a woman in marriage and, in place of the dowry he would normally be expected to pay, his sister would be given in marriage to the bride's brother.

Dalla: A small pyramid-shaped pot with a long curved spout and a long handle used for preparing Arabic coffee.

Deferred dowry: A deferred dowry is a sum of money specified in an Islamic marriage contract, which, in the event that the husband divorces the wife, the husband must pay upon their separation.

Dhikr ceremony: A gathering for worship common among Muslim mystics, or Sufis, which generally includes a sermon, Qur'anic and poetry recitation, repetition of the names of God, singing, and dancing.

"The evil's been broken!": An expression used when something breaks in the house, "The evil's been broken!" (inkasara al-sharr) is a way of expressing optimism. In other words, since something has broken, whatever evil force was behind the breaking has been spent, and all is well now.

Fatiha: The first chapter of the Qur'an, with which every ritual prayer in Islam commences: "In the name of God, Most Gracious, Most Merciful. Praise be to God, the Cherisher and Sustainer of the worlds; Most Gracious, Most Merciful; Master of the Day of Judgment. Thee do we worship, and Thine aid do we seek. Show us the straight way, the way of those on whom Thou hast bestowed Thy grace, those whose portion is not wrath, and who go not astray."

Fawzi al-Qawuqji: Born in Beirut under Ottoman rule, Fawzi al-Qawuqji (1890–1977) served as an officer in the Ottoman Army during the First World War, but was an Arab nationalist. He fought against the British during the 1936–39 Arab revolt against the British Mandate in Palestine. He served as a German agent in Palestine during the Second World War, and was the field commander for the Arab Liberation Army during the Arab–Israeli War in Palestine in 1948.

Glubb Pasha: Lieutenant General Sir John Bagot Glubb (1897–1986) was a British soldier who is best known for training and leading the Transjordan's Arab Legion from 1939 to 1956. It was Glubb Pasha who led the Arab Legion across Jordan to occupy the West Bank in the 1948 Arab–Israeli War. In a move to distance himself from the British, and to counter claims that Glubb Pasha was the one actually ruling Jordan, the late King Hussein dismissed Glubb Pasha in 1956. After having one son, Godfrey, in 1939, Glubb Pasha and his wife, Muriel Rosemary Forbes, adopted three Arab children. He died in Mayfield, Sussex.

Greek Orthodox Church: From its inception, the hierarchy of the Greek Orthodox Church in Palestine has been dominated by ethnic Greeks, thereby excluding the Arabic-speaking majority from the Church's upper echelons. In the early twentieth century, Arab clergy rebelled against this situation, and their cause dovetailed with Arab nationalism. In 1909, Arab Orthodox Christians formally petitioned the Ottoman authorities for inclusion in the higher ranks of the Patriarchate.

Habis al-Majali: Born in Kerak, Jordan, Habis al-Majali (1914–2001) served in the Arab Legion under Glubb Pasha. He later served in the Jordanian Armed Forces (1958–1975) and in the Jordanian Senate for nearly twenty years.

Haganah: Derived from the Hebrew phrase ha ganah ('the defense'), Haganah was a Jewish paramilitary organization that came into existence under the British Mandate of Palestine between 1920 and 1948, and whose initial purpose was to protect Jewish settlements and farms from attacks by Arab gangs.

Halawa: Literally meaning 'sweetness,' the term halawa refers to a crumbly sweet made of sesame paste and sugar to which pistachios are often added.

Harisa: A sweet semolina and honey cake, scored into diamond shapes and topped with almond halves.

Izz al-Din al-Qassam: Sheikh Muhammad Izz al-Din al-Qassam (1882–1935), born in Jablih, Syria, was an Arab militant under the British Mandate of Palestine who mobilized the Arab masses against the Jews and the British for the way in which they were dispossessing the Arab population of their land and livelihoods. By taking up arms as he did, al-Qassam set himself apart from other Palestinian politicians of the day.

Jamal Pasha: Jamal Pasha (1872–1922) was a Turkish military officer who served as an Ottoman military governor in Syria during the First World War. Because he was responsible for the execution of many Lebanese and Syrian Shi'a Muslims and Christians who had wrongly been accused of treason on 6 May 1916, he came to be known among local Arab inhabitants as "the Butcher" (al-saffah).

al-Khalil: Hebron.

Khalil al-Sakanini: Khalil al-Sakakini (1878–1953) was an Arab Orthodox Christian who became a leader in the Arab nationalist movement in Palestine. He wanted to reform and Arabize what he saw as the corrupt Greek Orthodox Church of Jerusalem.

Kunafa: A popular Middle Eastern sweet made from soft white cheese and a vermicelli-like pastry. It is topped with a thick syrup made from water, sugar, and a few drops of rose water, and sprinkled with crushed pistachios.

Mahmud Mukhtar (1891–1934): Looked upon as the father of modern Egyptian sculpture, Mahmud Mukhtar studied fine arts in Cairo and Paris, after which he went on to create the prototype of his famous statue, *Nahdat Misr*, or 'Egypt's Renaissance,' which was first unveiled in Ramses Square in 1928 and now stands across from the Cairo University Bridge. Mukhtar is also famous for his two large statues of Sa'd Zaghlul, one of which stands in Cairo, the other in Alexandria.

Mahmud Sa'id (1897–1964): Born in Alexandria, Egypt, Mahmud Sa'id practiced law until the death of his father in 1947, at which point he began pursuing his own dream, painting, on a full-time basis. Taking scenes from Egyptian life as his subjects, Sa'id left an indelible mark on contemporary Egyptian art. Many of his works are on display at the Modern Art Museum at the Cairo Opera House, and work is underway to transform his home in Alexandria into the Mahmud Sa'id Museum.

Majidi: An Ottoman coin worth twenty Ottoman piasters, the majidi was first minted toward the end of the Ottoman era and named after Sultan Abd al-Majid II, the last Ottoman caliph.

Maqluba: The term maqluba ('upside-down') refers to a dish made from rice, chicken, or lamb, which is inverted onto a serving platter before being eaten. It sometimes contains potatoes, and can also be made with cauliflower and carrots in place of the potato.

Millieme: A monetary unit equal to one-tenth of a piaster.

Muhammad Abd al-Wahhab (1900–1991): An Egyptian actor, singer, and composer who is said to have changed the course of modern Arab music by incorporating Western musical instruments, melodies, rhythms, and performance practices into his works.

Mujaddara: A rice-and-lentil dish.

Mulukhiya: A green leafy vegetable ('Jews' mallow'), which is made into a thick soup and served with chicken and rice.

Naji: The name 'Naji' literally means 'one who has survived or been delivered.'

Night of Power: Celebrated on the 26th and 27th of the fasting month of Ramadan, the Night of Power (Laylat al-Qadr) is believed by Muslims, based on Surah 97, to be the night on which the Qur'an was revealed.

Qunbaz: A long, sleeved garment worn by men, open in front and fastened with a belt.

Ratl: A unit of weight that varies widely from one region to another, from approximately half a kilogram to three kilograms.

Saleh Abd al-Hayy (1896–1962): A renowned Egypt singer who became popular in the 1920s.

Sayyid Darwish (1892–1923): An Egyptian singer and composer who, like Muhammad Abd al-Wahhab, introduced Western musical instruments into his performances.

The Sutriya clan: This clan is known as the 'Arabs of al-Sutriya,' the term 'Sutriya' being derived from a place known as al-Sutr near Khan Yunus from which they had emigrated, or 'the Arabs of Fadl,' because their lands are part of an endowment that had belonged to the Prophet's Companion al-Fadl ibn al-Abbas.

Taghribat Bani Hilal: Also known as *al-Sira al-Hilaliya*, *Taghribat Bani Hilal* is the longest Arabic epic poem in existence. Consisting of nearly one million lines of poetry and containing the contributions of numerous poets, it relates the story of the exile of the tribe of Banu Hilal from Nejd to Syria and Iraq, and from there to North Africa.

Modern Arabic Literature
from the American University in Cairo Press

Edwar al-Kharrat *Rama and the Dragon* • *Stones of Bobello*
Betool Khedairi *Absent*
Mohammed Khudayyir *Basrayatha*
Ibrahim al-Koni *Anubis* • *Gold Dust* • *The Puppet* • *The Seven Veils of Seth*
Naguib Mahfouz *Adrift on the Nile* • *Akhenaten: Dweller in Truth*
Arabian Nights and Days • *Autumn Quail* • *Before the Throne* • *The Beggar*
The Beginning and the End • *Cairo Modern*
The Cairo Trilogy: Palace Walk, Palace of Desire, Sugar Street
Children of the Alley • *The Coffeehouse* • *The Day the Leader Was Killed*
The Dreams • *Dreams of Departure* • *Echoes of an Autobiography*
The Essential Naguib Mahfouz • *The Final Hour* • *The Harafish* • *Heart of the Night*
In the Time of Love • *The Journey of Ibn Fattouma* • *Karnak Café*
Khan al-Khalili • *Khufu's Wisdom* • *Life's Wisdom* • *Love in the Rain* • *Midaq Alley*
The Mirage • *Miramar* • *Mirrors* • *Morning and Evening Talk*
Naguib Mahfouz at Sidi Gaber • *Respected Sir* • *Rhadopis of Nubia*
The Search • *The Seventh Heaven* • *Thebes at War*
The Thief and the Dogs • *The Time and the Place*
Voices from the Other World • *Wedding Song*
Mohamed Makhzangi *Memories of a Meltdown*
Alia Mamdouh *The Loved Ones* • *Naphtalene*
Selim Matar *The Woman of the Flask*
Ibrahim al-Mazini *Ten Again*
Yousef Al-Mohaimeed *Munira's Bottle* • *Wolves of the Crescent Moon*
Ahlam Mosteghanemi *Chaos of the Senses* • *Memory in the Flesh*
Shakir Mustafa *Contemporary Iraqi Fiction: An Anthology*
Mohamed Mustagab *Tales from Dayrut*
Buthaina Al Nasiri *Final Night*
Ibrahim Nasrallah *Inside the Night*
Haggag Hassan Oddoul *Nights of Musk*
Mona Prince *So You May See*
Mohamed Mansi Qandil *Moon over Samarqand*
Abd al-Hakim Qasim *Rites of Assent*
Somaya Ramadan *Leaves of Narcissus*
Mekkawi Said *Cairo Swan Song*
Ghada Samman *The Night of the First Billion*
Mahdi Issa al-Saqr *East Winds, West Winds*
Rafik Schami *The Calligrapher's Secret* • *Damascus Nights*
The Dark Side of Love
Habib Selmi *The Scents of Marie-Claire*
Khairy Shalaby *The Hashish Waiter* • *The Lodging House*
The Time-Travels of the Man Who Sold Pickles and Sweets
Miral al-Tahawy *Blue Aubergine* • *Gazelle Tracks* • *The Tent*
Bahaa Taher *As Doha Said* • *Love in Exile*
Fuad al-Takarli *The Long Way Back*
Zakaria Tamer *The Hedgehog*
M.M. Tawfik *Murder in the Tower of Happiness*
Mahmoud Al-Wardani *Heads Ripe for Plucking*
Amina Zaydan *Red Wine*
Latifa al-Zayyat *The Open Door*